WESTERN COLLECTION

The Rancher's Promise

New York Times Bestselling Author

Jillian Hart

Big Sky Family

Charlotte Carter

2 NOVELS
GREAT VALUE

Discover Love Inspired® Books

Whether you love
heart-pounding suspense,
historically rich stories or
contemporary heartfelt romances,
Love Inspired® Books has it all!

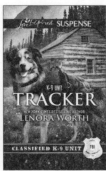

Praise for Jillian Hart
and her novels

"This first story about the Grangers of Wyoming is an easygoing romance about love, forgiveness, following your dreams and finding your way home again."
—*RT Book Reviews* on *The Rancher's Promise*

"It's a pleasure to read this achingly tender story."
—*RT Book Reviews* on *Her Wedding Wish*

"Jillian Hart conveys heart-tugging emotional struggles."
—*RT Book Reviews* on *Sweet Blessings*

Praise for Charlotte Carter
and her novels

"The reader can feel the characters' anguish. The importance of seeking God's guidance and the value of focusing on abilities, not disabilities, is evident."
—*RT Book Reviews* on *Big Sky Family*

"This is a heart-achingly poignant story that has many bright spots and an abundance of love."
—*RT Book Reviews* on *Montana Hearts*

"The characters' struggles are realistic, and Carter does a great job educating the reader on PTSD and the benefit of therapy dogs in this touching tribute to military men and women everywhere."
—*RT Book Reviews* on *Home to Montana*

Jillian Hart grew up on her family's homestead, where she helped raise cattle, rode horses and scribbled stories in her spare time. After earning her English degree from Whitman College, she worked in travel and advertising before selling her first novel. When Jillian isn't working on her next story, she can be found puttering in her rose garden, curled up with a good book or spending quiet evenings at home with her family.

A multipublished author of more than fifty romances, cozy mysteries and inspirational titles, **Charlotte Carter** wrote seven titles for Love Inspired. She also wrote for Harlequin Western Romance, Harlequin Romance, Harlequin Duets and Harlequin Love & Laughter as Charlotte Maclay and Charlotte Moore.

The Rancher's Promise

Jillian Hart

&

Big Sky Family

Charlotte Carter

⬧ HARLEQUIN® LOVE INSPIRED®

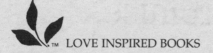 LOVE INSPIRED BOOKS

Recycling programs for this product may not exist in your area.

ISBN-13: 978-1-335-00668-4

The Rancher's Promise and Big Sky Family

Copyright © 2017 by Harlequin Books S.A.

The publisher acknowledges the copyright holders of the individual works as follows:

The Rancher's Promise
Copyright © 2010 by Jill Strickler

Big Sky Family
Copyright © 2011 by Charlotte Lobb

www.Harlequin.com

Printed in U.S.A.

CONTENTS

THE RANCHER'S PROMISE

Jillian Hart

My voice You shall hear in the morning, O Lord;
in the morning I will direct it to You,
and I will look up.
　　　　　　　—Psalms 5:3

Chapter One

"Justin, I finally got a call on the housekeeper job."

"Oh, yeah? That's a shock." Justin Granger hefted the feed sack, settling the fifty-pound weight easily onto his shoulder. As a rancher, he was used to heavy lifting and in his line of work, this wasn't considered heavy. He followed his dad out the open front door of the feed store, waved goodbye to Kit behind the counter and squinted in the hot late May sunshine. "I was beginning to think that putting an ad in the paper was a waste of time and money."

"I figure we got lucky. Not many folks want to cook for the likes of us." His dad, Frank Granger, swung two feed bags into the back of the white pickup parked curbside. "I made the interview for later today. If that doesn't fit your schedule, then I can interview the gal on my own."

"A gal?" That meant a woman. Not promising, not at all. Justin tossed the sack into the back and closed the tailgate. "I wish Aunt Opal hadn't gone to Arizona. She's about the only female I want to trust."

"Not all women are like Tia or your mom." Frank

gave the keys a toss. "I'm sure there's one trustworthy gal around these parts, at least enough honest to cook three squares for us and wash our socks."

"You're more optimistic than me, Dad." Justin hopped behind the wheel and turned over the engine. Cool air breezed out of the vents, a relief from the intense summer heat that had hit hard and early. Not the best thing for the crops. They mostly ran cattle, but they grew their own alfalfa, corn and hay. "I don't see why Autumn and Addison can't do it."

"Hey, if you want to tell your sisters to do *house*-work instead of ranch work, be my guest. I'm not touching that with a ten-foot pole. I'd rather wrestle a rattler bare-handed." Frank buckled up. "No, it's better we hire someone. I got a good feeling about this one."

"I hope you're right. I don't want to wind up with another closet drinker who falls asleep on the couch instead of fixing our supper." Justin checked the mirror. No traffic coming for as far as he could see, which wasn't a surprise. In a town the size of Wild Horse, Wyoming, it would have been a shock if there *had* been a car. He pulled onto the main drag, scowling. "If I remember, you had a good feeling about the drinker, too."

"Try to be more optimistic, son."

Justin rolled his eyes. Optimism was for birds and fools. He'd tried it once and hadn't liked it. He'd gotten his heart crushed and his illusions shattered because of it. In his view, it was wiser to expect the worst. Hard not to get disappointed or hurt that way.

"Looks like everyone's gettin' geared up for the festival." His dad sounded pretty glad about that.

"Guess so." Justin frowned, slowing down when the mayor held up a hand and walked into the road. Wild

Horse was a small town with a handful of necessary businesses and an equal number of others tottering on the edge of failure, like The Greasy Spoon, which had been The Brown Bag eight months before. Justin stopped, wondering what the mayor wanted.

"Mornin', Grangers." Tim Wisener strolled up to the passenger window. "Got some exciting news. Just heard it from my wife a few minutes ago."

"Don't tell me you're finally going to be a grand-daddy," Frank teased in his good-natured way. "Both your boys have been married for how long and no little ones?"

"Too long." Tim shook his head. "Don't know what it is with kids these days."

Personally, Justin got the Wisener sons' view of things. Facing the prospect of marrying a woman was tough enough—something he never wanted to do—but trusting one to raise a family in this remote ranching town and stick with it when times got tough was a whole different question. He didn't want to wind up like his dad, raising a family and making a living when a wife kept trying to bail him. That was one drama he wanted to avoid.

"Martha sold the old River Lodge. Deal closes right quick. It's a lady from back east, New York, I think, putting down cash for the place and the cottage and acres behind it."

"That is good news. This town could use something besides one sorry motel. Too bad it won't be up and running for the annual shindig."

Justin didn't tune in to the older men's conversation. This couldn't have waited? He hadn't the time or incli-nation to worry about the old lodge. He had a ranch to run and time was wasting. Now he had a new woman to worry about. Personally, the family did need a cook, but he didn't have high expectations.

His dad kept talking, and Justin really didn't listen until his ears perked up at the mention of horses. Along with a fine herd of Herefords and Angus, they raised and sold working ranch horses. That was his sister's love. She possessed a knack for working with animals that no one in these parts had.

"Martha will be thrilled." Tim backed away from the truck. "I'll tell her to get a hold of Autumn."

"You do that, Tim. See you around."

Now that his dad was done jawing, Justin put the truck in gear. Something familiar caught his attention. He swung back to look at the woman walking along the sidewalk up ahead. She had dark blond hair with gold highlights, blue eyes the color of hyacinths, and his heart skipped three beats. He would know that heart-shaped face anywhere.

Rori. His high-school sweetheart. His palms went slick against the steering wheel. His pulse lurched to a shotgun start and galloped like a runaway horse. What was she doing back in town?

Not his business, he decided, whipped his gaze away and hit the gas. The truck zipped forward, but he didn't let his eyes stray from the single yellow line. He was over her, done with romance and emotions that took a man up and down and lower still. White-knuckled, he prayed she didn't notice them as they rolled by. Too bad he knew the sheriff was parked behind the library sign with radar, or he'd get up some speed and leave her behind in his dust. In fact, maybe a ticket would be worth it.

"Slow down, son." Frank buzzed open his window. "Rori! What are you doin' walking around town?"

Leave it to Dad, who had to chat with everyone. Tempted to keep on going, Justin bit the bullet and hit the brake. He could man up and face the girl who'd broken his heart, who had as good as told him he wasn't good enough for her. No need to let her know how that broke him. Back then he'd been too young to know a smart man didn't let a woman into his heart. All they did was cause wreckage and ruin.

Yep, he could handle this. He shoved the gear into Park and pulled the brake. Might as well get this over with. Let her see she didn't have an effect on him these days.

"Hi, Mr. Granger." She looked a mite surprised, folded a lock of silken hair behind her ear and approached the truck. Her gaze cut through the windshield and when she spotted him behind the wheel, she winced. The way her top teeth dug into her bottom lip, worrying it, was a clear sign. She wasn't comfortable seeing him either. "Justin."

"Rori." No need to sound overly friendly. Likely as not she was back in Wyoming only to visit for a few days. Probably attending Terri Baker's wedding. Had he thought it through and realized running into her might be a possibility, he would have stayed on the ranch and let his dad run the errands.

"Looks like you've got a problem, missy." Dad leaned out the window to get a good look at something. "Your horse threw a shoe."

"He's trying to. It's come off just enough that I can't ride him back to Gram's. I can't get it off, wouldn't you know?" She was a master of the shy grin. "I didn't think to bring a shoe-puller with me."

Don't get sucked in by that grin, Justin told himself. No way, no sir. He'd stopped being immune to her smile when she'd taken his heart, stomped it to bits and shoved it back at him. He opened his mouth to tell her they'd be happy to call her grandparents for her, but Dad unbuckled and opened the door.

"We got some tools. We can improvise." Frank's boots hit the blacktop. "Justin, get out here and help while I dig through the back, will ya?"

If it were anyone else—*anyone*—he'd have done it before his father could volunteer him. Justin's grip tightened on the steering wheel. Why hadn't he kept driving when he'd had the chance?

Gritting his teeth, he yanked the belt loose and tumbled into the road. With every step he took, he felt the weight of her gaze. He didn't like it, but there wasn't much help around on a Sunday afternoon. There was no one handy to take over the task of helping the lady in distress. Most of the businesses in town were closed and aside from the mayor out for a stroll, there wasn't a soul on the streets.

"I'll go put in our lunch order." Frank handed him a flathead screwdriver, a pair of pliers and a battered roll of duct tape. "You can stay here and help Rori."

"No, Dad." He couldn't believe his own father would do this to him.

"Justin, you might as well go with your father," Rori spoke up, clearly not comfortable being left alone with the likes of him. "I can do it myself."

"That's not the way we do things, little lady. Justin, you can catch up with me at Clem's." Frank hopped in behind the wheel and pulled the door shut, looking pleased with himself.

He'd seen that mischief in his dad's eyes before. Playing matchmaker, was he? What, did he think that Rori with her model good looks and college education was going to take a shine to the same cowboy she hadn't wanted years before? Justin shook his head, vowing to give his dad a piece of his mind later. The pickup's engine revved and the vehicle took off, leaving him behind in the middle of town with the sun blazing and a hint of old anger beginning to brew.

"I'm really sorry about this." She did look sorry. Sorry about being forced to see him again.

That made two of them.

"Don't worry about it. This will only take a second." He stalked around her and approached Copper with an outstretched hand, palm up. "Hey there, old boy. Remember me?"

The gelding snorted, his tail swished and he nickered low in his throat.

"Guess you do." He stroked the horse's neck. "He's gone gray around the muzzle. He's gotta be what, twenty?"

"Twenty-one."

"Autumn's mare is getting up there, too." Justin's face softened as he stroked the horse again. "Looks like your grandfolks have been taking good care of him."

"He's happy on their farm. He rules the roost."

"At least that hasn't changed."

"Justin, you might as well hand over the tools and let me do this." She took a deep breath. Talk about awkward. Nothing could cover up the fact that she'd hurt him long ago, and the pinch around his dark eyes told her he well remembered. "I'll return your tools later."

"I don't mind." He looked as if he did. Tension corded in his neck as he ran one hand down Copper's back leg; his jaw went tight. A sure sign that he minded very much.

This was *so* not a good idea, especially when Copper refused to lift his hoof. She knelt at Justin's side. Being near him felt strange. Enmity radiated from him like the sun's heat off the earth. She wished she could elbow him aside and take over. "I know how to remove a shoe," she insisted. "Let me do it."

"Still as stubborn as ever."

"Are you talking about me or the horse?"

"Hard to say. Right now the both of you are giving me a headache." His grin belied his words.

She touched Copper's pastern, and the gelding obliged by lifting his hoof.

"That's more like it." Justin fell silent, head bent as he edged the screwdriver beneath a bent nail head and gave it a good tap with the pliers.

It didn't look as if he was going to relinquish the job. She scooped up the roll of tape he'd left on the pavement. It was hard to believe after all this time she was face-to-face with him. What were the chances she would run into him on her first trip into town? And it wasn't fair. She hadn't been prepared. She hadn't been back for more than a few days, and here he was in real life—not a dream or a memory—his ruggedly handsome face as emotionless as granite.

Time had been good to him. The old affection she'd once felt was like a light going on in her battered heart. Not that she loved Justin—no, there was no chance of that now and he would never feel that way about her again.

So, maybe it wasn't old affection she felt. *Lord, let this be simply a touch of nostalgia.* At least, she could pray it was so.

She studied the rugged cut of Justin's profile, the shock of dark hair spilling over his forehead, the straight slope of his nose and the spare line of his lips. Familiar and dear, but time had changed him, too. It had matured his face, sculpted hollows into his cheeks and fine lines in the corners of his eyes. His shoulders had broadened, he was a man in his prime and looked every inch of it.

With a few yanks, he pulled the last nail out of Copper's hoof and the horseshoe clattered to the pavement.

He plucked the tape from her fingers without meeting her gaze. He tore off a few strips and expertly lined them along the edge of Copper's hoof, working quick but competently, still an accomplished ranchman. There was something about Justin's combination of down-to-earth country, stoic strength and capability she would always admire.

"That ought to get you two home. Just go slow. No galloping." He lowered Copper's hoof to the ground and retrieved the shoe. "Want me to put this in the saddle pack?"

"Sure." The wind gusted in a hot airless puff, stirring leaves in the aspens that marched down the sidewalks. A dust devil whirled a thick funnel in the feed store's lot, giving her an excuse to look down the main street. The sidewalks were as empty as the road. Way down at the far end of town, the distant sound of kids' voices rose from the drive-in, known for its selection of ice cream.

What did she say to him? He didn't seem concerned about the silence as he unbuckled the pack slung behind the saddle and slid the shoe into it.

"Grocery shopping?" His brow furrowed as he inspected the pack's contents. "Wouldn't it have been quicker to drive?"

Okay, this was even more awkward. She felt the weight of his gaze searching her face for signs. Maybe he was noticing the discount-store T-shirt, the denim shorts she wore and the inexpensive flip-flops on her feet. Knowing how small-town rumors went, he was probably curious where her luxury sports car was and her designer clothes. Maybe even her wedding ring.

Humiliation swept through her. Likely as not he was holding back an "I told you so." Maybe he was waiting to hear that the life she'd left Wyoming to find after graduation had not turned out better, just different. And the man who'd taken her to the opera and symphony hadn't compared to the one she'd left behind.

"I suppose you miss riding." He filled the silence without a hint of an "I told you so."

"Something like that." She lifted her chin, wiser these days and stronger than she ever could have guessed, even if her knees were wobbly when she went to untie Copper from the hitching post. "I haven't been in a saddle for so long, I almost forgot what to do."

"You didn't have a horse boarded somewhere in Dallas?" A hint of surprise dug into the corners of his mouth.

"No." Life was like that. She'd wanted a horse; Brad had said it would be an outrageous expense they couldn't afford. Things simply hadn't worked out. She knew God was in charge, taking her where He thought she should be. "Besides, I still have Copper. How about you? Still riding Scout?"

"Now and then. He's retired from ranch work these days."

"You must miss him."

"Work isn't the same without him. I didn't know you were coming back for Terri's wedding."

"Coming home was a last-minute decision." She gathered Copper's reins and drew him away from the post. It was easier to concentrate on rubbing his nose than on meeting Justin's gaze. She didn't want her old beau to know how wrong she'd been and how stupid. A country girl like her hadn't suspected Brad's duplicity until it was too late.

"Hope you have a nice stay in town." He tipped his hat, walking backward. A gentleman, for he could have vented his anger at her, he could have asked questions about her life she did not want to answer, things she did not want him to know. He could have brought up how she'd hurt him and that would have torn at her conscience, but he didn't. He squared his shoulders, nodded goodbye and ambled away, tools and tape in hand.

Lost chances. They troubled her as she slipped off her flip-flops and stowed them in the pack. You chose a path in life and you followed it. You never knew if it would take you where you wanted to go. You just had to trust, even if the choice had been a mistake. She never would have guessed the road she'd followed would have led her back home, full circle, standing right where she'd started.

Copper blew out his breath impatiently, as if to remind her that time was wasting. The sun bore down on her, and the blacktop sizzled beneath her feet. She swung into the saddle, ignoring the burn of hot leather, and reined Copper toward the edge of town.

At least *that* was over. Meeting Justin. Recovering from the shock of seeing him again. Her palms went damp, and it wasn't from the midday heat. She wished she could rewind, hit delete and replay the past few moments. She should have apologized to him. She should have asked how he'd been. She should have explained that the reason she'd come back wasn't only to attend Terri's wedding, although she had planned on going.

"I hadn't been prepared to see him so soon," she explained.

Copper shook his head, plodding along the strip of Main reserved for parking, a totally understanding friend. She rubbed her free hand along his warm neck, his coarse mane tickling the backs of her fingers. She'd been reconciled to the idea of seeing Justin later today at the ranch, where he would probably be busy in the fields. She hadn't been prepared to talk with him, to look him in the eyes and see how much bitterness had taken him over.

She still owed him an apology. She didn't intend to shirk from it. As a Wyoming girl, she knew how to stand up and take a hit on the chin.

The front door of the diner swung shut. A new neon blue and yellow sign proclaimed the establishment to be The Greasy Spoon, but everyone called it Clem's. Clem had initially run the place beginning with the First World War, when he'd bought the building new. He'd made the best milkshakes in the county. Bittersweet, she remembered sitting in a vinyl booth sipping on a shake and laughing with her high-school friends with Justin always at her side.

Was he thinking about those days, too? As Copper circled around the new white pickup parked along the curb, she kept her gaze glued on the empty road ahead. She didn't want Justin to think that she was looking for him through the sun-washed windows. The afternoon would prove to be tough enough without adding the memories of their old romance to the mix.

Chapter Two

Justin swiped the last two steak fries through the puddle of ketchup on his plate and jammed them into his mouth, already rising from the kitchen table. Eating takeout was getting old, especially since the town diner's menu variety was limited, but it was better than the alternative.

"Hey, not so fast, bud." His sister Autumn, strawberry blonde and fragile-looking, unhooked her leg from the chair rung, snatched her tan Stetson from the sideboard and stole a wedge of pickle from his plate. "It's your turn to clean up."

"I'll do it after supper." He loped toward the back door and the mudroom, where his boots were waiting. "I've got fences to repair and a lupine patch I gotta spray."

"That can wait ten minutes. Dad, tell him, will you?" Autumn, two years younger and the bane of his existence when they were little, snagged a water bottle from the fridge. "If I'm stuck with a kitchen mess again, I'm going to chase you down, big brother, and rope you like a calf."

"Best listen to her, son." Frank glanced up from the current issue of a cattleman's magazine. "I wouldn't mess with a woman when she's got that tone in her voice."

Autumn shot him a triumphant grin on her way out the door. "And wipe down the counters and the table, too. Use soapy water, not a wet paper towel. Or my threat stands."

An empty threat, but still. What was the world coming to? He had a good eight more hours of work to do for the day, and the Sunday-morning service and errands in town hadn't helped. "What we need is to lure Aunt Opal out of retirement with a huge raise."

"Not going to happen. Don't think I didn't try it." Frank slapped the magazine shut. "Might as well clean up. Got that interview in a few minutes."

"Great." Justin stuck his head in the mudroom to give Autumn a few instructions on the yearlings, but she was already outside. Determined to catch her, he hit the screen door, sending it flying against the wall with a bang.

A horse neighed in protest, he heard a woman's "whoa!" and a thud of something hitting the dry dirt. A dust plume rose, shielding the rider who had taken a fall. Justin shrank a few inches, recognizing the red gelding skittish in the driveway.

Copper.

A tall, willowy figure rose up, at first a slim feminine shadow in the dust, but as the cloud began to settle, details emerged. The things about Rori he would never forget—the swirl of her long straight hair in the Wyoming breeze, the curve of her porcelain-cut chin, and the way she looked classy even wearing a battered baseball cap.

"What are you doing here?" He heard the venom in his words and winced. He hadn't meant to sound harsh. His thoughts had somehow influenced his voice, the same unexplainable way he had found himself mysteriously on the edge of the lawn without realizing he'd moved a single inch off the porch.

"I'm falling off my horse, apparently." She dusted herself off. "Copper still doesn't like loud sudden sounds."

"If you're out of practice riding, then you are out of practice falling." There were a couple of dried blades of grasses stuck in her hair and a streak of dirt on the hem of her shorts. "Hurting anywhere?"

"I'm tougher than I look." She smiled, but it didn't reach her soulful eyes. He didn't know what her life had been like in Dallas, but the bright sparkle that used to light her up was gone.

"Howdy again, Rori." Frank's voice behind him was deep with amusement. "If your grandfather wasn't able to replace that shoe for you, I can take Copper to the barn and get it done."

"Really? I don't want to put you to any trouble."

"Me? No trouble for me. I didn't say *I* would do it."

Yep, leave it to Dad. Not that he wouldn't have made the same offer, but his old man didn't have to sound so pleased about it. "I'll take the horse. Go back inside and finish your lunch, Dad."

But did Frank listen? No. "You and Rori go on inside and get settled. I'll be back to start the interview in a few."

"Interview?" His brain screeched to a stop. He meant

to set out after his father to take the horse and get Copper shoed, but his boots mysteriously stuck to the lawn. Rooted in place, he tried to shake the fog out of his head. He couldn't have heard that right. "Interview?"

"For the housekeeping position." Frank tossed over his shoulder as he took the reins from Rori. "Don't let his bark trouble you none. Justin's gotten cranky over the years. We manage to put up with him because he's family."

"I'm sure that's the only reason." Her laugh was like a trill of a creek, bubbling, quiet and inviting, leaving him thirsting to hear more. Unaware of her effect on him, she shoved a stray strand of hair beneath her baseball cap. "Thanks, Mr. Granger."

"If you're gonna be working for me, you've got to call me Frank." He clucked to the gelding, who followed him confidently, and the two set off down the gravel and dirt road to the horse barn.

"Thanks, Frank," Rori called out with a smile, earning a wave as man and horse turned the corner and disappeared from sight. She faced him, looking a little pale. "I guess you didn't know I wanted the job?"

"Would I be standing here with my jaw dropped if I did?" He jammed his hands in his jeans pockets, mostly wanting something to do with them. Throttling his dad didn't seem like a good idea, and it certainly wouldn't solve his problems with Rori. "Why didn't you say something in town?"

"I thought you knew."

"If you're looking for work, then that means you're staying around and this is not a quick trip home for Terri's wedding." Anger unrooted his feet and he marched toward the house. "You lied."

"No, I *am* going to Terri's wedding. I assumed your dad told you that I was here for an extended stay."

"Dad didn't tell me anything." Nothing unusual about that. He could guess at what his father was up to.

The wind gusted as if it were in cahoots with his dad because it brought the faint whiff of Rori's rose-scented perfume. He strode the same path they used to walk hand in hand. He marched up the back porch and ignored the swing where they'd spent many a summer afternoon sipping homemade lemonade and doing their homework.

Judging by Rori's silence, she might be remembering, too.

"Maybe I should ask. Do you want me to apply for the job? I understand if you don't." She swept past the screen door he held for her and waltzed into the mudroom like she'd done hundreds of times a dozen years ago. "The thing is that I need a job, and there aren't many positions available in town. Nothing else, as a matter of fact. That's the only reason I answered your dad's ad."

"Sure, I get it." He let the door slam shut and followed her into the kitchen, boots and all. "I suppose that fancy lawyer you married will be following you soon. Will he be putting up a shingle in town?"

"No. Brad won't be coming. I'm on my own." Raw emotion cut across her face and while she set her chin, straightened her shoulders and visibly wrestled it down, her sorrow remained. Sadness that was banked but unmistakably bleak in her violet-blue eyes.

Sympathy eked into him, and he did his best to stop it. No need to feel sorry for the girl who'd gotten everything she wanted. He yanked the refrigerator door open. "Sorry it didn't work out."

"Me, too."

He set his heart against her. He was no longer swayed by her emotions. He felt sorry for her. A failed marriage was nothing to celebrate. But that was as far as he was willing to go. He plunked the pitcher onto the table and went to fetch a glass out of the cupboards. He ought to say something more to fill the silence, but anything he could think to say would make him seem interested in her life.

Hardly. She'd made her decision, and now he made his. She might be thinking she'd settle for her second choice. After all, he was still available, right? Oh, he knew how women thought. They were largely a mystery, but he'd learned a thing or two over the years. The bottom line with them was wanting security, marriage and a man to pay the bills. The bigger the man's wallet, the better.

He slammed the glasses onto the table with enough force that the clunk reported through the kitchen like a gunshot. He glanced down, surprised that he hadn't broken them. That was when he realized half of the table was free of foam containers, plastic bags and the plates from lunch. "What do you think you're doing?"

"Clearing a place so we can talk about the job." Rori calmly set the armful she'd gathered onto the nearest counter, studied him with her steady gaze and backed toward the door. "But now that I see what you really think, I'm going to go. I thought we were adults and what we had was water under the bridge, but I was wrong. I'm sorry, Justin. I really am."

Uh-oh. His scars were showing, wounds he'd vowed

to keep hidden and buried. He hung his head. "Didn't mean to growl at you."

"It's okay. I know you well. Your bark is worse than your bite."

"I never bite."

"I'm glad that hasn't changed." She gripped the screen door handle.

"You don't need to go."

"Are you trying to tell me that you wouldn't mind me working here?" She'd been the one to leave. She'd broken his heart. That she was here at all showed how desperate she was. She didn't need to read minds to know what he was debating. She opened the door, fighting to hide her disappointment. "I don't blame you. I understand."

"No, wait. Give a fellow the chance to think." He paced after her, squinting at the sunlight when he joined her on the porch. "I haven't had time to prepare myself for seeing you again. I need to think this through. You, the interview, it was all sprung on me."

"I suppose that was your dad's plan." She could see that now. Frank had been downright cheerful on the phone when she'd first called. He'd been welcoming earlier that morning in town. And now he'd set them up in the kitchen together. He wanted to give them time alone. Frank had meant well, but this wasn't what she wanted or Justin, either, judging by the frown carved into his granite features. There was nothing else to do but to leave. She eased down the steps and into the burn of the sun. "Your dad is destined to be disappointed."

"I think I heard the front door shut." Justin cocked his head, listening. "Suppose he's sneaking in through the living room listening in to see if his plan is working?"

"I can't believe he would do this. Your dad is not a romantic."

"He always liked you, Rori. He said you were good for me."

"You were good for me. You were a great boyfriend. I'll always be grateful for that. We grew up together."

"Up and away." He hadn't forgotten. His face was set, his emotions stone. But had he forgiven?

She didn't think that was likely. She didn't blame him. She'd been overwhelmed when he, the quarterback of the football team, had asked her, a freshman, to go to Clem's after school for shakes. For as long as she had been able to remember, she'd had a crush on Justin Granger. Three years older, he'd been every girl's wish—smart, kind, strong, funny, popular and drop-dead gorgeous. There had only been one thing she'd wanted more in life than being Justin Granger's girl—a college education and the chance to study music.

"So, are you back to stay? Or is this a temporary thing?" Justin's deep voice hid any shades of emotion. Was he fishing for information or was he finally about to say, "I told you so?"

"I will probably go back to teaching in Dallas when fall quarter starts, but things could change. I'll just have to wait and see." The things in life she used to think were so important no longer mattered. Standing on her own two feet, building a life for herself, healing her wounds—that meant everything now.

God had given her no other option but to return to her grandparents' tiny house for the summer. She had to think He had a purpose in bringing her here. One of her favorite verses was from Jeremiah. *For I know the thoughts that I think toward you, says the Lord, thoughts of peace and not of evil, to give you a future and a hope.*

"And this man you married?" he asked. "Did he leave you, or did you leave him?"

"He threw me out." She adjusted her baseball cap brim and waited for Justin's reaction. Surely a man with that severe a frown on his face was about to take delight in the irony. She'd turned down Justin's love, and her husband of five years had thrown away hers. If she were Justin, she would want her off his land.

"You were nothing but honest with me back then." He leaned against the railing, the wind raking his dark hair, and a different emotion passed across his hard countenance. "I was the one who never listened. I loved you so much back then, I don't think I could hear anything but what I wanted."

"I loved you, too. I wish I could have been different for you." Helpless, she took another step toward the driveway. She didn't know how to thank him. He could be treating her a whole lot worse right now, and she would deserve it. "Goodbye, Justin."

"I suppose you need a job?" he called out from the railing, casually concerned.

"I'll figure out something." Needed a job? No, she was frantic for one.

How did she tell him the truth? That she'd been given enough money for a bus ride home. That she'd never thought twice about letting her husband handle the money, or the fact that he'd cleaned out the bank accounts and cancelled her cards before he'd replaced her with his plastic-surgery-enhanced receptionist.

"I haven't had a chance to get that shoe back on Copper," he called out.

"Gramps can do it tonight." Probably. If not, she could always call in the farrier. Costly, but it had to be done.

"Tell you what? You stay and round us up some decent supper, and I'll take care of your horse." Justin loped down the steps, his long-legged stride eating up the distance between them. "That will be the interview. If the food is edible, then as far as I'm concerned the job is yours. It's really up to my dad."

"Really?"

"I'll hardly be around most of the summer anyway. You know how it is. Long hours on the range."

"You're agreeing because you've figured it out, haven't you?"

"Discount-store clothes a size too large—probably your grandmother's. Am I right?"

Rori ignored the sting of her pride. The plain yellow T-shirt was Gram's, something the older woman had never worn much, and so were the flip-flops. "I didn't have a whole lot of time to pack."

"You don't have a car, do you?" Justin stalked closer. "That's why you rode Copper over here. No clothes, no vehicle and no money. That's my guess."

Shame scorched her face. She scrambled to hold on to her dignity. "I really don't feel comfortable discussing this with you."

"That fancy big-city fellow you married left you without a care." Anger dug into the corners of his mouth, making his high cheekbones appear like merciless slashes beneath his sun-browned skin. "You didn't deserve that."

"That's not what I expected from you." She stared at the grass at her feet to avoid the pity in Justin's eyes—pity for her. She couldn't blame her circumstances on anyone but herself. No pity needed. What she had to do was to wise up. Reach inside and find the tough, country girl she'd once known.

"Why don't we let the past stay where it belongs? Behind us." Justin hiked backward toward the barn. "It's gone. Done and over with. We'll just go on from here."

"Employer and employee, you mean?"

"That's it." He gave her a slow grin, the one that used to make her heartbeat flutter in adoration.

Maybe there was a tiny hint of a flutter—just old memories, nothing more as she watched him go. Looked as if she had a chance for this job after all. With any luck, there would be enough groceries in the pantry to whip up a supper the Grangers weren't likely to forget.

She hurried back to the house, glad to find Justin's dad holding a box of recipe cards left behind by his aunt Opal. It was nice to have some inside help.

"Is that Copper?" Autumn skidded to a stop in front of the corner stall. "Did Mr. Cornell bring him over?"

"Nope." Justin circled around her in the barn's main aisle, hefting his working horse's saddle. "Rori rode him over."

"Rori? You mean she's in town?"

"No need to look so excited about it." He'd done his best not to think about her all afternoon long. His work was tough and demanded all of his attention, but somehow she'd remained at the front of his mind. Patching up a calf, checking on his herd, hauling feed and playing vet, all the while bothered by the image of Rori

Cornell in a hand-me-down shirt and sadness deepening her violet eyes.

He mentally hammered up a barricade around his heart. Sure, he might feel sorry for her. She'd obviously come on hard times. But that was all he intended to feel for her. Ever.

"She's up at the main house." He shouldered through the tack-room door and plopped the saddle onto a sawhorse. He would wipe down the leather this evening. Not that he was in a hurry, but he knew if he didn't show up for supper, Dad would come out looking for him.

Frank had always thought the world of Rori. Probably because she had always been honest from the get-go. She'd always had bigger plans than settling down in small-town Wyoming. He figured she was always meant for something better.

"I can't believe it! Rori came back for the wedding, didn't she?" Autumn deposited her saddle, dancing in place. "I can't believe no one told me. Then again, considering the men around here, maybe I can."

"I can feel your gaze boring a hole in the back of my head." He gave Copper a nose rub on his way outside. "I'm not the reason she didn't call up and tell you she was back in town. Don't blame this on me."

"Who else?" Autumn padded after him. "Besides, that's what big brothers are good for. Taking the blame."

"Funny." He rolled his eyes. "And before you say it, I'm over Rori. It doesn't matter to me that she's here."

"There was a time when I would have called you a liar if you'd said that, but now I know it's true." Autumn caught up with him, the heels of her riding boots crunching in the grass. A sign of her determination.

"You've become a cold, hard man, Justin. I'm worried about you."

"Nothing new there." He'd been like this a long time. It had taken him a while to learn the important lessons about women, but he'd finally done it. "No need to worry about me. Go on up to the house and catch up with your old friend."

"*My* old friend?" Autumn sounded as if she was going to correct him but then decided better of it. "Aren't you coming, too?"

"Got a mare I need to check on first." He climbed through the board fence into a grassy paddock. A small band of expecting mares looked up from their grazing and wheeled in his direction. "I won't be long."

"Need any help?"

His sister stood there, the sun at her back, the only female he could count on. She did a man's work without complaint day in and day out come blizzard cold or blistering heat and still he couldn't trust her with the truth.

Help? He would need a ten-gallon bucket of it if Rori ended up working for the family. Yet how could he object? She wouldn't have left behind the city life she'd chosen if she had any other option. He wanted to keep his distance, but that didn't mean he wanted to see her hurting.

God had a way of keeping a man humble. Justin tipped his hat brim lower to keep the sun off his face, held his hands out to show the mares he'd come without treats and went on with his work.

Chapter Three

"Mighty fine grub, Rori." Mr. Granger—Frank—dug his spoon into the big bowl of chili in front of him. "We haven't eaten this good in months."

Judging by the look of satisfaction on his face, he was telling the truth instead of tempering it with kindness. Relieved, she turned back to the sink. She wasn't the most accomplished cook, since she and Brad had employed a maid who'd done most of the food preparation. "I've gotten rusty, but being home with Gram and Gramps has given me some practice."

"If this is rusty, I can't wait to eat what you fix when you're back in practice. Autumn, where did Justin get off to?"

"He had to check on a mare."

"He missed grace, and if he's not careful he's going to miss supper." He didn't look all that happy with his son. Probably it was disappointing work being a matchmaker.

"Do you want me to stick around, or should I take off?" She'd tidied the kitchen and put all the prep dishes into the dishwasher. "I can stay, but my grandparents—"

"Are expecting you." Frank nodded. "Sure, go ahead. It's Justin's turn to do dishes, since he left the lunch mess."

"Serves him right," littlest sister, Addison, piped up from her side of the table. It was hard to get used to her being so grown up. When Rori left town, Addison had been eight. Now she had just finished her junior year of college. The girl with the ponytails and freckles was only a memory replaced by a tall beauty. Addison frowned, wrinkling her perfect complexion. "Justin looks down on kitchen work."

"He does, and it's our job to keep him in line," Autumn added with a wink.

What Rori wanted to do was to get out of the house before Justin walked in. Not that she felt compelled to avoid him, but her dignity was bruised. He pitied her. No doubt, that wouldn't change. She grabbed her ball cap from the hat hooks by the back door. "Thanks. Have a good evening, everyone."

She slipped outside listening to the three Grangers at the table call out their goodbyes to her. The sunlight had tempered, the blazing heat kicked down a notch to hint at a beautiful early summer evening. She hopped down the steps and hurried across the lawn, the grass fragrant beneath her flip-flops.

The hills, the stretch of the high prairie and the rim of the breathtaking Tetons in the distance surrounded her. She trudged toward the barn, keeping a lookout for Justin. Best to avoid him if she could. That wouldn't always be possible now that Frank had offered her the job, but it was likely. Justin had changed, and she hated to think she had played a hand in that.

What I would give to go back and do it over again,

she thought, half prayer, half impossible wish. If she could turn back time, she never would have accepted his offer for their first fateful milkshake together. She would never have trusted or married Brad.

"Rori!"

She heard the wind carry her name. Through the lush green fields she saw Justin in the knee-high grasses, his hat shading his face and a gloved hand raised up to her. More than distance separated them. She waved back, hurrying to the barn, and freed Copper from a stall. The white-muzzled gelding nickered a warm welcome and pressed his face in her hands with unmistakable affection.

Warmth filled her—emotions she'd been battling since she'd come home. Copper's steadfast friendship, the sweet-scented grass and the earthy hint of dust in the air, the endless blue skies, it all overwhelmed her. Life may have led her away but her roots remained deep in this land. The days of long ago felt so close she could almost hear them. The sound of the radio in Dad's truck, running up the back steps to the whir of Mama's mixer in the kitchen, the carefree head toss Copper used to greet her with when he was young, bounding up to the fence.

"I missed you, too, old buddy." She leaned her forehead to his, her best friend. "C'mon. Let's ride home."

By the time she'd saddled and bridled him and mounted up, the yard was empty of all signs of Justin. He was probably inside finishing up the chili and cornbread she'd made. Maybe he was seated at the table and facing the windows overlooking the backyard and the mountain view.

Was he watching her now? she wondered as she

reined Copper toward the driveway. Or was he doing his best to avoid her? She sat straight in the saddle, glad when the curving road took her out of sight. It was sad how much had changed between them, when they had once been so close.

Of course, that was her fault, plain and simple. She drew her cap brim over her eyes and, squinting into the light, rode the low rays of the sun home.

"How is Wildflower?"

Autumn's question came from as if far away. Justin shoveled a steaming spoonful of chili into his mouth, hardly feeling the burn on his tongue. He grabbed a nearby glass, gulped down some milk to put out the fire, and realized everyone in the kitchen was staring at him. Addison struggled to hide a grin.

"Seems he's got something important on his mind, girls." Frank, grabbing a cookie from the stash they'd bought from Clem's, couldn't look happier. "Looks like Autumn had better ask her question again."

Justin cleared his throat. He was in no mood for ribbing, however well-intentioned. "Wildflower is fine. She's close to her time."

"Too bad Cheyenne isn't back from school yet. I reckon she'd like to be there when her mare foals." Frank grabbed his root beer off the table. "The Mariners are on. Anyone going to join me?"

"I will." Addison bounded up from the table, still coltish and energetic, her strawberry-blond ponytail bobbing. "Are you comin', Autumn?"

"No, I'm going to go sit with the mares and leave Justin with the dishes." His oldest little sister seemed pretty pleased with herself, too. "Have fun, brother dearest. I know what you think of housework."

"I don't have a bad opinion about housework," he argued. He had more outside work than he could get done in a day, the last thing he needed was more. "I just don't want to do it."

"Sure. We wouldn't want you to demean yourself," Addison joked.

"Not our brother." Grinning at him, Autumn stole her Stetson off the wall hook. "I don't know how you turned out to be so grumpy. You must have gotten a bad gene. It's a shame, really."

"A terrible shame," Addison agreed from the counter, where she was helping herself to a cookie. "Is it my imagination, or is he grumpier tonight?"

"He's definitely grumpier," Autumn agreed. "Let's hope his mood improves."

"Or it's going to be a long summer," Addison predicted, backing out of the room to join their dad. The TV droned to life in the next room.

"It will be a longer summer if you two don't knock it off." He scowled over another spoonful of chili. "Or else."

"Yeah, like we're scared." Autumn plopped her hat onto her head. "You're all bark, Justin."

"You never know. One day I might change."

"I'm not worried." She stole a cookie from the counter, too. "I've known you all my life. You're one of the good guys."

"Yeah? Haven't you heard? Good guys finish last."

"You're thinking of Rori?" She nibbled on the edge of the cookie. "What happened to her? She looks so sad. Is there something I should know? Her grandparents are all right, aren't they?"

"Rori didn't say Del and Polly were having health problems."

"Just checking." Autumn said nothing more, waiting a beat before she padded through the door, but what she hadn't said lingered more loudly than if she'd uttered the words.

Rori wasn't all right. She was hurting. Regardless of what he'd come to think about her and women like her, he didn't like that. Not at all.

Blurry-eyed, Rori bounded through the early morning kitchen, eyes glued to the coffeemaker in the corner. Thank heavens it was chugging away. The smell of caffeine lured her straight to the counter.

"Good mornin', Pumpkin." Gram's voice startled her. There was a clang of a pot at the stove. "Aren't you up early?"

"This isn't early. This is still technically nighttime." Dawn was a light haze at the rim of the dark world. "Do you get up every morning like this?"

"Early to bed, early to rise."

"That's your secret to being healthy and wise." She grabbed a cup from the cabinet. "I'm going to ride Copper over to the Grangers and leave you and Gramps with the truck."

"Oh, we were looking forward to running you over there." Gram flipped sausage links in the fry pan. "Del is so pleased to have you back, he's over the moon. I am, too. Your sweet face livens up our place."

"Not as much as yours does." She brushed a kiss

against her grandmother's cheek. "I won't be home until late."

"Should I keep a plate of supper warm for you?"

"No, but leave the dishes. I have to make myself useful some way." The sound of coffee pouring and the fragrant smell of the rising steam made her sigh. A few jolts of caffeine and maybe her brain would stop feeling heavy and foggy. She hadn't slept so hard in ages. It was all the fresh air and country living. At least being forced to come back home had a few perks.

"You know I can't let dishes sit around in the sink. Goodness." Gram laughed to herself. "The idea."

"Try it, would you?" Rori slid the carafe back onto the burner and reached for the sugar bowl. "I have to earn my keep, and I'll be mad if you don't."

"I don't want you mad." Gram slid a sausage from the pan onto a paper-toweled plate. "I want you stayin' around as long as you can."

"Me, too." Rori gave the coffee a stir and set the spoon in the sink. "There's no place like home."

"You remember that when you start thinking about leaving us at summer's end." Tears prickled in her grandmother's gentle blue eyes. "Not that I blame you, but I miss you and your sister when you're not around."

"Ditto." Rori squeezed her grandmother's frail shoulder, unable to say how hard it had been to stay away. Visits home weren't enough, and a part of her had been sorely missing. She loved her work at the private arts school where she taught piano and music theory, but it took coming home to remember how much she loved Wyoming's peace and quiet, the restful stretch of rolling fields, hills and endless sky of this farm and the family she loved. Her grandparents had taken her in and her younger sister when their parents had been killed in a blizzard. "Give me a call if you need anything. I won't be home until near dark."

"Have a good day, Pumpkin." Gran whipped open the oven door and wrapped something in a paper towel. "Here. You need breakfast."

She took the scrambled egg-white sandwich with thanks and headed outside. Things were simple here. Balanced meals three times a day, no endless hurrying, no pressure to measure up, no feeling like a Wyoming girl out of place in her husband's life.

It was an odd feeling to grab the jingling bridle from the barn, whistle to Copper in the pasture and slip between the barbed-wire fencing as she did when she was younger. If only she could take an eraser and wipe away that chunk of time she'd spent in Dallas, then maybe she could find a way to be happy again. Erase her mistakes and find some peace. Wouldn't that be a blessing?

"Good morning, old friend." She petted Copper's nose when he came up to her. She laughed when he tried to get a hold of her sandwich. "That's not for you. Sorry."

Copper gave her a sheepish look, as if he were saying he had to give it a try anyway. She slipped the bridle over his head, the bit into his mouth, and managed to get onto his back without spilling her coffee. They headed off through the fields surrounded by birdsong and the golden crown of the rising sun. Beauty surrounded her. The only shadow that loomed ahead of her was thoughts of Justin.

He wanted to leave the past behind them. Water under the bridge. He apparently had no problem doing that. He had probably gotten over her in a flash. Men were built that way, she feared. They didn't feel as deeply as women did. Love didn't rope them in as much, nor did it sink beyond the heart to the soul.

Justin had gotten hurt when she'd told him she couldn't marry him and set aside her dreams for him. But he probably hadn't shed a tear over it. He probably didn't feel racked with regret regardless of the number of years that had passed. He just probably turned off his heart like a switch, and she was sorry for that.

He would never know how much she had wanted to say yes. She took a bite of her sandwich and a sip of coffee. He would never know how afraid she'd been of living a life without having reached her biggest goals, ending up with nothing but a list of regrets. Losing her mom in junior high had affected her forever. Life was finite. You had to make it count.

Ironically, she'd racked up more regrets by running toward her future. One thing was for sure, there would be only smart decisions and careful choices from here on out. As if in agreement, the sun peeked over the rolling hills, bringing light to the shadows.

Justin heard the muffled clip of horseshoes on the hard-packed dirt outside the main horse barn. He stuck his head over the rail to see Rori riding in on a sunbeam. Dust motes danced in the soft yellow rays, hazing her like a dream.

Or, he realized, like an answer to a quick prayer. Wildflower was standing next to him, skin flicking, head down, panting heavily. "Rori, can I ask you to race up to the house and call the vet?"

"What's wrong?"

"My sister's horse is having some trouble." He kept

his voice calm and authoritative, letting the mare know he was confident and in charge of her. That was the best way to comfort the frightened creature. "The number's on the wall above the kitchen phone. Tell Nate it's Wildflower and he needs to get over here pronto. Oh, and fetch my dad, too."

"You got it." She wheeled the red horse around and with a touch of her heels, the gelding leaped into an all-out gallop. Head down, tail flying. It was good to see the old gelding still had his racing legs.

Wildflower blew out her breath to get his attention. She watched him with unblinking liquid brown eyes, staring so hard it was as if she were trying to give him an important message. Good thing he spoke horse.

"I hear you, girl." He rubbed her muzzle. "Let's try to walk you. Are you game?"

She followed him into the aisle, head down, winded. First foals could be tough on a small mare. He and his dad had kept a close eye on her and they'd caught her trouble as early as they could, but she had a hard row ahead. He wished Cheyenne had been able to make it back home from vet school. He could really use her help right now. He didn't want to be the one she blamed if things went wrong.

"Just keep it slow and steady, girl. I'm right here with you." He and Wildflower had made it to the end of the aisle and carefully turned around before hooves drummed outside. Rori rode up, dismounting in a graceful sweep. She was a welcome sight, as hard as that was to admit. "Did you reach Nate?" he asked her.

"I heard him running to his truck before he hung up on me. He promised to break speed limits on the way over." She patted Copper's neck and led him into the end stall she'd used yesterday. "Your dad said he's on his way, too."

"You're a lifesaver. Of all the mornings to forget my cell phone."

"It's hard to function properly before sunup." She unbuckled the old bridle and gated the horse in. "She's not looking so good. Is there anything I can do to help?"

"We'll see. If she holds off until the vet gets here, then you are free and clear. But if not, I'll need your help with the foaling."

"Okay." She reached over the rail to grab the empty water bucket from Copper's stall. "I'll fetch some water first, and then take over walking her if you want to get the stall ready."

"I'll take you up on that. Here." He ambled close and stole the bucket from her grip.

This close, she could smell the hay on his T-shirt and the soap from his morning shower. Without a hat, his dark hair stood up on end, still shower damp, and his lean cheeks were freshly shaven, showing off the deep groves bracketing both sides of his mouth, groves that transformed into dimples when he grinned but now they were grim set lines.

"Thanks ahead of time." He put distance between them. "It's good to have you here after all."

"Oh, you say that as if it had been a huge question? I thought we settled that."

"I know. I might not have been fully truthful yesterday. What I *want* to feel and what I admit to feeling are two different things." He handed over Wildflower's lead. "This is the truth. When I saw you ride through that door, I knew I could count on you."

"Back at you." She clucked to the mare, encouraging

her forward. "The vet is going to be here in a bit. Your dad is coming. She's going to be just fine."

"As long as we can get that foal turned first, she will be." Grim, determined, he hiked to the nearby sink. The walled-off room hid him from her sight, but nothing could diminish his steady, capable iron will and his endless decency.

It was heartening to know some things didn't change. That for all the prickly layers and cool granite Justin had become, he was still underneath the cowboy she'd always admired. His heart wasn't switched off completely, after all. She may as well face the fact that she would probably always be just a little bit in love with him.

She cooed soothingly to the struggling mare as they took slow painful steps down the aisle.

Chapter Four

Justin upended the bucket into the stall, letting fresh grain tumble into the feeding trough. The polite old gelding nickered what sounded like thanks and swished his tail before nosing in to lap up the treats. One animal cared for. He knuckled back his hat, watching Rori out of the corner of his eye. The bulk of his thoughts ought to be centered on the expecting mare, but his mind seemed drawn magnetically to the woman, fresh-faced and so wholesome she made his teeth ache.

She looked as if she belonged here with her light hair tied back in a single ponytail swinging slightly with her slow gait. The concern for the mare touching her face made her a hundred times more beautiful than any makeup artist could. With the sun spearing through the skylights above and through the open doors, she looked ethereal, too lovely to be true, and something straight out of his forgotten dreams.

Footsteps padded through the grass and dirt. Dad's gait, dragging a bit from a long night spent up and down checking on the mares. Frank came into sight. "Looks like she surprised you."

"Yep. I came out to feed the stock and Wildflower was down in the field."

"I wasn't talking about the horse."

Justin frowned. Impossible to miss the grin on his dad's face. He figured he would set them up, was that it? He shook his head at his dad. Now wasn't the time to hash this out. The horse was the concern. His boots carried him down the aisle and before he realized it he was at Rori's side, doing his best not to notice the light spray of freckles on her nose as he took the lead rope from her. As careful as he was, his fingers brushed hers. Her skin was warm and satin-soft, and a shoot of tenderness took root in his chest.

"You can go on up to the house now." His voice sounded scratchy and thick with feelings best left unexamined. "Thanks for your help."

"Any time." She stepped away, shy and graceful as always, as if nothing significant had happened between them. Of course she hadn't reacted to his accidental touch. Why would she? She backed down the aisle, glancing between him and his dad. "Call me if you need anything. I'll be back with some coffee."

"Bless you." Frank tipped his hat to her. "I could use some chow, too."

"I'll see what I can do." She ran her hand gently along Wildflower's swollen side. "It's going to be okay, girl."

Don't start liking her again, Justin told himself. He'd always been a sucker for a woman who was kind to animals. That's what had gotten him noticing her in high school in the first place. A few years ago, that's why he'd decided to trust Tia.

"Same old Rori." Frank ambled close and rubbed the mare's neck. "Good to see that it's true."

"What's true?" He turned his shoulder, afraid that his dad had noticed something Justin wasn't ready to admit to himself.

"You can take the girl out of the country, but you can't take the country out of the girl." Frank smiled as he spoke, as if he was greatly amused. "Why, what did you think I was going to say?"

"Let's just help the mare." His face heated. He didn't like that his dad *had* figured things out. Just because he liked Rori didn't mean a thing. Probably he always would like her. She was a nice woman. "Think we can wait for the vet?"

"Get Wildflower in the stall, and I'll scrub up." Frank gave the horse another caring pat, for the mare had nickered at the sound of her name. "It won't be much longer now, sweetheart. You go with Justin."

"Dad, you know nothing is going to happen between Rori and me, don't you?" He gently eased the mare toward the birthing stall.

"Is that what you think?" A barrel laugh rang out as he disappeared into the washroom.

"Isn't that why you have been trying to push me and Rori together?" Fresh hay crinkled beneath his boots and Wildflower's hooves.

"I figured the two of you ought to resolve things. It's not good to leave loose ends the way you have with that gal." Water rushed, pouring into a stainless-steel sink. "Don't you reckon it's time you forgave her?"

"For running out on me?"

"For doing what she had to do. For following the path the Good Lord set her on." The water cut off, and Frank ambled into sight, drying his hands and forearms on a fluffy blue towel. He tossed it over the top of an empty stall gate. "You're not so good at forgiveness, son."

"I don't want to be you. No offense." Wildflower lowered her head, heaving, her knees buckling.

"Let's get her on her side." Frank jumped to help. He had worked with animals all of his life, and it showed in the skill and comfort his touch seemed to bring Wildflower. The mare leaned her neck into his hands.

One day he wanted to be as good a man as his dad. The trouble was, he didn't want to be as gullible. Their mom had left Dad twice. Both times Dad had wrestled with a shattered heart, later accepted her apologies and let her back into their lives. Then he'd taken care of her when liver disease set in.

No one in their right mind would ever call Frank Granger a fool, but he did have a big heart. Too big.

That was something Justin would make sure he would never have. No way did he intend to let any woman tread on his dignity like Dad had allowed Mom to. At the time, Dad had young kids who missed their mom and wanted her back, too, but a man could only take so much. Justin had already reached that limit.

"Sounds like Nate's here." Frank stopped to listen. "Yep, tires in the gravel. Help has arrived."

Justin ran his hand down the mare's nose, murmuring low to comfort her, and forced his thoughts away from Rori.

But it didn't work.

"Need a hand?" Autumn swaggered through the mudroom and popped her head into the kitchen.

"No, I'm managing just fine." Rori slapped the last

omelet onto the last plate and turned off the burner. "How is Wildflower?"

"A brand-new mama." There was a *thunk, thunk*, presumably Autumn kicking off her boots before she strode into the room with two large thermoses. "She made it through just fine once they got things heading out straight. She has the cutest little filly. All long legs, bottlebrush mane and the biggest brown eyes. Cheyenne is going to flip when she gets home."

"Glad there's good news. I could tell your dad was worried. He was totally frowning. I didn't know he was capable of it." She rescued the platter of bacon and sausage patties from the warm oven and walked down the counter, filling plates. "I'll get you all some more coffee and tea in a jiffy. I was going to bring breakfast out to the barn."

"Sounds like a good idea. Dad was up half the night checking on the mare as it is, and you know Justin, grumbling about being behind with the morning chores." Autumn set the thermoses on the counter and rolled her eyes. Her light auburn hair tumbled loose around her shoulders. At first glance, no one would peg her as a tomboy, not with her china-doll complexion, deep hazel eyes and leggy stature, but Rori knew no one could outride her. She'd tried many times. "How is Bella?"

"Still the best horse in the history of the world." Autumn uncapped the thermoses. "I had to stop and say hi to Copper. He's looking good for his age. Your grandfather is pampering him."

"Gramps can't help himself. Once a horse lover, always a horse lover."

"That's the truth. It's the way God made us." Autumn yanked the coffee carafe from the machine and upended it over a thermos. "It has to be weird being back. You've been away for so long."

"I hadn't realized how much I've missed this pokey little town. Not one thing happens there." She did her best not to remember the past and the impatient girl she'd been. And how eager to experience something more exciting than dinky Wild Horse, Wyoming. "It used to drive me crazy, but I'm thankful for it now. It's reassuring when home always stays the same."

"Speaking of things that haven't changed. Clem's— now The Greasy Spoon—still makes the best burgers around." Autumn screwed the cap on the thermos and reached for the hot-water carafe. "Have any plans, say, middle of the week?"

"Are you thinking horse ride?"

"Just like old times." There was a quiet question hanging in the air between them, but Autumn didn't ask it. Instead she finished pouring the water. "I'll run this outside. Need me to take anything?"

"How about the muffins?" The sausage platter was empty and she set it aside to snatch the cloth-covered basket from the edge of the kitchen table.

"Yum. Smells good." Autumn hugged the thermoses and took the basket into the crook of her arm. "Hate to rain on your parade, but guess who's listening at the door?"

"I'm not listening," a man grumbled from the mud-room. "I'm getting some clean towels for the barn."

Justin. Rori's palms went damp, and she wiped them on her jeans. Great. Why hadn't she noticed he was there? How much had he overheard?

"Yeah, right." Autumn chuckled as she strolled out

the door. "You could have asked me to bring back the towels."

"Didn't think of it." Justin sounded easygoing as he spoke with his sister. "Did anyone think to call Cheyenne?"

"I'll do it," Autumn called out a split second before the screen door slapped shut.

Rori set the plates on a tray she'd found in one of the bottom cupboards and covered the steaming food. With every movement she made, she was infinitely aware of Justin in the next room, the faint shuffle of his boots on the tile floor, the muted squeak of a cabinet door closing and the rustle of fabric as he paced to the kitchen door.

"Need any help?" Hard to tell if he was being friendly or just helpful, as he might be to any hired hand.

"Nope, but thanks. I've got it."

"You could make us trudge into the kitchen to eat, you know. You don't have to bring food to us."

"I don't mind. You've all had a busy morning and it's not even six o'clock." She opened the drawer and began counting out flatware. This is just conversation, she told herself. Justin had meant what he said about letting bygones be. He was making an effort, and it mattered. She could, too. "Since you're standing there with a free hand, you could grab the juice on the counter."

"Good. I like to make myself useful." A faint hint of his dimples carved into either side of his mouth. He ambled into the kitchen, shrinking the room with his size and presence. He casually scooped up the pitcher and the stacked plastic glasses without complaint. "You need to come see the new filly."

"Autumn said she was the cutest thing."

"Foals usually are." He held the door for her, and

somehow the morning seemed brighter as they headed down the steps and along the path together. "You were calm under pressure, Rori. You helped a lot."

"I did nothing. I called the vet. I walked the horse." She shrugged. "Anyone could have done the same."

"Not anyone. I was afraid you had turned into a city slicker, but I can see you've still got some Wyoming girl in you. I'm glad you're working here. It's a big responsibility running this place, and it will be a burden off Dad's mind to know he's got someone in the house he can rely on. Someone to feed us and the hired men when we get hungry."

"I'm glad you think I'm a help." She held the tray steady, flatware and dishes clattering with each step, and squinted against the low slant of the morning sun. She'd forgotten her ball cap. Grass slapped against her shins, crunched beneath her shoes and barely hid a jackrabbit who startled away into the field as they approached.

"Rori." Frank hurried out of the barn to take the heavy tray from her and shot his son a telling glance. "That's too heavy for you to carry all this way."

"No problem. I'm stronger than I look."

"Oh, the problem wasn't with you. I thought I raised my son better than that."

"I offered, but she turned me down." Justin put the pitcher and cups down on top of a barrel.

"I did. I wouldn't have given up the tray if he'd tried to wrestle it away from me." She followed Mr. Granger and the tray to a walled-off room next to the tack room, where a sink and counter, microwave and small refrigerator sat as neat and as clean as any kitchen. A small battered dinette set huddled in the center of the area. Frank slid the tray onto the faded pink Formica top and the rest of the Grangers plus the vet descended on the table.

"Want to come see her?" Justin's voice rang low, but even with the clang of dishes, rise of voices and cheerful conversation it was the only thing she heard.

"I'd love to." She floated after him, excitement tingling through her. It had been ages since she'd seen a newborn foal. She loped down the aisle, the stalls empty this time of year, and felt the fingers of the past trying to grab hold of her. She was at home with the warm scent of horseflesh and grain in the air and the concrete beneath her feet. Maybe she'd never realized how much she loved country life.

"Hey, there, Wildflower." Tender-toned, Justin knelt down at the stall bars. "We just want to get a good look at your baby."

"Your beautiful baby," Rori corrected, wrapping her hand around the rail and kneeling beside him. Wildflower nickered low in her throat, a proud mama who turned to lick at her little filly's dainty ear.

Nothing could be sweeter than the little gold-and-white bundle curled up in the soft clean hay. The newborn stared at them with a surprised expression, as if she didn't know what to think about the strange faces staring in at her. She blinked her long eyelashes and stretched toward them as far as her neck would allow.

"That's a pretty girl," Justin soothed, holding out his hand, palm up, his motions slow.

The filly gave his fingers a swipe with her tongue and drew back, as if her own boldness startled her. Wildflower nickered gently to her baby and, as if encouraged, the little one's head bobbed down as she scrambled to get up on her spindly legs and point them in the correct direction.

Sunshine tumbled through the open top half of the stall door, gleaming on the mare and foal's velvet coats. Wildflower rubbed her chin on her daughter's shoulder, a congratulatory pat, and nickered proudly. The tiny filly wobbled on her thin, impossibly long legs and flicked her bob of a tail joyfully. She took a few proud steps. Her front knees gave out and she landed in the soft hay.

"Poor baby." Rori reached through the rails instinctively, making sure the newborn was all right. The foal looked up at her with big, wondrous eyes, and Rori felt her chest catch. Hard not to fall in love with the wee one. She couldn't help brushing her fingers across the soft velvet nose. "You will get the hang of it. I promise. Keep at it."

The foal's eyes drifted shut, as if she liked the gentle stroke.

"You still have a way with animals." Justin's low voice moved her like the brush of the summer air and the peace of the morning. Familiar, and it was what she'd missed over the years.

"I do all right." She didn't have a gift, just love for creatures large and small. "Not the way you do."

"I got it all from my dad." No way to hide the affection in his voice. "I learned a lot growing up at his knee. One day, I might be good enough to take over the place when he retires."

"Word is that he's cutting back, handing over a lot of the responsibilities of the ranch to you and Autumn."

"Your gramps was talking about me, huh?" He paused as the filly opened her eyes, set her chin with determination and positioned her front hooves for another go at walking. "Dad wants to retire, but truth is, he loves the work. It's not like he has anything else to do. He's single, and he's done raising all of us."

"It's good that you're close. You must spend a lot of time with him."

"A perk of the job." He'd sacrificed a lot for his dad and for this ranch that had been in his family for five generations. "It's what I like most about ranching. Long hours in the saddle talking with my dad."

"I can't picture you doing anything else but ranching." She gazed up at him with those big blue eyes.

He felt the impact like a touch to his cheek. Her gaze raked him, as if she were trying to see past the titanium barrier he'd put up.

"You still love the work," she stated, not questioning. That's how well she knew him.

"Truth is, I would have liked a lot of things, but this is what I chose." He paused as the filly pulled herself up and swayed, but what he was seeing was Rori. The changes in her—more mature and seasoned and longing for something he couldn't name. "Truth is, after you left town I couldn't take it. I missed you so much."

"You missed me? But you said—"

"That I wouldn't even notice if you were gone?" he repeated his horrible words, angry at himself for saying what could never be taken back. She didn't even understand what she'd been to him. "No one knew I applied to college and got in. A late admission for the winter quarter in agriculture sciences at Washington State University."

"Where I was." Her hand covered his, warm and comforting, a connection he did not break.

"I was all set to accept when Dad took a bullet. Rustlers. They got away with about a thousand head of cattle. I was too busy trying to save my father to stop them."

"I'd heard he was hit. I remember Gram and Gramps talking about it. I called several times, but no one was home. I didn't feel right about leaving a message. When I heard he was all right, I didn't call again."

"It was touch and go for a while there. We almost lost him. I ended up staying and pulling my weight around here, so Dad could recover. The bullet nicked his heart, so there was no question. He had to take it easy to heal right."

"You're a good son to him, Justin. A good man."

"Looks can be deceiving." He grinned, fighting the moment, because the way she peered up at him made him feel ten feet tall, the way he used to feel when she loved him.

Careful, knowing he needed to put the brakes on his thoughts, he extricated his hand from hers a little too quick and rough. Her face fell as if he'd slapped her, but he couldn't help it. The tenderness that had taken root in his chest ached, tenderness he had no right to feel, and he'd better figure out a way to pluck it right out. It would not be wise to have gentle feelings for Rori. When summer ended, she would be out of here. Wild Horse, Wyoming, was too small for her—*that* hadn't changed.

"Look at her go!" Dad's warm chuckle broke the moment, filling the silence that had fallen and chasing away the hurt look on Rori's beautiful face.

Justin tried to force his attention to the filly awkwardly loping the length of the stall. She skidded to an unsteady stop, swaying. She shook her head, flicked her tail and gave a little bleat of happiness. Victory.

"Cheyenne's gonna be sorry she missed this." Frank shook his head, moseying over to the rails. "Watch, she'll probably drive up this morning. What are you two doing here? Catching up?"

"Admiring the foal." Rori seemed to know what his dad was up to and wasn't intimidated one bit. "You are going to have to hold your horses, sir, because your matchmaking efforts are not going to work."

"Wasn't trying to matchmake. But since you put it that way, are you sure there isn't a chance?"

"Dad." Justin rolled his eyes, shook his head and counted his blessings. He wouldn't trade his father for anything, but he would like the right to keep a few things private. Judging by the knowing look on his father's face, Frank wasn't fooled. They both knew that what Justin felt for Rori wasn't gone—not by a long shot. Trying to be friendly with her wasn't working. Time for a new plan.

"I'd best get my breakfast and hit the range." He turned tail on Rori, determined to follow the path his life had taken and one he would not change—a path that led away from her. He didn't look back.

Chapter Five

Justin. She couldn't forget the warm moment between them or the way he'd jerked from her touch as if she had the plague. Not even prayer had helped. It was not easy to get him out of her mind when signs of him were everywhere she turned. There was his coffee cup with his name on it that she had rinsed and fit into the dishwasher's top rack. Blue towels she harvested from the dryer to fold, which had his name monogrammed on them. When she went upstairs to put them away, she was bombarded with the images of him in framed pictures marching up the walls of the stairwell. Justin as a baby, Justin as a toddler, Justin as a little boy.

I never should have taken his hand like that. She shook her head, wishing she had kept the urge to comfort him to herself. What had she been thinking? She hadn't, that's what. She'd reached out to him instinctively, as she would have done to anyone who was talking of something painful, but the way he'd jerked away from her had felt like a slap. Worse, it felt like a rejection.

After you left I missed you so much. His confession

in the barn stayed with her, lodged like a knife too deep to pull out. Obliterating everything she'd believed about him. Why hadn't he told her? She'd never known how he felt. He'd always kept his most intimate feelings private.

It looked to her as if he were still doing the same.

His room was spare and neat with no clutter on his nightstand or dresser. His bed was made, his blinds open to the panoramic Teton range. She set the pile of towels on the foot of his bed and continued on her delivery. When she was leaving a stack of brown towels on Mr. Granger's bathroom counter, the phone rang.

She dragged the empty laundry basket behind her as she raced the length of the hall, skipped down the stairs and plucked the cordless handset from the cradle.

"Hello? The Granger residence." She set the basket on the floor next to the kitchen counter.

"Uh, I'm looking for Stowaway Ranch?" A woman's pleasant voice hesitated across the line.

"You have the right place. How can I help you?"

"I'm looking to buy a horse, and the mayor's wife gave me this number. I need to speak with Autumn, please."

"If you don't mind holding, I'll be happy to check for you."

"Thank you so much." Her voice was polished-sounding, with a slight East Coast accent.

Curious. Rori hit hold on the multiline system and frowned at the radio. It had been a while since she'd used a two-way. She assumed it was on the right station as she unhooked the mouthpiece and hit the call button twice. "Justin?"

No reply. The dishwasher gurgled, the only sound in the silent kitchen. The window over the sink showed a sunny vista of sprawling meadows and a distant rising hillside. A bright white speck sat midway up the slope. Justin was working in the field, hopefully not too far from his truck. She clicked again. "Justin?"

"It's Frank. What's up?" The radio squawked.

"I've got a call for Autumn."

"Hold on, I'll go fetch her."

While she waited, she tried not to read too much into the fact that Justin hadn't answered her call. Chances were that Frank had been closer to the truck. That Justin was tangled up repairing a fence or busy feeding grain and it was easier for his dad to grab the radio. That was all.

If only the image of him striding away from her would amble straight out of her mind, along with the look on his face when he'd yanked his hand out from beneath hers. It wasn't quite terror or disdain, but it had been close.

"Rori? It's Autumn. What's up?" She sounded breathless, as if she'd been working hard and had run to the truck.

"I got a call for you." After she'd followed Autumn's instructions for patching the caller through to the barn, she hauled the basket back to the laundry room.

As she stuffed washed clothes into the dryer, she tried planning her shopping list for town, but her thoughts returned to Justin. He'd applied to college? She couldn't believe it. Justin, at college? She tried to imagine him living in a dorm, hauling a backpack jammed with books across campus and spending his time studying.

No way. Whenever she thought of him, she couldn't place him anywhere but right here on Granger land.

She grabbed the hundred-dollar bill Frank had tucked beneath a set of truck keys for her use, scribbled out a list and headed out the door. The instant her sneakers touched the top step, her gaze arrowed to the rise ahead, where Justin's white pickup was parked along the fence line.

Regret. It grew with every step she took, and it wasn't the only emotion haunting her. The old feeling she'd tried to explain away as nostalgia, as a fondness for what had been between them, trailed her to the garage. Even out of sight, a piece of her heart longed for him.

Lord, what do I do? She wasn't over Justin at all.

He wiped the sweat from his brow and watched the tan pickup amble down the driveway. Brake lights flashed through the growing dust cloud slowly stealing her from sight. If he were given to poetic notions, he would say he lost a chunk of his heart as she left. Good thing he wasn't prone to such nonsense.

"Son, are you going to daydream or grab the other end of the board?" His dad cut into his thoughts.

Justin shook his head, realizing how things must look, him staring after her like a love-struck fool. He grabbed his water bottle, took a healthy swig and went down on one knee. So his dad wouldn't jump to conclusions, he ground out with what he hoped was enough bitterness, "Did you *have* to hire Rori? Of all the women in the county?"

"She was the only one who answered the ad. What did you want me to do?" Frank hefted his end of the board, fit it in place and hauled his hammer out of his belt. "Besides, she needs the job. She looks down on her luck."

"No comment, Dad. I don't want to talk about her."

"You two were looking pretty cozy in the barn earlier." A few whacks of the hammer and Frank drove nails deep into the fence board. "I thought you two had a chance to clear the air. Maybe work out your differences."

"What's there to work out? She left, now she's back. It has nothing to do with me." That would be his new plan—indifference, distance and diversion. He drove a few nails into the post and hooked his hammer into his belt. "You didn't think I was still in love with her, did you?"

"No." Frank's denial rang with humor. "But a dad can hold out hope, can't he?"

"Don't tell me this has anything to do with talking with the mayor yesterday. Grandkids were mentioned. Remember?" He yanked his saddlebag off the ground and swung it over his shoulder. "You need to stop with the matchmaking."

"I admit to no such thing." The twinkle in his eye was a guilty one. "And even if I was, Rori was good for you, son. You can't hold what she did against you."

"She didn't want me." His work horse was grazing. He gathered Max's reins and swung the leather pack behind the saddle. "I proposed and she said no."

"If I remember right, she said for you to ask her again after she graduated from college."

"The same difference." Justin heard the growl in his tone and regretted it. Swinging up into the saddle gave him time to rein in his turmoil. "You're trying to polish up the past and put a pretty bow on it. It won't work."

"I didn't say it was perfect. What do you think, Scotty?"

Their hired hand Scotty, who had been on the ranch for as long as Justin could remember, looked up from packing his tools. "I say you're both wrong."

"Not me," Justin denied. Wrong? He wasn't going to stay and listen to this. His pride bruised, he eased Max through the tall wild grasses. "But I agree with you about Dad."

"Hey, now maybe I am wrong, maybe I'm not, but you're wound up pretty tight." Frank mounted up, not one to be left behind. "Don't you understand what happened?"

"I don't want to rehash this. I can't go back. I learned that from you always going back to Mom."

"The past will always be chasin' you unless you come to terms with it. *That's* what I hope you learned." He pressed Rogue to a trot. "Something tells me you missed the lesson."

"Not now, Dad."

"Now's as good of a time as any." He caught up to his boy and slowed his horse to a walk. Side by side, it was easy to get a good read on the boy. His oldest son, his firstborn, was the one most like him in temperament. He remembered not being much different at the same age, which seemed a lifetime ago. He'd been a husband and father trying to wrangle both jobs on top of making a living off this land. He'd been stretched thin, and he hated to admit it, just as prideful as Justin.

What would have happened if he had learned his lessons earlier? The lessons about pride and defensiveness, understanding and forgiveness may not have made a difference in his marriage. Lainie had her own set of problems. But those lessons might have made a tough go a little easier on everyone.

"Believe me," he told his son. "There will come a time when your pride isn't as important as other things. A time when you wish you made things right with the girl when you had a chance."

"I know what I'm doing, Dad."

"Yes, that's just what I said when I was your age." From the ridge he could see the faint dust smudge and the blot of the beige pickup as Rori turned onto the main road to town. It took two to make a marriage work, but it only took one to make it fail. He'd learned that the hard way, too. Relationships could tear the heart out of a man. "I want you to make peace with the girl, that's all. Whatever you think, I want you to be happy."

"I am." Chin up, shoulders straight, iron strength, that was his boy. "At least, I'm as happy as I'm going to be."

Stubborn. A chip off the old block, Frank mused. As he rode the crest of the hillside, the breeze rustled through grass and trees, the plod of the horses' gaits added a muted percussion to a glorious day. His fields rolled over hillsides and stretched along flatland for as far as he could see. A pair of eagles wheeled overhead in perfect synchrony and a jackrabbit darted ahead of the horses, leaping to safety, and stopped to take a look at the coming procession. The creature wrinkled his nose, eyes curious as they rode by. Up ahead a pasture of horses grazed in the sunshine, and in another cattle lounged in the shade.

Yes, he was a blessed man. He spotted another problem with the fence. Looked as if the bull had been kicking the fence again. He drew Rogue to a halt.

"Dad!" Autumn's call broke the relative stillness. She galloped in with a smile on her pretty face. To him she would always be the little girl with a ponytail and freckles, Daddy's girl. "I think I've finally found the right buyer for Misty, or as much as I could tell over the phone. We'll see next week when she drops by."

"Good." Autumn looked pretty happy. That always perked him up. He dropped Rogue's reins, swung down and hauled his saddle pack with him. The woman who had bought the lodge, he remembered from his talk with the mayor. Autumn had a gift with horses, and he liked to see her venture as a trainer taking off. He hefted his tools to the ground. "Tim said she'll be renovating the cottage behind the lodge, too. Could be she might need boarding for a while, before she gets some of that acreage fenced off."

"I'll be sure and talk to her about that. I'm psyched." Autumn dismounted, as pleased as punch. "What's with Justin? He looks like he sat on a bee."

"To my way of thinkin', he always looks like that." With hammer in hand, Frank gave the board a wrench, neatly removing a bent nail. When Justin protested, they all laughed until even he joined in.

Yes, Frank thought, he was richly blessed. Life was a tough battle for everyone, this he knew for certain, but there were so many parts of it that were worth the fight. This moment was one of them.

His daughter hiked over to help him replace the board, his son went to work on resetting the far post. The flawless blue sky above made him feel as if God were watching over all of them. Maybe there was a lot more good waiting on the road ahead for his family.

Encouraged, Frank swiped the sweat from his brow,

grabbed a few new nails and bent to his work. The ringing of hammers filled the air.

Was Justin really going to stay out there? Rori squinted through the darkening glass, the kitchen window offering her a fair view of the stubborn man.

He'd climbed into the corral with the expecting mares, and in the falling twilight they gathered around him with tails swishing and noses outstretched, beautiful horse-shaped shadows ringing a solitary man. With his Stetson, wide straight shoulders and cowboy's stance dark against the last fiery remnants of sunset, he could have been a scene from a movie come to life. Justin had always been a larger-than-life hero to her.

Didn't they say first love never died? As she dried her hands, the scent of dish soap on her skin tickled her nose. She had to admit this was true in her case. Old pieces of the love she once had for him were like dying embers she thought had gone out. But once stirred again, they gleamed with a light of their own.

She hung the towel on the oven handle so it could dry, her movements echoing in the lonely kitchen. Boot steps rapped up the steps and the screen door whispered open. A man's gait, but not Justin's. She could still see him out of the corner of her eye. The man who could be cold as steel was also gentle, his stance softer, his head bowed, his hands peaceful as he stroked one mare's neck and then another. The real Justin Granger revealed.

"It's gettin' late, missy." Justin's dad ambled into the room. "You put in a long day, longer than I wanted for you."

"There was a lot to do. I've got the main floor of the

house spic and span." She gestured toward the cookie jar. "A batch of snickerdoodles made."

"My favorite. You know how to make the boss happy, that's for sure." When Frank smiled, it was contagious. Rori found herself grinning, too, as he lumbered over to the counter. He lifted the top of the porcelain cow-shaped jar. "I don't want you feeling as if you have to compensate because of Justin."

"He doesn't like that I'm here."

"Darlin', it isn't what you think. He's been like that since the day he proposed to you." Frank bit into one of the two cookies he'd taken. "This is one great cookie. You did well today. This kitchen has never looked so good. Now get home, see your grandfolks and unwind. And don't let Justin worry you none."

"I'll try."

"No trying. Just do." Frank winked as he ambled away. A few moments later the TV's faint drone murmured from the living room. Sounded as if he was catching a sports show.

Time to go. She grabbed her baseball cap and burst out into the temperate night. A very forward cow leaned over a nearby fence and bawled at her, puppy-dog eyes bright with friendliness. Crickets sang in the grasses and a handful of deer looked up from grazing, their soft eyes watchful as she headed toward the barn. The path led her straight past the field with Justin and the horses. She didn't see him at first. The mares spotted her and several of the beautiful animals loped straight up to her, pressing their barrels against the white board fence and reaching their noses as far over as they could.

"I know, I smell like cookies." It was why she'd stayed late. Justin hadn't come in for dinner, and she wanted to wait for him. But he'd been exceptionally busy, considering the rest of his family and ranch hands had come in for the evening meal hours ago.

One horse nickered. Another whinnied. A white mare shook her head, as if demanding the cookies she could scent.

"Headin' home?" Justin's abrupt question rose out of the half dark, a disembodied voice that startled her.

"Yes. I suppose you're glad to be rid of me for the day." She meant the words to be light, but the man emerging out of the shadows did not smile.

"Dad seemed happier today knowing you were taking care of things at the house." He sounded gruff, a mix of anger and something colder. "It means a lot that you're here. For however long that lasts."

She squinted at him, not quite believing her eyes or her ears. He could have been a stranger. Had Justin really changed that much? Where was the gentler man she'd spotted among the mares? "Do you mean to do that?"

"Do what?"

"To compliment me for being here and then hit me with an insult."

"I only meant you might not realize it, but folks are counting on you. Not me, but my sister. My dad." His shoulders squared like a man ready for a fight.

Well, he wasn't going to get one. She could read him even in the shadows. She didn't need to see his features or to be able to see the emotion playing in his eyes to know he hurt every bit as much as she did. The past felt alive and the gap between them as wide and vast as the Grand Tetons. She could see the spearing peaks behind him, black against the encroaching night, dividing the past from the present moment. She wished she could forget that long-ago, flawless time when the two of them had been in love.

"Good night, Justin." She turned on her heel. The mares wrangled for her attention but she couldn't pet them without being near to Justin. She would not let him pull her back into their old conflict. She kept walking. "I left your supper warming in the oven."

"Don't do me any favors, Rori. I don't need them."

She swallowed hard, perhaps to keep down a gasp of shock. He sounded harder than ever, like a man who'd lost more than his heart. Maybe her working here was costing both of them more than she'd anticipated.

Bad decision, she realized as she hurried up the lane. But she hadn't had another choice. She needed to work. It was a puzzle why on earth the good Lord had brought her to the Granger ranch. She felt raw inside, wrung-out and worn. By the time she reached the barn, she realized Copper was tied in the aisle, saddled and ready to go.

Justin's work, no doubt, and his statement couldn't be clearer. Pain wrapped around her like a shroud, heavy on an evening rife with Wyoming beauty. She snuggled her horse, mounted up and didn't look back as she reined him into the meadows. She felt Justin's gaze as harsh as a hand to her spine pushing her from his sight. Stars winked to life and a warm breeze serenaded the trees, but not even the beauty of God's handiwork could lift the ache from her soul.

He watched her from the back steps, where the shadows behind the house were darkest. He had a good view of her astride Copper, riding tall and willowy. She'd always been a beautiful sight whether it was in the saddle with the wind in her hair or standing in the twilight looking ready to put him in his place.

He wished he could forget the hurt he'd put on her face. He'd been too harsh tonight, that was for sure. He raked a hand through his hair, feeling defeated. He'd only been trying to be proactive and protect his vulnerabilities. If he didn't put up his defenses, then she would waltz right in and wrap him around her little finger all over again.

He couldn't go through that brand of torment again. She'd brought him to his knees because he'd made the mistake of loving her so much.

He lifted his head, his gaze zeroing in on her instantly. He felt her presence in the dark, for he didn't need eyes to see. The night had claimed her, and she was only a hint of movement, a faint glimpse of an outline. Distance was stealing her from him, even the small beauty of looking at her, the only part of her he could allow himself to have.

Watch over her, Lord. He sent the prayer heavenward, just as he'd done every night since she'd left town years ago. Over time, she had become his only true prayer.

When he was sure she'd safely crested the hill, he climbed to his feet. The deer close to the house looked up from their grazing, watchful and unafraid as he reached inside the door. His fingers closed on a cool metal handle of the scoop he kept inside the mudroom door. Full to the brim with grain he carried it to the edge of the lawn where he dumped it, talking low to the creatures.

The pampered pet cows in the closest pasture began to bawl, begging for similar attention. The deer kept their space as he circled around them, giving them plenty of leeway, and handed over the last treats to the cows. Buttercup rubbed her nose against his hand, begging for a little petting. Usually he would oblige her but tonight he felt restless. He heard the house phone ring, the musical tones spurred him to action. He ran to answer it. No doubt it was Cheyenne calling to report in on her long drive home from Washington State. It took all his might to banish Rori from his mind.

Chapter Six

"I've noticed things haven't been going so great between you and Justin." Autumn dunked a golden steak fry into a puddle of tartar sauce. "What can I say? Sorry doesn't seem to cut it. There's no excuse for my brother."

"So it's true." Rori sat up straight on the faded red vinyl seat. "Justin *has* been avoiding me."

"Big-time."

Their booth at Clem's was in the back alongside the window, giving her a perfect view of the entire restaurant and the street, where Copper and Autumn's first horse, Bella, waited at the hitching post in the building's shade. Rori dipped a fry through the pool of ketchup on her plate, processing Autumn's confession. "I wanted to think he was just busy out in the fields. When I do see him, he's heading in the opposite direction. Every time."

"Like when you brought lunch out to the west quarter section today?" Autumn nodded, reaching for another fry. "He couldn't move fast enough. His lunch was cold by the time he came back and Dad had eaten half of his sandwich. Served him right."

"Maybe tomorrow I had better bring extra, just in case. He's bound to take off again."

"Sure. He'll suddenly remember something he needs to check on about the time he spots you riding up the hill." Autumn smiled. "I could calf-rope him, hobble him and force him to stay, but that's a little extreme. I promised Dad I wouldn't rope any of my brothers unless it was really, really necessary."

Rori burst out laughing. She couldn't help it. It was good to be home with her childhood friends. "Autumn, I've missed your sense of humor."

"Oh, you think I was joking? It's a threat I just might use one day. Brothers." She shook her head, scattering light auburn hair over her shoulders. "It wasn't easy growing up stuck in the middle of those two."

"I remember." She spooned a mouthful of strawberry milkshake out of the enormous glass. It was too thick to drink with a straw until more of the ice cream had melted. She knew that Tucker had moved off the ranch, looking to get out of the small town, too. "You were always trying to keep up with Justin and outdo Tucker. Look where it got you. Working alongside your dad and training your own horses."

"I do okay." Autumn shrugged, staring far off down the street as if lost for a moment in thought. "Not too many men in these parts are interested in a woman who can outride, outrope and outshoot them."

"All you need is one man. The right one."

"Finding him is the tricky part. Then when you think he's the right one, he always disappoints you."

"Tell me about it." Rori nodded in sympathy. The wounds of her failed marriage were still too raw to think about. "Or the right man isn't right for you."

"Justin's coming."

"What?" She nearly dropped her spoon. The icy concoction on her tongue hit the roof of her mouth—brain freeze. She blinked against the pain, her eyes blurring slightly so Justin strode into sight on the sidewalk looking as if he was riding on the slanting sunbeams.

"Oh, he hasn't spotted you yet. But look, he just noticed Copper." Autumn propped her chin on her fist, as if watching a particularly interesting part in a favorite movie. "Watch the panic spread across his face. He's stopped in his tracks. Now he's staring at the horse as if he's debating. Should he proceed or turn tail and run?"

"If he wants to avoid me, then let him." Maybe Justin was right. Maybe this was easier. The sun-glazed glass made the scene ethereal, like something out of a dream, like the past come full circle. She saw the handsome man with her schoolgirl's heart, the Justin she'd always loved—his strength, his goodness, his open laughter. How his voice would only drop a note when he spoke to her. Only to her. How special he'd made her feel, how safe and loved.

She'd been sure he would wait for her. Sure he would understand. But he hadn't loved her enough. And having that happen twice in her life was too much. Maybe she was meant to be alone. Maybe this was what Justin felt, too, whenever he looked at her.

He'd changed so much.

He must have sensed her because he pivoted on his boot heels, his gaze finding hers through the window. She could not get over how remote he looked, as if he were carved of marble. Only a muscle ticking in his jaw gave him away.

"I'm going to go pay." Autumn grabbed the ticket off

the edge of the table, holding up one hand prepared for a protest. "This is my treat for old times' sake."

She wanted to argue, but she knew what her friend was up to. "Thanks, Autumn."

When she turned back to the window, Justin had turned away, strolling out of sight, retracing his steps.

Message received, she thought, refusing to let her head hang. Amazing. His rejection hurt as much as it had done twelve years ago.

Lord, help me to handle this the right way. She pulled a decent tip out of her pocket, tossed the bills on the table and took both milkshake glasses with her.

"I'll get that." Sierra Baker in her checkered apron met her at the counter. She had two paper cups in hand and a friendly smile. Sierra might have been a few years behind Rori in school, but they'd been friends in the church's young life program. "It's good to see you, Rori. Terri is over the moon that you're going to be at the wedding."

"She has three days to go until the big day. How is she doing?" Rori handed over the milkshakes, grateful for the interruption.

Forget about Justin, she told herself. Let him go.

"It's crazy." Sierra transferred the milkshakes into the cups. "The usual last-minute things are falling through. The favors haven't arrived. Tom's mother is refusing to come. The church hall had a water heater break and the carpet is still wet. Let's face it, weddings are nerve-racking. Mine was no different."

"Or mine." Her stomach twisted at the thought. Hers hadn't been the wedding of her dreams mainly because of the horrible feeling she couldn't get rid of. That through the years when she dreamed of her future wedding, Justin Granger had always been the groom she wished for, the only man she'd wanted waiting for her at the end of a church aisle. The end of that dream was a wound that faded with time, but did it end?

No, her heart answered. After all this time, after everything she'd been through, that dream remained within her, something treasured that had been lost and found again. She wished she could stop it, but she couldn't.

"Maybe Terri will have her happily-ever-after. The good Lord knows that didn't happen for me." Sierra snapped lids on the cups and pulled two paper-coated straws from her apron pocket. No ring marked her left hand.

Sympathy swept through her, aware of the pain of a failed love and how deep it went. "I'm sorry, Sierra."

"You, too?" Sierra handed over the drinks. "Did you have any children?"

"No. You?"

"A little boy."

"And a total cutie." Autumn bopped over, stuffing change into her pocket. "Owen is the sweetest little boy."

"I think so, but then I'm biased." Sierra's eyes misted. "You two have someone waiting for you. I can feel him glowering from here."

"That would be Justin." Autumn rolled her eyes, as if both a touch amused and exasperated by her older brother. "Let him wait. He needs to learn to be more patient. This will be a good opportunity for him."

"Or a good opportunity for him to lose his temper." Rori bit her lip, nodded goodbye to Sierra and took a sip of her milkshake. Nothing came up the straw.

"I'm not afraid of that man's temper." Autumn plopped her Stetson onto her head and led the way out the door. Fearless, that was Autumn. She might look frail, but she knew how to hold her own. She marched right up to her brother, who leaned against the building, a harsh scowl somehow making him look more handsome.

Rori's pulse fluttered in admiration and in memory. She knew how tender Justin's voice could be when he leaned close to murmur in her ear. The memory of sitting on the porch swing rushed back to her, Justin's strong arm cradling her shoulder. The innocent thrill of being close to him whispered through her now, as sweet as the evening breeze.

The distance between them vanished when his gaze fastened on hers. Autumn stood between them, the rumble of a motorcycle rolled down the street, and Copper's whinny of greeting faded into nothingness. All that surrounded her, all that she could see, was Justin tall and strong in the golden evening light and his emotions revealed.

Was that regret she saw? A wish for what could have been? The concrete beneath her old riding boots faltered. She froze, unable to trust her next step. The moment stretched, timeless, and she felt the beat of his heart. Was he remembering, too? Was he wishing there was a chance? Her entire being leaned toward him and the past vanished. For one moment, it was as if there had been no breakup, no anger and hurt or disappointment. That no years separated them, and no distance. She felt his affection as unmistakable as the sun skimming her cheek.

Hope burst through her. "Justin, I—"

He closed up like night falling. His eyes shielded. His face hardened. He turned away, and she stood in darkness, cold where once she'd been warm, her hopes scattered like rattling October leaves on the ground in front of her.

"Autumn, I need to talk with you." Justin turned his back, hauling his sister with him by the arm.

Alone, Rori blinked against the sun in her eyes, the sun she could not feel. Humiliation washed over her. Had she been wrong? Had she only imagined what Justin felt, that he might be regretting his decision like she did and he was wondering if—

That was one *if* she could not let herself imagine. Not ever again. Marriage hadn't worked out so well for her, and she wasn't eager to do it again. She swallowed hard, willing down a pain she could not let him see. Copper nickered, stretching his nose as far as his tether would allow, reaching out to her as if he'd seen it all and had understood everything.

It was nice to have a champion and a true friend. She wrapped one arm around his neck. Burying her face in the velvet heat of his coat, she breathed in his comforting scent. He nickered low in his throat, as if offering sympathy.

"Thanks, buddy," she whispered so only he could hear. He tossed his head, craning to get a look at what she had a hold of. "Oh, right. I'd forgotten."

Where time went, she had no clue. But the years had changed so many things. This wasn't one of them. She popped the top from the cup, pulled out the straw and let him lap it up. Companionably, she licked the thick blob of milkshake that clung to the straw and the ache in her soul eased a little. By the time the horse had licked the inside of the cup dry, Autumn returned.

"Justin wants me to come home. Three out of the last four mares are about ready to foal." Autumn returned and untied Bella, her movements uncharacteristically jerky. "My one evening off."

"A rancher's work is never done?"

"I know, but I have the right to complain, don't I?" She grinned.

"Justin said something else that upset you," she guessed because Autumn loved her work.

"True." Autumn mounted up. "I'm sorry for Justin. He was rude to you."

"He was sending me a message." Her face heated. Had he recognized her affection? Had he guessed at what she'd been feeling?

Probably. Humiliation washed through her. As if she didn't feel badly enough. "Guess I'll see you tomorrow."

"I'm going to talk to him. He shouldn't be treating you like that."

"No, but we'll work it out. Don't say anything. Please."

"Okay, as your friend. But if he keeps this up, I won't be able to ignore it."

The back of her neck prickled. She tossed the empty cup into the nearby garbage can and caught sight of Justin's pickup idling a good ten yards away, brake lights lit. Obviously, he was waiting for his sister. There was a steel wall between them. She felt nothing, not even his coldness toward her.

"I hate leaving you like this," Autumn explained. "Dad is calling everyone in. They need me to help."

"I wanted to take the scenic ride home anyway."

She untied Copper's reins. "I'll be keeping you all in my prayers."

"Thanks." Autumn waved goodbye, wheeling her beautiful horse around in the street and taking off at a fast trot. The steeled horse clip-clopped on the pavement as she followed Justin's truck.

"Guess it's just you and me, buddy." She mounted up, the leather creaking as she settled into the saddle. Justin's truck grew smaller with distance until the sun's glare stole him from her sight.

She'd become lost in time today, her feelings tangled up with the past. She couldn't afford to get confused like that again. No more wishing for what might be, she told herself. Careful choices, that was her plan. There was no way Justin could ever be considered a good choice and certainly not Justin as he was today. Where did the gentle young man he'd been go?

That was the man she missed, she realized, gathering Copper's reins. A man who no longer existed. He was as lost to her as the young woman she'd once been, full of naivety and unrealistic expectations.

"C'mon, boy. Let's head home." Justin's rebuff still hurt, but she would have to get over it. He'd made his feelings plain.

Copper answered with a whinny and led the way, taking off down the street in a sprightly walk. Show horse that he'd once been, he held his head high and tossed his mane, earning admiration from a little girl and her mom climbing out of their four-wheel drive.

"Rori Cornell, is that you?" Eva Gibbs called out over the top of her Jeep. "Are you coming to Terri's wedding?"

"I am."

"Then I'm telling the old gang. I'll see you on Saturday."

"I can't wait." Yes, it was good to be home again. She'd missed the people and this way of life more than she'd realized. She dropped the reins over the saddle horn, giving Copper his head. As he broke into a cantor, she felt a little bit more like the girl she used to be.

"Go to bed, Dad." Justin grabbed the steaming carafe of fresh-brewed coffee. "I'll keep an eye on things tonight."

"No, that's not fair. We'll split the duty." Frank set a thermos on the counter, his face tight with strain. "I'll take first shift so you can get some shut-eye."

Justin snatched the thermos away from his father and filled it over the sink. "I'll be up anyway."

"Got trouble on your mind?"

"You could say that." No way was he letting his dad know what—or rather who—was troubling him. Dad probably already had it figured out. Besides, with one foal dropped and two more about ready, trouble was at the foremost of all of their minds. "Don't even mention Rori."

"Fine. I was going to say I think Sunny is about ready to go. I'll be staying out in the barn. If you stay with me, then Autumn can relieve you in the morning."

"So much for getting some shut-eye." Justin screwed the cup onto the top of the thermos and tucked it under his arm. The screen door slapped shut behind him as he padded down the steps.

The moon was full tonight, blazing the hillsides and meadows with luminous platinum and highlighting Autumn kneeling beside a mare in the corral.

"Is Paullina close, too?" He kept his voice low, but it carried easily in the midnight hush. That would be four out of four, an even busier night.

"No, she's resting. I spotted a pack of coyotes up against the tree line when I came out here. You will need to keep a close eye on her, though."

"I promise. I'll take good care of her."

"I appreciate it. Justin—"

He recognized the tone, and it meant she wanted to talk about something important. Ten to one that something important was Rori. "I don't want to talk about her."

"But—"

"No buts." He pushed away from the fence. "You can't fix everything, Autumn."

"Maybe if you tried to forget."

"Forget what? Her wanting something more than me?" He hid the pain as best he could behind a smile. "Take a look at me. Can you blame her? There was a reason she graduated top of her class. She's no dummy."

"No, but you can be one."

"No argument there." It mattered that his sister cared, but some things hurt too much. Like seeing Rori in town.

She'd come back and fit into life, looking right at home as if she had never left. As if time and their differences hadn't torn him apart. He could have almost believed that she was waiting for him, just as she'd done long ago, with a strawberry milkshake sitting on the table in front of her and Copper tied at the hitching post. Did she remember? Or had it all been easily forgotten?

As long as he kept himself as stone-hard on the inside, he wouldn't have to feel or hope or start wishing for what wasn't meant to be. Rori may be fitting in just fine, but she was still the same girl, ready to leave him behind.

Help me to remember that, Lord. He tipped his head and stared straight up at the heavens. Stars winked and the moon glowed against infinite black. Somewhere God was out there, watching over them all. He felt closer tonight.

Headlights broke the night darkness, hovering above the inky driveway. It took him a moment to place the truck.

"Cheyenne!" Autumn launched through the fence and pelted down the driveway. The truck halted a few yards short of the garage, and the driver's door flung open. His sister emerged, shouting with glee. Autumn launched at her and they hugged, jumping and squealing.

It was good Cheyenne was safely home.

"Is that you, girl?" The back door swung open, the porch light went on.

"Daddy!" Cheyenne shouted, extricating herself from Autumn's hug and racing across the yard. She jumped into her father's arms.

Dad's deep happy chuckle rumbled through the night. "Glad to see you, young lady."

"Cheyenne!" Addison stumbled out in her housecoat, hair tousled from sleep. "You're home! You've got to see the foal!"

Too much emotion for him, and besides, there was work to be done. Justin hiked toward the barn. He shut the doors behind him, cutting out all sounds of happiness and joy, of homecoming and family love that threatened to pull him back and remember dreams he'd lost along the way.

Alone, he ambled down the aisle, talking low and comforting to the mare awaiting his care.

Chapter Seven

Weddings. He didn't like them. Justin had wanted to avoid this one, but his entire family had dragged him along. Since Rori was attending the reception, too, his torture continued.

Why couldn't he block her from his mind? He accepted a dainty glass cup full of lemonade from elderly Mrs. Ford, doing his best not to grumble at the too-small handle he couldn't get his fingers through. His dad was having the same problem, but nothing seemed to trouble Frank. He cradled the cup in one hand, hardly noticing it as he chatted with the mayor's wife.

Great. This was what he got for agreeing to share a ride with his father. It didn't look as if they would leave any time soon. Justin ran a finger behind his collar, hating the tie that cinched him up like a noose. Social events didn't usually put him on edge, but this one was destined to. He spotted Rori standing alone on the periphery of the crowd.

She made a pretty picture in the dappled sunshine wearing a sleek blue dress that exactly matched her eyes and her hair rippling in the breeze. He kept his resolve in place. He had to turn his back on her. They couldn't be friends; he couldn't take it. So that didn't leave him with any other choice.

"Cady ought to be here." Martha Wisener's voice rose above the din of the crowd and the classical music screeching over in the corner. He was not a fan of the violin. He tried not to listen, but the mayor's wife was a gregarious sort with a voice to match. "She closes on the lodge on Monday, so she's staying at a hotel over in Sunshine until then. She's moved all the way from New York, can you imagine? She's never been out west before her one trip here."

"You don't say?" Dad seemed interested in that. "She and her husband just decided to up and move?"

"Oh, there's no husband. Cady Winslow is a single lady. Always has been. Just a real classy gal and as nice as could be."

Doubtful, Justin thought, fighting a sadness he didn't want to admit. It was easier to stick with the notion that no woman was trustworthy, that you couldn't depend on a single one of them.

Take Rori. She stood like an outsider who didn't belong, watching the kids dashing around trees and squealing down the sidewalk, playing tag in front of the church. She looked lonely. He'd hurt her the other day. He didn't like it, but he couldn't apologize for it either. Seeing her threatened the careful defenses he'd set up against her. Tiny curls of emotion struggled to escape, and a tough man wouldn't give in to those tender feelings. Nothing good could come of it.

"I'm still mad at you." Autumn sidled up to him, a plate of wedding cake in one hand and a fork in the other. "You're being impossible."

"No, I'm being smart." He'd been successfully avoiding Rori for days. He didn't see why he should break his streak now.

"Smart? I don't think so. How about cowardly?"

"I'm not a coward." He ground out the words. Maybe he was so prickly because they just might be true. He wasn't handling the Rori situation well at all. "I don't want to talk about her."

"You're going to have to eventually. She works on the ranch. She lives in the same town. You can't keep changing directions and going the other way every time you two meet. It might as well be sooner rather than later."

"I disagree. I'm perfectly happy standing here ignoring her."

"But she isn't. Look at her. She's alone. Now's the perfect opportunity."

"Don't you have someone else to bother?"

"No one as fun as you." She smiled up at him, understanding what he couldn't say. "I didn't realize how you still felt about her."

"And trying not to." Trying for all he was worth. He wanted those feelings to be gone. He wanted them crushed to bits, tossed over the edge of a high cliff and scattered on the wind never to be seen again. But wanting didn't make it so. Even with his spine set and his feet planted with determination something deep within him whispered to turn around and look at her. Somehow he could feel her loneliness and her misery. Not that she would admit to being miserable, but he could feel it. He'd put that misery there.

"Don't you say a thing to her, do you hear me?" He knew he sounded like a bear, but the thought of opening up riled him. Better to act angry now than to wind up heartbroken later. "You keep this secret between the two of us."

"Well, maybe the three of us." Dad ambled over, frowned at the itty bitty cup he held and drained it in a single swallow. "Couldn't help overhearing, mostly because I was trying to."

"I knew coming here was a bad idea."

"We've all known Terri since she was knee-high. It's not like we want to miss being here for her." He set the cup on the edge of a nearby table. "Do you want to know how I know you're still hung up on Rori?"

"You're wrong, Dad."

"Because you're working so hard to ignore her. Son, if you're really over her like you say, then you would have no problem going over there and asking her to dance."

"Like I need your romantic advice? You haven't dated a woman in over thirty years."

"True, but I was a charmer in my day." That was how he caught the prettiest gal in White Horse County. "Go on over there and ask the poor girl. If you do it, I won't say another word about the two of you."

"Unbelievable. Besides, Rori's not standing alone anymore. I'm through with the both of you. I'm gonna go get some cake." He stalked away, shaking his head, looking as if he was trying to work up a storm of mad to keep painful things at bay.

"What are we going to do about him?" Autumn stabbed her fork into her piece of cake and scraped off the frosting.

"I don't know. I reckon he and Rori will figure it out. What are you doing, kid? The frosting is the best part."

"Sure, but it's really bad for you."

"That won't stop me." He scooped a chunk of white fluff from the edge of the plate, using his finger since no one was looking.

"I wonder who that is?" Autumn asked, gesturing with her fork down the sidewalk.

"Who?" Instead of swiping another bit of frosting, he squinted into the bright rays of the sun.

A woman tapped their way, no one he'd seen before in these parts. She looked to be somewhere in her mid to late forties, tall and willowy, and she moved gracefully, as if the sun burnishing her slender shoulders shone just for her. Her light brown hair was shoulder length with a fancy cut and highlights—he had three daughters, so he wasn't unfamiliar with such things. She wore a simple slim green dress and matching heels. A few steps closer brought her face into view—heart-shaped, flawless skin and a radiance that could bring a man to his knees.

"Cady!" Martha, the mayor's wife, broke off from her crowd and hurried across the lawn. "You did make it."

"Barely. I'm so sorry I missed the ceremony." The woman named Cady smiled. She could have been a movie star with that wide, friendly smile, one that lit her up and everything around her. "I ran into road construction all through South Dakota, which made me a full day late. I just made it in."

"Then we're happy you're here safe and sound." Martha wrapped the woman in a warm hug.

"Must be the lodge's new owner," Autumn told him, as if he hadn't figured that out for himself. "I talked with her on the phone, so I recognize her voice. She's really nice."

He didn't need anyone's help to figure that out either. If he looked up "nice" in the dictionary, he wouldn't be surprised to see a picture of this Cady woman posted there. She looked like goodness walking, a dream men like him had forgotten to believe in.

The mayor hurried over, blocking his view, and Frank took it as a sign. No sense in watching the woman or in bothering to join the crowd greeting her. He was a practical sort with his feet firmly planted on the ground. He'd learned the hard way that dreams had a way of breaking a man. He'd been burned by a city woman before. He turned his back to her and headed for the dessert table, where he spotted his son working on a piece of cake. Cake. Now that was a good distraction.

"Maybe I'm wrong, but is Justin looking our way?" Eva Gibbs asked over the lilt of the string quartet playing on the church's side lawn. The hall's carpet hadn't dried out quick enough after all, so Terri's wedding reception had been moved outdoors.

Rori didn't dare look over her shoulder like the rest of her high-school friends. As if she wanted the man to think she might be talking about him! He'd made his feelings toward her crystal clear, and she intended to keep her distance and her dignity. The only thing left to do was to figure out a way to be immune to him.

"You're wrong, Eva. He's not looking at us, he's looking at *Rori*," Marjorie Long announced with a wink. "You know what they say about first love?"

"I do, but I don't believe it," Rori quipped. Her biggest fear was that her friends were going to read something into this, and somehow she had to keep unaffected and aloof. If he really was watching, she didn't want him to know how hard this was for her. "Besides, Justin isn't my first love."

"Then who was?" Eva wanted to know.

"Copper." That brought a round of laughter from the little circle of her oldest friends. She couldn't help laughing, too. "Copper is a good guy. He's loyal and agreeable."

"Plus you can tell him what to do and he does it," Eva added. "I wish my husband was more like Copper."

"Hey, I heard that!" a man called out from a nearby cluster of guys, who all looked familiar. Rori recognized Eva's husband, Gary, who'd been senior class president.

"See what I have to put up with?" he asked his buddies, his good nature ringing in his voice. "If you fellas will excuse me, I need to set my wife straight on a few things. Eva, may I have this dance?"

"Certainly." Eva beamed, allowing her husband to take her hand and escort her over to the shade beneath several ancient maple trees. They joined in with the others waltzing in the dazzling afternoon.

"I'm going to get a refill." Sierra held up her empty cup. "Can I get anyone else one?"

"I'll come with you." Marjorie drained the last of her punch and the two of them headed off with promises to return.

Alone again and with no one to distract her, she could feel Justin's piercing stare from across the yard. She shivered as if in warning, although the breeze was hot, and she wasn't surprised when footfalls padded behind her in the grass. She set her jaw.

"Rori?"

Her name on his voice still rumbled deep like harmony, the sound she had once most loved to hear. She didn't turn, taking a moment to gather her courage.

"Aren't you going to speak to me?"

Did he sound glad or sorry for her silence? She couldn't tell. Her fingers tightened on the glass handle of the cup she held and she turned toward him, dread rolling through her. Don't let him see it, she told herself. Don't let him know how much he hurt you.

"So, at least you're looking at me." No one was more handsome than Justin Granger in a suit and tie. He towered above her, dark hair tousled by the gentle breeze, as rugged as ever. "You're pretty ticked at me."

"No." She wasn't mad. Once, he would have been able to read her like a book but now he had no clue about her. She could see that plainly, too, and it was proof how much times had changed, how much *they* had changed. A touch of panic popped through her. All she could see was the image of him turning his back to her in front of the diner and of his empty chair at every meal she put on the Grangers' kitchen table. It wasn't as easy to hold back her feelings as she'd thought. How did he do it? She backed away. "Excuse me, but I have to go."

"Go where?" His hand snared her forearm, his fingers banding her wrist. His touch burned through her like a brand that would not yield and, worse, with recognition. One kindred soul recognizing another.

We are no longer like souls, she argued and wrenched away from his grip. But he held on, iron that would not relent.

"If you leave, then this awkwardness between us stays. And I don't want that." A muscle ticked in his jaw. At least she wasn't the only one tense; at least this was hard on him, too. He blew out a frustrated sigh. "Do you think it was easy for me to come over to you?"

"I don't understand what you think might solve this. We can agree to get along, but we tried that before, remember?"

"I remember. Friendly didn't work. That was my fault. I didn't realize how hard it would be." He told her the truth.

"It was hard to be friendly to me?"

Of course she had to take it the wrong way—and that was his fault, too. He counted to three and tried again. "Being friendly makes me remember the way things were."

"Me, too." She softened, her violet-blue eyes full of emotions that could tempt him to fall for her all over again. "Why is it that the bad times stick?"

"You mean like the time when you wouldn't accept my engagement ring?" How a decade-old wound could hurt as if it were new was a mystery he could not explain, but he felt the blow of it deep in his chest.

"You mean the way you didn't offer to wait for me?" The same wound was mirrored in her eyes, on her face, in her voice. "It was only four years until I graduated."

"You wanted me to wait?" That had never occurred to him. He hung his head, disbelieving. Hard to believe he'd been that stubborn and unable to see what she'd needed. There was proof right there he would have made her a lousy husband. Maybe that was his real fear deep down, the one that had made him run and kept him running.

"I don't know about you, but I've had enough of bad times."

Her chin went up, and she gave nothing away. Not

a hint of just how angry she was at him or of any other emotion. She was stronger than he realized.

"Then we'll concentrate on the good ones." He tugged her closer. "Come dance with me."

"Did I hear you right? You couldn't have asked—"

"I did." He led her along, stumbling across the grass. "Look at everyone. My family. Half our friends."

"They're watching us." She went pale, and he felt her tremble with nerves.

So, she wasn't as unaffected as he'd thought. Her vulnerability touched him. He couldn't let his defenses weaken. No tenderness allowed. He straightened his spine, determined to do this right. "If we don't do this, then you know what happens?"

"We're the talk of the town."

"And my family will never let me live it down. They will never leave the subject of you and me alone. But if we have one waltz, and you go on to dance with someone else and I do the same, then it's over. No one is going to keep wondering." He no longer was. "I want to put an end to this. Do you?"

"Yes." They were in the shadow of the maples surrounded by other dancing couples, and she placed her free hand on his shoulder.

You feel nothing, he ordered as he took the first step, guiding her to the sway of the music. Be cold. Be distant.

"The last time we danced like this was at my grandparents' fortieth wedding anniversary." Her voice teased him, pulling him back to what might have been.

He gritted his teeth, his will unyielding. He would not remember.

If only he could forget. The sound of the big band,

scratchy on the old record player, the scents of honey-suckle blooming in her grandparents' garden and of berry punch from the big bowl on the porch table carried on the wind. How Rori, sweeter than sugarplums, twirled in his arms in a slow waltz beneath a fiery sunset.

"That was one good time." She could lull him into remembering more, if he let her.

It had been quite a night. She'd looked like a princess in a white dress, all that had been missing was a tiara and the storybook ending to go with it. Even a man as cautious as he had believed that's where they were heading, for her hand had been cradled softly in his and her head rested on his shoulder. Tenderness had swept him away more strongly than any fairy tale.

"Surely we can think of another." She gazed up at him more lovely for all the years that had passed. She captivated just as much as she'd had in their school days. Rori had an open honesty that reeled him in against his will.

"There was that time we rode the horses to the river." He had more common sense than to bring up that stellar afternoon, but he did it anyway. The buried memories unearthed, he felt the heat of the late summer afternoon, smelled the sun-ripened grass and cotton-woods and maples baking in the hot wind. Heard again the hushed gurgle of the swift current and the horses blowing out their pleasure at the sight of the sparkling water up ahead.

"We rode to the river a hundred times." Amused, little dimples bookended her grin and he wondered what had put the brightness into her at the memory. "You aren't going to remind me of the first time I tried going off the rope swing, are you?"

"Guilty." He kept their three-step slow and easy and enough space between them so everyone was clear, especially his family, that this was a dance for old times' sake. There was nothing between them. Back then, their first trip to the river had been their first time alone together without family or friends from school tagging along. "You were afraid to jump."

"I was," she agreed. "After you talked me into giving it a try and I finally climbed onto that rope and put one foot on the big knot in the end, remember?"

"Sure do." As if he could ever forget the way she'd clung to that sturdy hemp, her hair tied back in a single ponytail, wearing a pink T-shirt and ragged cutoffs, the gold cross around her neck glinting in the sun. He'd been treading water, ready to help her to shore, and tried to talk her through it. He'd been chagrined to learn she was afraid of heights and between the tree, the rope and the steep cut of the bank, it was a fair way to the river.

"If I recall correctly," he drawled. "I said trust me, I won't let anything bad happen to you."

"And I closed my eyes and jumped. I trusted you."

"Bad decision," he quipped, surprised when a chuckle rumbled through him. She laughed, too, and the sounds merged like melody and harmony and in perfect synchrony. Just like old times.

"I remember Gram packed us a tasty picnic lunch and after you rode home with me, you kissed me." Her blue-as-dream eyes resonated with the innocence of that time and the beauty. "Not a peck on the cheek, as you had done before, but a real kiss. It was everything a girl's first kiss should be. Sweet and gentle and reverent."

"The Granger men are gentlemen, even if we spend most of the day with horses and cattle." Humor was the best way to hide the fact that he recalled that kiss, too, how she'd looked too lovely beneath the lilac tree in front of her grandparents' house. When their lips had met for the first time, he'd seen his future loving her, protecting her, taking care of her and making sure she spent the rest of her life happy.

But he never got the chance. They never got their ever after. The music began winding down and couples around them broke apart, and a prayer rose straight from his soul. *Lord, please don't let this moment end.*

Chapter Eight

"You were always a perfect gentleman to me." Rori gave in and let her eyes drift shut. Justin led her in the final few steps of the dance. They were the only couple on the dance floor still together, as if trying to hold back the last notes of the music. "I never thanked you for that."

"No need." His voice was a few notes deeper than that of the boy from that long-ago night, his shoulders wider, a hint of a five-o'clock shadow on his jaw, but his strength of principles remained. The dance was over, the last note faded into the brilliant May afternoon.

She opened her eyes, the moment broken, the past vanished. All that stood between them were the remnants of a shared past that could no longer be. Their chance was gone, but she couldn't stop the piece of her soul that wished and whispered. What would have happened if she'd accepted his proposal?

When she opened her eyes, she realized he hadn't moved away. Couples surrounding them were chatting and the kids' shrieks of delight carried above the roar and rumble of conversations. The sunshine, suddenly too bright, made her eyes burn.

"Are you okay?" Justin asked, towering above her, his baritone buttery warm with concern.

If he'd been cold or distant or dismissive, she could have handled it better than his caring. How had she gotten carried away? A dignified woman gathered her feelings, hid them carefully for none to see and pasted a polite smile on her face. "Thank you for the dance."

"It was my pleasure." He turned away as if it were the easiest thing in the world and offered her a small smile, neither cold nor caring but one of recognition of what they'd once been. Beyond the bitterness, beyond all hope.

"We had better stick to the plan," he said over his shoulder, tossing a glance toward the punch table.

His family must be there, she surmised, because she wasn't about to look. She tried to make her feet work so she wouldn't seem like a fool staring after him, as if she still carried a torch, but she didn't move fast enough. Justin had asked Eva to dance, stealing her away from Gary as the first notes of the next waltz filled the air like a new beginning.

Alone, Rori hurried out from beneath the maples, wondering just who had noticed.

"You're lookin' mighty lonely, young lady." Frank Granger called her back. "You wouldn't want to give an old cowboy like me the pleasure of this dance?"

"I would be honored. Under one condition." Out of the corner of her eye, she saw Justin guiding Eva step by step, talking easily. She'd let go of the past. Now it was time to move on. She was grateful to Justin's dad for his offer. She knew what he was doing, helping to ease her embarrassment and keeping her from deciding to head home. "We don't mention Justin."

"Deal." Frank offered his hand. "I figure I'll be lucky to get a few turns around the dance floor before the young bucks in this town start taking a shine to you. Look, there's one now."

It turned out Frank was right. Less than a minute into their dance, Troy Walters cut in. She did her best not to notice Justin, who had relinquished Eva to her husband's arms before he wandered off. She had to close her heart against him. It was better for both of them that way.

His dad did that on purpose. Justin grabbed a handful of cashews from the bowl on the table and popped a few into his mouth. Asking Rori to dance and then handing her over to Troy. The cowpoke was still dancing with her and judging by the look of things, she enjoyed being with him.

Shouldn't he be glad? His plan was working. His dad and sisters had said nothing about him and Rori. He took a swig of punch to wash down the nuts and they caught in his throat. Truth be told, he wasn't glad at all. Rori looked right at home in Troy's arms, and the crimson staining the edges of his vision was jealousy, plain and simple.

The current dance ended, and Justin watched as his dad escorted his dance partner back to the circle of folding chairs set out in the church's shade. Elderly Mrs. Tipple beamed with delight as she joined her friends. Another elderly widow spoke hopefully to Dad, and he nodded, offering his arm to her.

"Saw you and Rori dancing." Blake Parnell moseyed up to the table and grabbed a handful of cashews. "Guess old high-school sweethearts can still be friends."

"Guess so." He couldn't stop from noticing that Rori had stopped dancing and accompanied Troy off the dance area to a group of friends. Since he didn't want to get caught staring after his old sweetheart, he focused in on Blake. "The Marines let you off for good behavior?"

"Me? I'm never good." Blake's severe military haircut and drilled-in soldier stance belied his statement. He was special forces, the elite of the elite. He was Terri's cousin. "I flew in last night. Almost didn't make it for Terri's big day. With her dad gone, I'm not sure what she would have done to me if I hadn't been able to walk her down the aisle."

"She and Tom make a good pair." Small talk kept his mind busy. Maybe there was a chance he could forget about Rori entirely. "How long are you home for?"

"The weekend. I head back on Monday."

"Didn't you just get back from Afghanistan?" Something blue at the corner of his field of vision caught his attention. Rori. He gritted his teeth, refusing to look.

"Yep. I'm about ready to leave for a year in Okinawa. Looks like Terri's almost ready to go. They're bringing around the car. See you later, Justin."

"See ya." Sure enough, a brown sedan decorated with ribbons and bows glided to a stop in front of the church. Shouts rose up, folks cheering as they headed over to line the concrete pathway.

Time to go, he decided. His obligation here was done, and just in time because his sisters had clustered around Rori, pulling her toward the front step.

He could still feel her in his arms.

"Single ladies! Up front!" the mayor's wife hollered above the din. "Time for the bouquet."

The bride pounded onto the top step, her elaborate white gown swaying. As if he needed to see this, he thought, hiking off toward the quiet side of the church. He didn't need to think about Rori single again and how she'd laughed in her gentle way when Troy had whirled her waltz after waltz.

"Hold up, son." Frank jogged after him. "I'll come with you."

"I don't want to leave the ranch unattended for long." The only concern was Paullina, their last expecting mare, although she wasn't the most important reason why he wanted to leave.

A roar rose up above laughter and hoots and hollers as the bride feigned a throw. A few of the town's more aggressive single ladies leaped into the air like NFL quarterbacks at the Super Bowl. Rori wasn't one of them.

At the sight of her, the memory of her in his arms returned.

"Guess I was right," Frank said in that affable way of his. "All you and Rori needed to do was to clear the air. You look more like your old self."

Maybe his father thought so, but Justin didn't agree. It was hard work to hide his scowl. The rising tide of jealousy just kept coming at him and he couldn't shake the feeling he was leaving something important behind, something he might never find again.

"Isn't that Mrs. Tipple's car?" Frank knelt down beside the 1963 Falcon, which was still in showroom condition. "She's got a flat."

"I'll check her spare." Justin opened the driver's door

and pulled down the sun visor. He caught the set of keys that fell from it and unlocked the trunk. "She has a jack and a tire iron in here, but the spare is flat."

"Then I'll roll it down to the gas station."

"No, I'll do it." He didn't mind helping out. He would rather be busy, that way he didn't have to think about Rori and Troy, or Rori and any other bachelor in these parts.

All he wanted to do was to forget her.

"Okay, this time is for real!" Terri called over her shoulder, clutching the bouquet in both hands. She bent her knees deep, as if ready to hurl it into space. "One, two, three—"

The beribboned spray arced into the air, thudded against the underside of the entrance's awning and ricocheted straight toward the flowerbeds. Rori, having chosen the outer perimeter of the crowd hoping to avoid the bouquet, looked up just in time. Bachelorettes were leaping, others shouted and arms reached out and fell short as the flowers jettisoned straight at her head.

Duck. That was her first instinct. She did *not* want to catch those flowers. But who knew what unsuspecting elderly widow was standing behind her innocently chatting with her friends? So, to avoid any accidental injuries, she reached out and caught the bunch of perfect roses.

"Rori! You did it!" Autumn shrieked, clapping enthusiastically. "Congratulations."

"Looks like you're going to be next." Cheyenne tossed a lock of dark auburn hair behind her shoulder before she gave Rori a hug. "And before you say that your divorce isn't final yet, you don't know what God has in store for you. Maybe happiness is waiting just around the corner."

"That's awfully optimistic." Rori shrugged. "The flowers hit the awning, that's why it came to me. The bouquet was probably destined for one of you. Addison was standing directly behind Terri."

"Hey, I was dragged there. I don't want to get married." The youngest Granger sister spoke up, scrunching her button face in an amusing sneer. "Are you kidding? I don't want to give up my freedom. I don't want some man telling me what to do."

"She watches too many daytime talk shows," Autumn joked as they all moved together to the side of the pathway.

"Congratulations, dear." A frail voice, hardly audible in the din, made Rori turn. Mrs. Tipple was one of her grandmother's dearest friends. "I saw you were the belle of the ball, dancing with a few handsome men. I'm sure one of them will sweep you off your feet."

She'd been swept off her feet and she didn't know how to tell the dear lady that falling in love was the last thing she wanted to do again. From now on her motto was both feet on the ground and no one—not even Justin—was going to get control over her heart. She'd lost her illusions of love. Shattered, they could never be made whole again.

"I'll be praying for you." Mrs. Tipple patted Rori's hand consolingly before she turned away to join her circle of friends.

Terri and Tom, arm in arm, alight with profound joy, paraded down the walkway to their waiting sedan.

"Have fun, you two!" someone called out to the happily married couple. Flower petals sailed up into the air, twisting and dancing to the ground like colorful snowflakes.

Cheers rose up, and Rori tucked the bouquet into the crook of her arm so she could clap. She prayed for every happiness for them. She truly hoped their love would never waver and their ideals never fall.

"She is a beautiful bride," Autumn breathed as Tom held the door for his new wife and helped her onto the passenger seat. "When I get married, I want it to be just like this, at the church where Mom and Dad were married."

"And we were baptized," Cheyenne added. "I haven't given a thought to my wedding day. I need to get through my last year of vet school first. It's the toughest, and it's looming ahead of me. Maybe after I've graduated, I'll think about marrying the right guy."

"Are there really any Mr. Rights these days?" Rori brushed a fingertip over one fragile rosebud. Breathing in the fragrance, she remembered her wedding day. Her bouquet had been made of roses, too.

"Is being here hard for you?" Autumn asked as the newlyweds motored away.

"Not much." Fine, it wasn't the entire truth, but she wanted it to be. She wanted to be over the pain and the humiliation of having a man fall out of love with you—two men, actually. "Water under the bridge. Are you going to get married here, Cheyenne?"

"It depends on whether or not I get proposed to."

Was that a twinkle? Rori wasn't the only one who saw it. The remaining two Granger girls instantly began talking.

"What do you mean? Is it getting serious with Edward?" Autumn asked.

"Are you totally in love with him and you haven't even told us?" Addison demanded. "Now's the time. Inquiring minds want to know."

"Inquiring minds will just have to wait." Cheyenne shook her head, scattering her long red curls over her shoulders. "School comes first for both of us. But I don't think either scenario is out of the realm of possibility."

"I knew it!" Autumn held up a fist, and Cheyenne bumped it with one of hers.

"We're taking it slow, so there's no need to get so excited. Honestly." Cheyenne did look pleased. "Rori, how about you?"

"What about me?"

"You're going to marry again, right? Or would you want a home wedding this time around?"

"I'm not planning on getting married again." She hoped not one of the sisters would notice her gaze straying to the disbursing crowd. Or the fact that she felt disappointed there was no sign of Justin. "Two failed relationships are enough for me."

"Won't you get lonely?" Cheyenne wanted to know.

"Cheyenne!" Addison planted her hands on her hips. "I can't believe you. A woman doesn't need a man to be happy. In fact, show me one woman who is happier with a man than without. That's what I want to see."

"Well, there's my grandmother." Rori couldn't help pointing out the truth. "I've watched my grandparents most of my life, and they are truly happy."

"Fine, there's one stellar exception," Addison relented. "But I'm talking about generalities here."

"All I want is a man who doesn't turn tail on me when I outride him," Autumn added. "I haven't had a date since I was nineteen. That's ten years. I'm about to give up hope completely."

"I guess we'll both wind up as old single ladies." Rori bent down and held out the bouquet. Eva's little girl had been staring at it wistfully and came forward, eyes hopeful. "At least I'll be in good company."

"I feel better all ready." Autumn smiled, and it was like the sun shining. It was hard to believe she would never find true love.

Then again, true love was a scarce commodity in this world.

"For me?" the little girl asked, hands reaching for the roses. "Really?"

"Every little bride needs a bouquet." Rori knelt down, relinquishing the perfect blossoms.

"Thank you!" With a flip of her blond hair, the girl darted away.

"That was nice." Cheyenne took Rori by the arm. "I guess big-city life hasn't changed you any."

"I guess not that much." She let Autumn take her other arm and they headed into the church to help with the cleanup. There were so many things she'd forgotten over the years—the ladies' aid, simple weddings and country girl friendships—the kind of friendships that nothing, not even time, could diminish.

"Rori, no one expected you to stay and help clean up." Martha Wisener strutted up to Rori in the hall's wide entrance. Being the mayor's wife had become such a habit that she naturally took charge whether she was actually appointed or not. "It was good of you."

"Just helping out like old times." Pitching in had felt like the right thing to do. Her grandparents had left long ago, and Autumn had promised to drive her home. Rori grabbed her purse and her sweater from the stack on the nearby tabletop.

A tall, slim woman wearing a designer dress and three-hundred-dollar heels joined her at the table. Rori recognized the shoes since she'd had a similar pair. The woman didn't look familiar and she certainly didn't seem to be from around here, not with that upscale salon cut and color. She had to be somewhere in her forties, but her skin was flawless and smooth. Her blue eyes sparkled in a friendly way.

"I can't seem to find my purse. I wasn't sure about just leaving it like this, but everyone else seemed to be doing it." Her quiet alto resonated with kindness and a sense of discovery. "I also hear most people do not lock their doors here."

"And some even leave their car keys in the ignition." A habit she'd been trying to break Gramps of, but he was stubborn. She spotted a designer bag, probably worth much more than the shoes, and grabbed it by the butter-soft leather handle. "Wild Horse is a pretty safe place. Is this yours?"

"Yes, thank you." The woman smiled and took the bag.

"Cady!" Martha boomed. "I can't believe you stayed and helped, too. You don't officially live in this town yet."

"It will be official tomorrow."

Oh, the new lodge owner. Rori had heard about her from Autumn and the grapevine. Even her grandparents had talked about it. Back in the day, they had honeymooned at the once luxurious inn. She hooked her purse strap over her shoulder and turned, ready to join

Autumn outside. But something outside the back window froze her in place.

Justin. He knelt with his father beside an old Falcon, tapping a hubcap into place. Frail Mrs. Tipple stood nearby, her hand on her heart, crooning her thanks.

"I don't know what I would have done if you boys hadn't changed my tire for me." Her voice thinned, betraying her emotion. "The tow truck would charge me more than a week's groceries to have it changed."

"You'll still need to replace the one tire so you will have a functional spare," Justin explained, rising, his work done. "That ought to do for you now, ma'am."

"Frank Granger, you've raised a fine son." Mrs. Tipple nodded her approval. "And you aren't so bad yourself."

"I thank you for that, ma'am." Frank, tire iron in hand, rose to his six-foot-plus height. "You have any trouble, you can always give me a call."

"Isn't that nice of that man," Cady Winslow said, joining her at the window. "He isn't a relative of hers, is he?"

"No, he's just helping out. Frank's like that." It was Justin she couldn't take her eyes off, taking the tire iron from his dad and stowing it in the trunk.

You don't want him, she told herself. You don't want to care for any man.

"Oh, that's Frank Granger and his son." Martha squeezed in close to assess the situation. "They live out of town a ways."

"Granger? That's the name you gave me for the horses." The lady lit up. "I have an appointment on Monday with Autumn to look at a mare."

Outside the window, Justin shut the trunk, gave it a

pat and lifted his hand in farewell to Mrs. Tipple. Rori's pulse lurched. What if he sensed her spying on him from the window? Thankfully he didn't look her way as he strode out of sight.

"You and I spoke on the phone the other day." Her brain kicked into gear and the conversation around her began to make sense. Now she could place the well-modulated voice, remembering her first day at the Grangers'. "I cook and keep house for the family."

"Oh, you answered the phone. I remember." She smiled. "You were so helpful."

"Just doing my job." She opened the door. "You are going to love Autumn's horses."

"That's good news."

"They are the most gorgeous creatures, with the sweetest disposition. I don't think you'll be disappointed."

"I appreciate knowing that. When it comes to horses, I'm completely out of my element. I've wanted my own mare since I was a little girl. I'm already so excited, I could burst." Had she said too much? She may as well have a neon sign around her neck shouting "city girl." But no one faulted her for being indecorously enthusiastic. The door swished shut and Cady returned to the window.

Her gaze didn't waver from the view of the robust, steady-looking man with a touch of gray at his temples. The elderly lady offered him a handful of dollar bills. Frank refused with clear denial and kindness softening his ruggedly handsome face. The way he stood with his boots planted and the well-cut suit framing his wide shoulders made him look like a Western legend who had just walked off the silver screen.

"Cady, are you all right? You look lost in thought," Martha spoke, startling her.

"I'm perfectly fine." Heat stained her face. She jerked away, hoping her feelings weren't transparent.

"You must be hungry. Why don't you join Tim and me for supper?" Martha held out her hand, the big diamonds and rubies of her many rings glittering. "The maid promised to have a roast waiting. There will be plenty."

"Thank you, but I need to get settled at the motel." Funny how she couldn't seem to tear her gaze away from the man, who opened the door for the frailest elderly lady Cady had ever seen. After the woman had folded her tiny frame into the front seat, Frank Granger closed the door cordially.

My, wasn't he something?

Not that men were interested in a woman her age. She'd celebrated her fiftieth birthday three weeks ago. Cady sighed, staring down at her hands that not even the most expensive lotions could keep young. She forced herself to turn away from the window, when all she wanted was to look at him one more time.

Chapter Nine

"So, did you and Justin clear the air?" Autumn asked behind the wheel as she guided her pickup along the ribbon of country highway. Town had disappeared from the rearview and Jeremy Miller's fields stretched far and wide on one side of the road, the Parnells' in the other. Still irrigation wheels adorned the growing sugar beets, hay and wheat and at the top of a rise a green and yellow tractor churned up dust.

Rori took her time answering. "Do we have to talk about your brother?"

"Believe me, there are days I feel the same way about him."

"And what way would that be?"

"Like he's the most irritating, hardheaded man alive." Autumn shook her head, her red-gold hair dancing in the breeze from the window. She might be trying to look annoyed, but it was only a front. Beneath the annoyance was a sister's love for her brother. "Justin is just like Dad. You have no idea what it's like to work with the pair of them. It drives me nuts some days. They refuse to listen. They always think they are right. Dad has gotten better, but Justin just keeps getting more impossible."

"The years have changed him."

"It hasn't been for the better." Autumn said nothing more, although a frown creased her forehead.

Rori wanted to ask what that meant, but she bit her lip. Maybe it was wrong to be curious about Justin. She wanted to know more, but why? And what good could come of it? Their waltz was supposed to be a sign of moving on, and that's what she wanted to do. So why wasn't her heart listening?

The truck's windows were down, and she let the grass-scented air breeze over her face. It felt good, bringing up memories of riding to town with Gramps in his old truck, the radio crackling and spitting static, the radio that had always been persnickety. Before that, she remembered riding shotgun with Mom behind the wheel of their old Ford, her little sister standing on the hump on the floor behind the front bench seat, talking excitedly about what kind of ice cream she wanted at the drive-in.

How could she have forgotten how much she loved this place? When she'd left for college, a piece of her had always stayed behind here. She'd always intended to come back, but the Lord had seemed to lead her in another direction. And truthfully, there was another reason she'd stayed away. The thought of running into Justin in town, seeing him at church as a matter of course had been too painful. Her love for him, as young as she'd been, was true.

"He took it pretty hard when you wouldn't say yes." Autumn broke the silence. "I don't blame you. You were right. You were just out of school, and I think that's too young to marry for most folks. Look at my dad. He married Mom right out of high school and no matter how hard he tried, how hard they both tried, they couldn't make it work."

"But I hurt him."

"It's true. Justin was never the same after you left."

"Neither was I." Justin had been so hurt and angry, her quiet refusal had surprised him as much as it had her. So she'd earned her degree, applied for jobs and the teaching position at a reputable arts school had seemed heaven sent. She'd met her future husband and settled for a second-best life with Brad. Knowing the outcome made her feel as if she'd made the worse decisions.

Is there a way to find peace, Lord? The need for it rose like a storm within her, so powerful her throat closed up. Turmoil became a physical pain, needles twisting behind her ribs.

"About four years ago," Autumn said as she slowed the truck. A cow was standing on the road up ahead. "Justin starting seeing this gal from the next town over. Tia seemed nice enough. I never did feel comfortable with her, but she made Justin happy. He started whistling again when he worked, and he stopped being bitter. He was almost a pleasure to be around, the way he used to be."

Rori's stomach coiled tight. She knew there couldn't be a happy end to the story. The truck rolled to a stop and she opened her door. Hot air puffed over her as she dropped to the pavement. "What happened?"

"He never said. He simply ended it." Autumn climbed down and circled around the front of the truck. The cow, intent on trying to dislodge the reflective yellow marker in the middle of the road, looked up and casually flicked her tail. Autumn shook her head as if in disbelief. "Buttercup, is that you?"

The cow mooed as if to say, "Yep, it's me," and went back to work on the marker.

"How did she get out?" Autumn plodded up to the cow. "She's spoiled rotten. We can't herd her home. You wouldn't happen to have any candy on you?"

"Maybe some mints in my purse."

"Let's look. I don't have any molasses treats in my truck. Justin got stingy at the feed store last week." Autumn circled back to the truck, and so did Rori.

The cow watched them go and blinked her long curly lashes, waiting to see if something more interesting than the bright yellow square was going to appear.

Rori dug into her purse, hauled out her wallet and her cell and a stick of lip gloss. A roll of butterscotch candies sat in the very bottom along with a bit of spare change. She handed the candy to Autumn.

The cow's head came up as she scented the air. She bolted into action the moment Autumn tore open the roll. With an excited moo, she clattered across the pavement, grabbed a butterscotch with her long tongue and crunched on it happily.

The hum of an engine broke the serenity of the valley. Rori glanced behind her and, sure enough, there was a second truck approaching—a white truck.

Justin. Nerves prickled through her as if she'd fallen into a nettles patch. Sweat broke out on her palms and a longing to see the steady strength of him surprised her, the wish for him rising up unbidden and so powerful she could not stop it.

"Is that you, Buttercup?" The passenger door swung open and Frank hopped down. The fact that he wore a suit and tie didn't stop him from holding out his hands to the heifer. "What do you think you're doing, girl?"

Buttercup's chocolate-brown eyes melted as she spotted her favorite person. She streaked past Autumn and burrowed her rather substantial-size head into Frank's chest. He patted the cow's neck, talking low to her.

"Do you want me to walk her home?" Autumn offered, but her words came as if from a far distance.

Although Justin remained in the truck, disguised by the sun-glazed windshield, Rori could feel his gaze and his distance. She had to remind herself that she was moving on, but did her heart listen?

Not a chance. How did she force it to? She had no idea. Autumn's story about him rang in her mind, playing over and over like a song. He'd had his heart broken twice. Was that the reason he'd become so hard?

Sympathy for him filled her, and she didn't notice that Autumn was talking to her until the truck door shut. She blinked, realizing that Frank was on his cell, Autumn was behind the steering wheel and she was standing in the middle of the eastbound lane.

"Dad will take Buttercup in. She'll follow him like a puppy. The rest of us wouldn't have an easy time budging her." Autumn waited while Rori climbed in and buckled up before she hit the gas. The road carried them around a corner and to her grandparents' driveway.

From out in the field, Copper spotted them. His head swung up from the grass, his tail arched, he whinnied and took off at a full gallop for the corner post.

"I see he's still racing trucks." Autumn smiled as she pulled into the driveway and eased off the gas. "It's good to see he's still got the spirit at his age."

"Yes. Some things don't change. At least not yet."

She prayed Copper had a lot of good years left. He surely looked as if he did. He sped along the fence line, ears back, stretched out in a dead gallop, his joy as tangible as the hot puff of breeze on her face. It lifted her up to see her beautiful boy stretched out like a Thoroughbred at the homestretch. Autumn was kind enough to ease off the gas the last few yards of the driveway so that Copper sailed ahead, the clear winner. He knew it, celebrating with a rear kick and a flick of his mane.

"Good boy!" Rori congratulated when she climbed down from the truck, her heels a little wobbly in the loose gravel as she approached the fence. "You did it. You are my good winner."

Breathing hard, Copper preened before leaning over the fence for a well-deserved hug. Autumn wobbled over on her heels to pet the champion.

"Did you girls get everything squared away at the church?" Gramps called out, hauling a ladder as he came into sight.

"We sure tried to," Rori answered. "Gram has you changing the bird feeders."

"She surely does. Those hummingbirds get better treatment than I do." He winked. "Howdy, Autumn. Good to see you here again. I'm sure Polly has some lemonade and sugar cookies in the kitchen if you girls are interested."

"Maybe when we were ten," Rori teased.

"Right, I forget you two are all grown up. My apologies." Gramps shook his head. "I guess you'll always be those little girls riding in the fields to me. I forget how much time has gone by."

"Del? So *that's* where you've got off to," another voice called out cheerfully. Gram appeared around the apple tree, hands on her hips. "The hummingbirds are bombing me. They aren't happy their feeder isn't changed yet."

"I just took a moment to chat with the girls." Gramps shook his head as if he were perturbed, but in truth there was no mistaking the affection lighting him up. "Look at Autumn. Was she always that tall?"

"Goodness, she was at the wedding today. She's at church every Sunday." Gram shook her head good-naturedly. "Men. Don't see what's right in front of their noses. Oh! Did you see that?"

"I sure did. Kamikaze hummingbird. He nearly got you." Gramps chuckled. "It's a laugh a minute around this crazy farm. If you girls will excuse me, I'd best go change the feeder before those birds circle around for their next air strike."

"I should say so!" Gram's face wreathed with mirth. "Say, wasn't that a lovely wedding? Brings back memories. We had pink and white roses, too. Remember, honey?"

"Like it was yesterday," Gramps called over his shoulder as he trudged up to the house, Gram hurrying to join him.

"Well, I'd better go help Dad. If Buttercup is out, others could be, too." Autumn pushed away from the fence, her forehead furrowed. "Maybe we've got more problems than we think."

"I hope not." She knew this part of the county hadn't seen major rustling problems in a long time, but all things changed. "I'll see you in church tomorrow?"

"Count on it, although I might not be bright-eyed and bushy-tailed. We'll see." She climbed up into her truck. "Have a good evening, Rori."

"You, too." She waved her friend off, glad of Copper's company as the dust cloud faded. There was nothing like a little quiet time between a girl and her horse. "How about I go inside and change, grab something to read and come outside and hang with you?"

Copper tossed his head, as if to offer his horsy approval. She crunched through the loose gravel toward the house, where Gramps had placed and climbed the ladder. Gram waited nearby, offering helpful advice.

"You're tipping it, Del."

"What's a bit of spilled sugar water?" Gramps didn't seem troubled.

"It's wasteful, that's what, and I don't want ants congregating on my porch." Gram's eyes twinkled as she gazed up at her husband. "Over fifty years and I have to tell you every time."

"That's why I keep you around, Polly. To tell me things I don't have to bother to remember," Gramps quipped.

"Oh, you!" Gram laughed. "Rori! Did you girls have a fun time?"

"Very. Even the cleanup was fun. I got to catch up with old friends while I dried dishes."

"I was talking about all that dancing," Gram warbled, looking pleased.

Time to blush. Rori rolled her eyes. She should have guessed it would have been impossible to get through the evening without discussing Justin at least once.

"My, but you're popular." Gramps began his descent of the ladder. "No surprise there. You always were."

"I danced with two guys, that's it." And one only because it would prove to Justin she wasn't falling for him again.

"One is all it takes." Gram beamed. "There's plenty of fine young men in this county. You'll be happily married in no time."

"You did catch that bouquet," Gramps pointed out, carefully transferring his weight from the bottom rung of the ladder to the ground. "I saw the way Justin Granger was looking at you. That boy's still sweet on you. Woo-wee."

Her defenses went up, but one look at the wishes sparkling on her grandparents' faces stopped her. How could she fault these people who had always championed her and who radiated their hopes for her happiness?

"No comment." She pleaded the fifth, since it had to be safer than trying to convince these two she wasn't falling in love with him again. It took everything she had to try to convince herself.

"Looks like we've got a problem," Justin said into his cell, staring at the cut wire and downed posts at the Granger/Cornell property line.

"You're not telling me something I don't already know." On the other end of the call, Frank was at a computer, and Justin could hear the rapid *tap, tap, tap* of the keys.

"Did the girls find any more cattle out?"

"Not that we can tell. I sent every hired man we had checking roads, driveways, you name it. Nothing."

"But we're still missing three cows?"

"So far. I got a call in to the sheriff, for all the good that will do. Autumn and the hired men are doing head counts and I'm going through records to make sure no other cows are missing."

"Maybe they just took the ones with access to the road."

"That's what I'm afraid of." The two-year-olds had been bottle-fed and hand-raised, orphans who'd lost their mamas and were so tame anyone could walk up to them. Tame enough and well pedigreed so that they would fetch a high price at any auction in the state. "What did you find, son?"

"I know where they got in. Looks like a pair of motorcycle tracks. There's a lot of foliage here, a lot of cover from the road. No one would have noticed anything."

"Sure, since most everyone in these parts was at Terri and Tom's wedding."

Justin knew what his dad was thinking. Whoever had stolen from them had to know about the wedding, which would include half the county. Instead of an organized strike, this looked like a couple of people who probably hadn't been armed. He remembered the last time rustlers had troubled them. His dad had spent six weeks in intensive care. "At least they waited until everyone was gone."

"Thank God for small favors."

"I'll follow these tracks and see where they lead. You'll tell the sheriff?"

"Sure, when and if he shows up. Be careful, Justin. Whoever did this is probably long gone, but it doesn't hurt to play it safe."

"I know." He flipped shut his phone and swung up into his saddle. Max gave a mane toss, as if to say he was annoyed at this slow pace of things. Justin guided him through the downed length of the fence, careful not to disturb evidence should the sheriff want to take a look at it.

From his vantage in the saddle, he caught glimpses of the Cornell place through breaks in the trees. He spotted Copper grazing in his pasture, cropping the grass close to the house. His red coat shone in the sun and for some reason a memory burst into his mind, of Copper grazing next to Scout, both horses without saddles, their bridles trailing in the grasses. Again he heard the mighty sound of water splashing as Rori disappeared into the shining river, and droplets whooshed upward like pieces of crystal. He caught the rope, the hemp coarse in his hand, as he waited for her to surface.

She popped up, hair sleek and dark gold, her eyelashes damp and curling, delight turning her eyes a clear lavender. Her laughter trilled, his most favorite sound, as she treaded water and spotted him on the bank. "Your turn."

"You'd better watch out. I feel the need to cannonball." That was his only warning as he pulled the rope back, jumped up and held on tight. The world spun away beneath him, exhilarating and free. He sailed from the bank and high above the water, the hot June wind puffing against his face. He let go at the highest arc of the rope, spotting Rori in the river below, and curled up into a ball. Gravity pulled him down into the cool, refreshing wetness. He dropped down into the sun-streaked waters, where a trout scurried out of his way and Rori's pretty little feet were treading water.

Was it his fault his hand snaked out and grabbed her ankle? He gave a tug, drawing her down with him. He heard her shout of surprise, muffled by the water, and waited a beat so she could get a mouthful of air before he dragged her down with him. Her arms came around his shoulders, her hair loose and flowing like a mermaid's—his mermaid. The tender love that scored his soul was immeasurable. He swung her in a fast circle, the water whirling around them before he kicked up, lifting them to the surface. She came up laughing, her joy alive in his heart. She was his heart.

"I can't believe I'm graduating tonight." She took one hand off his shoulder to swipe at the water streaming into her eyes. Her church youth choir T-shirt glowed red as the sunlight found her. A dragonfly hovered close to check out the color before buzzing away.

"You're graduating in less than three hours." He checked his watch, which was waterproof, of course. "Your grandmother is going to kick me across a month of Sundays if I don't get you home soon."

"My gram has never kicked anyone in her life."

"That's what I mean. She'll bring out the special punishment for me. Tonight's important to her." He folded a lock of hair behind her ear. Her hair was like satin, her skin like silk. "One more jump and then I'm taking you home."

"Why? What's special about tonight?" She squinted at him, searching for the tiniest hint. "Don't tell me she has a party planned. I told her I didn't want a big fuss."

"I'm not saying a word. You can't get anything out of me." Laughter rumbled through him. He'd never been happier. The pieces of his life were coming together. He could finally see God's purpose for him—working the land as five generations of Grangers had before him, marrying Rori and taking care of her. Keeping her safe and happy and protected. Doing his utmost to give her a joyful life with all the love he possessed.

"Not a party." She rolled her eyes. "I suppose no one could stop her."

"Your grandmother is a determined woman." That was a fact. "You can be, too, Rori Cornell."

"True, but that's not all in all a bad thing. At least I'm not stubborn like you. Set in my ways." Gentle teasing. The love for him in her eyes was priceless. She had no idea how much it meant to him. How much he would give up for her, do for her.

"I'm not stubborn," he denied, although maybe it was true. Everyone said it was, but he couldn't see it. "I just know what I want."

And he wanted her. He wanted to spend every day, every season, every year with her for the rest of his life.

"Justin?" she asked, arms still looped around his neck. The laughter faded from her beautiful face, seriousness dulcet in her voice. "Tell me that nothing is going to change."

"Darlin', everything changes. But change can be for the good." Like weddings and starting a family and living happily ever after.

"Tell me that we aren't going to change. That no matter what, it will always be you and me."

The gurgling melody of the river, the blissful sunshine and the peace of that long-ago afternoon faded. Justin blinked, realizing something had pulled him from his daydream. He was surprised to find that he'd drawn Max to a stop and was staring at a perfect view of the Cornells' backyard. Del and Polly were side by side on a porch swing, Del reading a farming magazine, Polly her Bible.

Was Rori nearby? He had to search for her, scanning the knee-high grass before he found her in the pasture on the far side of Copper, curled up with her nose in a book. She could have been that girl in his memory, untouched by time. Or maybe that was the way his heart saw her.

Everything in this earthly world changed but one— he loved her. He had always loved her. He would forever love her.

He signaled Max, and the horse bolted forward. He rode into the falling twilight, glad for the shadows that hid him from sight.

Chapter Ten

"**D**ad and Justin are out with the sheriff," Addison explained as she grabbed a pancake from the stack on the table, rolled it around a sausage and a spoonful of scrambled eggs. "Dad's none too happy. Sheriff Todd refused to work on Sunday, which I understand, but it's frustrating. It's not like the town can afford a deputy or something to fill in."

"That's too bad. I hope the trail isn't too cold." Rori had heard Gramps's view before on the big-city sheriff. She finished browning the last batch of sausages for the Granger sisters and carried the fry pan to the table. "Your dad has to be worried about his cows."

"His pet cows." Cheyenne clarified as she tromped into the room, dressed to ride. All that was missing was a Stetson. "They're worth a good five or six grand a piece."

"Times are hard for a lot of people." Rori tipped the pan, rolling the links onto the paper towels. "It doesn't sound like a big band of rustlers."

"That's what we think, too." Autumn grabbed a pancake and rolled up a to-go sandwich the way her sister had. "But we're riding patrols to be safe."

"We'll stay in cell range," Addison added, stepping into her boots in the mudroom.

"You'll have to man the main phone." Autumn snatched a travel mug and carried it to the coffeemaker. "I'll be back in time for Cady's appointment. In case she shows early, would you mind offering her coffee and giving me a jingle?"

"Will do." Rori considered the platters of food, largely untouched, on the table. Maybe she would plate up and keep breakfast warm in the oven for Justin and Frank so she could start cleaning the kitchen. "Which horse are you going to sell to her?"

"I'm hoping she and Misty will take a shine to each other." Autumn finished filling her mug, replaced the carafe and reached for the carton of coffee creamer. "I've been trying to find the right person for that mare for a long time. No one has been the right fit. For my other horses, sure, but not her. I'm hoping Cady is the right match."

"I guess we'll see. Misty is the palomino paint?"

"The most gorgeous horse ever, and sweet as the day is long. She doesn't just go to anyone." Autumn worried her bottom lip, protective of the horses she loved. "After I see Cady around horses, I'll know if I can trust her with Misty."

"No one understands the bond between a girl and her horse." Rori set the fry pan on a cold burner. "Not unless you've been there."

"That's right. It takes one to know one." She capped her thermos and headed toward the door. "My advice is to keep the coffee hot and fresh. My suspicion is that when Dad comes back, he's not going to be in a good mood."

"Thanks for the heads-up." Rori opened the dishwasher. "Maybe I'll bake blueberry muffins. He hinted they were his favorite."

"That would earn you big points with him." Autumn disappeared around the corner. "See ya later."

"Bye." Alone in the kitchen, she picked up two clean plates from the racks and carried them to the table. The picture window framed the backyard and half of the hillside perfectly. For as far as she could see foals pranced under the watchful eyes of their mothers in the nearby field and Buttercup, picketed on the back lawn, mooed and ran at Autumn as far as her generous rope would allow. When the heifer ran out of slack she tugged against her restraint with all her might, stretching her neck as far as it would go and then her long pink tongue toward Autumn's pancake rollup.

"You already have breakfast." Autumn's voice carried across the silent yard. "Sorry. You'll have to wait for Dad to spoil you."

Buttercup mooed pleadingly, sounding so pitiful Rori gathered a few molasses treats from a small bag in the mudroom. When she pushed through the screen door, the cow, bright-eyed as a puppy, ran straight at her. It was a little like looking a runaway train in the grill until the rope tautened. Buttercup skidded to a stop and danced in place, already knowing the treats were hers.

"You *are* the most spoiled cow ever."

Buttercup appeared to feel no remorse at this, so Rori held out one of the goodies on her palm. With a single swipe of that tongue, the treat was gone. The cow chewed it happily, jowls working.

"I'm glad you're here safe and sound." She patted Buttercup's neck. She hated to think what could be happening to the other missing cows. Where were they, and were they frightened? Being mistreated? Rori guessed that was what ate away at Justin and Frank. Sheriff Todd, whom she'd only seen at church, was from Detroit, and he might not understand the value of a farm animal, sometimes something that went far beyond their monetary worth.

She fed Buttercup the last treat and rubbed her poll. The cow's short coat felt bristly against her fingertips. Content, Buttercup flicked her tail and closed her eyes.

"What are you doing sweet-talking my best gal?" Frank called out across the yard.

Rori whipped around, unprepared for the sight of Justin on horseback riding in on the sun. He dismounted alongside his father and left the horses standing in the back yard.

"You've caught me red-handed." She cleared her throat, hoping her voice sounded unaffected. "I'm spoiling Buttercup."

"Like she needs more of that." Frank moseyed up to the cow, who batted her long curly eyelashes at him and pressed her forehead against his chest. "Thanks for it, though. You wouldn't still happen to have breakfast on the table?"

"And it's still warm."

"Bless you, girl. I'm so hungry I could eat my own boot." He gave the cow a final pat and broke away to the house, leaving her alone with Justin.

It was a total shocker he wasn't walking away from her. Nor was he doing his best to avoid her. Instead, he strode toward her with purpose. Larks sang in the nearby maple and Buttercup lowed a cheerful hello as the span of lush green grass separating them diminished. His shadow fell across her, and she shivered. Every step he took toward her felt as if it brought them closer to what could be.

You don't want a future with him, she told herself. She wasn't ready for him or anyone. Falling in love with him would be the biggest mistake. Hoping that he would love her in return was an even bigger mistake. All she could see was heartbreak brewing.

"That's nice of you to pamper Dad's favorite cow." Justin shoved his hands into his pockets, looking about as uncomfortable as she felt.

"It was my pleasure." She stroked Buttercup's nose. "What did the sheriff say?"

"Not much. He says because the trail is cold, there's no sense in trying to solve this thing. That we should collect the insurance money and get different cows."

"But those were special animals."

"Todd said a cow is a cow. His attitude might be the reason the town council is so unhappy with him." Justin shrugged. "Maybe they'll hire someone better come November, but in the meantime, we've got motorcycle tracks and hoof prints exiting our property near the main road. They could have loaded the cows into a trailer from there. Not a soul would have seen them. There are no other leads."

"Isn't the sheriff going to check with the auction houses? Maybe some of the county slaughterhouses?"

"He said he would, that's standard procedure, but I'm going to finish making the calls myself this morning. I don't trust him to do it fast enough. The cows were branded, so if they're found we have proof of claim. Other than that, there's nothing we can do."

"I'm sorry, Justin." She could read the strain and worry on his face and his concern for their animals. She fisted her hands to keep from reaching out to him. She didn't have the right to help smooth away the furrow in his brow or the tension tight in his jaw.

"In the meantime, we're going to start branding early." He tugged his hat brim lower to keep the sun out of his eyes. "That means we'll need you to haul the food out to us."

"Sure."

"Dad will give you the particulars. I just thought you might want a heads-up before you grocery shop." He stared down at the ground between them, kicking his toe into the thick grass. "We'll probably bring in more hired hands to keep an eye on things. That will mean more mouths to feed."

"It's all fine, Justin."

"Good." Did she feel torn up, too, remembering how it was to be close and knowing it could never be again? She sure didn't look it. He squared his shoulders, determined to seem at least as unaffected as she was. But one look at her hit him like a punch to the gut. He backed away. "It was good of you to coddle Buttercup. She's missing her cow buddies."

"Spoiling animals is my specialty." She brushed the cow's face one more time, her kindness revealed. Buttercup responded, her big brown eyes melting as she gazed up at her new friend. "Well, I've got to get back to work. Dishes are waiting in the sink and your breakfast is getting cold."

For a second he didn't realize she'd been speaking

to him. He'd been so caught up in watching her lips move as she spoke, the gentle smile at the corners of her mouth, the innocence of sunlight on her creamy skin. Embarrassed that he'd been staring so hard at her, he nodded, his boots turning toward the back porch but his feelings and his spirit did not turn from her.

Her voice spoke to him from his memory, so strongly he could hear the babbling river and the leaves singing in the wind. *Tell me that we aren't going to change. That no matter what, it will always be you and me.*

Strange it was that God had brought her back home to Wyoming and at the same moment they'd needed a cook. Once, he would have believed that God had fated them to meet again. Now, he wasn't sure what God wanted from him, but surely it could not be to break him down to the soul over Rori one more time. There had to be a different answer.

He held the screen door for her, and Buttercup mooed her displeasure at being alone. When he glanced over his shoulder, the cow was straining at her rope in their direction. First chance he had, he intended to fix Buttercup's pasture.

"I think that heifer would come into the house if she could untie herself." Frank looked up from the table, a fork in hand. "Rori, I don't know for sure if that picket line will hold. You won't mind keeping an eye on her this morning, will you?"

"Not at all." She left Justin at the door, breezing away as if she had no clue what she did to him or how something deep in his soul leaned after her, wanting what could never be.

"You'll have to put her in the barn when you bring lunch out to us. Would you mind?" Dad cut into his pancake stack. "I'd do it, but I don't want to shut her up all day."

Justin noticed Rori didn't state the obvious. That Buttercup could be let out into the upper rangelands with the rest of the cattle or in with the expecting mares. He liked that she understood Buttercup was special to them all. The cow was used to being near the house.

"I don't mind at all. I'll lead her in with a trail of molasses treats." She went straight to the sink.

"You catch on quick. And I have to say, young lady, this is the tastiest breakfast I've had in some time."

"I'm glad you're happy." She turned on the faucet, looking like an image straight out of his long-ago dreams. Rori at his sink, in his kitchen, looking happy and relaxed and right where she belonged. Had he married, Dad would have given him this house. They would have lived here, been happy and raised their children here.

Why was he thinking of that now? Pain slammed into him like a spike to his chest and he put on the boot he'd just taken off. His stomach growled something fierce, so he grabbed a few pancakes and sausages off the table and headed straight out the door before any more foolish notions came to mind.

Rori Cornell had left him once. He had to believe she would do it again. Loving her or not had never made a whit of difference.

Buttercup spotted the food in his hand, mooed hopefully and then sadly when he bypassed her. He went straight to his horse, mounted up and put distance between him and Rori as fast as he could.

Cady Winslow adjusted her sunglasses. She'd stopped her SUV and glanced around. She saw nothing but a long ribbon of two-lane paved road behind her and stretching endlessly in front of her. There was no one else around, not unless you counted the hawk sitting on a telephone pole ahead, watching her with great interest.

She squinted at the directions Autumn had given her. She'd written them down carefully and followed them to the letter, but Cady had a terrible sinking feeling she was lost anyway. The fencing on one side of the road rising up to a rocky ridge had been going on for miles. Black cows glanced up from their grazing to stare at her. On the other side of the road, a field of something green and growing stretched as far as she could see. Huge metal wheels the size of semitruck tires were connected by pipes, spraying water onto the crops. Dozens of tiny rainbows glistened in the watery mist.

She checked the speedometer. She'd only gone nine miles, and the notes said a stone's throw past nine miles. How much was a stone's throw? Maybe she ought to go a little farther before she turned around. She felt like the only person in the entire county—there was nothing but silence and open space and the big bold sky. She was used to blasting horns and people everywhere and buildings crowding out the sky. Not for the first time did she have to wonder. Was she making a mistake?

Well, only time would tell. She'd left a secure job, her friends and family and nearly everything she knew to move to Wyoming. The right decision? It certainly was a scary one. She'd prayed over it, searched her soul and in the end she had followed her heart. Probably that wasn't very wise because in her experience, that's what brought a woman problems every time.

"Remember today's devotional," she told herself,

holding on tight to the morning's verse from Proverbs she'd studied over breakfast at the motel's diner. *A man's heart plans his way, but the Lord directs his steps.*

She had to believe the Lord was showing her the way in the grand scheme, but for now she really needed to find the way to the Grangers' ranch. Why hadn't she sprung for the GPS option, she asked, and would it even work all the way out here?

The cows to her left bolted, running swiftly up the rising hill. Their sudden movement piqued her curiosity. What inspired cattle to run? Did they spot some sort of danger to them, or did they like to stretch their legs?

She had no clue, not until she spied a familiar man on horseback cresting the ridge. She recognized him, the man from the church parking lot. Frank Granger. Like a Western hero in the films she'd grown up on, he wore a black Stetson. With the brilliant blue sky framing him he looked larger than life, able to right wrongs and stay the distance.

If her pulse skipped three beats, she ignored it. Riveted, she could not take her eyes from him. He wore a white T-shirt and jeans, and he was the reason the cows were running. Tails up, they flocked to him like children to an ice-cream vendor and milled around his brown horse.

The man towered above them, hands reaching down to rub a nose here and the top of the head there. It was obvious the animals adored him. As if he felt her gaze, he looked up, the angle chased the shadow from his face and where sunlight touched it she saw high cheekbones, a straight nose and a handsome square jaw.

His hand shot up in a manly wave. As if he knew who

she was—probably Autumn had told him she would be arriving—he gestured down the road and nodded.

Warmth rolled through her heart, a hint of awareness for this man she did not know. How embarrassing. She didn't have her hopes up, that was for sure! She waved her thanks, careful not to smile too much. She did not want her interest to show. She had gotten used to rejection over the past few years, when whatever bloom she'd had faded. She hadn't become as successful as she was without being a sensible, practical woman. So she swallowed a hint of disappointment and turned her attention to driving. She did not look into the side mirror for a chance to see him again. She kept her gaze firmly on the road and after it took a long curve, the driveway came into sight. Wooden fencing marched down the way and an overhead sign proclaimed, Stowaway Ranch.

Cottonwoods and maples shaded a lazy stream near to the driveway, and the gravel lane ribboned around a low hillside. It felt as if she were driving through a storybook picture as horses lifted their heads from grazing in an emerald green meadow to watch her go by. A two-story house with brick and wood facing, a wide front porch and plentiful large windows crowned the rise, inviting her to come closer. Tree leaves tossed shade into the front yard, a porch swing rocked in the breeze and the white screen door opened as she pulled to a stop.

"You're right on time." Rori, whom she'd met at the church, smiled a greeting. Although she wore a simple cotton shirt and denim shorts with sneakers on her feet, she looked every bit as sweet. Cady knew if she'd taken a different path in her life, she would have a daughter about that age and hopefully one as nice.

Oh, these midlife questionings were getting worse!

Cady shut off the engine, left her purse on the seat and stepped out into the pleasant sunshine. She felt over-dressed in her blouse and boot-cut trousers.

"I know Autumn is on her way in to meet with you. Would you like some coffee? Iced tea? Juice?"

"No, thanks. This is a lovely place."

"I think it's the prettiest property in the county, al-though I just work here." Rori breezed down the steps. "I live next door."

"Next door?" She laughed, glancing around. The horses that had been grazing were still watching her, obviously curious. As far as she could see there were no other buildings other than a large seven-bay garage tastefully set off to the side. There was not another house in sight. "You must mean the next ranch over?"

"Yes. My grandparents' farm isn't as grand as this, most spreads in these parts aren't." Conversationally, Rori led the way to a white picket fence and a gate, which she opened.

Cady gasped at the garden, where old-world lilac trees stood watch over canes of climbing roses. Cabbage roses that had grown taller than she was lined the fence, and miniature shrubs lined the pathway that skirted the side of the rather grand house. The wind lazily lifted the most delicious fragrance from the colorful blossoms.

Once, the walled garden had been grand, but now the blooms were in need of deadheading and the shrubs of a good trimming. Cady sighed down to the bottom of her soul. It reminded her of a garden she'd read about in a book when she'd been young. As a school girl she'd always had her nose in a book, to her mother's con-sternation.

"Here's Autumn now." Rori opened the far gate and

led the way to an expansive backyard. The grass, neatly trimmed, was flawless except for the black cow with a white face who stood in the middle of it, mooing loudly.

"Buttercup, no one has forgotten you." Autumn paraded into sight, Stetson shading her face. "Hi, Cady. Sorry about Buttercup. She's rather loud. She's Dad's favorite pet cow."

Not that she'd ever heard of a pet cow, but she could certainly see the animal was used to attention. She'd never thought of cows as happy, but this one beamed dog-like joy with those bright eyes and smiling expression. Cady remembered the man on horseback swarmed by his cows. Frank Granger appeared to be such a strong man, capable and rugged, but obviously kind to animals and elderly ladies.

Very hard not to like that.

Chapter Eleven

"Dad?" Justin raised his voice. Maybe then his father could hear him, but Frank Granger seemed to be off in his thoughts. Maybe he was worried about his missing cows. Justin nudged Max up the rocky slope into the shade of a few sparse evergreens. The five hundred head of mother cows in this field ambled along with babies at their sides. Across the milling black and white herd, he spotted Cheyenne and Scotty, barely visible through the dust cloud rising up like smog.

"Dad!" He bellowed louder.

Up ahead, his father startled and twisted around in his saddle. "What is it, son?"

"You want to stop here?"

"What?" Frank looked around as if realizing where he was. Pretty strange, since he wasn't a man given to daydreaming. "Got a lot more on my mind than I figured. We'll stop for grub and then we'll separate the herd."

"Autumn should be back by then," he agreed. He was a good cutter, but the work went faster with Autumn at his side. "You want to take a break, Dad? Ride down to the house. Maybe call the sheriff again?"

"No." A sharp, quick answer, not at all laid-back Frank Granger's manner.

Wow. His father was agitated about something. But what? His first guess would be a woman, but that didn't make any sense. His father was an avowed bachelor.

Maybe he was projecting his own troubles, Justin wondered. He certainly did have a woman on the mind—Rori. And he couldn't stop wondering and remembering. Fortunately a cow darted from the herd with her little one at her side. He wheeled Max around. Something to take his mind off the woman. "Let's get 'em, boy."

Up to the challenge, Max dug in, lowered his head and roared down the grade, executing a perfect turn that cut off the cow's escape and drove her back to the herd. He hadn't been gone more than a few minutes at most, but Frank was still staring off into space.

Something was definitely up. Justin rode up to him. Once he'd reached the top of the ridge he realized that his dad wasn't staring off into space but down at the backyard. A mile away, it was nearly impossible to make out details, but a gray SUV was still in the driveway. The lodge lady come to buy the horse?

No, why would Dad be interested in a city woman? Justin dismissed that out of hand. Something else had to be wrong. It wasn't like Dad to keep things bottled up for long. He would talk about it in time. That was the benefit of being your father's best friend.

"Hey," he said, knuckling back his hat. "Want to ride down and fetch lunch?"

"No, Rori's on her way up. She's behind the trees. I

saw her leave the house. We'll wait here for her because I feel like staying put. Must be old age." Frank winked, back to his lighthearted, laid-back self.

"You're not so old, old man." A joke between them but it was soon forgotten when Rori rode into sight, appearing round the copse of trees.

She sat straight in her saddle, rocking gently with Copper's gait, talking to her horse and the horse she led, carrying the bundles of food and drink. By the look of things, she was enjoying whatever it was she was saying to the horses, chatting away as Copper nodded in agreement. She might look amazing in a dress and heels, but this was how he liked her best. With her hair pulled back in a ponytail and a ball cap shading her face, his country girl.

"Justin? Do you hear me, boy?"

He shook his head, unaware of how much time had passed. "What did you say?"

"Go down and help her, son." Understanding layered those words.

Justin blushed, aware his dad had known all along what he had just figured out. He whistled Max to a walk, cutting a path through the cattle to the gate. His sisters had dismounted and were giving a few calves their attentions. Maybe Cheyenne or Addison called out to him, he didn't exactly notice, because he couldn't take his gaze off Rori. She was still a fair distance away, far enough that her voice couldn't reach him. She drew him anyway, making him hunger for the melody of her words and her gentle presence.

Boy, am I in big trouble. He headed down the incline toward her, sure the grass was greener, the birdsong sweeter because of her. This moment was like a piece of the future he'd once wanted—the moment when she looked up and saw him riding toward her, the way she lit up with gladness and made his world brighter. He drank in the moment—the jingle of the bridle, the placid clomp of horse hooves and the Wyoming landscape stretching out all around them. His love for her lifted like hope on a prayer.

Lord, help me not to show it. You have to know this is a love that's not meant to be.

"Justin," she called across the closing distance. "Autumn said to tell you she's on her way."

"I take it things went well with the lodge lady?"

"Cady Winslow. Yep. She fell in love with Misty."

"Autumn must be glad." All he had to do was to play it cool, not be too remote or too interested, maybe frown a little and that ought to hide the fact that instead of taking the pack horse's lead from her, he wanted to take her hand in his like he used to do.

"She said she's been waiting for the right owner for Misty, and once I met the mare I knew why. Gorgeous."

Don't look at her, he told himself, staring as hard as he could at the ground ahead. If he didn't look, he wouldn't be captivated by the adorable way she tilted her head when she talked. He wouldn't be tempted to want to recapture the past, which was gone, or to wish for the soft warmth of her smaller hand in his.

"And sweet," Rori went on, talking about the horse, unaware that he was thinking the same thing.

Gorgeous. Sweet. So rare that he'd never felt the same way about another woman. Once, that had been why Tia had been so attractive to him because she hadn't held the power over his heart, she never could have claimed a part of his soul.

"Not that any horse is better than Copper, of course," she went on.

Copper snorted as if to say, "Of course."

"But Misty is definitely the second best."

"The third," Justin found himself arguing as Max nickered as if to say he was a touch insulted at being left out.

"Sorry, Max." Rori apologized and the gelding seemed satisfied. "You must miss riding Scout all day."

"It was a hard thing when he got too old for ranch work." He bowed his head, looking down instead of at her. "He started getting winded easily and dragging by day's end. It broke my heart to retire him, but I think he knew. He was ready."

"You miss him."

"We miss each other." He shrugged as if he wasn't troubled by anything as pesky as an emotion, but she wasn't fooled.

"He was down in the paddock watching me saddle up," she confessed. "He kept glancing up at the ridge. He knew you were up here. It nearly broke my heart to leave him behind. I gave him a handful of those treats he loves."

"Thanks. I'm sure he appreciated it. I know he gets lonely. He and I spent all day every day together for more years than I care to count."

"I know. I missed Copper when I was away. There wasn't a single day I didn't wish he and I were galloping through a field together or just sitting close reading while he grazed."

"Were you happy in Dallas?"

"It wasn't a bad life, but it was second best to life here."

"Are you sorry you left?" His question came quietly, hovering in the air between them like an undetonated bomb, one about to go off at anytime and destroy their tentative peace.

But it didn't. She heard a deeper layer to his question, one she'd never known before.

"No," she answered honestly. "I'm just sorry I didn't come back sooner."

They'd nearly reached the ridge, so he didn't answer and she stayed silent. As the horses plodded up the rocky trail, a hawk circled overhead, calling out as he sailed wide, hunting. The smaller birds went silent, disappearing from sight. Nothing but the wind moved the grasses as they circled toward the fence.

It felt comfortable riding quietly at Justin's side, like all the times they'd gone off together on horseback. She breathed in the fresh air, enjoying the companionable silence, God's nature spread out before her and the pleasure of Justin's company. All that was missing was the way he used to take her hand in his when they rode.

Some things were lost forever. She did not reach out to him but drew Copper to a halt. Justin rode up to open the gate, tall and confident in his saddle, a man who took her breath away.

No doubt about it. Justin had grown up into a fine man.

A man she could not let herself love.

She pressed her heels against Copper's side, urging him forward where Cheyenne and Addison were calling out welcomes to her, surrounded by adorable baby calves.

All afternoon long and into the evening the image dogged him, the one of Rori cuddling up to the calves.

The delight on her face as the doe-eyed creatures gathered around her, eager for head pats and handfuls of grain the girls were giving out like candy. Her cheerful alto, the fun she seemed to be having, and how comfortable she looked among the animals. Not what he might expect from a girl who'd spent a significant chunk of time living an urban life.

She was just passing time until summer's end. They both knew it. She'd never said a word about staying. When she was back on her feet and recovered from the blow of her marriage falling apart, she would be off again, leaving him behind. He had to keep that truth front and center in his mind. He could not afford to forget it.

"That's the last one." Dad straightened up. "That's one herd tagged. We did good today, son."

"Desperation." He released the ropes hobbling the bleating calf, who scrambled to his feet crying for his mama on the other side of the sturdy fence. The desperate mother answered, mooing long and worried. She did not like being separated from her baby.

"That's all right, Moonshine. Your little guy is gonna be with you in a second." Dad rubbed the cow's nose and she quieted, anxious until he opened the gate just enough to let the calf leap through. Once reunited, the mother inspected her little one with great care.

Long day. Justin squinted at the sun low in the sky, tossed his hat onto a fence post and stretched his back. He hurt everywhere. They had moved up branding a month so the youngest cows wouldn't be vulnerable. A brand was proof of ownership. That wouldn't discourage any returning rustlers, but it would limit the way they could profit.

"I'm beat." Cheyenne dismounted, leading her cutting horse, Lulu, by the reins. "I spent all school year missing being here in a saddle on the back of my horse. But I forgot about these kinds of days."

"Makes you miss the classroom." Justin took a swig of his water. He was too hot for a swallow to make much of a difference, so he upended the bottle over his head. That was better. "I think we should leave the herd down here by the barn for the night. Run them back up come morning."

"Sounds like a plan. I'm going to go soak in the tub." Cheyenne limped away. "I hope Rori left us something good for supper."

"Not that it's probably still warm." Autumn rode up, streaked with dirt and sweat, wearing a wide grin. She was still in a good mood over selling her mare. "Or if Rori did leave food to keep warm in the oven, it's probably dry by now."

He hadn't seen her leave, and he'd been looking. But Copper wasn't in his stall. He hated that he'd missed seeing her.

He hated that he'd wanted to see her.

"I'll take care of the horses." Addison trotted up. "I got the easiest job today, so I don't mind. Justin, I'm taking Max."

"Thanks, Addy." He grabbed his hat, patted a cow straining through the slats of the fence, extracted the hem of his T-shirt from her mouth, and walked on aching feet to the barn. The hot breeze didn't help cool him one bit, and even in the shaded main aisle, sweat kept rolling down the back of his neck.

Scout nickered, running in from the paddock to his stall, head up, dark eyes hopeful.

"You want to take a ride, buddy?"

The one excited nicker said it all. Justin grabbed Scout's bridle from the tackroom. The thought of taking a swim in the river put a bounce in his step.

Rori knew she should be home weeding Gram's garden, but she'd had to escape. She needed fresh air to clear her head. The last thing she wanted to do was to expose her dear grandparents to more of her troubles. They thought she was doing well, and she wanted them to keep thinking that. They didn't need to waste time worrying about her. She'd made a mess of her life, but that was her problem. Besides, they had been completely enchanting together, sitting side by side in the old porch swing, chatting about the upcoming bake and rummage sale at the church. Gram was planning on baking her renowned angel food cake for the event.

"Looks like we're here, boy." She slid off Copper's bare back, her sneakers sinking into the fragrant grasses. Wildflowers dotted the small meadow with the brilliant yellows of dandelions and buttercups, the reds of Indian paintbrush and a few purple coneflowers.

Copper rubbed his head against her, an affectionate gesture, and she stroked her fingers through his mane. The hot wind lifted her bangs from her forehead and she lifted her face. That felt so good. The silence, the aloneness, the beauty all coalesced into perfection. She'd missed the realness of a life on the land.

If she had come back after college, would she have been happier? She didn't know, but the restlessness remained, unanswered questions that made her uncertain about the decisions she'd made in her life. She'd tried to follow where the Lord led, but maybe she'd been wrong.

The package that had come in today's mail was proof enough of that.

The swimming hole looked the same as it always had. The water's melody, the thick knotted rope hanging from a sturdy maple bough, the feeling of solitude and peace were all just as she'd remembered it. Time stood still here. She felt as if she were eighteen again as she kicked off her sneakers and grabbed hold of the rope. Leaving her troubles behind, she pulled it as far as it would go, tightened her grip and took a leap, swinging out over the grassy bank.

Out of the corner of her eye she saw something big and dark breaking through the foliage. Adrenaline spiked through her as the ground fell away and water winked up at her. Copper tore one last mouthful of grass before his head shot up, scenting the intruder. She couldn't help him.

"Rori?" A familiar baritone rolled like thunder across the small clearing.

"Justin?" It was startling to see him riding out of the clutch of the shadows.

Her grip slipped, the rope slid between her palms, and the friction burned so she let go. The last thing she remembered was shrieking as she fell unprepared into the river below. She grabbed a bite of air just before water cascaded over her head and pulled her down.

What was *he* doing here? Hard and stoic Justin Granger was no longer the type to cannonball into a river. She kicked, sputtering to the surface and swam to the bank.

"Sorry about that." He towered over her, amusement relaxing the hard planes of the face she knew so well. "I didn't mean to startle you."

"Well, you did." Not the best comeback in the world, but she was startled. That had to be the reason why her brain wasn't functioning properly and *not* because he was standing before her looking like the best of blessings in a pair of cutoffs and a T-shirt advertising a rodeo. She said the first thing that popped into her mind. "I didn't know you were a bronco rider."

"No, but Tucker is. We always head over to Cheyenne for the rodeo. The girls compete in the horse events." He grabbed her elbow to help her up the bank.

His touch felt comforting, like coming home after a long journey. Tension slid out of her muscles. This was not exactly like old times, she realized as she landed in the soft grass. Everything had changed between them, even the way he looked into her eyes. Was it the lost past she ached for? Or something else?

Don't think about that, she warned herself. She feared the answer wasn't what she wanted it to be. She shook her head, and droplets flew into the air. "Don't tell me you came to play in the river?"

"What if I did? And there's a bigger question here. Why are you on my family's land?"

"I figured the no-trespassing signs along the property line didn't apply to me. They never have."

"You did notice the other signs. The ones that said owner will protect with force?"

Oh, she spotted that twinkle of amusement he was working so hard to hide. "Just try it, buster. Country girls know how to hold their own."

"Is that so?" he challenged, grabbing her into his arms before she could do more than squeal. He was warm from the sun and smelled of hay and summer. "Looks like you can't hold your own against me."

"I'm in a slight predicament, that's all. I could break your hold easily, I'm sure." She was laughing too hard to speak. "Justin, you aren't going to—"

"Take a deep breath," he interrupted as two quick steps brought him to the bank's edge. The river burbled below, swift and refreshing, and both horses watched curiously as he rocked her toward the edge. "One."

"Don't you throw me," she told him.

"Two. It seems to me that you don't have much say-so." He held her safe against his chest, right where she belonged.

"You put me down this instant." She laughed, the past melted and there were no wounds between them, no breakup, no lost years, no regrets.

"Three." He swung her with care, launching her safely over the bank and out of his arms.

"Justiiin!" She squealed as the momentum of his toss sent her up into the air and then down, down toward the rippling waters.

A splash silenced her and when she disappeared beneath the river's surface he kicked off his shoes and joined her.

Chapter Twelve

"I can't believe you did that." She was waiting for him when he surfaced, swiping water out of her face and doing her best to look mad at him, which she wasn't. She had to bite the inside of her mouth to keep from laughing out loud. "What were you thinking?"

"That it would be fun to dump you in the river."

"Oh, and do you think this is fun?" She launched out of the water like a bouncing tiger, her hands landing squarely on his wide shoulders. She shoved hard enough to dunk him beneath the water. His dark hair swirled in the current before he disappeared.

Something snaked around her wrist and tugged. With a shriek she was hurled down beneath the surface, spitting water out of her mouth as she went. That Justin, he was grinning at her looking like ten different kinds of trouble as he took off down the river, holding her captive and carrying her with him.

Good thing she'd managed to get enough air! And if he thought she would go along for the ride, he was sorely mistaken. That Justin hadn't changed much, he was still as bossy as ever. She grabbed his hand holding her wrist and searched for the pressure point in his palm that would make him release her.

He knew what she was up to because his arms came around her, trapping her against his chest as he soared upward. They broke the surface, water droplets tickling like music all around them.

"Ha!" Justin laughed. "Try to get away from me now."

"I'm sure I could if I wanted to." In truth she was stuck, caught like a fish on a line, and her heart was, too.

Water clung to her lashes, framing the edges of her view like light through diamonds. Although the current was carrying them away, she felt safe in his arms. He was her champion, a man who chased away her every sadness and all her regrets. Her pulse skipped a beat. Her entire being stilled.

His gaze dropped to her mouth and lingered, as if he felt this, too. Did he want to kiss her, or was he simply remembering how amazing their kisses had been?

Please kiss me. The wish lifted like a prayer from her soul. Was there a way to recapture the past? Her beliefs in true love had shattered, her trust that love could last, but in his arms, in the moment, gazing into the midnight blue of his eyes, she began to hope.

He ripped away from her. Answer enough. She floated freely on the current, but he put a hand to her back and kept her from drifting away. She stayed at his side, treading water, feeling the push of the current, the inexorable pull of what could be.

"I don't want Copper thinking I've taken off with you." His explanation was a thin one.

She didn't comment. Instead she took after him,

keeping her head above water and swimming at a diagonal against the river's force.

"I didn't know you still came up here," she said when they'd reached the bank. "I would have thought your playing in the river days were behind you."

"Now and then I have a rough day and I feel the need."

"You don't normally brand the calves for another month."

"We'll have to de-horn, vaccinate and cut them then. Doubles the work." He offered his hand to help her up the bank. "I should have spent the day in the fields in the air-conditioned tractor."

"Sounds like a better chore, as long as your iPod is charged." She laid her palm on his, ignoring how familiar it felt to let him help her up the rocks and onto the cushiony grass.

"Are you kidding? We have satellite radio and a stereo system to keep me grinning even on a long day." The horses continued to graze side by side in companionable silence, friends catching up.

"You rode Scout," she noticed.

"Just like old times."

"Yes." She could almost believe nothing had really changed. Did he feel this, too, the push of the future, the pull of the past? The earth was springy beneath her bare feet, the ground radiating the sun's warmth and her spirit as light as a nearby lark's song. She felt whole, as if grace and not the wind breezed over her.

"You never said what you were doing here." Justin pulled back the rope as leaves rustled a quiet symphony. "A tough day for you, too?"

"Not at work, if that's what you're asking."

"It crossed my mind. It's a lot of work keeping care of us all. Only my aunt Opal would do it and she did it out of love, because we were family."

"You all feel like family to me." She blushed, realizing too late what she'd said.

"What happened today?" He stepped back, allowing her room to step in and take the rope.

"I received my divorce papers." She curled her hands around the thick hemp, holding on tight. "I sign on the designated lines and acknowledge the biggest failure of my life."

"It can't be the biggest." He felt her sadness as if it were his own, and he hated that she was hurting. "Wasn't turning me down your biggest mistake?"

"Some people might think so, but I'm not one of them." At least she could still crack a joke.

"You're right. I should have waited for you." The admission killed him because a man never liked to be wrong, but it was time he lowered his pride and let in the truth. "I never even thought of it. I shouldn't have made my proposal all or nothing. Proof I wasn't ready to be a husband."

"I wasn't ready to be a wife." Pain filled her. He knew, because it was his, too.

"And when you were ready, it wasn't with me." He swallowed against the rising tide of emotions too strong to name, ones he did not want to bear. "What happened to your marriage?"

"I wanted kids, he didn't. I wanted to focus on our marriage, he wanted to focus on his career. I wanted to move out of the city and live on a little acreage, he wanted to stay near his country club."

"You wanted different things." His parents were like that and it had torn them apart.

"Yes, and one day the differences were too great and he no longer wanted me."

"How could any man not want you?" Unbelievable. He couldn't imagine it.

"Brad decided he had more in common with his receptionist and surprised me by having the locks on the house changed, canceling my cards and moving all the money out of our joint bank accounts." Humiliation. She tried to hide it from him with a careless shrug.

Was he fooled? Not a chance. He brushed a wet tangle of hair away from her cheek and laid his hand there, his palm curved against the delicate line of her jaw and cheek. Tenderness, an emotion he'd long ago banned from feeling, ebbed through him, gentle and sweet and powerful enough to drown him.

"I'm sorry, Rori." He truly was. "You didn't deserve that."

"It's not so bad to start over. It's turned out all right. I haven't been this happy in a long time."

"Marriage is hard, and the wrong marriage is harder." His dad had always said this, and Justin had seen it with his own eyes. "There's something to be said for being single."

"Especially when you aren't the kind of woman a man will give everything for." She winced, as if she believed that. She blushed, as if she'd confessed too much.

Not to him. Never to him. He curled his hand to the back of her neck and drew her against his chest. Caring roared through him like the leading edge of a twister, but he couldn't let it devastate him. He had to be strong. He had to hold on to his resolve.

"Don't think there was anything missing in you." He wanted her to know the truth. "The right man would give up anything for the privilege of loving you."

"Oh, Justin. You said exactly what my heart needed to hear." Her arms wrapped tight around his ribs, holding on tight, as if she hadn't had anyone to steady her in a long, long time.

His arms went around her, too. He wasn't ashamed to be the shoulder she needed to lean on, her soft place to fall and if only for this moment in time. He leaned his cheek against the crown of her head, breathing in the fragrance of her hair and the faint scent of strawberry shampoo. Immeasurable emotions threatened to break down the dam he'd put up.

Please, Lord, let those walls hold. Since I can't help loving her, at least don't make me feel it.

He wasn't too sure if the Lord could help him with that, but he prayed anyhow. Disaster was coming on the road ahead, there was no doubt about that. Hadn't Rori just told him that she was starting over? That she was ready to build a new life for herself? Obviously that would be back in Dallas.

"Now that I've all but cried on your shoulder." She tilted her head back, searching him as if she wanted to see his truths buried within. "Why haven't you let some woman snatch you off the market?"

"Because this woman I was seeing a few years back, Tia was her name." He released Rori so she wouldn't be as close, so that maybe he could try to hide from her how disillusioned he'd become. "We were talking on the phone, like we did every evening after I'd get in from the fields. She had another call and she put me on hold to take it. Except she didn't put me on hold. She must have hit the wrong button because the line didn't switch over."

"Uh-oh. That doesn't sound good."

"No. The next thing I heard her say was, Oh, Sarah, thank goodness you called. I'm on the phone with Justin. He bores me to tears and if he wasn't worth millions of dollars..." He took a breath, but the bad taste lingered. "That's when I broke in and told her we were done."

"I'm sorry she hurt you." Sincere, she laid a hand over his chest.

"I cared just enough about her to wind up bitter, but not more." His pulse beat betrayingly. Could she feel it? Would she guess that he'd never truly loved anyone but her? No matter how hard he'd tried, his heart kept circling back to her. "That's when I decided to stop dating. I've been good with it, but Dad suffers."

"Your father wants you to be happy. Sometimes happiness and marriage go hand in hand."

"Sometimes." His hand covered hers, tenderly. "My guess is that it's killing Dad. No grandkids. Autumn scares away every eligible bachelor."

"She scares them away? She's not frightening."

"No, but there have been men stopping by and I see at first their interest. But the minute they see her rope an animal, or work a horse or once we had the new farrier drive up during shooting practice, that's it. They are no longer interested. Cheyenne's got school to finish, and Addison, you've heard her views on marriage, I'm sure."

"She's pretty vocal about it."

"That leaves Tucker. He's competing on the rodeo circuit and always on the go. We hardly see him as it is. He's not going to settle down. Dad's never going to get those grandkids he wants."

"Poor Frank." She tried to move her hand, but he held it firmly, as if he didn't want to let her go. "But you can never know what the Lord has in store for you. Things might change. Autumn might find a man who doesn't scare easily. Cheyenne will finish school. Addison could meet someone who changes her mind."

"Tucker might come home," he finished.

"And you might lose your bitterness."

"Then we had all better pray for a handful of miracles because that's the only way those things are going to happen." He hated the bitterness that had built over the years, because he had let it. He could feel it now, dark the way a storm brewed on the horizon, threatening to take over until everything was dark. Until he'd driven everything away.

Rori was like the sun shining into his world, pushing back the clouds. And as much as he needed her, he could not lean on her. He could not count on her. With her hand, so small compared to his, resting on his chest, he wondered if she could feel how much he loved her. How much he wanted to draw her into his arms again and kiss her with all the tenderness he possessed, the way he used to do long ago under the shade of these very trees.

Should he do it? Everything inside him wanted to reach out to her, ask her to stay in Wild Horse and choose him this time around. But he let go of her and reached for the rope, swinging forgotten beside them, and offered it to her.

"Ladies first," he said.

Chapter Thirteen

The Greasy Spoon rang with noise and busyness, so Rori suggested taking their after-supper milkshakes to go.

"Good idea," Autumn said as they pushed through the queue at the entrance, where folks were standing to wait for a booth—a rarity in Wild Horse. "I guess this year's Frontier Days are off to a booming start."

That was an understatement. The festival used to be a small celebration over a single weekend, culminating in a local rodeo. But now the event had grown into an impressive affair with folks coming out from Jackson to join in the fun. Colorful vendors' booths lined the main street through town, closed off to traffic. Crowds of people milled from booth to booth admiring everything from branding irons to crocheted blankets to hand-blown glass. The scent of cotton candy and roasting hot dogs filled the air as kids dashed by, calling out to their parents.

At the hitching post, Copper raised his head as if trying to catch her attention. He looked worried. Maybe all the noise was bothering him.

"I've got to check on my buddy," she told Autumn, turning her back on the temptation of the booths full of things to buy.

"It is a little loud," Autumn agreed, coming with her. "We could tie him down by the feed store. It looks quieter there."

"Just what I was thinking. I'll see if he's all right first." Rori took a sip of her milkshake. "Ever since Monday he's been dragging."

"Have we been working him too hard? You could use any of our horses to bring out meals to us."

"I know, but I think it would break his heart if I did that. Right, fella?" She laid a hand on his flank before she circled behind him.

He nickered, sounding as if he were in need of a little sympathy.

"I know how hard that is," Autumn agreed, running a hand along her mare's coat. They met at the hitching post, both separating the extra cups from their milkshakes. "I am very blessed to have the horses I do. I love everyone, but there's something special about a girl's first horse. There's something special about you, Bella."

The mare nodded, tossing her platinum forelock and mane.

"Very special," Rori agreed, laughing when Copper nibbled a kiss to her check. "I got your favorite. Strawberry."

"They aren't spoiled at all," Autumn quipped, pouring half her milkshake into the second cup. Bella was already lipping the rim, anxious for the treat.

"Not one bit," Rori agreed, holding the cup for Copper. He dipped his tongue into the icy drink, lapping it up hungrily. She leaned against the hitching post, enjoying the moment. There was so much to savor. The light shadow of dust in the air, the stunning blue sky and the milling sounds of people talking and laughing and having a good time. Above all the noises, one stood out from all the others. The faint steady gait of a certain cowboy.

"Why am I not surprised?" Justin asked, shaking his head at Copper's milkshake mustache. "I was going to call you, but when I thought about it I knew right where to find you."

"What are you doing here?" Joy rippled through her at the welcome sight of him strolling closer. "I thought you hated all this fuss and the crowds."

"I do, but I figured I might make an exception this year and check things out. Isn't that what we agreed to?" He sidled up to her at the post. The old wooden bar groaned a hint when he leaned on it. His elbow brushed her shoulder as he relaxed at her side. "Autumn, don't say one word."

"I'm doing my best to hold it back, but no guarantees," came the amused answer from the other side of Bella.

Out of the corner of her eye, Rori saw Autumn grinning wide, but she remained silent, working on the last of her milkshake.

"There's Dad." Justin inclined his head. "He got sidelined by Martha again."

Rori craned her neck to see around Copper. Sure enough, the gregarious, pleasantly plump Mrs. Wisener chattered away at Frank in front of the engraved horseshoe stand, clutching one of his shirtsleeves to keep him from getting away.

"Poor Dad," Autumn sympathized. "Should I go over and rescue him?"

"Someone better," he answered. As Autumn gave Bella a final pat, held out her hand for Copper's empty cup, and left with the *clip, clop* of her sandals, Justin crossed his arms over his chest. "She's probably trying to get him to join the town council. She's been lobbying hard and she doesn't want to take no for an answer."

"Why didn't you offer to go drag him away from her?" she wanted to know.

"Because I was afraid she would give up on Dad and decide to try angling me into the job. Can you see me as a politician?"

"No." She threw her head back and laughed merry and bright, her golden hair dancing in the wind.

"Well, you don't have to laugh so hard. It's not that funny."

"Sure it is."

"I happen to disagree."

"I hate to break it to you, but I can't see you sitting indoors and still for the length of a town meeting. I can't see you listening patiently to everyone's point of view," she quipped breezily. "You would hate it."

"True, I'm a man with flaws. But I'm improving." Oh, that interested her. He could see her light up. "If you stick around, you might see just how much."

"Maybe I've noticed." She rubbed her free hand over Copper's nose.

She noticed? That put a good feeling square in the center of his chest. For the past few days he'd been trying to put less importance on their meeting at the old swimming spot, but he couldn't do it. The evening had been stellar, a memory emblazoned upon his soul. And tonight, with the soft light of the sun casting across her like gold, she could be a princess with her country-girl charm and timeless beauty—that's what she would always be to him.

"You were right." Rori leaned closer conspiratorially, bringing with her the scent of strawberry milkshake and fabric softener. "Martha looks like she's trying to recruit Autumn for the job."

"I was smart to avoid that woman." He laughed. He hadn't expected Autumn to get roped in for the cause, but it looked as if she were extricating herself all right. She tugged Dad away, shaking her head politely. Neither of them looked as if they could escape fast enough.

"Woo-wee." Frank kept his voice low, but swept off his hat and rubbed at a few beads of sweat. "That woman knows how to put on the pressure. I was going to grab a bite a Clem's, but it's packed. Son, I was going to offer to buy you a hot dog, but it looks like you've found better company."

"Yes, but I'm not sure if I'm going to keep him," Rori quipped. The wind tossed a lock of gold across her face.

It took all his willpower not to push it out of her way. Once, touching her had been his right. Caring for her, letting her know how he felt, that was his to do. But no longer. Sorrow hit him hard, and he hoped it didn't show as he added his own teasing line. "Did you hear that, Dad? You might be stuck with me after all. If I hang with you, I'm bound to hurt your image."

"That you will, boy."

"I was just about to check out the branding iron booth." With a wink, Autumn patted Bella. "Dad, did you want to come with me?"

"Sure. You're a mite better for my reputation." Frank

winked, donning his Stetson and joining his daughter. "I look like a good father when I'm with you."

"And what about me?" Justin asked above the round of laughter.

"I'll let my reputation take a hit," Rori offered. "I don't mind being seen with the likes of you. *Too* much."

"Good to know." He might be laughing, too, but he recognized the steady message in her eyes, the quiet connection that had always existed between them.

"Then you've got me," he told her. What he didn't tell her was that she had him for tonight or forever. It was her choice.

"Where do you want to go first?"

"I want to check out the pottery booths. Gram needs a new butter dish." She gave Copper a final pat, studied him carefully as if to make sure he was all right, and then held out her hand.

Nothing felt more right than twining his fingers through hers. Nothing felt more like a blessing than having her at his side.

"Look at Justin and Rori."

At his daughter's words, Frank set down an iron, glanced down the way and spotted his son in front of a bright red awning. Hard to see much, since Justin's hat brim was down, shading his face, but he knew his boy and he knew the signs. The way he leaned toward Rori, protected her from the passersby and watched her as if she were the most precious thing on earth. It all meant one thing.

"Seems to me they're havin' a good time." He cleared his throat and hoped that his prayers for his son weren't showing.

"Are you kidding?" Autumn stepped away from the stand. "It looks like old times. Remember?"

He did. He'd been still grieving Lainie when Justin had started dating the girl. Back then Rori had been a timid thing, but she had fit right in with the family as time went by. It was happening all over again, and he was thankful to the Lord for that. Justin was almost back to himself, and Frank saw hints of the man Justin was meant to become. Rori was good for him.

"Do you think she'll stay?" Autumn asked.

"Why wouldn't she?"

"Oh, she might want a job where she can use her music degree."

"We like music. She could play our piano."

"Yeah, but that might not be the same as at an actual school." Autumn dodged the crowd, zeroing in on some stand with jewelry. "Maybe this time Justin won't blow it."

"We can hope and pray." He did every night for Justin's happiness, as he did for all his kids. He loved them. He'd do anything for them. It killed him that he couldn't pave their way to a fulfilling future. Had he failed them? He'd married the wrong woman, or so time had proved in the end, and everyone had paid the price for it.

"Maybe love will be enough." Autumn's words were more of a question than a statement. She was a good girl, strong in all the ways that counted, and she had a tender spirit. It was showing now.

Sure, he knew what she was asking. If love could be enough. Frank shrugged. It sure hadn't been in his case. "I hope so, sweetheart."

He jammed his hands in his pocket, waiting while she checked out shiny crystals and polished stones on display. Folks milled around them like a river's current around a rock, always streaming. Across the way, Justin put his hand on Rori's back as they walked along. The girl was laughing and his son looked happy.

Happy. That's all he'd ever asked of the Lord. Frank nodded, filling with an intense hope he hadn't felt in a long time. He hadn't been a hope-filled man in a long time. Right there was proof that God did work out all things for the good. A man just had to be patient.

"Oh, look, there's Cady." A plastic shopping bag crinkled as Autumn rolled it and jammed it into her pocket.

"Cady?" His heart slammed to a halt in his chest as he spotted her sauntering their way. The woman was grace personified. Her light brown hair was down, framing her face in a sleek bouncy way. She looked like a catalog page come to life.

"Autumn." A smile of pleasure changed the city woman from beautiful to stunning. She began weaving through the crowd with speed and intention.

"Oh, Dad, you have to meet her."

Before he could escape or at least think of a decent excuse to stay behind, Autumn caught him by the wrist and tugged. He stumbled forward, his pulse drumming so hard his blood pressure had to be in the red zone. He didn't want to meet the woman because he didn't want to see her reaction to him—maybe a quiet dismissal or a tactful lack of eye contact. Whatever it was, she wasn't going to feel this way for him, a country boy who spent his days with cattle and horses.

"Cady, this is my father, Frank Granger." Unaware, Autumn plunged ahead as if eager to introduce him.

Might as well make the best of it. He tipped his hat. "Nice to meet you, ma'am."

Here it comes, he thought. Brace yourself. He waited the split second it took for the woman to really look at him. He might be fit for his age from a life of hard work, but he had to be honest. He wasn't in the same league as she was used to. The sun had weathered him—not bad, but not good either. He came with a lot of baggage— five kids, five hundred thousand acres and a failed marriage. His best friends were his children, his horse and his cows. Plus, he didn't have a fancy education. There hadn't been time for college, only the hard work of running a ranch and raising his family.

He figured Cady Winslow would see all this in an instant, give him a tepid but polite greeting, and focus back on his daughter. It sure would have been less painful to have avoided her, just as he'd done on the ridge the other day. He didn't think women like her would understand that his baggage and shortcomings were what he was proud of most.

"Nice to meet you." Her smile brightened. She met his gaze and held out her hand.

She had the prettiest green eyes. They could make the world's finest emeralds look dull. The impact of her gaze hit like lightning. Her hand felt fragile in his, delicate and refined and so soft, she had to be a dream.

"Good to meet you." His voice sounded strained, and he prayed to high heaven he wasn't blushing.

"Your daughter has told me all about you." She withdrew her hand, speaking quietly and a little rushed.

Maybe he made her uncomfortable. It wouldn't be the first time. He knew he was a big man, rough-and-tumble-looking, his hands scarred and callused from a lifetime of ranching. "I hate to think what she'd told you."

"Only good things," Cady assured him, as Autumn rolled her eyes.

"I told her I have the best dad. When I was ten, he bought me a champion quarter horse. Bella cost more than our house was worth at the time." Autumn didn't pause when surprise passed over Cady's face. "I competed throughout high school. That's how I earned money for Misty's mother."

"Everyone has told me what a fine horse I'm getting. I thought she was lovely," Cady explained. "I did some research because I wanted to understand about pedigrees and her parents and the kind of rating that she has. She's amazing. I'm so excited to start riding her."

"Do you know where you want to board her?" Autumn asked.

Glad the women were engaged in conversation, he could simply drink in the sight of Cady Winslow, bask in the gentle melody of her voice and wish—just a tad— for her. Not that she could be interested in him. But she hadn't dismissed him either. That spoke well of her character.

"Hey, Dad." His middle daughter popped up at his side. "I wanted to meet Cady."

"You must be Cheyenne." The woman held out her hand pleasantly, looking pleased to meet the girl.

Now that surprised him. Maybe she was that way with everyone. That had to be it. The sinking sensation in his chest made no sense. It couldn't be disappointment. He'd only been doing a little wishful thinking and nothing more. It was a fact he couldn't get tangled up with a city girl.

"Oh, and before I forget." Cady reached into her slim, fashionable shoulder bag and pulled out a folded-up check and held it out to Autumn. "This is for you. Misty is now officially mine. I'm so thrilled."

"So am I." Autumn pocketed the check without looking at it. "You two are perfectly matched. She needs someone as gentle and quiet as she is. She's sensitive. Don't worry, I'll go over everything you need to know."

"And I'll take notes. I want to do this right." She clasped her hands with excitement. "My contractor tells me the fence will be the last to go up, so it doesn't get knocked down accidentally by the heavy equipment they are bringing in. I think the wait will about kill me."

"I'll email you a list of the best places to board," Autumn promised. "And I include free delivery, so if you don't want to go with us I totally understand. I'll trailer Misty wherever you want."

"I promise to let you know as soon as I decide. I'm juggling a lot between the remodeling and the move."

"How is that going?" he broke in.

"I hired the Wiseners' son. He came with the best references and a fair price for the work." Nerves fluttered in her stomach. The man was even more handsome close up.

"It must be hard to know who to hire when you don't know folks in the area." His deep voice rumbled with a blend of strength and kindness. "Seems like you did everything right. The Wisener boy does good work."

"I'm relieved to hear that for sure." It was such a big project. So much could go wrong.

But that wasn't the reason the flutters in her stomach went from butterfly to buffalo-size. Her years working her way up from junior associate to full partner in one of the best personal injury firms on the East Coast had taught her to handle her nerves. Yet standing before Frank Granger had her knees knocking. Good thing she was wearing jeans so it wasn't noticeable.

She couldn't ever remember wanting a man to like her before. Not like this. The deepest places within her heart ached for the sight of his smile and prayed to see a light of interest in his lapis-blue eyes. She knew full well it was foolish of her, but a tiny flare of hope filled her anyway.

"I told Autumn I was impressed by your family's ranch." Self-conscious, she slipped her hands into the front pockets of her jeans, trying to hide them. "I've never been on a working ranch before. It was interesting."

"Glad you thought so." He said it politely enough, but he said nothing more. He didn't directly meet her gaze but looked a little past her right ear.

She could have told him that when she'd petted Buttercup staked in their yard it was the first time she'd been so close to a cow, or her trip to his ranch was the first time she'd ever stepped foot inside a horse barn. She'd been entranced by the foals, how Wildflower had allowed her to stroke her baby through the fence, and how wonderful it must be to live in such a beautiful, vibrant place.

She *could* have said all those things, but she kept silent. Perhaps he wasn't interested in what she had to say. He clearly didn't seem interested in her.

"I don't want to keep you from your family time." She backed away, praying to the Lord above that she was adequately hiding her disappointment. "I'll be in touch, Autumn."

"You don't have to go. You could hang with us." She was such a nice girl, but was that sympathy in her voice?

Cady truly hoped it wasn't. She couldn't bear it if anyone had guessed her feelings. She didn't let herself hope very often, and she had been wrong to do so tonight.

"Thank you, but I have plans." She pasted on what should pass for a smile. "It was nice meeting you, Cheyenne and Frank."

"It was great meeting you," Cheyenne enthused. "You and I will have to get together. I want to go over some basic veterinary care, just things you should know and stuff to watch out for. Since this is your first horse and all."

"That's nice. I would appreciate that very much." She swallowed hard when Frank tipped his hat to her. That was all—no word of goodbye, nothing—before he led his daughters away. She forced her feet to carry her forward to the next vendor and stood unseeing at the booth's contents, trying to calm the ache in her soul.

That's what a woman her age deserved, she feared, for wishing as if she were young again, wanting a young girl's dreams. Love had passed her by in life, she had to accept it. She set her chin and the electric branding irons in front of her came into focus. She'd learned the hard way you could not live your life looking backward. The past was gone. Only the present mattered.

She thought of her morning's devotional verse. *This is the day the Lord has made; we will rejoice and be glad in it.* Those comforting words strengthened her as Tim Wisener Junior's wife called out to her, rushing over to say a friendly hello.

Chapter Fourteen

"**W**hat was that?" Autumn demanded, her voice pitched low so that it wouldn't carry, but Justin heard it. She was coming closer through the crowd, looking upset. She skidded to a stop at a stand showcasing hand-woven horse blankets. "Dad, you were rude to Cady."

"Yeah, Dad. Totally rude," Cheyenne agreed.

"No, I just didn't have much to say." Frank's color was high, as if he was mad or upset. A muscle ticked along his clenched jawline.

What was going on? Justin pulled his wallet out of his back pocket and tossed two twenties onto the table.

"Justin, what do you think you're doing?" Rori shook her head, scattering locks of honey and gold. "I can't let you pay for this."

"Just try to stop me." He took the aqua-blue blanket the sales lady had folded and bagged.

"You're spoiling me." She might be protesting, but her eyes said she appreciated it. When Rori was like this, her worries forgotten, her guards down, she took his breath away.

"A little spoiling won't hurt you." He kept his tone

low, hoping his family couldn't hear, but he knew that was a pointless hope. Both of his sisters were grinning ear to ear and even Dad looked a little less upset at seeing them together.

"I saw you talking to Cady." Rori turned to Autumn. "Was that a check she gave you? Is the big sale official?"

"Yes. No buyer's remorse with her. I like that about her." Autumn patted her pocket where the check resided safely. "Plus, it was a personal check for forty thousand dollars. She didn't even haggle."

"That's class," Rori agreed. "She really must want Misty."

"I think it was love at first sight," Autumn answered, her voice low, shoving past him to talk with Rori. "I didn't want to take advantage of Cady, so I had to make sure she wasn't just carried away by the idea of owning a horse. It happens to a lot of people."

Dad's face was redder than ever, and he took a sudden intense interest in a pink horse blanket. What were the chances he didn't even see what was directly in front of him? And why did the girls talking about Cady Winslow seem to upset him? Justin glanced over his shoulder, searching the crowds for the woman. There she was, chatting with Tim Junior and his wife. She was elegant and friendly and if Autumn would sell one of her favorite mares to her, she had to be a good person. Autumn checked references extensively. Could his dad like the lady?

No. Impossible. Dad hadn't shown any interest in dating since they'd buried Mom. Justin accepted change from the vendor and pocketed it. What was bothering his dad? Maybe the missing cattle was troubling him more than he'd let on.

Dad jerked away from the blanket, realizing the color at last, and hurried to catch up with them.

"Is Frank all right?" Rori leaned in, concern layered in her hushed tone. "He seems distracted."

"Must have a lot on his mind." And maybe it was Cady Winslow, after all. He caught his dad looking at the far end of the street, past the crowd, to where the two women were chatting. Cady Winslow lifted her hand in a wave and left the Wiseners behind, heading down the street into the setting sun. The long low rays of light seemed to swallow her and, judging by the look on his father's face, Frank Granger had never seen a more beautiful sight.

Now that was interesting.

"You rode Scout?" Rori had only seemed to notice the bay gelding at the far end of the hitching post. A good two dozen animals stood drowsing in the shade all waiting for their owners.

"I always ride him in the evenings. Dad drove, but I didn't ride with him because I'd promised Scout a trip to town." What he didn't say was that he'd hoped to ride along with her home. The lowering sun, the warm evening, the privilege of her company sounded like a mighty fine way to pass the time. Just so she wouldn't guess how much it meant to him, he kept his tone offhand. "Scout and I might as well keep you company, since we're all heading the same way. If you wouldn't mind hanging with us."

"I suppose Copper and I could tolerate it." She sparkled up at him, brilliant and precious. Every moment spent in her company made him want to believe in happily-ever-afters and second chances. But did she feel the same way? She didn't appear to be. Unaffected, she sauntered beside him, her stride relaxed and easy, her hand brushing his to take the shopping bags he was carrying for her. "It would be nice to ride home with you."

The link between his heart and hers strengthened until he could feel what she did not say. The evening had been like a gift, one he'd never figured on having again. Maybe she didn't either.

This isn't a second chance, he reminded himself. He couldn't assume that it was. He laid a hand on Copper's flank, letting the animal know who was standing behind him, and held open the leather flap on Rori's saddlebag. She carefully packed her purchases inside, and he took the time to adore her. The slope of her perfect nose, the smiling shape of her lips, the tiny cleft in her chin that was impossible to see unless he was kissing close. He knew her so well, he'd dreamed of her face every night when he knelt down to pray. Could things change? Could they make this their second chance?

Please fall in love with me, he pleaded. Not that she would. Not that he could trust her again if she did. But he wanted nothing more than a future with her, one he could not let himself see. He caressed a stray curl from her forehead, just so he could be closer to her.

Goodbyes rang out. He hardly noticed. Rori was the center of his world. She was all he could see, all he knew. Vaguely he was aware of Dad heading off toward the truck he'd parked on a side street, saying he'd best get home and check on Addison, since she'd offered to stay and keep an eye on the last mare about ready to foal.

Cheyenne and Autumn mounted up and trotted away. The clatter of steeled hooves on blacktop faded. His pulse pounded and pattered, because he was alone with

Rori. The thinning crowd, the vendors beginning to close up for the night, the other horses drowsing nearby hardly existed for him as he untied Copper's reins from the post.

Rori hopped up and settled into her saddle, no longer just the girl he remembered, but so much more. A woman of substance and beauty, gentleness and grace, laughing as she chatted to Copper, who reached around to lip her ankle affectionately, glad to see her. With her ball cap shading her face, her hair dancing in the wind, she made him believe. She chased away the bitterness within him and he saw promises of long-lost dreams. If he could spend his days at her side, simply serving her, then he could ask for nothing more.

"Hurry up. Copper and I are ready to roll." She'd come alive, no longer sad and lost, more confident than he'd ever seen her. Gently, she reined Copper around, the old horse chipper, too. He arched his neck, showing off for his mistress, and the pair launched forward, not bothering to wait.

"You had better hurry up, Justin," she called over her shoulder. "Catch us if you can."

He loved her just like this, the Rori he'd never seen before. Strong and sure, she rode off like the wind, impossible to fence in, golden hair flying behind her. Away she went, his heart.

Scout stomped his hooves, anxious to step up to the challenge. Not one to be left behind either, Justin loosened the knotted reins, swung into the saddle and gave the gelding his head. With a flick of his tail, Scout was off, plunging down the street, ears back, churning into a smooth, swift gallop. Town rolled away behind him, and he moved Scout onto the dirt shouldering the road and crouched low, urging Scout faster.

Up ahead, Rori glanced over her shoulder, spotted them and drew her gelding to a walk. She twisted around in the saddle. "Copper and I decided to give you a break. If we didn't stop, you would never be able to catch up with us."

"We were making good progress," he quipped. "Seems to me you stopped before we could show you two up."

"Let's call it a draw."

"Deal." As he caught up to her, Scout and Copper touched noses, old friends exchanging sentiments. "Thanks for coming along with me tonight."

"It was my pleasure. It's been a long time since I've enjoyed a small-town street fair. Especially in the presence of such a handsome guy."

"Why, thank you." He winked.

"I wasn't talking about you." She couldn't help ribbing him. She felt light and joyful, as if everything had changed. "It's surprising how everything has changed, though tonight was like it used to be. But better."

"True. The branding iron booth and the hand-braided harness booths make a real nice addition to the festival." A curve tugged at the corner of his mouth, a sure sign that he knew what she was too shy to speak of.

Was he going to make her say it?

"I wasn't talking about the street vendors." Surely he knew that. Her face heated, the skin tightening as she blushed. She looked away so he wouldn't see it.

"I know." His assurance rumbled comfortingly and he sidled Scout closer. His much larger hand covered hers where it rested on the pommel, and she closed her eyes. Caring ribboned through her, and she twined her fingers between his.

Just like they used to do, they rode toward home through the heavenly path of low slanting light, side by side and hand in hand.

Her grandparents' house rose into sight when Copper turned into the graveled driveway. Their ride was almost at an end. She pushed aside a knot of disappointment because she wanted the moment to last forever. Did he feel this, too? she wondered. How on earth had she ever been able to hold back her love for him? It whispered through her like the quietest of hymns, somber and reverent and life-affirming. Everything she'd accomplished, every decision she'd made, every day she'd lived had been in an effort to forget him, and it had failed. Through the years, her affection had remained, changed and now renewed. Justin had grown into the man she'd always known he would be, and she loved him more.

Please, she prayed. *Lord, don't let this moment end.*

As if Justin felt the same way, his hand remained clasped in hers, swinging slightly between them as he slowed his horse to an even slower walk. She did the same. Seconds ticked by, but they could delay having to part ways for the night.

"I don't suppose you have plans for Saturday?" His question stirred seeds of hope.

"The rodeo is on Saturday."

"Yes, it is." Dimples cut deep as his grin widened, whole and carefree. "Would you like to go with me?"

"I'd love to." She felt breathless, like a schoolgirl

again, dizzy because handsome Justin Granger was asking her out. "But can you leave the ranch unattended?"

"Scotty will keep an eye on things. I figure Dad won't be away for long." His hand tightened around hers, just enough that it felt as if he didn't want to let go.

Please want me the way I want you, she wished. She wasn't prepared to feel this way. She didn't know if she wanted to trust any man, even Justin again, but her feelings for him were impossible to deny.

"There's still no word on the missing cattle." He changed the subject smoothly.

"It's got to be hard worrying about their welfare," she answered. "Buttercup keeps bawling for her friends. She nearly drove me nuts when I was baking this afternoon. I kept having to come outside and bribe her with molasses treats."

"Which only makes her bawl more often," he pointed out, chuckling.

"Right, well, then I'm really hoping the sheriff finds the cows. That's the best solution."

"Todd isn't too motivated to find three heifers. He didn't bother much with the evidence they left behind."

"Gramps says he put in a complaint to the town council."

"He's not the only one. A lot of ranchers aren't happy with this guy. The Greens on the other side of Mustang Lane were hit by rustlers about nine months ago. Professionals, who brought in helicopters and semis, the whole nine yards. Wiped them out." It was easier to talk about the county's problems with the sheriff instead of asking Rori the one question he'd been holding back.

Was she going to stay? He didn't want to admit it, but he suspected he knew the answer. They'd reached the fork in the driveway, where a well-traveled path was worn into the grass from the road to the small barn. Time to let go of her hand. He hated the sensation of her fingers slipping way from his and the empty feeling inside as he turned away from her. He reined in Scout and dismounted. They'd reached the end of the line.

"I had fun tonight." The best evening he'd had in over a decade because he'd spent it with her. He waited while she swung down, her movements graceful and poised. He could spend a lifetime watching her and he would never tire of seeing her adjusting her ball cap and sparkling with quiet happiness.

She was healing, which was what she'd come home to do. Don't open up to her, he thought but his warning had come too late. The strength of his affection for her was like a flash flood striking without warning, crashing down the protective walls he'd built and laying bare his heart.

"I had the best time." Wide-eyed and vulnerable, she laid her hand in the center of his chest. "It's so good to be home and with you."

If only her bottom lip hadn't vibrated as if with uncertainty, as if she were hoping to be kissed. Then maybe he wouldn't have dipped his head and claimed her. A smart man would proceed with caution, but he wasn't thinking. Emotions drove him to fit their lips together in the softest, most reverent kiss.

She held on tight to him, the sweetest woman on earth, and for that one moment in time she was his. Nothing could come between them—not the past or the unknown future. He felt so close to her as he cradled her cheek with his hand, clinging to her, refusing to break their kiss.

Could she feel how much he loved her? How he'd finally learned what true love was? Could she know just from his kiss that his heart had left with her years ago and now she'd brought it back to him? He was whole because of her. If he ended this kiss, the moment would end. The past would matter and the future she was planning without him. It took all his courage to withdraw from her tender kiss.

Please love me, too, he prayed. But the moment was gone and rational thought returned like an icy wind on the summer's evening. The bright sun could not warm him when he gazed into the violet-blue of her eyes. Had he gone too far? He didn't know, and she didn't say anything. She gazed up at him, maybe it was tender, or maybe she had simply been carried away with the moment.

He didn't like being vulnerable. Wanting her was like flinging open the door to his soul and he stood undefended, wanting what she had never been able to give him.

"Maybe that shouldn't have happened." The words were out before he'd thought them through, words hovering in the air between them.

"Oh." She looked down for an instant, the long shadows hiding her expression.

For one tiny hopeful second he imagined she might be trying to hide her disappointment. That she was attempting to find the words to tell him how important their kiss had been. He wanted her to choose the best course not for his sake but for hers. It was up to her to decide if she wanted him or not. He was not going to make the same mistake this time. As hard as it was, he steeled his spine.

Please choose me, he wished and searched her lovely face for the smallest sign she might want him. He found none.

"If that's the way you feel." She tossed him a carefully controlled smile. "We can always attribute that kiss to the power of the past."

Not to the pull of the future, he realized. Disappointment floored him. He didn't hang his head, and he prayed the agony punching through him didn't show. Drowning in it, he did his best to give her a come-what-may nod and tipped his hat to her.

"Guess so," he said, managing to sound as if he wasn't choking, as if the wind and his unspoken dreams hadn't been knocked out of him. "Guess we got carried away."

"Yes." Polished by the glow from the sunset, she seemed luminous. Or perhaps, he realized, he'd never seen as deep inside her before. It was as if they stood together, hearts open and souls revealed. She did not reach out for him.

He was afraid of reaching for her. If he enfolded her in his arms and kissed her again, would she push him away? If he offered her his love, would she refuse him? She'd done it before and he'd survived it, but he carried the scars with him still. Every day without her had been empty, and if he dared to say the words, to give voice to what he wanted most, a life honoring her, it would crush him if she said no.

Surely, she would say no. He had nothing to offer but life on a working ranch, which meant day after day of hard work and commitment to the animals in his care. In his experience, most women didn't choose that kind of life. He wanted her to be happy. He wanted her to follow her bliss. And if that was in Dallas, then he may as well get it over with now before another day went by and he found himself more in love with her.

"Maybe it would be best if we didn't ride together again." He said the words with regret and because they needed to be said. "Since old times keep getting confused with the new."

"Right." She swallowed hard, holding herself very still. Copper nudged her affectionately, nickering low. "That tricky nostalgia keeps getting in the way. That can't be good."

"That's my thinking, too." He sounded distant, as if he were talking of the weather or of the latest crop report. "It isn't smart for us to confuse what is with what was. That's how people get hurt."

"Sure. Neither of us want that." She blindly felt for Copper's reins, although the gelding was leaning against her and he would follow her without reins if she asked. She needed something to hold on to, something to do with her hands that felt normal and familiar. The earth seemed to be crumbling at her feet, and she had to hold it together long enough to get safely inside the barn. "I have to get Copper cared for. Thanks for the walk down memory lane tonight. I hope you have a good evening."

"Wait. Are you all right?" He held himself like a mountain, tall and unyielding, larger than life, but his question made her pause. He swept off his Stetson, revealing the rugged planes of his face and a poignant question. Unspoken, he waited for her reply.

No, I'm not in love with you, she wished she were able to tell him. But it wouldn't be the truth. She longed for the shelter of his arms and the light of his love. But she feared he did not feel the same. "I'm fine."

"Oh. Well, good." The question vanished and he looked uncertain for a moment.

Had he wanted a different answer? If she had gathered up her courage to risk her heart, would it have changed things? Or would he still be turning away from her?

Please love me, she wished. If she could have one prayer answered and only one, that's what she would ask for. But true love took two, it was not a one-way street, and so she watched as Justin donned his hat, swung into his saddle and reined Scout away from her.

"Good night." He tipped the brim of his hat, a Western man to the core, looking like everything a woman could ever dream of. He was strength and integrity and what a man ought to be.

"Good night," she managed to say without a single hitch to betray the sorrow building within. She was thankful he wasted no time in disappearing from her sight, galloping down the drive until the shadows stole him. Only then, when he was far enough away not to hear, did she let her heart bleed.

Chapter Fifteen

The fire of sunset lingered long after the sun went down. Atop the ridge overlooking home and stables, Justin spun Lightning in a slow circle, surveying the rise and fall of Granger land stretching beyond sight. After leaving Rori behind, he'd stopped long enough at the house to grab a thermos of coffee. He had to caffeine up for first watch, then he'd rubbed Scout down and settled him in his box stall with a good meal. He'd left the old gelding, then assured a tired-looking Max that he'd worked hard enough on the day shift and chosen one of the quarter horses Dad and Autumn had trained.

The radio strapped to his saddle squawked. Cell coverage in the north hills was patchy, so that meant it was Scotty calling in. Sure enough, the familiar voice crackled to life. "All's quiet here. Do you want me to send Louis to you?"

"No." Justin palmed the handheld. He couldn't keep his mind on his work. "Go ahead and send him home for the rest of the night."

"Roger." The radio squawked out.

In silence again, Justin stowed the radio and searched

the dark stretch of land for Cheyenne. He lifted his
binoculars for a better look. He'd spotted her horse.
She was riding Dreamer tonight and his saddle was
empty. It wasn't hard to figure out where she'd gone.
He scoped the nearby herd and found her rubbing the
bull's poll. The big animal had his forehead down so
she could reach it and his eyes closed, looking as if he'd
found heaven.

No doubt about it. Cheyenne had Dad's gift with
cows. It was their joke that the Grangers were a family of cow whisperers. The Hereford pressed his huge
face against Cheyenne's middle, nearly obscuring her
from sight. Appearing content, she wrapped her arms
around his enormous neck.

If there were any danger around, the bull wouldn't
be calm. Justin dropped his binocs and pressed Lightning into a quick walk, heading the length of the ridge.
There was another herd to check on before he felt right
about taking a coffee break. But as hard as he tried,
work didn't keep his thoughts from Rori. They followed
him like shadows in the night.

I was right, he told himself as he sat back in the saddle, balancing his weight as Lightning began to pick her
way down the steep side of the ridge. He'd been smart
to end things. He couldn't go through that again. The
bleak grief when he'd lost her had smashed his entire
world. He'd never been whole again, his life never right.
Something had always been missing and now he knew.
She was more than his heart. She always had been and
would always be. His devotion to her was absolute.

But she wanted different things. And just as she'd
said, when the differences between two people were so
great they couldn't be compromised on, heartache was

the end result. He remembered his mom and her misery. She'd resented Dad's long hours in the fields and barns. She'd grown bitter at the animals always needing care and attention. She'd felt trapped on the ranch because vacations were nearly nonexistent. The closest mall was a two-hour drive one way. There was no luxurious day spa nearby, just the Glam-A-Rama beauty parlor next to the feed store.

Rori was a country girl, sure, but she'd thrived in a city. She had taught music at a private arts school. There was nothing like that around here. She'd admitted wanting to live in the country maybe on a few acres outside Dallas, but that wasn't the same as living on a remote working ranch. The few options in Wild Horse and on this ranch would limit her. Would she be happy with that?

This evening, she'd been amazing, dazzling him every moment they'd been together. The images of being with her today drove away his doubts and he savored them—the play of the wind in her hair, the notes of her laughter, the harmony of walking at her side. They'd discussed this and that—items in a booth, the funny antics of a kid nearby in the crowd, just small stuff as they bantered back and forth. Happiness filled him as he remembered how she'd captivated him. Her presence was like the first ray of light at the day's beginning and the last gleam at day's end. He was in the dark without her.

He lifted his face to the heavens where stars were blinking to life, one by one, precious light in a universe of darkness. The Lord was out there somewhere in the vast night, a caring God to guide him. But where was he going? He wanted to keep his heart closed, his vulnerable self protected because all signs led to Rori leaving in a few months. Leaving. He did his best not to feel the pain. He adjusted his balance as Lightning skidded the last few steep steps to the grassy floor below, and the meadow lay out ahead of them.

Lord, I don't think You are guiding me to her and it's tearing me apart. He searched the stars, prayer lifting through him. *Dad needs me here. I'm sure this ranch is where You mean me to be. Wherever You are leading Rori, please let it be to somewhere good.*

Dressed for work, Rori tucked her iPod into her pocket and closed her bedroom door behind her. She fumbled her way down the creaking stairs in the dark, drawn by the faint ray of light at the bottom of the stairwell. Kitchen sounds grew louder as she skirted the old upright piano in the living room. Her fingers itched to sit down and play as she'd done last night until bedtime, but two hours of music hadn't chased away her devastation. There was nothing to be done but to hide her heartbreak and face the day.

"Good morning, Pumpkin." Gram turned from the stove, spatula in hand. "Did you get enough sleep?"

"Enough to get by on." She made a beeline straight to the coffeepot, filled a cup and took a sip. In a few seconds the caffeine would kick in; until then she only had to try to seem awake. She saw no need to mention she'd had a hard time settling down last night. Her brain kept going over what Justin had said and what he hadn't.

"It was a pleasure to listen to you play last night." Gram gave the sausages a turn. "You know how I love Beethoven, but I worried about you. You didn't get any wind-down time. I worried you wouldn't be able to get right to sleep. And look at you this morning, all groggy."

"I'll be fine." Hot coffee burned down her throat. "I just wanted to get in some practice. I've been falling down on the job lately."

"I'll say. You haven't touched the piano since you've been here." Gram scooped an omelet from the fry pan, wrapped it around a sausage and packaged it neatly in a paper towel. "Here's your breakfast to go. I ran into Ellen Gibbs at Frontier Days yesterday and do you know what she asked me?"

"I have no idea." Rori kissed her grandmother's cheek and took the breakfast wrap in hand.

"She wanted to know if you would consider giving her granddaughters piano lessons. You know Mrs. Simpson retired last year, and there's no one around to take her students."

Rori recognized the sweet meddlesome look on Gram's face. She hesitated at the door, one hand on the knob. "Are you asking me to stay and teach piano?"

"I'm not the one asking. I'm mentioning it, is all. I told Ellen you already had a job in that fancy music school in Dallas, but she didn't want to listen." Gram grabbed a paper-towel-lined plate and plucked sausage after sausage from the pan. "You have a good day at the Grangers', dear. I suspect you'll see Justin?"

"It would be hard to miss seeing him." Oh, she knew good and well what Gram was getting at. And pointing out the alternative life she could have here instead of returning to Dallas come September wasn't going to change her mind. It wasn't Dallas she was fond of, but she loved teaching and she liked having the assurance of her teaching job waiting for her now that her divorce was all but final.

And it wasn't as if she had a reason to stay. Not if Justin was going to kiss her and then call it a mistake.

Wrestling down heartbreak, she crossed the porch, tripped down the steps and followed the path to the barn. Copper's head came up from grazing, his ears swiveled forward and he nickered a cheerful greeting.

"Hi, handsome!" she called and he came running up to the fence. He lipped her forehead in affection and then tried to steal her omelet. Good thing she was too quick for him. Laughing, she climbed between the fence boards.

You don't get mornings like this in the city. She breathed in the fresh air rising from the growing grass, scented by the apples in the trees nearby. Life here was good. She'd missed the wide-open feeling, of having Copper walking at her side, of never hurrying, and she loved the commute. She grabbed Copper's bridle.

Fine, she could be honest with herself. She'd missed this way of life. It was part of who she was and would always be. And if an inner voice whispered that she would be happy here, that she had a good paying job cooking for the Grangers, then she tried to deny it.

No, it would never work, she thought. Justin would be there and *then* how could she try to drive away the memory of his kiss?

"Hey, Pumpkin." Gramps ambled into sight toting a small pail. "I was just on my way to feed the hens. You look a sight this morning. Didn't you get much sleep?"

"I'm fine, Gramps." Really. It wasn't as if he could mend what was broken. This wasn't a skate or a saddle needing repair, but her heart. "I've just got a lot on my mind."

"Sure. Sending those divorce papers off yesterday had to be wearing on ya." He hesitated, as if he had something he wanted to say but wasn't sure if he should. He tipped back his hat like a cowboy of old, one of the good guys. "Bein' out with that Granger boy had to make things a bit better for you, I suspect."

"Oh, nothing is easy when it comes to Justin Granger."

"That's spoken like a gal in love. I can tell. I've known you since you were yay big." He held up his hands, two feet apart, the small bucket swinging. "I don't suppose it's your feelings that are the problem, but his?"

"I lost my chance with him long ago." She set down her cup, laid her breakfast wrap on top of it, and gently eased the bit into Copper's mouth.

"What are you talkin' about?" Gramps shook his head as if in disbelief, scattering fine gray hairs. He gave his overalls a hitch. "That boy's never fallen out of love with you. Everyone in these parts knows it. Why can't you see it?"

"Because that's just wishful thinking on your part, and I won't be tempted into believing you're right." She tossed him a smile as Copper tried stealing her breakfast again. "Besides, I'm going back to Dallas in two months."

"Is that what you want?"

"Sure. Why wouldn't it be?" She would have earned enough money working for the Grangers to buy a used car and to put down a deposit and first month's rent on an apartment. She would be back on her feet and back to her life.

Except it had began to feel as if her life was right here.

Gramps tilted his head, listening. "That's your grandmother calling me. Guess I'd better go see what bee she's got in her bonnet."

She smoothed a saddle blanket across Copper's withers, carefully making sure there wasn't a single wrinkle before she shouldered the saddle in place. As she worked, her grandparents' conversation drifted faintly through the open barn doors.

"Hey! Who's that good-looking woman standing on my back porch?" Gramps whistled.

"The woman who has your breakfast ready and waiting, you sweet talker."

"I'm glad you think so. Want me to whisper sweet nothings in your ear?"

"You've been dragging your feet this morning and now I'm waiting on you. What I want is for you to put down that pail. You can feed the chickens later. Get in here before the eggs get cold. And, no, a kiss isn't going to charm me."

"Then how about two?"

Copper stomped his foot, eager to be off, as she tightened the cinch and lowered the stirrups. Rori led him out of the barn just in time to see Gramps taking Gram's hand. He lit up with adoration as he helped his beloved up the porch steps, his devotion to her strong and flawless.

They made love look so easy. She watched with a touch of wistfulness as the couple bowed their heads together in soft conversation. Whatever Gramps said made Gram brighten like dawn. Happiness wreathed her lovely face as she passed through the screen door he held open for her and they both disappeared from sight.

Could love like that ever be possible for her? She swung into the saddle, juggling her coffee and breakfast, and reined Copper toward Granger land. Justin was the only man she wanted to love with all her might for the rest of her life. No other man, not even the one she'd loved enough to marry, had even come close.

She felt infinitely alone as she rode into the peaceful fields accompanied by lark song, alone and with some decisions to make.

Justin stumbled down the stairs, fighting grogginess and a headache from lack of sleep. This afternoon he was interviewing a half dozen applicants, but until he hired a few extra hands he would be pulling double shifts. Although their herd was insured and losing them would be a hard blow to the ranch, he was more concerned about the animals. Men ruthless enough to steal weren't usually the sort who put the care and needs of cows ahead of their own. That was the reason for the tension headache, but not his sleeplessness.

After he'd checked on the expecting mare, given Dad and Autumn a report and stumbled to bed, he hadn't been able to turn off his brain. He'd kept thinking of Rori, going over and over their kiss. It had felt right, as if it were meant to be. The way she held on to him, the way she kissed him back with all the innocence she possessed.

But it hadn't been right. Going over and over the moment stirred up regrets and wishes that tore at him. He should have known better than to have let down his guard. What were the chances she would leave? That she wouldn't choose him? He should have kept his distance, never relented on his decision to keep far away from her.

He pounded into the kitchen and the scent of brewing coffee was a clue. Too late to put on the brakes and find another way out of the house. Rori and Autumn looked up, caught in the middle of a conversation. He tore his gaze away but not before he noticed Rori's paleness and the dark circles beneath her eyes. Hadn't she slept much, either?

"I was telling Rori about Paullina," Autumn explained as she popped the last bite of a muffin into her mouth. "It could be any minute now, so she needs to be watched."

"I can do it," he clipped out, fully aware the woman in question had turned her back and was breaking eggs into a fry pan at the stove.

Pain rolled through him. He didn't know what he expected. He'd been the one to tell her he didn't mean that kiss—a lie if there ever was one. He was not a lying man, and he hadn't thought of it as one at the time. But a lie it was because he'd meant that kiss, he was no longer sorry about it. If he thought it would change the courses of their future, then he would haul her into his arms and kiss her as much as it took for her to stay.

But he wouldn't because he wanted what was best for her. He wanted her to be happy. She'd chosen a life away from him and small-town life once. No, he had to be practical. Why would she want anything different this time around?

"Good," he ground out to Autumn's explanation and pounded straight to the mudroom, bypassing the pot of coffee. His head pounded worse at the thought of a morning without it, but he didn't want to get any closer to Rori than he had to. It hurt too much.

He jammed his right foot into his left boot. Great. He sat on the bench, yanked it off and grabbed the right boot. A movement in the doorway had to be her. He'd know her willowy grace anywhere. He kept his gaze on his laces as he tied a quick knot.

"I thought you might need this." The soft melody of her voice rippled through him, beauty he did not want to feel. There was a scrape as she set the travel mug on the bench beside him and the air crackled from her nearness. He breathed in the scent of roses and lost dreams as she moved away.

Don't look at her, he thought. Maybe that would keep him from hurting. He willed steel into his chest.

"Thanks," he grumbled. Knowing full well she'd paused in the archway between the rooms and stood waiting for a better response from him, he grabbed the left boot, jammed his foot into it and fumbled with the laces. He hated that show of weakness, the proof of how much she meant to him. He grabbed the cup, hopped to his feet and pounded out the door.

"Justin?"

One word from her stopped him. He froze in the threshold. Don't turn around, he ordered even as everything within him wanted to face her and to savor every moment with her for as long as he could.

She isn't going to stay, cowboy, he told himself and kept going. "I'll be out in the fields, but close enough for you to call if any trouble comes up."

"I, uh—" She'd obviously wanted to say something

else, but changed her mind. "Okay. I'll keep a breakfast plate in the oven in case you need it."

"I won't," he said flatly, marching across the back porch. He'd eat the months-old energy bars in his saddlebag before he'd let hunger drive him into the kitchen alone with her. He was trying to be smart, in control, to follow the path God had laid before him.

But it didn't make him happy as he felt her pain. Regardless of how much distance grew between them that hurt remained, an unbearable connection he could not break.

Buttercup bleated, front feet braced, putting all her might into her plaintive moo. Her chocolate eyes implored him to come keep her company and to let her check out his shiny metallic cup.

"Sorry, sweetheart," he told her, striding on by, fighting with himself to keep from turning around to catch a glimpse of Rori one more time. He had to keep on going. It was the only smart choice.

Stop thinking about him, she told herself as she wiped down the counter and hit the start button that set the dishwasher to gurgling and whooshing. The big, pleasant kitchen echoed around her. Everyone had rotated in on shifts to eat and had gone back to their work, except for Justin and a few of the hired men who left for home and a bit of sleep.

It was grocery day. She'd penned a long list. Running around-the-clock shifts, Frank had asked her to make hearty meals to keep everyone alert and full of energy. She planned on making granola and homemade trail mix, perfect for snacks that packed well in saddlebags, and was debating on whether to make brownies or chocolate-chip cookies when the screen door made a strange sound.

Curious, she put down her pen and peered around the edge of the island. Buttercup stood on the porch, her rope tangled on the boards. The cow, caught in the act of mouthing the door handle, stopped and flashed her innocent eyes. A puppy couldn't have looked sweeter.

"What do you think you're doing?" She abandoned her list and crossed the room. "You've pulled up your picket stake. Don't tell me you're trying to open the door."

As if to say, "Okay, I won't," Buttercup fluttered her long curly lashes and tried not to look guilty.

"You're awful pleased with yourself." She turned the handle, as Buttercup grinned with delight and watched the door open a few inches with wonder. "You're not coming in, pretty girl. Excuse me, out of the way. Let's get you—"

Buttercup interrupted with a loud moo, glanced over her shoulder toward the horse pasture and mooed again. Rori noticed that Paullina, the mare she'd been checking on throughout the morning, wasn't in sight.

"Funny, she was there a few minutes ago. Back up, Buttercup." Since the cow had a mind of her own, Rori managed to wedge her arm through the crack between the screen door and the jamb and push on the cow's sturdy shoulder. Grudgingly, the animal stepped back enough to allow Rori to slip through. She grabbed Buttercup's halter. She didn't like the twist of worry in her stomach. Something felt wrong. "C'mon, girl. Let's go check on Paullina."

As if in agreement, Buttercup mooed, awkwardly turned around in the relatively small space and clomped down the steps as if she were no stranger to them. Rori didn't even want to know how many times previously Buttercup had tried to let herself into the house.

She led the cow across the front lawn, no sense wasting time fussing with the stake, and tried to calm the quivery feeling shaking her knees. Where was the mare? All she saw was lush green grass and the otherwise empty field.

"You were a good girl to come get me," she told Buttercup, tying her quickly to one of the fence posts. Buttercup nodded as if she were already aware of that fact and watched as Rori climbed through the fence boards.

"Paullina?" she called gently. "Are you all right?"

Insects buzzed lazily around her in the midmorning air and a killdeer squeaked, startled, as Rori crunched through the soft, crackly grass. The bird cried out and tucked her wing at a strange angle. Feigning a broken wing, she ran away from a hidden nest. Rori ignored her and kept going.

"Paullina?" she called, her voice echoing back to her. "Where's the good, pretty girl?"

No answer. She found the mare down in a hollow of grass, lather flecking her beautiful white coat and groaning in pain. Rori dug her phone from her pocket and dialed Justin's number without thought, her heart reaching out to him. She knew it always would.

Chapter Sixteen

The wide-open spaces felt good, just what he'd been needing to chase away the lingering effects of Rori's presence. Sorrow had lodged deep in his chest, whether it was hers or his he could no longer tell.

Justin reined Max to a halt along the fence line and dismounted to check on the newly branded calves. He knew Cheyenne and Addison would be along later to check the little ones for any signs of infection or discomfort, but he needed to walk a bit to clear his head. Somehow he had to find a solution to Rori and how much he wanted to love her.

"Hey, Clancy," he crooned to the bull. At the sound of his name the big Hereford ambled over, head up and proud to be in charge of his herd. "Everything all right?"

The bull lowed, a comforting sound deep in his throat, and offered his poll for rubbing. Justin obliged, and the satisfaction of being where he belonged rolled through him.

Could he leave this place? he wondered. His dad wanted to retire in a few more years, and the ranch had grown by thousands of acres over the time he'd helped to manage it. So had the number of cow/calf pairs ranging it. The ranch had grown to be too much for one person to run alone, if he left Autumn to do the job.

Family had always come first, but which family did he choose—the one he'd grown up with or the one he wanted to find? He tried to consider his life elsewhere. Not that he was going anywhere, but it didn't hurt to wonder what if. Selling out his share of the herd would make him very comfortable. He could go where he wanted and do what he wanted.

He could be with Rori.

Lord, surely this isn't You putting doubts in my head. Justin felt a tug on his jeans leg. He looked down to find two cows grabbing a hold of him, teeth locked on the denim hem.

"Did you ladies want some attention, too?" Apparently they did because they tugged harder. He didn't have time to lift his free hand to oblige them with a pat and a stroke. Other cows came up from behind him, affectionately lipping his shirt, licking his boots, stealing his hat.

Okay, maybe that was answer enough. He was happy here, and considering leaving a life he loved on the hope that Rori's feelings for him had changed was a fool's course. As much as he wanted her, the memory of being twenty-one and proposing to the love of his life returned, the one obstacle he could not defeat. When she'd whispered no, she could not, it had been the end of his world. A man couldn't take that kind of a blow a second time no matter how much he wanted to.

Or could he? Was it worth the risk?

An electronic chime sounded from his jeans. One of the cows, curious about the noise, attacked his pocket.

He snatched back his hat, thumbed out his phone and frowned at the screen. Rori. His thumb hit the answer button before he could think about it. "What's wrong?"

"It's Paullina." Panic snapped in her voice, an urgency he'd never heard before. "She's down. I've checked her and I think everything is all right, but please come. I don't want to do this by myself."

"You won't be alone as long as I'm near." Every fiber of his being responded. Instant tension telegraphed through him as he extricated the hem of his T-shirt from one cow and his untied bootlace from another. He raced straight for Max. "Keep her calm. This isn't her first foal, so she knows what's going on."

"Should I call the vet?"

"I've got Nate on speed dial." He swung into the saddle and wheeled Max toward home. As if the gelding understood, he broke into a hard gallop. The ground flew by in a blur. "Hang tight and I'll give him a call."

"Thanks, Justin." She sighed, a rush of relief that told him she'd been worried he might have refused to help.

Didn't she know he wasn't made that way? She ought to know him better than that. He wondered exactly what circumstances had changed her back in Dallas. Lord help him, but he had to fight to keep the sympathy from his voice. "No worries. I'm four minutes away."

Maybe this was God's answer, he pondered, as he and Max raced home.

"That's it, Paullina." Rori stroked her fingertips across the horse's neck. She sat in the sun-warmed grass next to the mare, doing her best to keep the animal comforted. She'd never found herself alone with a foaling mare before. Assisting wasn't the same as helping, she realized, glancing toward the corral where Wildflower grazed with the sprightly filly Cheyenne had named Rosebud.

"You're going great," she reassured her. The horse's head came up and she stroked her cheek, gently calming her. "Just lie back. You are such a good girl."

Paullina nickered low in her throat, as if she were grateful for the company. Her sides heaved, and she thrashed a little in pain. Four minutes away, Justin had promised. She checked her watch. Only three minutes had ticked past. It felt as if a century had gone by.

Maybe because she was dreading being alone with him. She couldn't forget the way he'd been this morning, hardly looking at her. His painful aloofness puzzled her. How could he have kissed her so perfectly with endless affection, and where had that affection gone? Last night, just when she'd been ready to believe again, just when she could see a glimpse of his tenderness, he'd turned away. He'd called it a mistake.

Would he ever be able to open up to her?

Hoof beats echoed across the long expanse of sloping hillside and verdant fields. She whipped around. Justin rode with the sun at his back, wide shoulders braced and invincible. Her most cherished dream.

Max approached the fence and Justin dismounted while the horse was still moving. Buttercup bellowed to him, as if to explain the circumstances. Was that a smile cracking the stony line of his chiseled mouth? He patted the cow's neck, ducked between the fencing and strode her way.

Remember to breathe, she told herself. Somehow she had to keep her feelings firmly reined in. But as his long-legged stride brought him closer, her pulse skipped beats. Her palms went damp. Last night's kiss tingled across her lips.

You can do this. She lifted her chin and hoped she looked dignified. "She's progressing fast."

"I got a hold of Dad and Autumn, too. We'll see who gets here first, the foal or everyone I called." Nothing rattled Justin. He was solid and steady as the earth beneath her, a Western hero of old striding in to save the day. He halted where the vulnerable horse could see him and held out a hand to stroke the mare's nose.

"Hey, girl, looks like you're about to become a mama." Low, soft tones as smooth as molasses. He moved in slowly, carefully aware of Paullina's steeled hooves. "I plan on helping you out. Is that okay with you?"

Paullina answered with a part nicker, part groan. Lather flecked her beautiful white coat as she struggled against the pain, caught in the grips of a contraction.

"This won't take long at all." His hand covered hers completely, and Rori startled. The contact struck her like lightning all the way to the soul. Was it her imagination, or was there a hint of affection in his dark blue eyes? Caring in his sun-warmed touch?

Her heart swooped right up in adoration, knowing it was true.

"Are you doing okay?" he asked.

"I'm fine. Do you need me to get anything?"

"We should be fine for now. I want to make sure we've got both hooves pointing in the right direction. You keep doing what you're doing." The connection between them remained even after his hand lifted from hers and he moved away, talking softly to the mare.

For the first time in a long time she didn't second-guess her choices or feel the need to examine the decisions she'd made in her life. The regret and fears of mistakes vanished, leaving only Justin kneeling nearby. The warm sun beat on her shoulders, the pleasant wind whispered through the grass. Dandelions and daisies fluttered nearby and Paullina groaned, straining against her pain.

She couldn't see what was going on as she stroked the mare's neck in reassurance, but she had a perfect view of Justin helping to deliver the foal. Straightening front hooves, helping to pull with each contraction, cleaning the little nose when it appeared.

"Welcome, little one." Justin's deep tone rumbled through her like homecoming. He was stroking the tiny creature, who lay panting in the grass glistening and miraculous. Infinitely gentle, the big man reassured the newborn, who gazed up at him as if he were an amazing sight.

Truly amazing, Rori decided, giving Paullina one last stroke of comfort before easing onto her feet. She moved slowly as she didn't want to startle the baby. Nothing could be cuter. She twisted up inside with love for the foal, a precious bundle of new life, all long legs and big brown eyes.

"She's as pretty as her mama." He chuckled when the filly shook her head, ruffling her bristled mop of mane and blinked her lashes, as if she couldn't believe her eyes. Apparently she was very surprised to see a second human.

"She's adorable." Rori eased down in the grass on one knee next to Justin. It felt like a century ago when she and Justin had admired Wildflower's foal and the pain of the past had been an unbreachable wall between them. Where had it gone?

She did not know. Somehow it had vanished. Justin's unguarded gaze found hers. She felt the impact like a hook to her soul and she was caught, bonded to him for all eternity. Only this moment mattered and the unspoken comfort of a love that nothing could diminish.

He felt it, too—she knew he did—for he reached across a cluster of daisies and cradled her hand in his. The hook deepened in her soul, binding them with a strength only grace could do.

"Rori, I—" That was as far as he got. Paullina whinnied, recognizing Frank, who was striding through the field, his horse Rogue lathered and waiting alongside Buttercup and Justin's Max.

"Looks like I missed the big event." Frank bounded up to check on Paullina. The mare struggled to her feet and with a quiet nicker, put her head in Frank's hands. "That's one fine baby you've got, sweetheart."

Justin released her, and Rori felt awkward sitting there. Autumn was riding into sight, and the rumble of an approaching engine told her the vet was moments away. No sense sitting around instead of lending a hand. She rose, aware of Justin's silence as she backed away. There was no distance far enough nor any defense strong enough to hold back her love for him.

The men stood by as Paullina licked her baby affectionately. The precious filly rested fawnlike in the grass, watching her new world with fascination and taking it all in. At the sidelines, Buttercup bellowed as if to announce the birth to the entire ranch.

Larks sang and a hummingbird hovered above a honeysuckle bloom next to the porch step as she skipped by.

When she glanced over her shoulder, Justin was watching. Maybe it was the distance or maybe it was wishful thinking, but she saw love on his face, the sort of love a woman dreamed of finding, a once-in-a-lifetime gift.

"There you go, girl." Justin dumped the measure of grain into the feed trough in the comfortable box stall. Paullina dived in, sweeping up the treat, leaning her shoulder against him in affection. He patted her velvety neck before moving away. Rori kept returning to his thoughts like a favorite song playing over and over.

"Looks like you've got a lot on your mind, son." Frank held open the gate, looking serious. "You okay?"

Not much got past his father, Justin had to give him credit for that.

"Fair to middling." He waited for Frank to latch the gate, watching the little foal, as perfectly white as her mother. Addison had named her Snowflake. "I'd better get back to work."

"Come with me." Frank inclined his head toward the door, a single nod, but his gaze was grim. "Just got off the phone with the state patrol. Seems a truck and trailer broke down on the interstate near the Montana line. They found our girls inside."

"The cows?" Dad didn't look happy, so something was wrong. Justin passed a hand over his face, preparing for bad news. "Are they okay?"

"Starved, dehydrated, beaten and Jasmine is down. She couldn't get up. Don't know why yet, but the patrolman said they had a vet on the way. It's possible they are going to need my authorization to euthanize."

"Ah, Dad, I'm sorry." He was sorry for the animal and for his father who had bottle-raised the cow. "I'll hitch the trailer and we can be on the road in ten minutes, tops."

"I've already sent Addison to the house to pack for us. It'll be an overnight trip, so we'll need enough feed in the trailer. I'll see to that."

"What about Rori?" He glanced toward the house, where large windows winked in the noontime sun.

"She's in town grocery shopping."

"Oh." He hadn't noticed her leaving because he'd been getting the stall comfortable and cozy for the new mama and her baby. The strong sunshine burned his eyes as he broke away from his dad. Buttercup was now in the brood mare's empty meadow, drowsing after an exciting morning.

He wanted to talk to Rori before he went. He couldn't tell her he loved her, that he wanted to spend his life with her because nothing had changed, well, nothing between them. When he'd thundered into the yard on Max and spotted her sitting with the horse, love had hit him so hard he could not breathe. Every step he took toward her had doubled it. She sat unknowing with the wind tangling her hair and the sunlight blessing her. All that mattered, all that would ever matter, was her.

He hopped into his truck, started the engine, backed out of the garage and up the lane along the lawn, speeding up the stretch to the second stable behind the barn. Dad had opened the bay doors and stood beside the trailer, hands up and gesturing, guiding him in. He kept his father in the side-view mirror, turning a tad to the left, easing up on the gas, hitting the brake, and where was his mind?

On Rori. On how serene she'd looked this morning and her awe making her even more compelling when she saw the new foal for the first time. She understood the wonder of life on this ranch, the miracle of each life, the importance of safeguarding God's creatures and the emotional reward that went with it. For a moment, he'd almost believed she might want to share the journey with him.

Alone in the truck, he tossed his hat on the crew seat behind him. The truck's shocks dipped slightly as his dad made quick work of hitching up. Justin had just enough time to decide to be honest. There was one more thing troubling him, one problem he'd refused to face so far. He would leave this ranch for Rori, and he hoped she would want to stay here. But finding out was a risk that shook him to the marrow. How did a man as closed off as he'd become open his heart? Take a risk, when he'd been playing it safe for so long?

The passenger door swung open and Frank climbed in. "We're hitched and ready to roll." He hit the dash with the flat of his hand. "Let's go, pilot."

"Will do, copilot." Justin put the truck in gear and eased out into the lane, the trailer rattling slightly behind them.

Addison met them near the house with two small duffel bags, an insulated food carrier and two cans of root beer. "I've said like ten prayers for a safe trip and for our cows. You'll call and let us know as soon as you see them?"

"Promise." Justin dropped the bags in the back and handed the carrier and one of the cans over to his dad. After a quick exchange of last-minute ranch concerns and goodbyes, Justin nosed the truck down the driveway.

"You and Rori looked mighty cozy when I rode up."

Frank popped his can open and took a slurp. "It's good to see you two together."

"We're not together." He glanced in the rearview. The light dust cloud rising up behind the truck obliterated home from his sight.

"If you two aren't an item, then what are you?"

"I don't want to talk about this, Dad." He turned onto Mustang Lane, heading away from town and away from where Rori was. He imagined her pushing a cart through the only grocery store in town, checking prices, her hair tumbling down from her baseball cap and so precious he would give his life for hers. What if she didn't feel the same way?

"Sure, I get that." Frank took another sip of root beer. "But don't forget life is about risks. God sets a path for us, but if we don't take the first step then we are hurting ourselves and disappointing Him."

"And did I ask for your advice?"

"No, but you're going to get it anyway." He grinned and put his can in the cup holder. "You and that girl are made for each other. Everyone knows it. Don't you think God might be giving you two a second chance? If you don't get this right, Justin, maybe God doesn't have another chance lined up for you. Maybe this is it."

"Fine by me." It wasn't, but he sure wanted it to be. He wanted to be invincible steel so nothing could hurt him again.

"Do you want to end up like me?"

"What's wrong with ending up like you?"

"A lot. Is this my fault? Is that what I've done?" He blew out a breath, holding in the torment that only the truth could bring. "You've been learning by my example."

"Dad, what are you talking about?"

"I've been a widower for nearly sixteen years. Being single is a lonely road and not one I want for you." He may as well be honest. "I don't even want it for myself."

"You said after we lost Mom, never again."

"I did." Truth be told, the marriage had torn him into pieces and he'd needed time to heal up. A lot of time. "Just because things went so wrong with me and your mom, doesn't mean I wouldn't do it all over again."

"What? I was there. I saw how miserable you both were. Mom hated this ranch, at least in the end."

"It didn't start out that way." Bittersweet to remember those years and the risk he'd taken in asking the pretty new girl just moved to town to have a milkshake with him at Clem's. "If I hadn't married Lainie, then I wouldn't have had the privilege of raising the five best kids in the world."

"Rori is going to leave at the end of the summer. It's not the same situation."

"Then I guess what I'm trying to say is this. Life is a demanding trail ride. The pain and the struggle is part of the experience. Sometimes you get knocked to the ground, but what happens if you don't get up? You don't finish the ride, you don't get to your destination. Maybe the reward you find there is worth the pain and the risk." He thought of Cady Winslow, and his own fears of taking the first step on the trail of romance again. "When you get it right, that's the best life has to offer. Love is the greatest thing there is."

"Maybe that's true." His son smiled, actually smiled, and Frank believed that life was going to work out just right for his boy. God would make sure of it.

Chapter Seventeen

Rori wrapped her arms around Copper's neck, holding her best friend close. The old horse nickered warmly, leaning into her, too. She treasured the moment with him, for they did not need words to communicate and drank in the companionable silence. She kissed his warm coat and let go.

"I'll be back with a treat in a bit." She climbed through the fence, already missing him. She'd longed for him every day of every year she'd lived away. She couldn't stomach the thought of doing that again, which was why she'd made a few calls. Why she had liked the idea of becoming a private music teacher.

The grass crackled beneath her shoes as she crossed the back lawn. A robin watched her from a low branch of the apple tree. A hummingbird zipped past her left shoulder on the way to the red feeder swinging from the porch eave. Gramps was nearly through filling a wheelbarrow at the garden's edge, where Gram sat on a low wooden stool, yanking weeds.

"I thought you were supposed to wait for me." She

marched beneath the shade of two ancient plum trees. "What did you promise me when I moved in?"

"That we would let you earn your keep." Gramps winked at her, taking hold of the wheelbarrow's grips and pushing it forward. "Don't look at me. I tried to tell her, but you know women. Don't listen to a thing us poor men have to say." He winked, heading off to the compost pile behind the garage.

"That man." Grams laughed, shaking her head. The bonnet she wore shaded her face and looked dear on her. "He doesn't want you working too hard either. You've put in a long day at the Grangers. I'm used to pulling my own weeds."

"Yes, but I'm here now." She knelt between the rows of lacy green carrot leaves and began plucking at the familiar fronds of a budding dandelion. "You could have at least waited for me."

"Gardening is a pleasure. Feeling the earth between your fingertips, tending God's green growing things, looking forward to the day I can pull these carrots and put them in a salad. It all makes me happy."

"I see that." Gram did have the secret to happiness, that was for sure. Regardless of what life tossed her way, she remained strong and optimistic and sure of her course. "Can I ask you something?"

"That's what I'm here for." Gram set down her trowel, ready to listen.

"When you have two choices in front of you, how do you know which is the right one?" She'd been pondering her decisions all day, but her regrets haunted her. Before she made a move, she had to be sure. "I've prayed on it, I've asked for guidance but I'm not sure of the signs. I've made so many mistakes already in my life. I don't want to make any more."

"What mistakes have you made?" So caring and wise, Gram reached out and covered Rori's hands with hers. "You have done wonderfully, Pumpkin. Your grandfather and I are so proud of you. Besides, what we often call mistakes are really God's way of teaching us what He most wants us to learn."

Tears burned her eyes. "The marriage was a failure, Gram. You know it is. My failure. What if I do it again?"

"God makes no mistakes. The best anyone can do is to trust the Lord and follow your heart. If you do those two things, then you will wind up where you most need to go. And that's never a misstep, dear one." Gram's grip tightened with loving comfort in the perfect evening's light. The approaching sunset cast a golden glow that crowned their piece of Wyoming as if with a promise from heaven.

Follow her heart? Rori swallowed hard, lifted her chin and rubbed at a smear of dirt on her grandmother's cheek. Her choices were suddenly clear.

"There you two are!" A familiar baritone broke through the crowded Wild Horse main street, where the weekend festivities of Frontier Days were in full swing. "Cheyenne told me to keep an eye out for you."

Justin squinted at Tucker, the younger, nearly identical copy of their dad moseying their way. His little brother was dressed in typical Western wear: Stetson, plaid shirt, Levi's and boots. A sight for sore eyes. "Glad you could make it, Tucker."

"My boy." Dad clapped his prodigal son in a one-armed hug and patted his back. "Didn't expect you'd show up."

"I dislocated my shoulder last weekend so the doc ordered me off the circuit for a few weeks." Tucker didn't seem too troubled by it, although his left arm was in a blue sling. "So I figured I might as well drive home for the big shindig. I got in this morning while you were away. Autumn put me to work keeping guard on the north ridge. Did you get the cows put up all right?"

"Yep, and Nate's been to check on them, too," Justin answered. It had been the first thing they'd done when they'd arrived home a few hours ago. "We have Jasmine in the barn recovering."

"Nate thinks she's bruised a few organs but ought to heal up just fine." Frank shrugged, an effort to hide how upset he'd been. "They've been through an ordeal, but they are all right now."

"Already spoiling them, huh?" Tucker winked.

"That's my job," their dad answered with a wink.

Autumn and Addison wandered into sight, colorful snow cones in hand, and they weren't alone.

"Look who we found by the snow cone booth," Autumn announced. "Cady's decided to board with us after all. Isn't that great news?"

Justin was the only one who noticed that their dad went pale.

"Now I have to learn how to ride." The elegant lady blushed, as if that were an embarrassment. "It seems everyone here knows how. I've heard there's nothing to it. But it seems I have a lot to learn before I get onto the back of a horse. That is a long way to fall."

"I'm sure Autumn could teach you what you need

to know," their dad spoke up. "Since you'll be coming around to the ranch and all."

"That would be nice." Cady Winslow smiled, blushing a little when her gaze met Frank's.

Well, this is going to be interesting, Justin thought. He caught sight of Rori's golden hair in the crowd, standing with her back to him while her grandfather bought two cones of mint chocolate-chip ice cream. Seeing her made the world, even his family, fade into the background until there was only Rori, his one true love.

"Cady's here all alone," Addison said as if from a great distance. "So we invited her to come sit with us in the stands. We'd better start heading over. Cheyenne's event starts in fifteen minutes."

"You go on ahead without me," he told his family, hardly noticing as they drifted away. He didn't remember crossing the street, only that he was suddenly close enough to hear her conversation.

"No, that's great, I'll take it." She was on her cell, chatting away with a smile in her voice. Her hair, down today, fluttered lightly with her movements, brushing against her back like the finest silk. "First and last month's rent and a security deposit? Sure. I'll write a check and get it to you."

That was the first hit of uncertainty, but he kept on going, his chin up, his spine braced. Hearing his boots on the pavement, she spun around, flipping the phone shut in one hand. She lit up when she saw him. The brilliance of her beauty both inside and out was unbearably bright, and he was no longer standing in shadow.

"Justin, good to see you, young man." Del Cornell

handed one mint-green waffle cone to his wife and kept the other. "Heard you found your stolen cows."

"We did, sir. We were lucky the truck hauling them broke down. They were taking them out of state to sell."

"Guess at least those hooligans won't be bothering the cattle around here again." Del nodded, his eyes glinting with understanding. "We'll leave you two young people to talk. I've got a hot date with the prettiest gal in White Horse county."

"Going over to the rodeo isn't a hot date," Rori's grandmother pointed out merrily. "If you want to make this a date, then you better take me out to supper, Del."

"As you wish." The two ambled away, arm in arm, their lifelong love another reason to believe.

"I couldn't help overhearing," he said, jamming his hands into his pockets so he didn't reach for her. He yearned to draw her into the shelter of his arms and hold her there, to never let her go. "Sounded like you found a place to live."

"Yes, I did." She slipped her phone into her back pocket, adorable in a pretty summer top and matching shorts. Her flip-flops kept rhythm as they turned in unison and headed slowly down the street. "I've found a place where I can take Copper with me."

"He'll like that." His palms had broken out in a sweat and a knot of doom had formed and taken over his stomach, but he knew the Lord had brought him here for a reason. Dad was right, this was his second chance. He could open up and show her how he felt. He could be vulnerable. It was the only way to have a happily-ever-after with Rori. He took a deep breath, gathered his courage and opened his heart. "Don't move to Dallas."

"Dallas?" She stopped, turning toward him, an adorable crinkle of surprise marring her forehead.

"At least not without me." He seized the opportunity and got down on one knee, fumbling in his shirt pocket for the ring he'd dug out of the safe back at home. He took hold of her left hand. "You are the love of my life, Rori Cornell. I will move to Texas if that's what you want. Or we can stay here and build a house, say on the quarter section next to your grandparents' property. All I care about is you. Marry me. Please don't leave me again."

"I wasn't going anywhere." Her hand in his trembled. "I rented a little house on the edge of town. I've decided to stay in Wild Horse."

"You have?" That was news to him. She'd decided to stay, but she hadn't given him a yes or no answer.

"My grandparents are getting older and they need a little help around the place. With the garden. Helping with the housework. That kind of thing." Her fingers curled through his, holding on so tight.

"That's good." This is where she rejects me, he thought, waiting for the blow of pain. She hadn't said yes to him. His love for her was so strong, surely it was not a one-way street? "No wonder Del and Polly looked so happy. They're glad you will be nearby."

"Yes." She bit her bottom lip nervously, her violet-blue gaze so intense she could see his soul. "Yes, Justin."

"Yes?" It didn't sink in at first. It took him a few beats before realization hit him. She had agreed to marry him. She wanted to be his wife.

His wife. Joy burst through him, stronger because his heart was open, his walls were down. Happiness filled every piece of him. Every dream he'd ever had burst to life—dreams of her, of their wedding day, the birth of their first child. Hopeful images of years to come paraded across his soul. They could do this, he thought. They could be happily-ever-after.

"I was prepared for this to go the other way," he confessed.

"Why would I say no to you?" Her voice softened, layered with all of her love revealed. "Long ago I asked you to wait, and you did. You let me come back to you."

"I never stopped loving you." Apparently it was a day for confessions. Now that he'd started, he couldn't seem to stop.

"I didn't either." She stared at the ring he slipped rather shakily onto the fourth finger of her left hand. "That's a beautiful diamond."

"It was my grandmother's." His gaze searched hers with one single question. "She and my grandfather had a long and happy life together."

"That's what I want with you." Like the sun's heat against her cheek, she could feel the assurance from heaven. This was their chance to get it right. She intended to do just that and give him her whole heart without reservations. "I love you, Justin Granger."

"I love you more." The truth of it rang in his voice and in the chambers of her heart. He rose to his full height, towering over her, tenderness transforming him. "I promise that I will never stop loving you. Everything I am and everything I have is yours forever."

He took her into his arms, oblivious of the crowd around them buying waffle cones and sun catchers and weather vanes. Kids ran and shouted while parents watched, couples held hands and the mayor called out a hello to the minister. With the sounds of life surrounding them, Justin's arms enfolded her gently against his chest. She closed her eyes, snuggled her cheek against his cotton shirt, joy spiraling through her. She felt full up and brimming over with gratitude.

Thank You, Lord, she prayed. All of her trials and life lessons had led her back to Justin, to the love of her life. She knew exactly how precious he was, this good man who would not falter, who was the other half of her soul.

"Break it up!" the mayor commented with good cheer as he strolled by. "Justin, isn't your sister competing soon?"

"Pretty soon," he agreed.

"Then get a move on to the stands!" Whistling, Tim Wiscner went on his way, calling out to others, reminding them of the barrel race about to take place.

"I guess we should go watch Cheyenne compete," she said, loath to let go of him.

"We should," he agreed, but he didn't move either. "There's one thing I'd like to do first."

"Which is?"

"Kiss my fiancée."

"This is my favorite part," she quipped.

His smile became a kiss, flawless and sweet, his unspoken promise of their happiness to come—enough happiness to see them through a lifetime. She wrapped her arms around his neck and held on tight.

* * * * *

Dear Reader,

Welcome to my new family, the Grangers. I hope you can sit down, get comfortable, put up your feet and set your worries aside for a few hours and let the story of Rori Cornell and Justin Granger carry you away to a very special place. Stowaway Ranch is the Granger family's Wyoming ranch, which has been in their family for generations. I also grew up on an original family homestead, where I spent my days caring for cattle and enjoying the beauty of God's countryside. I've hidden several memories from my own childhood on these pages—kamikaze hummingbirds, deer grazing in the fields and a terribly spoiled pet cow are just some of them. Writing the Grangers' stories is like coming home for me, and I hope you feel the same. I also hope you enjoy falling in love along with Justin and Rori as they try to listen to the Lord and figure out where He is leading them.

Thank you for choosing *The Rancher's Promise*.

Wishing you the best of blessings,

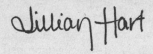

QUESTIONS FOR DISCUSSION

1. At the beginning of the story, how would you describe Justin's character? What are his weaknesses and strengths? What are his issues?

2. What is Rori's reaction when she first sees Justin in town? What does this tell you about her character? What are her issues?

3. In the beginning of the story Rori wrestles with regrets. She wants to go back in time and do over parts of her life. Have you ever felt this way? How has it affected you and how have you handled it?

4. Why does Justin decide to let Rori interview for the job? What does this say about him?

5. What role does the past play in the story? How does it support both Justin's and Rori's faiths? How does it develop and renew their romance?

6. Why is it painful for Justin to be around Rori? How does this change throughout the story? Why does it change?

7. What are the central themes? How do they develop? What meanings do you find in them?

8. How does God guide both Justin and Rori through their pain and fears?

9. Rori fears that men do not love deeply the way women do, and she fears she will wind up alone. How is this challenged through the book? What causes her to change? What does she learn about love and regrets?

10. What role do the animals play in the story?

11. What happens to make Rori let go of the past? How does she find self-forgiveness and understanding?

12. What do you like most about Rori and Justin as a couple? How do you know they are meant for each other?

13. How would you describe Frank and Cady's romance? What fears keep them apart?

14. Why does Justin finally take down his guard and open his heart to love? What makes him believe in true love again? What does he learn about love and life?

BIG SKY FAMILY

Charlotte Carter

Special thanks to my editor, Emily Rodmell,
who made this book so much better.

Then Jesus said to his host, "When you give a
luncheon or dinner, do not invite your friends, your
brothers or sisters, your relatives, or your rich
neighbors; if you do, they may invite you back and so
you will be repaid. But when you give a banquet, invite
the poor, the crippled, the lame, the blind, and you will
be blessed. Although they cannot repay you,
you will be repaid at the resurrection of the righteous."
—*Luke* 14:12–14

Chapter One

Her heart as thick in her throat as if she'd swallowed a ball of yarn, Ellie James drove the van over the cattle guard of the O'Brien ranch. She had once loved the man who had owned the ranch—and had abandoned him eight years ago.

Guilt pressing in on her, Ellie glanced in the rearview mirror and smiled at her six young preschool passengers. She'd been their teacher at Ability Counts Preschool and Day Care Center in Potter Creek, Montana, for a week. She already loved each of the four-year-olds in her class. Three had physical disabilities—cerebral palsy, spina bifida and a prosthetic leg. The remaining three were simply normal kids, including her own daughter, Victoria.

All the youngsters were the best of friends, which proved the value of mainstreaming disabled children early.

"There's horses!" Carson, her spina bifida boy, screamed.

Billy and Shane echoed Carson's high-pitched announcement.

Ellie flinched. "Inside voices, please."

A dozen quarter horses grazed in a beautifully fenced pasture to the right of the drive.

"Carson's getting anxious," her daughter, Torie, said.

"Yes, he is." She glanced at her sparkly eyed, little minx of a daughter, the child's hair almost the same shade of auburn as her own. She counted God's blessings, as she had every day since Torie had been born. "I bet you're excited, too, Torie."

"I wanna ride a great big horse, not a pony."

"We'll have to see what kind of horses they have, honey. And remember, you'll have to take turns with your friends."

Ellie followed her employer's van, filled with another half dozen preschoolers, down the long, dusty drive toward the core of the ranch. Up ahead, the sun glistened off the two-story white farmhouse. The nearby barn appeared sturdy and well maintained, and beyond that a new house was being built, the framing in place.

Her nerves settled a bit. The ranch was not the run-down, shabby place she remembered. Instead, this ranch was a prosperous enterprise.

Surely Arnie O'Brien was gone by now, had moved away, found another life, the ranch sold. The new owners would be the ones who welcomed the pre-schoolers.

She parked behind the van driven by Vanna Coulter, the owner and founder of Ability Counts. In the corral a mixed group of six saddled horses waited for their young riders.

"All right, children. Let's remember to help our friends." She activated the special lift that would enable Carson to exit in his wheelchair. Anne Marie, who used crutches, stepped onto the lift, as well. Ellie lowered the lift, and the other youngsters exited in a more traditional fashion.

"Hold hands with your partner." The children were so excited, their eyes wide, that she had trouble keeping them together. "Let's see what Miss Vanna has for us."

Her little clutch of youngsters started forward, Torie helping to push Carson's wheelchair. Jefferson, her quietest boy, stayed close to Anne Marie. The morning was already warm, and most of the children were wearing shorts. Ellie suspected by the end of this outing, she'd be happy to trade her lightweight slacks for a pair of shorts, too.

As they reached Vanna and her group of students, a man in a wheelchair rolled out of the barn and came toward them.

Mouth open in stunned disbelief, Ellie watched in amazement as Arnie O'Brien approached.

Each stroke of his hands on the wheels of his chair propelled him forward. The muscles of his darkly tanned forearms flexed and corded. His shoulders were broader than she remembered. Beneath his ebony Stetson, the tips of his silky black hair fluttered in the breeze he created by his sheer strength and power. His sculpted cheekbones and straight nose spoke of his Blackfoot Indian heritage on his mother's side.

A beautiful golden retriever mix trotted along beside him.

"Hey, kids. Who wants to ride a horse?" he called out.

The children sent up a cacophony of "I do! I do!" and raised their hands, waving them in the air.

Torie tugged on Ellie's hand. "Mommy, the man gots a doggy. Can I pet the doggy? Can I?"

"I… I don't know." Her head spun. By coming back to Potter Creek, she'd assumed her path might cross Arnie's again—*if* he was still living in the area. But she'd thought that would be a long shot. To find her former love still at the ranch so many years after his brother's reckless driving had paralyzed and nearly killed Arnie shocked her. She'd expected…

She shook her head. She had no idea what she'd expected.

But she hadn't expected the familiar fluttery feeling around her heart or the sense that she'd given up something special by leaving Potter Creek eight years ago. No matter that Arnie, barely out of a medically induced coma, had told her to leave. To go away. She'd deserted him when he most needed her. She'd broken the trust they'd had in each other.

Torie broke away from the group. She made a dash for Arnie and his dog.

Before Ellie could call her back, Torie slid to a stop right in front of Arnie.

"Hey, mister, can I pet your doggy? I love doggies. Does he like little girls? Can I pet him, huh?"

Arnie quirked his lips into a half smile. "Everyone can pet Sheila, but you have to do it one at a time. Okay?"

Not waiting for additional encouragement, Torie squatted down in front of Sheila, who sat calmly while the child stroked her head and ran her fingers through her golden coat.

"She's bea-u-tiful," Torie crooned.

The other children edged forward. Ellie moved with them until she was only a few paces away from Arnie. Unconsciously, she fingered the silver cross she wore around her neck, a gift from her father the year she graduated from eighth grade. Only after Torie was born and Ellie had made her peace with the Lord had she begun to wear it again.

"Hello, Arnie." Her mouth as dry as the sandbox at school, she spoke in a voice that was little more than a whisper.

His attention remained focused on Torie for a moment before he lifted his head. He squinted as he looked up at Ellie. There seemed to be no spark of recognition in his eyes. Only a blank stare.

"I'm sorry my daughter was so forward. I'm afraid she's quite an animal lover." Reaching for Torie, she said, "Give someone else a turn now, honey."

Awareness flickered in his eyes, and he shot the child an assessing look. "Same red hair. I should've known." His voice was as flat as his eyes, yet she read an angry denunciation in them.

"It's been a long time," she said.

"Yeah." No smile. A single word in bitter acknowledgment.

The sting of his response forced her to look away. She had no reason to expect anything more, but it still hurt. "Who wants to pet Sheila next? Remember to be gentle."

She drew Torie to her side, a protective hand on her daughter's shoulder.

"Sheila's a very nice doggy, Mommy. Maybe someday we could have a doggy, too?"

"We'll see."

As Carson approached Sheila in his wheelchair, Arnie's brows tugged together in apparent confusion. He glanced back at Ellie.

"Why are you here?" he asked.

"I'm teaching at Ability Counts Preschool. I started this week. Four-year-olds."

"That's ironic, isn't it?"

Before she could explain how she'd worked hard to earn her degree in early childhood education and added an elementary school teaching credential to her résumé, Arnie's younger brother, Daniel, sauntered out of the barn. Easily recognizable with his long legs and the cocky way he wore his hat on the back of his head, he called to the youngsters.

"Hey, what's taking you guys so long? Isn't anybody planning to go riding today?"

Instantly, the children lost interest in Sheila. They walked, ran and wheeled their way to the barn. In a quick maneuver, Arnie turned his wheelchair around and drove purposely after them.

Vanna and Ellie followed more slowly. A woman in her late sixties, Vanna stood nearly six feet tall and wore her gray hair closely cropped. But it was her smile and obvious love for all "her children" that endeared her to those who attended the preschool as well as their parents.

"The two young men hosting us have been a wonderful help to the school," Vanna said. "Arnie's on our board of directors, a very valuable resource. He's also on the Bozeman Paralympics board. He's trying to start a regional program to train local teenagers with physical disabilities for Western riding events. All the organization offers currently are English-style equestrian events, which leaves some of our kids without an event that appeals to them."

At some level, Ellie wasn't surprised that Arnie was

involved with programs for people with disabilities. Of the two brothers, Arnie had been the serious, solid one, often at odds with his wilder, more rambunctious brother.

As a nineteen-year-old, Ellie had been stretching her wings, ready to try anything, while Arnie generally watched with amusement as she tried to break her neck with some half-baked stunt Daniel had cooked up.

Arnie, in his quiet way, had given her balance when she needed it. She hadn't had that anymore when she first moved away to Spokane, to her regret.

Arnie and Daniel separated the two groups of youngsters. Daniel took his clutch of four-year-olds into the corral to ride, while Arnie lined up his kids for a lesson in grooming horses.

Needing to keep her distance from Arnie, not wanting to feel that tingle of excitement or the slashing pain of guilt, Ellie followed Daniel into the corral. He introduced the children to Marc, an older teenager who would assist the kids.

Daniel turned to Ellie. "If you can help out, that'd be…" He stopped midsentence and frowned. "Ellie?"

At his recognition, her first smile since she arrived at the ranch lifted her lips. "The bad penny has returned."

"Hey, no, it's great you're back." He glanced toward the barn and frowned. He hesitated. "Does Arnie know?"

"Yes, we've said hello." Barely. His greeting had been less than enthusiastic, which she should have expected.

With the ease of a working cowboy, Daniel picked up Carson and hefted him into a special saddle on a sorrel. He began securing the grinning boy so he couldn't fall off. "Yeah, well, that's Arnie for you. The quiet brother. I know who'll really be glad to see you again."

"Who's that?" Most of her high school friends had moved away, and she'd lost track of them.

He instructed Carson to sit tight until everyone had mounted. "Mindy. You know, Aunt Martha's grand-niece? She's Mindy O'Brien now." He stood a little taller, and his chest puffed out with pride.

Ellie's eyes popped open and her jaw dropped. "You married Mindy?" A couple of years older than Ellie, Mindy had helped her learn to knit one long-ago summer, when Mindy was visiting her aunt.

"Yep. Tied the knot last spring." He bent a little closer to her. "We're expecting a baby come the end of the year."

She gasped with delight and covered her mouth with her hand. "Oh, that's wonderful! We were friends only that one summer, but I remember her well." She glanced around. "Is she here now?"

"Nope. She manages Aunt Martha's Knitting and Notions shop. She'll be back in time for supper."

Daniel moved on to boost Torie into the saddle of a buckskin who'd been waiting patiently for a rider. Her skinny, bare legs poked almost straight out to the sides.

"What's my horse's name?" Torie asked.

"This is Patches. He'll take real good care of you."

"I like Patches!"

As Ellie helped Shane mount, she promised herself she'd stop by the knitting shop as soon as she could find the time. It'd be great to see Mindy again. She certainly hadn't expected her friend to return to Potter Creek after she'd gone back to Pittsburgh without say-ing goodbye to anyone.

Then again, when Ellie left Potter Creek, she hadn't expected to return home to stay, either.

But fate—and in Ellie's case, a good dose of stupidity—had changed the best-laid plans. An unintended pregnancy plus a man who had no intention in being a father changed a lot in a woman's life.

She sincerely prayed this current change was one for the better.

Chapter Two

Talk about being skewered by a wild bull!

That evening on the back porch of the ranch house, Arnie forked the three T-bone steaks he'd barbecued onto a serving platter. He'd spent the better part of the afternoon thinking about Ellie James and how she'd showed up out of nowhere. He could've been knocked over by a newborn calf.

She taught handicapped kids.

She'd walked out on him after the accident, unable to face life with a cripple. *Probably a good decision*, he admitted. *The best thing for her. But not for him*, he thought selfishly.

Was she living some sort of a twisted penance now? Forcing herself to care for those who repulsed her?

She had a daughter, a beautiful sprite of a child with Ellie's lush red hair that captured sunbeams and the same hint of freckles across her nose.

Where was her husband? The child's father?

Arnie had no answers to his questions and assured himself that he didn't want any. Ancient history. Better to leave it that way.

Daniel pushed open the screen door. "Hey, bro, Mindy's got the salad and rolls on the table. Are we gonna eat those steaks sometime tonight, or are you gonna let Sheila scarf 'em down all by herself?"

"I'm coming." With the serving platter across his lap, he rolled into the kitchen. Always his faithful companion, Sheila was right beside him, her toenails clicking on the tile. She'd get her share of steak on the bone he'd give her after dinner.

"Oh, those look delicious." Mindy was already seated at the round oak table, the same table where Arnie and Daniel had eaten since their childhood. The same table where their drunken father had yelled and railed at them for no particular reason and had sometimes slapped them silly.

Daniel, a rebel at heart, had always gotten the worst of it.

But those days were long gone, and even better days lay ahead.

Blonde and blue-eyed, Mindy had had a certain glow about her since she'd married Daniel. That glow had blossomed even more once she discovered she was pregnant. Having lost a child from her first marriage, she cherished the new life growing in her.

A stab of envy zinged Arnie right in his solar plexus. Why did Ellie have to come back to Potter Creek, reminding him of all the things he'd never have, like a wife and children of his own?

He selected a steak for himself, put it on his plate and passed the platter to Mindy.

"I don't know what I'm going to do when you move into your new house," Mindy said. "You'd better promise to come here for dinner every night."

"You only say that because you want me to be your kitchen slave," Arnie teased.

She laughed. "Never a slave. A highly valued chef is closer to the truth. And a great brother-in-law," she added.

"I vote for the slave part." Daniel plopped the third steak on his plate.

Arnie snorted. He reached for Daniel's hand and Mindy's, and they linked hands with each other. Arnie bowed his head. "Dear Lord, thank You once again for the food You have provided. Bless us and keep us safe, including little Rumpelstiltskin, who's growing in Mindy's tummy. Amen."

Choking, Mindy grabbed for her glass of water. "We're not going to name our baby Rumpelstiltskin!" she croaked.

"Well, you'd better come up with something better pretty soon." Cutting into his steak, he gave Mindy a wink. "Uncle Arnie is growing quite fond of little Rumple."

Laughing, she shook her head.

They ate in comfortable silence for a while; then Daniel asked Mindy, "How was the shop today?"

"Busy for a Friday. The knitting and needlepoint club is getting ready for the church's Autumn Craft Fair. All the ladies want to have items to sell to help raise money for the church. Baby caps and sweaters are the most popular for the knitters. I had to place a new order for baby yarn this afternoon."

"Sounds good. My wife, the entrepreneur." Daniel forked another bite of meat into his mouth and talked around it. "Hey, I forgot to tell you. Ellie James is back in town."

For a frozen moment, Arnie held his knife poised over his steak.

"Ellie? I remember her," Mindy said. "Is she here to stay or just visiting her mother?"

"I guess she's here to stay. She's got a job with the preschool that comes out for Friday riding lessons. She was with them this morning."

Mindy turned to Arnie. "She was such a fun person. So energetic I could barely keep up with her. She used to hang out with your crowd."

Keeping his eyes focused on his dinner, Arnie nodded as he cut his steak. "Yeah, she hung out with us." And as she got older, she wasn't just hanging out. Mindy had been gone before Ellie and he had become a couple. She wouldn't have known how Ellie had kicked the possibility of a future together to the curb when she cut out for Spokane.

"Well, isn't that interesting?" Mindy's suddenly chirpy, singsong voice grated on Arnie's nerves. "Maybe we can all get together again. It'd be fun to double-date sometime."

He turned on Mindy, glaring at her, his pulse thundering in his ears. "That's not gonna happen. Not ever."

Just because Ellie had moved back to Potter Creek did not mean he had to see her. Or think about her. Or remember the numbing pain in his chest he'd lived with since she left.

Nope. He intended to stay far away from Ellie James. He imagined she felt the same way about him.

The house where Ellie grew up, just outside of Potter Creek, was a one-story white farmhouse with bedrooms added onto the back, a covered porch along the front and a mudroom stuck onto one side like a wart. A detached, oversize garage and workshop had served to shelter farm equipment, and a small barn and corral had once housed Ellie's horse, Samson, but had remained unused for years.

After Ellie's father died two years ago, her mother had leased out all the surrounding farmland, retaining only the one acre where the house and outbuildings stood.

With a sigh of relief to be home, Ellie parked her compact car near the side entrance. As she had expected, the first week of school had been a challenging one.

Seeing Arnie this morning had been even more difficult.

He hadn't been at all pleased to see her. Anger had simmered right below the surface of his detached manner toward her. *Rightfully so*, she admitted.

She'd been the one to leave. *She'd* started a new life hundreds of miles away. *She'd* felt so guilty about what she had done, she'd made some foolish mistakes.

None of which meant she had forgotten Arnie.

He'd told her to leave more than once.

Torie popped open the back door of the car. "I gotta tell Grandma BarBar about my horse." Slamming the door closed, she raced up the steps and into the house to relate her adventures to her grandmother Barbara.

Briefcase in hand, Ellie followed at a more leisurely pace.

"...rode a horse named Patches around and around. I kept saying 'Giddy up,' but the man wouldn't let Patches run fast." Torie paused only briefly to take a breath. "Then another man gave us brushes, and we brushed and brushed a horse. The horse was very dusty. That made Carson sneeze."

Sitting in the kitchen, at the long white-pine table, Grandma BarBar listened to Torie's tale, nodding where appropriate and making encouraging noises. A little overweight, Barbara wore wire-rimmed glasses, and her hair had lost most of the auburn color it once had. The permed curls were nearly all gray.

Ellie set her briefcase on the counter and idly checked the day's mail, which her mother had dropped in the woven basket.

"The man with the brushes showed us how to clean the icky stuff out of the horse's hoof. He had a doggy he let me pet, and he said he had to sit in a wheelchair all the time 'cause his legs didn't work anymore. I told him Carson's legs didn't work, either, but I still liked him."

Barbara lifted her head. "Ellen? Where did the school take the children to ride?"

Without glancing toward her mother, Ellie tucked a wayward strand of hair behind her ear. "Turns out it was the O'Brien ranch. I'd been so busy all week, I hadn't thought to ask Vanna where we were going."

"The man in the wheelchair was real nice, Mommy."

"Yes, honey, I know." Ellie returned the mail to the basket. Bills and a newsletter from the agricultural extension service were of no interest to her.

"It was Arnie O'Brien, wasn't it?" Barbara said, a stunned expression on her face.

A guilty flush warmed Ellie's cheeks. "Yes, Arnie was helping the children. So was his brother. Daniel's married now, and they're expecting a baby."

"Mommy, if I learn to ride a horse really, really, really good, can I have my very own horse? Please, can I? I would loooove to have my own horse."

"I'm sure you would, honey. But horses are expensive and take a lot of care." Working in the child care business was not exactly a lucrative profession, though it should be. What made it ideal for Ellie was the opportunity to work with mainstreamed handicapped kids and live at home with her mother, mostly rent-free. Being near her mother, who'd been depressed since she'd become a widow, was an added bonus. Ellie hoped having an exuberant child around would lift her spirits.

"We could ask the man in the wheelchair to come take care of my horse. He was very nice."

Ellie swallowed hard. *Not a good plan, sweetie.*

"Little Miss Chatterbox," Barbara said, "why don't you go wash up? It's almost supper time, and I want to talk with your mother."

Torie's slender shoulders slumped. "I know. You want to talk about grown-up things."

"Go on, Torie," Ellie said, although she wasn't eager to pursue the topic her mother no doubt had in mind. "Wash your hands and face, and don't forget to use soap."

Skipping and hopping, Torie did as she'd been told.

"I'd better go clean up, too," Ellie said, eager to avoid any discussion about Arnie.

"I do hope you won't be taking up with that young man again."

Ellie bristled. "No worries on that score, Mother. I doubt that he'd be interested." Her actions eight years ago had shut that door permanently. Actions her mother had advised and encouraged.

"Just as well." Barbara sniffed.

After Arnie's accident, Ellie's mother had encouraged Ellie to move away from Arnie. Barbara's brother, Bob, had been born with cerebral palsy and was severely handicapped. Watching a loved one suffer pain and humiliation haunted Barbara. She didn't want her daughter to endure the same difficult experience.

To her shame and regret, her mother's constant concern about Arnie's future had added to Ellie's ultimate decision to leave Potter Creek and move to Spokane.

The first of a long litany of mistakes she'd made that had changed her life.

With the Lord's help, she'd turned her life around. But that didn't mean that a proud man like Arnie would ever be able to forgive her for turning her back on him.

Early Saturday morning, a gang of volunteer construction workers showed up at the O'Brien ranch. Most of the guys were from Potter Creek Community Church. As the half dozen pickups pulled to a stop, Arnie rolled out to meet them.

"I've got a big pot of coffee ready," he announced. "And Daniel went into town early for fresh doughnuts. Help yourselves."

Like a pack of ravenous chowhounds, the men gathered around the coffeepot on what would someday be Arnie's back porch. Their wives and girlfriends would show up around noontime with picnic baskets full of lunch makings. Building his new house was like an old-fashioned barn raising, and he was grateful for every bit of help he got.

Since Daniel had announced he was going to marry Mindy, Arnie had planned to move out of the old ranch house and into his own home. Now that Mindy was expecting, providing his brother and his wife some extra space was even more important.

Given the cost of construction, bringing the plan to fruition would have been impossible without the help of his friends. In fact, half the community had lent a hand in one way or another.

Coffee and doughnut in hand, Tim Johnson, a licensed contractor and good friend, sauntered over to Arnie. "We're gonna start putting up the exterior plywood sheathing today. If that goes well, next week we could be adding the siding."

"That's terrific, Tim. You know how much I appreciate your help. All the guys' help."

"No problem. If the situation was reversed, you'd be there for us."

"I'd sure try to be." But Arnie knew he'd never have a chance to return the favor, at least not in the same way.

"I got my chimney guy to say he'd come next week so we can get the flashings in before the siding goes up. He's giving you a good price."

"Thanks, Tim. I appreciate it." One of the lessons he'd learned after the accident was that he'd never be as independent as he had been before. For some things, he'd have to rely on others. That had been a hard truth to swallow, and it still didn't go down real smoothly.

Daniel came striding across the distance from the barn, a tool belt around his waist. Apparently he had finished mucking out the horse stalls and was ready to go to work on the house.

"Hey, you guys," Daniel said to the men still hanging around the coffeepot. "You can't stand around drinking coffee and eatin' doughnuts all day. We gotta get this house sealed up tight before the first snow flies."

"Yeah, yeah. We know, Danny boy."

"Hey, who made you the boss?"

Amid a lot of friendly joshing and gently barbed comments, the men set to work. Guys grunted as they lifted heavy loads of plywood. Hammers banged nails home. Orders were shouted out. Power saws whined.

The heat of the day rose. Sweat darkened the back of the men's shirts and dripped from their chins.

Arnie wheeled his chair up the temporary ramp into his living room and looked around. His pride, his gratitude, were tempered by the knowledge that he'd never share this house with someone who could be his partner in making it a home.

A sense of betrayal rose bitter in his throat.

Ellie!

Even knowing she'd done the right thing to leave him, he couldn't quite accept that the woman who had cried at his bedside and held his hand for five solid days after the accident had actually walked out of his life. She hadn't stayed to fight for their love.

Now she was back.

And he couldn't stop thinking about her.

Chapter Three

The white steeple soared above Potter Creek Community Church, glistening in the morning sunlight, a beacon of hope and a promise of the Lord's love.

Holding her daughter's hand, Ellie followed the path to the building that housed Sunday school classrooms. She'd grown up attending this church, and now her daughter would enjoy the same experience.

Somewhere between her sixteenth birthday, when she decided her friends were far more fun to be with than attending church, and her surprise pregnancy at age twenty-one, Ellie had lost her faith. Or, more accurately, she had simply ignored the teachings of the Lord.

Nothing like realizing you were going to be a single parent to drag a woman back into the folds of the church. That and praying for forgiveness of her sins.

"Will I know anybody in my Sunday school class?" Wearing a summery dress and her shiny Mary Jane shoes, Torie stretched her little legs in order to step over the cracks in the sidewalk.

"We'll have to see, honey."

Ellie introduced herself and Torie to the teacher. In

less than two minutes, Torie was playing with the other children in the class.

Kissing her daughter goodbye, she went in search of her mother, who was saving her a seat.

Off to the side of the main entrance a group of churchgoers had gathered around a table. The banner on the wall behind the table read Support Paralympics.

Ellie's steps slowed. Her mouth dried. As though she had no control over her own feet, they angled her directly toward the table and the person she instinctively knew would be sitting there.

As she drew closer, the two men who had been blocking her view stepped aside. Arnie spotted her the moment the men moved away. His dark eyes flared momentarily before he could shutter them and coax his expression into one of disinterest. His short-sleeved sport shirt revealed the deeply tanned column of his neck and his muscular arms.

"Looks like you're all dressed up for church," he said.

Ellie's tongue swept across her dry lips. "Yes. I just left Torie in the child-care room."

"I didn't know you ever went to church."

"I don't remember you as a regular churchgoer, either."

"Good point. Having a near-death experience forces a guy to take a look at his life, make some changes."

"Having a baby out of wedlock does the same thing." She cringed, wondering what Arnie would think of her. Wondering if he would condemn her for sleeping with a man outside the sanctity of marriage.

His brows lifted slowly but not in condemnation. "No husband?"

She held herself very still. "Turned out he wasn't interested in being a daddy." Or a husband, for that matter. Foolishly, she'd given herself too easily to a man who couldn't or wouldn't cherish her.

A small V formed between his brows. "Torie's a cute kid. He's missing something special."

She smiled, and some of the tension that had kept her nerves as taut as a piano wire eased. "I think so, too."

"So do you want to be one of my sponsors?" He shoved a glossy brochure across the table to her. "I'm trying to raise a couple of thousand dollars for the Bozeman Paralympics organization. We're hosting a marathon race in a couple of weeks, and I've entered the wheelchair division. I want them to start a Western riding event. You know, cow cutting and trail riding. Events like that. The money will help them do that."

"Sure, I'll sponsor you. Vanna said something about you working with the Paralympics group."

"A couple of years ago some guys in the organization dragged me to Bridger Bowl outside of Bozeman and took me skiing." He handed her a pledge form.

"Skiing? How could you—"

"I'm on a wheelchair basketball team, too. We won the regionals last year." He lifted his chin, challenging her to question him.

"Congratulations." Her admiration for all he had overcome kicked up a notch.

"Paralympics is like Ability Counts Preschool. It's not your disabilities that matter, only your abilities."

She heard chastisement in his voice and knew she deserved the rebuke. She opened her mouth to apologize, but he stopped her.

"The prelude's started. We better get inside." He put some paperweights on the stack of brochures and pledge forms. "You can bring that back to me after church, if you're still interested."

"Of course."

He wheeled out from behind the table and gestured for her to precede him inside, a gentlemanly courtesy. She stepped in front of him, fully aware that he was right behind her. His eyes were on her, his unseen gaze raising her temperature, sending a rush of heat to her face and a wave of guilt to her conscience. Her hand shaking slightly, she took a program from the greeter at the door.

Why on earth had she walked right up to his table? She'd vowed to steer clear of the man. With a firm grip on the church program, she promised she wouldn't forget again.

She spotted her mother in a pew halfway down the first aisle and slid in beside her.

"Did you have problems with Torie?" Barbara whispered.

"No, she's fine."

"What took you so long?"

"I, uh, stopped to talk with someone I knew," Ellie hedged.

"Oh, that's nice, dear."

Pastor Redmond, who looked to be in his fifties, stepped out onto the stage and raised his arms, asking the congregation to rise for the first hymn.

Fumbling for the hymnal, Ellie dropped her program and the pledge form Arnie had given her. Barbara bent to pick them up.

The organist played the first few bars of "Just a Closer Walk with Thee;" then the congregation and choir joined in.

Barbara nudged Ellie with her elbow and handed her back the pledge form. "With a daughter to raise, I didn't imagine you had extra money to give away. I don't think it's a good idea for you to get involved with him again."

Ellie's face flamed hot. Her jaw clenched, and she put the pledge form on the pew beside her.

Other than being a paraplegic, there was nothing wrong with Arnie O'Brien. He was trying to support a worthwhile organization, a worthwhile cause.

In Ellie's view, that made him more able-bodied and *worthwhile* than the good-time Charlie who had impregnated her and then deserted her, leaving her to raise their child alone. She should have steered clear of Jake Radigan.

Just as she should stay clear of Arnie now, but for a far different reason.

Before his accident, Arnie O'Brien would never have deserted a woman or his child. That nobility, that sense of responsibility, hadn't changed simply because he was confined to a wheelchair.

She believed that with all of her heart.

In contrast, Ellie had walked away from the man she'd loved. Scarcely the action of a noble woman. Rather the foolish action of a nineteen-year-old girl.

Propelled by her anger at her mother, and maybe at her own mindless decisions, Ellie scribbled in a larger pledge amount for the Paralympics than she could strictly afford and wrote a check on the spot.

After the church service ended, she ducked out the side door while her mother waited to speak to the minister. She hurried to retrieve Torie from her classroom and returned to find Arnie back at his table, raking in more pledges from his friends.

"Look, Mommy. Arnie's here!" Breaking away from Ellie, Torie beelined it across the patio to Arnie's table. Instead of stopping in front of the table, she squeezed in behind it, next to Arnie.

Sheila stood, backing away from her spot next to Arnie to avoid being stepped on by Torie. Arnie leaned back in his chair, equally startled by child's sudden arrival. "Hey, squirt. What's up?"

"I want to ask you an im-por-tant question."

He glanced toward Ellie, his lips twitching with the threat of a smile. "Sure, ask away."

Torie's face scrunched into its most serious expression. "If my mommy bought me a horse of my very, very own, would you come take care of it for me?"

Ellie choked. "Victoria James! You're not supposed to—"

"I don't know, squirt," Arnie said with equal seriousness. "That would be a big job to take care of a horse."

"I know, and I'm too little. I get a dollar a week allowance. I could pay you that much."

By now those standing around Arnie's table were fully engaged in the conversation, to Ellie's mortification.

"High time you earned an honest dollar, Arnie," a man said.

"Isn't she cute?" a woman said. "I bet when she's a teenager, her father will have to guard the door and lock the windows to keep the boys out."

Ellie had heard enough. "Come on, Torie. We have to find Grandma."

"But Arnie hasn't said he'll take care of my horse yet."

"You don't have a horse, so why don't we worry

about who's going to take care of it if and when you have one?" With an apologetic smile, she handed the pledge form and check to Arnie.

He glanced at the form and the check, then looked up at Ellie. "Preschool teachers must earn more than I realized."

"No such luck, but a guilty conscience can make a person feel generous."

"No need for you to feel guilty."

That was nice of him to say, but she knew it was a lie.

He held up the check. "Don't you want to hold off on this in case I don't actually finish the race?"

"You'll finish. I don't doubt that for a moment." She took Torie's hand. "Tell Arnie goodbye, honey. Grandma's waiting for us."

With her daughter in tow, Ellie hurried toward the parking lot. Having such an outgoing child had its disadvantages.

A muscle pulsed in Arnie's jaw as he watched Ellie and her daughter scurry away. His hands grasped the armrests of his chair, turning his knuckles white.

He had to get a grip on his volatile emotions—a boiling mix of anger, longing and grief—whenever Ellie showed up.

In eight long years he still hadn't figured out how to do that.

Chapter Four

"Shane, we don't throw sand at our friends." Ellie quickly corrected the boy's behavior Monday morning, during outdoor playtime at the preschool.

It was the second week of classes, and she already felt more comfortable with her students, knew all their names and their differing personalities.

They seemed more at ease with her, as well.

On this hot September day, most of the children wore shorts and a T-shirt, their arms and legs darkly tanned from a summer in the sun.

Squinting, Ellie scanned the play yard to check on her other students just as a van pulled into the parking area. A moment later, Arnie rode the wheelchair lift down to the ground. Sheila hopped right off and waited for him.

Ellie's heart stuttered an extra beat and her breathing accelerated. She wondered what had brought Arnie to the school.

Some of the children recognized him and his dog. They raced to the wire fence, shouting his name. Torie was there first.

"Arnie! Arnie! Did you bring your horses?" she cried.

"Not today, squirt." He reached through the fence to tweak Torie's nose. "Hey, kids, you having a good time at school?"

They clamored to answer him all at once, a chorus of high-pitched, excited voices.

Without giving it any thought, Ellie strolled toward the fence and Arnie. He looked dressed for wrangling cows, well-worn, faded jeans, blue work shirt and black Stetson firmly in place. Despite the wheelchair, he managed to radiate sinewy strength, constrained only by his self-confidence.

"Good morning." Her voice a little husky, she forced a smile. "I hope my check didn't bounce already."

His lips twitched, and a sparkle appeared in his dark eyes. "No one has deposited it yet. Should I be worried?"

"No, of course not," she gasped. "I just thought—"

"I came by to see Vanna. There's a school board meeting Thursday night. They're going to vote on Vanna's request to turn Ability Counts into a charter school, kindergarten through third grade."

"Yes, Vanna mentioned that to me." Vanna's dream of expanding Ability Counts from four preschool classrooms to a school for all primary grades was a big reason Ellie had been so eager to accept the job here. The school board hearing was a first step.

"I'm going speak to the need for specialized services for disabled kids. I wanted to touch base with her before the meeting, and I was in town, anyway."

"I think she's in the office."

"Good. See you later, kids." He started to roll up

the ramp, then stopped. "Are you coming to the board meeting?"

"Yes. Vanna wanted as many supporters as possible to attend. We've asked all the parents to be there if they can."

He held her gaze for a moment, making Ellie wonder if he was pleased or dismayed by her answer. Then he nodded. "I'll see you Thursday night."

He wheeled away, Sheila trotting along with him. Ellie exhaled. After all these years, he shouldn't have any effect on her. No racing pulse. No shallow breathing. No ache for what might have been.

But he did affect her. Like a direct shot of caffeine into her veins. A shot she'd better get over soon, before she made a fool of herself.

"All right, children," she said, shaking off the image of Arnie's muscular arms and his sweet smile for the kids. "Let's go inside for story time. Can you all please line up at the door?" She gently herded the youngsters toward the classroom.

Before she had the children settled down, Peggy Numark appeared at the classroom door. Short and petite, Peggy looked like a pixie and would never be taken for the fifty-year-old teacher that she was. More like a mother of one of the children.

"Ellie, Vanna would like to see you in the conference room. She asked me to take your kids for a few minutes."

Ellie frowned. "Now?"

Without any further explanation, Peggy said, "Come along, children. Miss Peggy has the best story she's going to read to you."

Dutifully, the children trailed after the energetic teacher.

With a puzzled shake of her head, Ellie headed for the conference room, located near Vanna's office. She arrived to find Arnie still meeting with Vanna.

Ellie slowed her pace. "Peggy said you wanted—"

"Yes, come in, please." Vanna waved her in the door. "I need to pick your brain a bit."

"She already picked mine," Arnie said, deadpan. "And discovered it was empty."

Ellie's lips twitched. "That's hard to believe."

"Not when you know I spend my days talking to a dog and a bunch of cows," he countered.

Sheila shook her head, rattling her collar, as though she disagreed with Arnie's statement.

Choosing a chair opposite Arnie, Ellie sat down at the long table. "What did you need?" she asked Vanna.

"I want it to be obvious to the school board members at the meeting Thursday that we have a lot of support in the community," Vanna said. "I'm not quite sure how to do that in a subtle, but very visible, way."

"I suggested everyone could wave little American flags," Arnie said. "I think Nate at the grocery store probably has some."

"I'm not keen on that idea. Not specific enough." Vanna's brows lowered in thought, and she rubbed her left arm.

"Maybe a campaign-style button," Ellie said. "Something big enough to be seen at a distance, with Ability Counts printed on it."

Vanna brightened. "Well, now…" She turned to Arnie. "What do you think?"

"I've always thought Ellie was more than just a beautiful woman. She's smart, too." His steady gaze latched onto hers, but he didn't smile.

For a moment, Ellie couldn't breathe. Was that what he'd really thought of her? Could that possibly still be true? It was impossible to read his thoughts when he sent such a mixed message.

Vanna eyed Arnie with interest and smiled. "Then I'd say we have a winner. Can you find out where to get those buttons made?" she asked Ellie.

"I may have to drive to Manhattan, but a copier store should be able to do the job."

"Perfect," Vanna announced.

She stood to end the meeting, and Ellie followed suit, still hearing the echo of Arnie's words in her head. *Beautiful and smart.*

After school, Ellie drove the ten miles to Manhattan. She made the arrangements for the buttons to be ready in time for the meeting, then decided to stop on the way home to say hello to Mindy at her shop in Potter Creek.

"How come we're going to a knitting store?" Torie asked.

"A friend of mine works there. I want to say hello to her and have her meet you." Ellie checked the rearview mirror and eased out of her parking spot.

"Does she have any kids I can play with?"

"I'm afraid not." Reversing direction, she drove out of the parking lot and turned west, toward the center of Potter Creek. The small town served a population of maybe five thousand people in the surrounding area. For any major shopping excursion, the locals drove to Manhattan, or all the way to Bozeman. "Maybe she'll have some yarn crafts you'd like to make."

"Are you going to buy some yarn to make me something?"

"I might. You could use a new sweater for fall."

Main Street looked much like it always had: grocery, hardware and drugstore on one side of the street; a diner, real estate and newspaper offices on the opposite side. At the far end of town, a brick building served as city hall and was adjacent to the popular public swimming pool. A stark contrast to downtown Spokane or even to the suburbs of that sprawling, big city with its traffic congestion and the press of a growing population.

To its advantage, however, Potter Creek was a size that a person could get her brain wrapped around, a comfortable, friendly place to live. Schoolkids rode their bikes on Main Street, and neighbors caught up with local news while lingering in front of the grocery store.

Home, Ellie thought. She'd stayed away too long.

She pulled up in front of Aunt Martha's Knitting and Notions. The front window featured posters of class offerings and autumn specials on wool yarn. A cute knitted vest adorned a clear-plastic mannequin.

"We're here," Ellie announced. "Out you go."

Dozens of memories flooded Ellie. Aunt Martha teaching her to knit, despite Ellie's initial lack of enthusiasm. Making friends with Mindy, dragging her into attempting new things, like floating down the river on a homemade wooden raft. When the raft fell apart, they both nearly drowned. The ever-responsible Arnie had to rescue them.

A frown tugged at her forehead. The reckless driving accident with his brother behind the wheel had stolen so much from Arnie, not just the use of his legs, but his self-image, as well. Adjusting to his new circumstances had to have been difficult.

Guilt tightened a knot in her stomach. *You should have stayed to help him*, she thought.

Holding Torie's hand, Ellie stepped inside the small knitting shop, setting off tiny wind chimes above the door.

"Oh, my…" she murmured. Over the years the shop had been upgraded and was chock-full of merchandise. In addition to bins of all types of yarn, one whole corner area displayed needle-craft samples and bins of thread in every color imaginable.

Mindy appeared from a back room. "Ellie? It's you, isn't it!" Arms open wide, she rushed forward to embrace Ellie. "Oh, my goodness. Daniel said you were back in town, but I wasn't home when you came to the ranch and I missed seeing you at church. I'm so glad you dropped by."

"I had to check out my old haunts, right?" One of those smiles that comes from the heart and lightens your spirits lifted Ellie's lips. "I can't believe the changes you've made to the shop. And by the way, I understand double congratulations are in order, Mrs. O'Brien, on your marriage and your pregnancy."

A quick flush colored Mindy's cheeks as she laughed. With her blond hair and fair complexion, blushing had once been the bane of her existence, particularly when Daniel had flirted with her.

"And this must be your daughter Daniel was telling me about," Mindy said. "I understand she wants a horse of her own."

"I'm afraid that's not in our immediate future. Victoria, say hello to Mrs. O'Brien."

"Hello." Torie shook hands with Mindy. "Do you like horses, too?"

"I certainly do. My husband raises some of the finest quarter horses in the whole state."

Torie put on her most serious expression. "Maybe someday my mommy could buy a horse from you."

Ellie hooked her arm around her daughter's shoulders and gave her an affectionate squeeze. "I'm afraid Torie's a bit fixated on horses these days."

"Most kids around here are."

"I told Torie you might have some craft projects suitable for her."

Mindy brightened. "I do. I'll be getting more in before Christmas, but come see what I have now." She took Torie's hand and walked her to the back of the shop.

Ellie followed. When she was living in Spokane, working full-time as a waitress and taking as many college classes as she could manage, plus caring for Torie, it had been hard to make friends.

Coming back to Potter Creek meant she'd have more time and have the chance to renew old friendships. Perhaps that was what coming home was all about.

"Do you run the shop all by yourself?" Ellie asked.

"Mostly. Sometimes Aunt Martha fills in for an afternoon or two to give me a break, and I have Ivy from the diner stand in for me occasionally."

Ellie frowned. "How are you going to handle things after the baby arrives?"

She smiled brightly. "Oh, I may close down for a few weeks. Then I'll bring him or her along with me. That should work for the first year or so."

"Watch out for those toddler years," Ellie warned,

thinking her friend might not fully realize what an energy drain a child could be. "There's no keeping them corralled in a playpen then."

"I suppose you're right," Mindy conceded.

While Ellie and Mindy caught up with their respective lives Torie searched through the assortment of craft possibilities.

"So, um, where's Torie's father?" Mindy asked.

"I haven't a clue. Apparently, being a father wasn't on his to-do list." Jake Radigan hadn't been a college student, but he'd hung out with some of the guys, showing off his motorcycle, revving the engine. Apparently he was a good mechanic, because he kept his friends' junker cars running, working out of a garage behind his rental house.

His "wild side" had attracted Ellie, she supposed. His lack of roots.

That same lack of roots meant that he rode off into the sunset on his bike virtually the moment he learned Ellie was pregnant.

In retrospect, that was probably for the best.

Torie returned from her search in the back of the shop with an "Old Woman in a Shoe" craft that she could lace with red yarn and hang on her bedroom wall.

"I found some yarn that would make a pretty sweater for me," Torie announced.

"Well, then, let's take a look." Ellie followed her daughter to a wall filled with bins of yarn. Mindy joined them.

Torie held up a skein of emerald green sport-weight yarn. "The green goes with my eyes."

"Yes, it does, sweetie," Mindy announced.

Ellie thought so, too. The pale green eyes were the only trace of Torie's father she saw in her daughter.

"All right, honey. We'll have to pick out a pattern you like." During the evenings, sitting with her mother, watching TV, would be a good time to knit.

After pouring over pattern books and making a selection, Ellie was paying for their purchases when Mindy said, "You'll both have to come out to the ranch for supper one day soon."

Credit card in hand, Ellie stiffened. "Oh, I don't know."

"You must. My favorite brother-in-law is the best cook in the world. He and Daniel remodeled the kitchen years ago, so it's totally accessible for him. You should taste his chili." She brought her fingertips to her lips and kissed them. "Absolutely delicious…if you don't mind burning your tonsils out, as Daniel would say."

A nervous titter escaped Ellie's lips, but eating dinner with Arnie—at the ranch or anywhere else—wasn't on her to-do list. Or, more important, on Arnie's list, despite what he'd said about Ellie's intelligence and looks. Those words had been for Vanna's benefit, hadn't they?

"It's sweet of you to ask. But you know, I'm still settling in." She gave Mindy another quick hug. "We'll get together soon, I promise." *Sometime when Arnie is far, far away.*

"But you and Arnie used to have a thing going. I thought you'd want to—"

"That *thing* was a long time ago, Mindy." Ellie didn't imagine for a moment that Arnie would want a repeat of their past. "Sometimes you just can't go back."

Waving goodbye to Mindy, Ellie ushered her daughter outside.

A few minutes later, as she pulled into the driveway

of her mother's house, she thought about how the tension between her and Arnie—the undercurrent of anger he exuded—was her fault.

In a small town such as this, she would be seeing him often. She needed to clear the air. Apologize. Whether he acknowledged or accepted her apology was up to him.

She needed to make the effort.

Chapter Five

Wiping her sweaty palm unobtrusively on her skirt, Ellie braced herself Thursday evening for whatever might happen at the school board meeting. She kept a smile on her face, desperately trying not to let her nerves show. Whatever happened tonight was important to the future of Ability Counts.

Standing at the back door of the Potter Creek Elementary School multipurpose room, she greeted parents and supporters of Ability Counts as they arrived. She gave each person one of the campaign-style buttons she'd ordered in Manhattan so they could demonstrate the community's support to the school trustees.

They were, after all, elected officials.

"Hello, Mrs. Axelrod," she said, handing Nancy's mother a button. "Thank you for coming tonight."

Mrs. Axelrod pinned the red, white and blue button on the lapel of her lightweight jacket.

Smiling, Ellie turned to greet the next parent coming in the door.

Instead of a parent, however, it was Arnie who wheeled into the multipurpose room, Sheila trotting proudly along beside him. Dressed in a long-sleeved Western-cut shirt with a turquoise bolo tie, Arnie looked every bit the contemporary Indian chief come to take charge. His white shirt set off his sun-burnished complexion, and the squint lines formed a fan at the corners of his eyes.

"Looks like you're the flower girl passing out roses at a wedding," he said.

Her eyes flared at his mentioning a *wedding*, and she struggled to dismiss the comment as meaningless. "As you know, we're hoping for a sea of red, white and blue to influence the board members."

"Hope it works." He patted his chest right over his heart. "Pin away."

She hesitated. Everyone else had pinned on their own button.

Trying for casual, she handed Arnie the box of pins, took one and bent down to pin it on his shirt. Her face close to his, she caught the hint of mint on his breath and the faint aroma of a woodsy aftershave on his smooth cheeks.

Her fingers trembled as she slid the pin through the fabric of his shirt.

"Careful. I bleed easy."

She lifted her gaze from the pin to his eyes. Dark. Deep as a mountain pool. Captivating. They immobilized her with their intensity.

She pricked herself. "Ouch!" Stepping back, she sucked on the tip of her finger, tasting blood.

His lips curved up ever so slightly. "Maybe I ought to pin it on myself."

"Good idea." A tremor shook her voice, and she

licked her lips. She handed him the pin, which he attached to his shirt with ease.

"Nothing to it." The amused crook of his brow caused a little flip of Ellie's stomach.

Only when he wheeled down the aisle did Ellie take another breath. That man had the most amazing effect on her, not that it mattered. Obviously, her effect on him was negative, a keep-away-from-me reaction, as though she were the carrier of a dreaded disease.

Except he'd asked her to pin the button on him.

The closest she'd been to him in the past eight years.

A shiver raised gooseflesh on her arms. *Close enough for a kiss.*

The multipurpose room had begun to fill, and the school trustees were beginning to take their places on the risers at the front. Five of the six trustees were men; two of them she recognized as merchants in town. The one woman, who looked to be in her sixties, was wearing an Ability Counts pin. No doubt Vanna's friend and a supporter.

When the chairman gaveled the meeting to order, Vanna signaled Ellie to come sit next to her in the front row. She started forward before she realized she'd have to squeeze past Arnie, whose wheelchair was parked at the end of the row, in order to get to the seat Vanna had indicated.

So be it. Being up front to support the expansion of Ability Counts was part of her job. Her career. Arnie would simply have to live with it.

So would she, Ellie thought as she eased past first Sheila, then Arnie, to take her seat.

"How'd we do for supporters?" Vanna asked.

Ellie showed her the box of pins. She'd started with fifty, and now there were less than ten.

Vanna smiled and gave her a thumbs-up. "Our families are loyal. The trustees have to give us that."

Ellie agreed. But that didn't mean the trustees would vote their way. Based on her research, no school board in the state of Montana had yet approved a charter school, claiming all the limited tax dollars should be used to support public schools. If Vanna could pull this off, it would be amazing.

It didn't take long to get through the agenda to the request from Ability Counts.

"I believe Ms. Coulter wishes to speak to her request," the board president said.

Vanna stood. "I do, Mr. Wright. Thank you." She made her way to the podium.

Ellie remembered having Patrick Wright as her government teacher in high school. Retired now, he'd been an adequate teacher, she supposed, although the subject hadn't been of much interest to her. Now she wished she'd paid more attention.

"Honorable trustees, ladies and gentlemen," Vanna began. "I'm sure most of you are aware of Ability Counts Preschool and our specialized program to integrate disabled youngsters and mainstream them with 'normal' children. Although, in my view, every child is an individual with unique abilities, so using the term 'normal' is a misnomer. I'm grateful that a good many of our parents and friends are here this evening to support turning Ability Counts into a charter school." She turned to the audience. "Thank you all for coming."

Vanna went on to describe studies that proved the value of early mainstreaming of disabled children, the benefits to the normal students as well and the advantages to the community such a school would provide.

Then she invited Arnie to speak.

He wheeled himself to the podium. Vanna handed him the microphone before she took her seat again with an audible sigh and an expression that suggested she was bone weary.

Ellie gave her employer an encouraging smile.

Arnie addressed the trustees with Sheila sitting alertly at his side, almost as though she was witnessing to the need for special programs for the disabled, as well.

"As most of you know, I became disabled as an adult. I'd already ridden a horse, played football, gone out on dates. But imagine what it's like for a child who spends his entire life with his peers literally looking down on him, running faster, jumping higher than he can. How does he gain his self-esteem when he is so different? Not by shunting him off with others who have the same problems. No, he or she has to be accepted and befriended by those who don't see him or her as different.

"That's what Ability Counts accomplishes by integrating young children in a way that makes them all feel normal."

Ellie's heart expanded with pride in the school's accomplishments and in Arnie's ability to communicate the value of Vanna's dream. She knew the audience didn't see Arnie as disabled. Not in any way that mattered. He was far too competent and confident, a natural leader. A man to be reckoned with.

She wished her mother could see Arnie as she did. Surely she'd realize how lucky any woman would feel to be loved by such a man.

And how stupid Ellie felt for having walked away from even the possibility. At nineteen, she'd been too young to fully realize what she was giving up.

A few parents took a turn at the microphone; then the trustees stated their positions.

The one woman on the board supported Ability Counts. The men, however, cited practicalities: budget limitations, public funds for public schools, adequate existing programs.

The final vote was five to one against creating a charter school.

Dipping her head in disappointment, Ellie closed her eyes and tried to accept the trustees' verdict. In the past few years, she'd learned that God's will didn't always coincide with what she wanted—or thought she wanted. But in the end she had to trust the Lord knew what He was doing.

That was a leap of faith that didn't always come easily.

Vanna patted her on the shoulder. "Chin up, my dear. This was only the first skirmish. The battle has barely begun. Let's have a cup of coffee and mull over our strategy for the next round."

She smelled of citrus. Oranges ripening in the sun, he thought.

Using the hand controls of his specially equipped van, Arnie drove to the diner after the meeting. He chided himself for letting Ellie get so close. For agreeing to have coffee with her and Vanna. For risking the temptation of being near her again.

What had he been thinking?

He had to be the biggest glutton for punishment this

side of the Continental Divide. If he kept this up, it would be all downhill from now on.

"Your master isn't the swiftest wheel on the chair," he said to Sheila, who was safely harnessed on the floor behind him.

Apparently agreeing, Sheila whined and laid her head down on her outstretched paws.

Vanna and Ellie had beaten him into town. Vanna held open the diner's door, and he wheeled inside.

The interior of Potter Creek Diner was decorated in early Western decor with paneled walls, old photos of rodeo cowboys and stuffed animal heads mounted around the room. Although Arnie had done some deer and elk hunting in the days when he'd been able to walk, he'd never been eager to have the animals stuffed and mounted in his house. It was enough that they'd provided meat for the family and neighbors.

"Hey, Ivy." He wheeled his way through the maze of tables to where the owner's daughter had made room at a table for his chair. No other customers were around, and it was only an hour until closing. "Not much action here during the late shift this evening."

"It was busier early." In her early twenties, Ivy had dark eyes and brunet hair, which she wore in a ponytail when she was working. "I don't mind working late. When it's quiet, I can get my homework done."

"College, right?" he asked.

A flash of pride shone in her eyes. "I'm majoring in fine arts, but I've gotta take a whole bunch of art history classes if I want to graduate."

"Good for you," Vanna said, taking the seat opposite him. "Do you know Ellen James? She grew up in town and came back to teach in my preschool. This is Ivy Nelson."

The two younger women greeted each other.

Ellie sat down in the chair next to Arnie. Close enough that he could see the reflection of the overhead lights in her striking blue eyes. He inhaled, wondering if he could catch that citrus scent again, then chided himself for being such a fool.

"What can I get for you folks?" Ivy asked.

"Just coffee for me," Vanna said.

"I'd better have decaf," Ellie said.

Arnie looked up at Ivy. "Make mine the leaded variety, and I'll have a dish of your double dark chocolate ice cream."

"You got it." Ivy headed back behind the counter to round up their order.

An "I remember" smile tilted Ellie's lips. "You and Mindy always were chocoholics."

"Some things never change," he said, his voice low and filled with the same memories.

She glanced away. "And some things do."

An ache bloomed in his chest for what might have been. He forcefully tamped it down. "So, Vanna, what's our next strategy?"

"I didn't really believe the trustees would go for the charter idea, but it was worth a try." She rotated her head as though trying to loosen the tension in her neck. "Their denial means we'll have to fund the expansion from some other source and run Ability Counts as a private school."

"That will be pretty expensive, particularly for families already burdened with medical bills for their children," Ellie commented.

"That's why we need a generous funding source. I don't want to have to turn any child away."

As Ivy delivered their coffees and his ice cream, Arnie considered the difficulty of raising large sums of money both for expansion and ongoing support. The need posed a gigantic hurdle for Ability Counts. More so than for Paralympics, which was a national organization.

Vanna blew on her coffee before taking a sip. "I had an architect produce a concept drawing of the expanded building and grounds. Our next step is to convince the city council to approve a building permit."

"Do you own the land?" Ellie asked.

"The Ability Counts corporation does. Two years ago Willie Tompkins donated enough adjacent land for the buildings and a play yard."

Arnie spooned some ice cream into his mouth and felt the kick of a sugar high. He knew Tompkins. The octogenarian was said to be related to the original Caleb Potter, who founded the town. Vanna must have done some fancy schmoozing to get the old guy to deed the land to the school.

"I've already talked to the mayor," Vanna said. "Arnie, do you know any of the council members personally?"

He shrugged. "I've had some business dealings with Ted Rojas. He's an okay guy."

"Good. See if you can get an appointment with him." Vanna turned to Ellie. "Why don't you try to meet with Jeffrey Robbins? Try to find out where he would stand."

Alarm bells went off in Arnie's head. Jeffrey Robbins was the slickest guy in town, not someone Arnie wanted Ellie anywhere near. From the stories he'd heard, Robbins had broken a dozen women's hearts from here to Bozeman. "Robbins has been involved with some shaky real estate development deals. Maybe I ought to talk to him."

Ellie's forehead pleated and her brows drew together. "If I only have to find out his position, I think I can manage that."

"Yeah, well, he's sort of a ladies' man. If he gives you a line… Well, don't fall for it." That was a stupid comment, he realized. Knowing it was none of his business who Ellie saw or what line she fell for, he turned his attention back to his ice cream. The rich flavor of chocolate suddenly tasted bitter on his tongue.

"Thanks for the warning, but I think I'll be able to handle it."

A stab of what had to be heartburn caught Arnie in the chest. He shoved his ice cream dish aside. "Sure. No problem."

"Well, you two…" Vanna stood, which caused Sheila to scramble to her feet, as well. "I've had a long day, so I'll be on my way home. Enjoy your coffee." She placed a ten-dollar bill on the table to cover the check. She quickly turned and headed out the door.

Surprised by Vanna's abrupt departure, Arnie said, "Guess I should get back to the ranch. Morning chores come earlier than I would like."

Ellie's hand covered his on the table. "Don't go just yet. I think we need to talk."

He looked at her hand, her fair skin almost white against his darker complexion. Her fingers delicate compared to his work-roughened hands, all nicks and scratches. Her nails short and neatly trimmed. Her palm like a soft, cool caress on his skin.

His throat tightened and he withdrew his hand. "What's to talk about?"

"I owe you an apology for how I handled things after your accident."

"A wise man once said an apology was about as valuable as an empty bowl of sugar."

She visibly flinched, and Arnie chastised himself for being so rough on her. She was trying to do the right thing. What had happened to his ability to forgive and forget?

"I'm sorry." Her voice was low and filled with regret. Her eyes focused solely on his, darkening in their intensity. "There's no excuse for what I did. I was young and frightened. Those first few days you were in the hospital, I'd never seen you so helpless. When you told me to go away, I panicked."

He straightened and lifted his jaw, his defenses on alert. "I never said any such thing." He wouldn't have, couldn't have, told her to go away.

"You were in and out of consciousness for days. How do you know what you said or didn't say?"

Whatever happened he couldn't sit there watching her pain thin her lips and wrinkle her forehead and tears glitter in her eyes. He was a coward when it came to Ellie. Too chickenhearted to take a gamble and lose.

Shaking his head, he rolled back from the table. "Forget about it, Ellie. It's ancient history. Nothing has changed. I'm exactly what you were afraid I'd become. I've got a handicapped license plate on my van to prove it."

Not wanting to hear what she might say, he charged toward the door, pressing hard. The thought that she might agree was too painful to contemplate. Too painful to risk hearing the words from the woman he had once loved.

The woman who had left him when he needed her the most.

When he'd worked his way behind the wheel of the van, he glanced toward the diner. Ellie was standing in the doorway, her hand covering her mouth.

Guilt nailed him in the sternum, driving the air from his lungs.

I'm sorry. How much courage it must have taken for her to speak those two simple words.

How much more courage would he need to accept them?

Chapter Six

The pain started in Ellie's chest, radiating outward until it throbbed at her temples. Her throat was so constricted, she could barely breathe. A tremor had shaken her body as she watched Arnie storm out the diner.

Fighting tears, she'd followed him as far as the door. Saw him get in his van. A minute later, the van's headlights shattered the darkness and spotlighted Ellie.

Spotlighted her failings.

Dear God, how could I have hurt Arnie so badly? How can I make it right again?

She rubbed her temple with her fingertips. He hadn't accepted her apology. From the way he acted, he never would.

Guilt was the hammer that pummeled her conscience, made her blood pulse icy cold through her veins and blurred her vision. *I'm so sorry.*

The last day she'd seen Arnie in the hospital, he had made it abundantly clear she should leave him alone. A part of her had not wanted to believe him. She could be stubborn. Wait it out until his injuries had healed. By then he would change his mind, she'd hoped.

Then he'd rolled over, turning his back on her, and she'd lost hope. Her foolish pride had demanded that she do just as he'd said. She'd leave him alone.

Exactly as her mother had encouraged her to do.

Now she knew she'd been wrong. Lacking in trust that she and Arnie, together, could have made a go of it.

Now it was too late.

With a discouraged sigh, she drove home. She found her mother in the small living room with its aging, over-stuffed furniture, watching a police story on TV.

"How did the school board meeting go?"

"They turned down our request." Beaten and dejected, Ellie shrugged out of her lightweight jacket and draped it across the back of the couch. "Did Torie get to bed on time?"

"Oh, yes. We read a book together. She really is reading, you know. And here she isn't even five yet. Of course, you were an early reader, too. I remember when you were four, the librarian was so impressed with you."

"I remember. Sorry, but I'm really tired. Thanks for watching Torie, Mom. I'm going to bed. See you in the morning."

Ellie fled to the bedroom that had been hers growing up. The twin bed with a trundle for company, the spread navy-blue with red-and-white squares. Posters of punk rock and heavy metal musical groups she had once favored had been removed, but the marks left by masking tape were still visible. She needed to repaint the room, make it a reflection of who she was now, not the impulsive girl of her youth.

She sat down heavily on the side of the bed.

Tears blurred her vision as she opened the drawer in the bed table and retrieved her Bible. The faux leather cover was worn from repeated use over the past five years, the gold lettering flaked away.

She laid the Bible in her lap. It opened automatically to the passage she had long ago committed to memory: Proverbs 3:5, Trust in the Lord with all your heart and lean not on your own understanding.

All Ellie could do was to lead as Christian a life as she was able and ask for forgiveness when she fell short.

That ethereal goal had never been harder than it was tonight.

She couldn't change the past. But how could she make the future right?

"Will I get to ride Patches again?" Torie asked from the back of the school van.

It was Friday morning, and the preschoolers were on their way to the O'Brien ranch for their weekly riding lesson. A knot of dread tightened in Ellie's stomach at the thought of seeing Arnie after the way things had been left last night.

"I don't know, honey," she said.

"I hope I get to go fast this time. I don't like a poky horse."

Torie received a chorus of agreement from her classmates.

"Just remember you all have to do what Daniel and Arnie tell you to do. We want you to be safe."

Ellie's heart accelerated as the van bumped over the cattle guard at the entrance to the ranch. A few head of beef cattle grazed near the roadway. They looked up, slowly chewing their cud. Ellie sincerely wished she could be that calm.

She inhaled a bracing breath. She'd done what she

could to make amends. If that wasn't enough to restore a bit of the friendship she'd once shared with Arnie, she'd have to let it go. Let God handle it. If He didn't think she deserved to be friends with Arnie, then she'd have to live with that knowledge.

As she parked, she noticed plywood now covered the framing on the house under construction and a riverstone chimney had been erected. Cutouts in the plywood showed where the windows would be. Progress was definitely being made.

"All right, we're here," Ellie said.

The children cheered and scrambled for the exits.

"Go join Miss Vanna and her class."

Keeping an eye out for Arnie, Ellie trailed along behind her students. By the time she reached Vanna, Daniel had appeared out of the barn, his young helper right behind him.

"Good morning, kids. You ready to ride?"

"Yes!" they responded in a shrill chorus.

"Great!" He grinned broadly. "Let's start with Miss Vanna's group. You go with Marc. He'll help you mount up. The rest of you can come with me."

"Where's Arnie?" Torie asked.

"He had some business in Bozeman this morning."

Relief and disappointment battled for primacy, the former easing the tension in Ellie's neck and shoulders, the latter dropping like a rock to her stomach.

Was he avoiding her? Or did he really have business elsewhere? She didn't know and tried not to care.

Daniel led her flock of children into the barn. "You all remember where we keep the brushes?"

Nancy, on her crutches, led the race to the Peg-Board

where brushes, hoof picks and other grooming tools were hung in place.

Ellie experienced a moment of pride at the independent streak Nancy was beginning to exhibit.

Gathering the children around a placid buckskin mare named Marigold, Daniel put the children to work combing her mane and brushing her coat. Ellie steadied the step stool Billy was using to reach the horse's mane.

"Sorry to hear the school board turned down the charter request," Daniel said, standing next to Ellie, where they could both keep track of the children.

"Evidently Vanna expected they would. She's starting to look for private funding."

He eased a child away from the back of the mare. "Don't get so close. She can kick you," he warned.

The child made a wide pass around Marigold's rump so he could work on the other side.

"Mindy asked me to invite you, Torie and your mother to Sunday supper after church," Daniel said.

Ellie's head snapped around. "This Sunday?"

"Sure. Assuming you don't have other plans."

"Um, no, but—"

"Mommy," Torie whispered. "If we come to supper, maybe Arnie will let me ride a horse again."

Amazing what little ears can hear. "We'll talk about that later, honey." Ellie stepped back away from Torie and her classmates. "I'm not sure us coming to dinner is a good idea," she whispered to Daniel.

His dark eyes widened, raising his brows. "Why not?"

She puffed out a weary sigh. "Arnie is still angry with me for leaving town after his accident."

"After all this time? I know you two were once an

item, but I thought he'd gotten past you leaving town and all."

"I'm afraid not. I've tried to apologize, but he wasn't interested in hearing it."

Taking off his Stetson, Daniel ran his fingers through his raven-black hair before resetting his hat. "It's not like him to hold a grudge."

"It's not a grudge, exactly." Far more personal than that, she suspected. More like a deep wound that refused to heal.

Carson wheeled up to Daniel. "I'm done brushing the parts I can reach. Can I feed Marigold an apple now?"

"Sure." He fetched a plastic baggie of cut-up apples from a nearby workbench. "Okay, kids. Put away your brushes, and you can give Marigold a treat. Remember, one at a time."

The children delighted in the graze of Marigold's soft lips on their palms as she delicately plucked a quartered apple from their hands.

By the time each child had a turn feeding Marigold, it was time to switch with the children who had been riding.

"I look at it this way," Daniel said to Ellie before she went out to the corral. "Mindy's your friend. She's invited you to have dinner with us on Sunday. Arnie's invited, too. If he doesn't want to come, that's his choice."

Ellie wished the decision was that simple. She didn't want to compound Arnie's bad feelings toward her or hurt him all over again. But she did want to renew her friendship with Mindy. Daniel, too.

She had no idea how her mother would react to the invitation.

"Let me think about it. Tell Mindy I'll give her a call or stop by the knit shop."

As soon as Ellie and her daughter returned home that afternoon, Torie went running into the house to find her grandma BarBar. Ellie followed her inside.

"I got to ride Patches again, and the boy let me steer by myself, but he didn't want me to go fast."

A warm smile creased Barbara's face. "That's nice, dear."

"And, Grandma." Torie bopped around from one foot to another like a Mexican jumping bean. "Mr. Daniel invited us to dinner on Sunday, and maybe I can ride on the horsey again. Can't I, Mommy?"

Ellie cringed inwardly. She'd planned to approach the dinner invitation when she and her mother were alone.

"I'm not sure we're going to accept the invitation, honey."

"But, Mommy, I want to ride Patches again!" She planted her fists on her hips like an angry fishwife and glared at Ellie.

"We'll talk about it later," Ellie insisted.

"I want to talk about it now!"

Controlling her own temper and her roiling emotions regarding Arnie, Ellie forced patience into her voice. "I don't want to give you a time-out, Victoria. You know you're not allowed to talk to me like that."

"But, Mommy…"

Ellie held up one finger as a warning.

Her daughter's face crumbled into a despairing expression, and tears bubbled to the surface.

When Ellie held up a second finger, Torie sobbed aloud, whirled and ran to her bedroom, slamming the door behind her. Given that show of temper, Ellie could only imagine what fun having a teenager in the house would be.

"You're going to dinner at the O'Brien ranch?" her mother asked.

"We've all been invited. I was going to discuss it with you later."

"Is he going to be there?"

"If you mean Arnie, I don't know if he'll be there or not. The invitation was extended by Daniel on Mindy's behalf and includes you."

Her hand shaking slightly, Barbara picked up a pair of Torie's jeans that she'd been mending. "I can't think of any reason they'd invite me."

"Mindy stayed at our house a couple of nights that summer when she visited Aunt Martha. I'm sure she doesn't want you to feel left out."

"Well, I don't want to interfere with you young people. You'll enjoy yourselves more without an old lady around to cramp your fun."

Ellie exhaled a weary sigh. "Mother, I wish you'd get to know Arnie better. He isn't nearly as incapacitated as Uncle Bob was. Yes, he has some limitations, but he's every inch the man Dad was." Smart. Good with children. Except for his paralysis, physically the equal of any man. And heart-stoppingly handsome.

Barbara's face turned red, and Ellie knew she'd gone too far. Her and her quick retorts. When would she ever grow up?

"I'm sorry, Mother. I didn't mean to—"

"It's no matter. You go if you must, but give Mindy my regrets. I'll manage Sunday supper on my own."

The larger question was, how would Ellie manage sitting at the same table with Arnie without making a fool of herself?

* * *

A warm breeze swept in through the window openings of Arnie's unfinished house Saturday afternoon and blew the roll of blueprints off the worktable.

"Sheila, pick up," he commanded.

He needn't have bothered. Sheila had moved almost before the blueprints hit the floor, retrieving them for Arnie.

"Good girl." He nuzzled his face against hers and scratched behind her ears. She was an extension of his arms, a substitute for his legs, and made his life easier in a thousand little ways. Getting a service dog was an admission of his limitations and one of the smartest things he'd ever done.

A load of drywall had been delivered that afternoon and was stacked in the corner. Arnie would start putting it up this coming week, when he had some free time.

Pride drove him to be a part of the construction of his own house. He couldn't climb a ladder or install shingles on the roof. But what was between the floor and as high as his arms could reach would be his own doing.

After a day filled with the sound of his buddies installing siding and insulation and making smart remarks, the house was quiet now. Peaceful. On the breeze, the occasional birdsong or quiet low of his cattle reached him, the nicker of Daniel's quarter horses and the buzz of flies nearer at hand. There'd been a time when he hadn't thought he'd live to hear the sounds of the ranch again.

The moment he realized Daniel had lost control of his truck. The sight of the boulder filling the windshield just before they crashed.

The excruciating pain that followed.

And then the darkness that had cocooned him. He hadn't wanted to leave that darkness. There was safety there. A kind of peace.

But they brought him back, the doctors and nurses. Daniel. And Ellie, holding his hand every time he broke through the surface of that black, bottomless hole.

Tears burned in his eyes, and he swiped them away with the back of his hand.

Sheila whined.

"It's okay, girl. It's okay."

At the sound of approaching footsteps, Arnie shook off his morose mood.

"Hey, bro, Mindy says dinner's ready in ten minutes."

He wheeled toward Daniel. "Be right with you. Gotta clean up first."

"No problem." Daniel stepped out of his way. "Ellie called a few minutes ago. Mindy invited her and Torie to Sunday supper. She accepted."

Arnie braked his wheelchair hard. "She's coming to dinner? Tomorrow?"

"Yep. After church. Her mother was invited, too, but she declined."

Anger pounded against his ribs like a four-pound hammer. "So what am I supposed to do?"

"Come to supper, like you always do. Mindy's slow cooking a roast. All you have to do is show up."

Show up and face the one thing he could never dare dream of having—Ellie.

"I'll eat at the diner tomorrow." He gave the wheelchair a shove. His chair didn't budge.

"What's with you, man? You can't go on avoiding

Ellie. It's not like she was the one who put you in that chair. I did that."

A muscle flexed in his jaw. "Let go of my chair."

"She's the best thing that could happen to you. You've been wearing your heart on your sleeve since she showed up. Give it a chance, bro."

Whipping his chair around hard, Arnie broke Daniel's grip and wheeled away from him. "I'll decide what's good for me, Danny boy. Not you. Not Mindy." And not Vanna Coulter, who, he suspected, had matchmaking on her mind, too. "Stay out of it, all of you."

He would not be coerced or cajoled into playing gracious host to Ellie and her daughter. And he wouldn't be suckered by well-meaning matchmakers into courting her, either.

That was not how it was going to be.

Chapter Seven

Upset with himself, Arnie knew his conscience, and maybe his good sense and sleepless night, had gotten to him. He decided not to eat Sunday supper at the diner. He couldn't be that rude to Ellie and her daughter. It wasn't their fault he was no longer the man he used to be.

He'd seen Ellie at church this morning. She'd had a bright, friendly smile for everyone she greeted. Her shiny auburn hair swung loosely at her shoulders as she walked, catching the sunlight like warm flames, and stirring thoughts he didn't want to entertain.

Didn't dare entertain.

Because the truth was, he wanted to touch her hair, lace the silken strands through his fingers, inhale the citrus scent. Coward that he was, he knew the flames caught in her hair would burn him.

He changed into jeans and a work shirt after he got home from church, and maybe took a little extra time combing his hair. He'd excuse himself as soon as the meal was over, retreat to his house and start putting up the drywall. No harm done.

"You need any help with supper?" he asked Mindy as he rolled into the kitchen, Sheila trotting beside him. The room smelled of beef cooking and freshly baked bread.

"No, I'm good. Thanks." She wore a butcher-style apron printed with colorful quarter horses over her church clothes, which didn't quite hide the growing paunch of her pregnant tummy. "I'll just pour the iced tea and milk and serve everything once Ellie and Torie get here."

"Okay. Let me know if you need me." He wheeled into the living room, where Daniel was sprawled on the couch, reading the Sunday paper.

Glancing out the front window, Arnie spotted Ellie's compact coming up the drive. The dust that rose behind it hung like a brown banner in the still afternoon air.

He swallowed hard and licked his lips. His fingers tapped a syncopated rhythm on the arm of his wheelchair. Maybe he should've gone to the diner, after all.

He beat a retreat to the kitchen. "Ellie's coming down the driveway. I'll pour the iced tea for you."

Mindy whirled and leveled a frown at him. "Why don't you go open the door for her instead?"

"Daniel's in the living room. He'll let her in."

Shaking her head, Mindy tugged off her apron and tossed it over the back of a chair. "Men! Humph! I'll do it."

Temporarily rescued from another face-to-face meeting with Ellie, Arnie blew out a sigh. *Coward!*

The house suddenly filled with girlish laughter, as though Mindy and Ellie were teenagers again. The sound took Arnie back to lazy days spent at the river park, water fights and strolls along the trail on moon-lit nights.

He squeezed his eyes shut, but the memories couldn't be easily vanquished.

"Come on into the kitchen," Mindy said. "Every-thing is ready to go."

"Oh, I love your hardwood floors." Wide-eyed and smiling, Ellie walked into the kitchen. She'd changed into slacks and a sleeveless T-shirt that bared her tanned, slightly freckled arms. "And look at this. Talk about top-of-the-line appliances and miles of counter space. My apartment in Spokane was so small, the whole thing would have fit inside your kitchen."

"Daniel and Arnie did most of the remodeling them-selves. They didn't think they needed a formal dining room, so they created a family kitchen."

Ellie came to a halt near the table. "Hello, Arnie."

"Hi." *Great conversation opener*, he admonished himself, not proud that he had turned tongue-tied.

Torie pushed her way past her mother. "Can I sit next to Arnie and his doggy, Mommy? Can I?"

"You'll have to ask Mindy. She's our hostess."

The child looked up at Mindy with her innocent green eyes, her expression angelic, her request impos-sible to deny.

"Of course you may, sweetie." Mindy handed two glasses of iced tea to Daniel, who put them on the table, then poured two more and a glass of milk for Torie.

Torie plopped down on her knees and started to pet Sheila. "She's such a pretty doggy. Will she ever have babies? Maybe my mommy would let me have one of Sheila's puppies."

Arnie heard Ellie make a choking sound, and he

swallowed a laugh. "I'm afraid not, squirt. No puppies for Sheila."

"That's too bad. I think Sheila would make a very, very good mommy."

Daniel carried the roast on a serving platter to the table. "Okay, gang, take a seat and let's eat. I'm starved."

Torie hopped into a chair next to Arnie's place.

"I have to warn you, Ellie." Mindy delivered serving bowls heaped with potatoes and vegetables. "These two cowboys eat enough at one seating to feed the whole population of Haiti." She took her place next to her husband, leaving the other chair next to Arnie vacant.

"Torie may need help cutting up her meat," Ellie said. "If you'd like to scoot over, I can—"

"I think I can handle it." His voice gruffer than he'd intended, Arnie sounded like he had a frog in his throat. Or a chip on his shoulder. "It's okay," he said more gently.

They all held hands while Arnie said grace. He wasn't sure what words he spoke, aware only of Ellie's slender fingers enclosed by his on one side and Torie's small, trusting hand in the other.

Beads of perspiration formed on his forehead and dampened his palms. This could have been his.

His stomach knotted. *Don't think about that.*

Conversation flowed around him as they ate. Talk of the kids they'd known years ago. How much Ellie enjoyed teaching. The success of Knitting and Notions. How well Daniel's breeding program was going for his quarter horses.

Arnie didn't participate much, only answering questions when he was asked.

When they were almost finished eating, he glanced at Torie and caught her slipping Sheila a bite of carrots.

"Oh, oh," he said quietly. "Somebody doesn't like carrots?"

"Sheila likes 'em."

"Maybe so, but it's not good to feed her at the table. She has her own food."

Torie's lower lip puffed out. "It was only one bite."

He winked at her. "No more, okay?"

Her defeated sigh would have blown out a hundred candles on the biggest birthday cake in Potter Creek.

After dinner, Mindy took Ellie and Torie upstairs to see the nursery, a work in progress. Daniel and Arnie cleared the table and put the dishes in the dishwasher.

With that accomplished, Arnie slipped out of the house and wheeled over to his place. He wasn't hiding out, exactly. He simply wanted to get started on the drywall.

With his tool belt hanging on the back of his wheelchair, he hefted a sheet of drywall and rolled to the corner of the living room where he planned to start. Sitting sideways, he settled the sheet into place over the insulation and held it there while he drove in the first nail. It went easily through the gypsum plaster and into the stud with a satisfying thud.

My house, my work.

Backing up, he set more nails in place to hold the board in place. That accomplished, he retrieved another sheet and repeated the process.

When he reached the window opening that looked out over the pasture, he used a straight edge and a utility knife to cut the board to fit.

"Whatcha doing?"

Torie's question startled him, and he nearly stabbed himself with the knife.

He glanced over his shoulder. "I'm putting up drywall so the house will stay nice and warm in the winter."

"Can I help you?"

"I don't think so, squirt."

She squatted down next to Sheila, petting her. "I got bored looking at the baby's room. One time I asked Mommy for a little brother or sister, but she said she couldn't make a baby all by herself. She needs a daddy to help her make one."

Struggling to keep a straight face, Arnie said, "That's right."

She sat cross-legged on the bare floor, and Sheila put her head in Torie's lap. "How come you don't have any childrens? You'd make a good daddy. My daddy didn't want to stay with us, but it's okay. Mommy and me have each other."

He wheeled across the room for another sheet of gypsum wallboard. Torie's conversation was touching on a sore subject. Arnie didn't think he was up for that.

Carrying the board, he wheeled back to the spot where he'd been working. "You're lucky to have your mom. She's a nice lady."

Ellie stepped into the house at just that moment. Her breath caught when she heard his compliment.

"I hope I'm not interrupting," she said, not wanting Arnie to think she'd been eavesdropping.

His head snapped up. She saw him swallow hard, and color raced up his neck to his cheeks.

"Mommy, we were talking about babies."

Ellie's blush rose hotter than Arnie's. He turned away, and she knew it was to hide his laughter.

"Victoria! I…" she sputtered. "I came to tell you Daniel will take you riding on Patches if you'd like."

Like a clown in a music box, Torie popped to her feet, dislodging Sheila, who scrambled out of the child's way.

"Oh, Mommy, I looove to ride Patches. Come see me."

"I will in a minute. Go find Daniel in the corral. He's saddling your horse."

When Torie was out of sight, Ellie said, "I apologize for Torie. I'm afraid she's a bit outspoken."

"She's a real pistol, all right." He lifted his shoulders in what was surely meant to be an easy shrug but looked as stiff as a cardboard cowboy. "No harm, no foul."

Hesitating, she crossed her arms in front of her chest. "Your house is going to be lovely. Lots of open space."

"Easier for me to get around in the wheelchair."

"Of course." She shifted her weight from one foot to the other and glanced outside.

Her curiosity riding high, she didn't want to leave just yet. She wanted to see what his new home looked like, wanted to be able to picture him here in his own place.

"I decided to go for three bedrooms and turn one into my office," he said. "Don't know what I'll do with the third. Probably just pile my extra junk in there."

She knew exactly what she'd do with that extra room. "It's smart to build bigger than you think you'll need. My dad was always adding on rooms or another porch. The house is like a jigsaw puzzle with too many pieces that don't quite fit."

"Do you want a tour?"

Her heart stuttered an extra beat. "I, um, sure."

"Okay." He leaned the gypsum sheet against the wall. "Obviously, this is the living room. That'll be the kitchen." He rolled across the room. "There'll be a breakfast bar here sort of separating the two areas and a view of the mountains out the window over the sink. And down this way are the bedrooms."

She followed him down the hallway, picturing the furniture that would fill the rooms—leather couches with bright throw pillows in the living room, an oak table in the kitchen that would expand to seat a dozen guests. Walls the color of sandstone with family photographs mounted on them. A family history built step-by-step.

"The master suite is pretty big. There'll be a Jacuzzi in the bathroom, plus a big roll-in shower with a bunch of showerheads." He paused at the bedroom doorway. "Across the hall is what I'll use as my office. Between it and the other bedroom is another bathroom with standard equipment."

"Very nice. I'm sure you'll be happy having your own space."

Wheeling around, he looked up at her. In the interior shadows, his eyes seemed darker than ever. They held a haunted look she couldn't translate. Of wanting? Of need? For her? She couldn't be sure.

"I, um, shouldn't keep you from your work any longer." Her fingers trembling, she touched the silver necklace around her neck. "I'd better rescue Daniel before Torie drives him crazy with questions."

"She does ask some real doozies."

"Yes, she does. Sorry about that." Her face still flushed, she backed up a few steps. "Between horses and doggies and babies, she seems determined to embarrass you with her questions."

"I don't mind. I like kids."

She smiled. "It shows." They'd never gotten as far as talking about the children they might have. She doubted that Arnie had considered the idea, while she... The possibility had more than crossed her mind. For fear of scaring Arnie off, she'd never mentioned their making a family together.

Too late now, she realized with a renewed pang of regret.

"As I said, I'd better go check on Torie." Her heart heavy, she backed out the door.

Minutes later, Arnie saw Ellie emerge from the barn. Daniel had saddled her a horse, and the three of them rode out of the corral, Daniel leading Patches, Torie sitting proudly in the saddle. Ellie laughing as she tried to rein her mount out the gate.

Regret washed over Arnie for the things he couldn't do. Like take Ellie and Torie for a horseback ride out to the creek that ran through the ranch. Or even saddle a horse for her or Torie.

Frustration burned in his gut.

He yanked the tool belt off of his wheelchair and slammed it across the room, where it banged against the wall. He had to get out of here. Not dwell on what couldn't be. He needed the wind in his face to blow away the cobwebs of regret.

He rolled out of his house and into the barn, where he kept his specially equipped ATV. Using the lift bar Daniel had jerry-rigged for him, Arnie levered himself into the seat. Sheila jumped into the back right behind him.

He punched the starter on the ATV, twisted the hand accelerator and rocketed out the open barn door.

His only doubt was that he might not be able to go far enough or fast enough to forget.

Ellie hadn't ridden a horse in eight years. She'd forgotten the feel of her thighs stretching across the saddle, the rhythmic movement of the horse beneath her, the sense of freedom riding a horse gave her.

Later she'd likely remember in detail the penalty for not having ridden in a long time—lots of aches and pains. She was already looking forward to a good soak in a hot bath.

They rode three abreast, Torie in the middle, jabbering about horses, the crows that rose cawing from a stand of pine trees and anything else that flitted through her mind.

Torie's constant chatter didn't seem to bother Daniel, for which Ellie was grateful since her own thoughts remained with Arnie. Wondering if he'd returned to his drywall task. If he was thinking of her.

She eased her mount around to the other side of Daniel so they could talk. "You and your brother seem to get along better now than you did eight years ago," Ellie commented.

"I nearly killed him in that accident. I figure I owe him big-time."

"Does he resent what happened to him?"

"Most days he's okay with what happened. Figures God has some sort of a plan."

Ellie thought that was very generous of Arnie, more so than she might have been under similar circumstances.

"Lately, since Mindy and I got married, I think Arnie's feeling left out," Daniel said.

"Is that why he's building his own house?"

"Yeah. Mindy and I didn't want him to move out. The main house is his, too. But he insisted."

Perhaps Arnie felt more resentment than he wanted to let on. Or perhaps he was planning ahead for his own future.

She licked her slightly dry lips and asked the question that she'd been afraid to raise. "Has Arnie been seeing anyone?"

"You mean a girlfriend? He hasn't dated since the accident. Frankly…" He glanced toward Torie, who seemed to be fully engaged in a discussion with Patches about not stepping on any snakes in the grass. "I think he'd be a lot happier if he found himself a woman and married her."

Apparently not as engaged in her conversation with Patches as Ellie had thought, Torie perked up at Daniel's comment. "When I grow up, I could marry Arnie, and you and Mommy and Mindy and Sheila could come to the wedding."

Daniel covered his bark of laughter with a cough. "I think we ought to leave that up to Arnie, okay?"

For a moment, Ellie couldn't breathe, as though all the air had been sucked out of Montana and replaced with hope.

Hope that Arnie would find happiness with a woman.

Hope that she would be that woman.

And fear that she wouldn't be.

Chapter Eight

By the middle of the week there was a hint of autumn in the air and the poplars near her mother's old barn were brushed with a touch of gold. This was Ellie's favorite time of year, except her nerves were on edge and she hadn't been sleeping well.

She hadn't seen Arnie since Sunday, but the memory of the horseback ride and Daniel's comments about his brother had stuck in her head as if they'd been glued to her brain.

It's none of your business, Ellen James. Get it out of your head right now!

Ellie had arranged to meet city councilman Jeffrey Robbins at city hall to talk about permits to expand Ability Counts and get his support, if possible. A one-story brick building shared with the police department, city hall was easy to navigate and Ellie had no difficulty finding Councilman Robbins's office.

From the moment he greeted her, Ellie developed an uncomfortable feeling about the councilman. Her instincts told her Arnie was right. She didn't want anything to do with this smooth talker.

He seated her in one of the two guest chairs in front of his impressive desk and sat down beside her. Leaning away from him, Ellie told him about the plans for the school and gave him the printed materials she'd brought with her. He placed those on his desk without even glancing at them.

"I've heard something about her plans," he said. "You'll be requesting a building permit, I imagine."

"Yes, Ms. Coulter is putting the request together. I've been asked to get a sense of where you might stand on the permit."

"I didn't see the request on the agenda for next week."

"I think Vanna is working out some of the specifics before she brings the package before the city council."

"Ah, good. Then we'll have some time to get acquainted." He slid his arm along the back of her chair. "It will take me a day or two to read your material. Why don't we get together Friday to discuss it, say, for dinner? There's a nice little place I know—"

Ellie stood. "No, thank you, Mr. Robbins. I'm sure if you call Ms. Coulter, she can answer your questions."

His expression darkened, and she could tell he wasn't used to being rejected by a woman. Personally, she'd pick a rattlesnake for a date before she'd go out with him. "Thank you for your time, Mr. Robbins."

Her head held high, she marched out of his office.

"You may be sorry, Ms. James," he called after her.

"Not in this lifetime," she mumbled under her breath.

Arnie had been only partially right about Robbins. He might think of himself as a ladies' man, but any woman who fell for his phony lines should go back to Dating 101. She knew enough to stay clear of a guy whose ego was bigger than the Titanic, because sure as the sun comes up in the morning, he'd sink to the bottom from the weight of all that false pride.

Ellie had learned that the hard way—from Torie's father, Jake Radigan. Smooth as silk and slippery as winter ice when it came to commitment.

By the time she gave birth to Torie, Ellie realized Jake's hasty departure had been the Lord's way of teaching her a lesson and giving her a blessing she'd never forget.

She drove back to the school to report on her meeting and lack of success with Robbins.

Sitting in her employer's office a few minutes later, she told Vanna about the meeting. "I'm really sorry. I think I blew it. In fact, Robbins might vote against the project out of spite because I refused his advances."

Sniffing in disdain, Vanna shook her head. "I knew he was full of himself, but I didn't know Jeffrey was a sleazy character, too. I'm glad you put him firmly in his place."

"Which may be firmly against the expansion," Ellie warned.

"There are seven members of the town council, including the mayor, who has been a personal friend of mine for years." She gazed out her office window toward the play yard, where extended-day-care children were engaged in trying to climb a thick rope hanging from a sprawling oak tree. "With any luck, I think we can count on at least four votes."

"Unless he can persuade others to vote against us."

"I think we'll start a letter-writing campaign," Vanna said, still watching the children outside. "If we get enough support from the townspeople, the council will have to listen to them. Democracy at work, as they say."

"Do you think a few letters will be enough to sway the council members?"

Vanna turned back to Ellie with a resolute smile. "You've got to have faith, child. That's what has kept me going all these years. I'm not ready to quit just yet, the Lord willing."

Something ominous in Vanna's tone, like a flat bass note on a piano, sent chills down Ellie's spine.

Vanna's expression hadn't changed, her determined smile still in place. Even so, Ellie felt a pain so sharp, she feared it was a harbinger of the future. And prayed it was only her imagination.

A group of Paralympic athletes had taken to training at a Bozeman high school track during evening hours. The school's coach had arranged for lights and the use of the shower facilities.

"Come on, O'Brien. God gave you two good arms. Use 'em." Carrying a stopwatch in his hand, Coach Milton ran along inside the track, on the grass, badgering Arnie, cutting the corners to keep up with him. "You're wheeling that thing like a girl. Dig, man, dig."

Despite the cool air, sweat ran down Arnie's face and pooled under his arms. It felt like he was back on the Potter Creek football team, only the workouts were ten times as rugged. He dug into the wheels so hard, the friction burned through his gloves and his lungs labored for air. He'd gone nearly forty laps, ten miles, around the track, and all of it at full throttle.

"You got ten days, O'Brien. Ten days until that

Thompson character from Billings is gonna try to whup you good."

Not this time, Arnie thought as he rocketed around the final turn. Thompson would eat his dust.

A man in his fifties, the coach wore a school sweat-shirt and running shorts that revealed his prosthetic left leg, the result of a motorcycle accident. "This is where you sprint, O'Brien. Don't let up now. It's the final hundred yards. Dig, man, dig. He's gonna catch you."

From somewhere, Arnie found one more ounce of strength he hadn't yet used. He poured it on, pushing hard past the finish line. Only then did he lean back and coast, drawing in great gulps of air to fill his over-taxed lungs.

The coach jogged after him. He held the stopwatch to show Arnie his finishing time.

Totally spent, Arnie managed a weak smile. "My personal best."

"You did it, son." He slapped Arnie on the back. "This weekend you'll have to make the same time on a hilly course and keep it up for twenty-six miles."

Arnie groaned. The coach was a lunatic. He never let up, never let anybody say "I quit." His high school athletes had to hate him, but they kept coming back year after year. Because they kept winning.

Arnie planned to do the same. Right after he bought a couple more pairs of gloves.

"I've been thinking about our letter-writing campaign," Ellie said. She'd arrived at school early and gone directly to Vanna's office. All night her head had been spinning with ideas, and she'd gotten little sleep. "I thought we'd have our best impact by having our children draw pictures of the school that we'll build, and each picture would be signed by the student. We can put those in a thick folder. With any luck, the pictures will be so touching, council members won't be able to tell our little darlings no to expanding the school.

"Then we have to encourage our parents to write actual letters." She handed Vanna the sample letter she'd composed that morning, along with a memo to parents. "And finally, we need to reach out to the community to write letters, too. I made up a flyer to distribute around town. I thought I'd ask the pastor at church to say something from the pulpit, too."

Leaning back in her desk chair, Vanna scanned the letter and flyer, nodding as she read.

"Young lady, you've been holding out on me. You're a born politician, and I mean that in the most complimentary way."

Laughing, Ellie shook her head. "Politics hold no interest for me. But I do want to see the school built. That's why I jumped at the chance to join your staff and move back to Potter Creek."

"You may not want to get involved in politics, per se, but you have the political instincts necessary to run a successful nonprofit organization. And believe me, a lot of politicking is necessary when you're the director of a school like this."

"Which is exactly why I'm content to teach the children and let you do the politicking."

Cocking her head, Vanna eyed Ellie in a way that unsettled her. "We'll see, my dear. We'll see." Standing, Vanna said, "You talk to the teachers about having the children draw pictures for us. I'll make copies of the letter to send home with the children this afternoon, and I'll do up some flyers to post around town."

"We could get something in the newspaper, too."

"Excellent idea. I'll put you in charge of talking to Amy Thurgood at the *Potter Creek Courier*. Give her copies of the material you gave Councilman Robbins. Maybe Amy will write up a story for us."

The rest of the morning sped by. Ellie's class of four-year-olds decided they wanted lots of swings and slides at the new school, a vegetable garden, plenty of books to read and a piano. On top of the school building they wanted to see an American flag flying.

Individually, they used crayons to create a picture of the school of their dreams, then added their name in their childish handwriting. Each artistic effort carried a powerful message no adult could match—or deny.

During the lunch period, Ellie met with the other teachers in the conference room. She showed them the pictures her students had drawn.

"I think if you let your students have free rein with their ideas, I'm confident they'll come up with some very touching arguments in favor of Ability Counts."

Dawn pulled the folder closer. "These are really great. Was this your idea?"

"Vanna wanted something that would persuade the council members," Ellie said. "Kids seem to know instinctively what buttons to push."

Peggy laughed out loud. "Don't you know, when my own two darlings were young, they could wrap anyone around their little fingers without half trying."

Torie was pretty good at that game, too, Ellie acknowledged. Not only with her, but with Arnie, as well.

It seemed her daughter could turn Arnie to mush with the crook of a baby finger. Regretfully, Ellie didn't have the same power over him.

With her fellow teachers briefed, Ellie left Torie in extended day care during the afternoon. She went into town, to the newspaper office, located on Main Street in a one-story stucco building with wooden siding. The headline on the most recent edition of the newspaper, which was posted in the front window, announced School Board Approves Principal's Contract.

Given that world news mainly involved wars, floods and general mayhem, Ellie decided Potter Creek was as close to perfect as she could get here on earth.

A cowbell clanked as she opened the door, and she caught a whiff of printer's ink and old newspapers. After a single step inside, she halted abruptly, freezing in place. Her heart ping-ponged around in her chest, and her face flushed, as though she'd spent too much time in the sun.

Arnie! Sitting in front of the counter, talking with Amy Thurgood, editor of the *Courier.* A woman in her fifties, she had her glasses perched on top of gray hair.

Dressed in a work shirt and jeans, Arnie turned slowly toward her. His eyes flared momentarily before he could disguise his surprise. "Hey, Ellie." Beside him, Sheila stood and wagged her tail in recognition.

Swallowing hard, Ellie forced herself to regain her composure and walked the rest of the way inside. "Hello, Arnie." Her throat was so tight, her voice rose to a higher pitch than usual.

"What brings you to the hallowed halls of the *Courier*?" he asked.

"I, um, wanted to talk to Amy about the expansion

plans for Ability Counts." She placed the file folder of information on the counter.

Lifting her glasses from where they'd been perched on top of her head, Amy flipped open the folder. "I reported the school board turning down the idea of making it a charter school. Vanna's going to expand, anyway?"

"That's the plan. We hope to build some community support before bringing a permit request before the city council."

Adjusting the position of his wheelchair, Arnie tried to read the material in the flyer upside down. "Vanna's one smart lady. I got a pretty lukewarm reception from Ted Rojas when I talked to him last week. A little pressure from the public could nudge him over to our side."

Amy skimmed the statistics about disabled students in the region, then closed the folder.

"So you want me to write an article about how you're moving on without the school board's help?" she asked.

"Plus the importance of the school and how the community can help, if you can work that all in," Ellie said.

Shrugging, Amy glanced at Arnie. "And this guy wants an article about the Paralympics marathon in Bozeman that's a week from Saturday. Looks like I'm going to be spending a lot of time at the computer the next couple of days."

After making her contribution in support of Arnie's race, Ellie had forgotten all about the event. She hadn't even put the date on her calendar.

"We're hoping to get a big turnout of people watching the race," Arnie said. "The wheelchair division starts at eight o'clock. At eight-thirty we've got about a hundred runners signed up to participate—guys and gals with prosthetics, some blind runners with sighted partners. It's going to be quite a scene."

"Is Sheila going to run with you?" Ellie asked.

"No, going that far on mostly asphalt would be too hard on her paws. I'll leave her with Daniel."

Ellie imagined Sheila wouldn't much like that. She was too attached to her master to stay behind when he went riding off on his wheelchair.

"I thought I'd cover the event in person," Amy said. "I'd like to get a few photos of our local athletes. Particularly since I figure Arnie here is a good bet to win his division."

"I'd like to come see the race, too," Ellie said before she stopped to think how Arnie might react.

Arnie's expression clouded and he frowned. "You don't have to do that. You'd be bored standing around for half the morning."

His words grated, and she fought to not lash back at him. "I don't think so."

Despite her vow to keep her distance from Arnie, he wasn't going to stop her from attending the race and cheering for him, win or lose.

With a stifled sigh, she realized down deep that she'd never be able to keep her distance from Arnie.

Chapter Nine

Their business completed at the *Courier*, both Ellie and Arnie decided to leave at the same time.

Arnie tried to do the gentlemanly thing and hold the door open for her. But when he pushed open the door, his chair was in the way and she couldn't get past him.

"Go ahead," she said, holding the door for him. "I've got it."

His awkward exit over the raised threshold made her wince. *The town ought to require businesses to be accessible for handicapped people*, she thought, miffed at the town fathers and the owner of the newspaper.

"Where you off to now?" he asked.

"I have some flyers I want to deliver to local businesses. The school needs their support, too."

"I'm sure Mindy will put up a flyer at Knitting and Notions."

"She's on my list to harass before I pick up Torie from after-school care."

One of his reluctant smiles appeared, the slightest curve of his lips, which brought a mischievous sparkle to his dark eyes, a look she remembered from their old days together.

His expression grew pensive. "I guess Torie's spent a lot of time with sitters and in day care since she was born."

Ellie tensed. Was he criticizing her and the way she was raising her child? "That's what a working mother has to do. I don't think she's suffered from the experience. In fact, that may be why she's so outgoing."

He held up his hand in defense. "I was just thinking how hard it must be for you, taking care of her on your own. She's a great kid, which means you've done just fine with her."

The unexpected praise caught Ellie off guard. For a moment, tears of gratitude pressed at the back of her eyes. "I do what I have to do. It hasn't always been easy for either of us, but we've made it so far. Now, living with my mother, she can look after Torie if she doesn't want to stay for extended care at school. And, of course, I'm right there at school if Torie needs me during the mornings."

"Sounds like a good arrangement."

"Better than most single mothers have."

"Yeah." He rolled his chair back and forth as though he was indecisive about something.

"Are you headed back to the ranch?" she asked.

His motion halted. "Afraid so. We're culling the herd for winter, and that wallboard isn't smart enough to put itself up. There's always something to do around the ranch."

"Well, then…" She knelt to give Sheila a few scratches behind her ears. "I guess I'll see you around."

When she stood, she was nearly eye to eye with

Jeffrey Robbins, who had just come out of the diner
next door. Wearing a blue, long-sleeved shirt, matching striped tie and chinos, he looked all business and
more than a little slick.

"Well, hello there, Ms. Ellie James," he drawled in
a surgary sweet voice. He swept a straying lock of hair
off his forehead with his hand. "What a pleasure to see
you again."

She greeted him with a simple nod.

"Robbins," Arnie said.

As though the man hadn't noticed Arnie's presence,
Robbins shot a surprised look in his direction. "Hey,
my man. How's it going?" He extended his hand, and
the two men indulged in a silent battle of who had the
stronger grip.

"If you two will excuse me," Ellie said. "I've got
some things I have to do."

Robbins released his grip. "I hope you've reconsid-
ered my invitation, Ellie. I can promise you a lovely
evening."

She gave a quick shake of her head. "Sorry. I'm not
interested."

Anger flared in Robbins's eyes.

"The lady said she's not interested, Jeff. So back off
and leave her alone."

Sheila, sensing the antagonism between the two men,
braced her legs and pulled her lips back into snarl.

Ellie stepped between Arnie and Robbins. In her
most stern schoolteacher voice, she said, "That's
enough. Both of you are acting like little boys on the
playground, fighting over a ball that doesn't belong to
either of you. Stop it."

Robbins's head snapped up, and he gaped at Ellie.

Arnie had the good sense to look chagrined.

"I'm sure both of you have business elsewhere." She planted her fists on her hips. "I suggest you leave now."

She stood her ground until Robbins broke eye contact, whirled and marched away. She sighed. *Men!*

"I'm sorry, Ellie." Arnie wheeled closer to her. "I was out of line. I have no right to stick my nose in your business. If you want to date that guy—"

"Arnold O'Brien! Don't you realize you are ten times, a hundred times, more of a man than Jeffrey Robbins is or ever could be? I wouldn't go out with him if he promised to make me the queen of England."

Slack-jawed, Arnie stared at her without uttering a single sound.

Throwing up her arms in frustration, she marched down the sidewalk and into the diner to deliver one of her flyers. What did she have to do to get Arnie to trust her again?

The man was as dense as a fence post and twice as impossible!

She was a fool to even try to get back into his good graces. And an idiot to make the shocking admission, even to herself, that she was falling for him all over again.

Openmouthed, Arnie watched Ellie vanish into the diner. She was the strongest, the toughest woman he'd ever known, and she'd just whupped him and Robbins, but good.

Where had she gained that kind of inner strength? Eight years ago she'd been a beautiful, impulsive bubblehead, or so he'd thought. Boy, had she changed.

Her passionate defense of Ability Counts and her students had made her even more appealing.

He finally snapped his mouth closed.

"Come on, Sheila. Let's go home. We have some serious thinking to do."

Back at the ranch, Arnie joined Daniel, who had already started culling the herd in anticipation of the coming winter, when the grass would be under as much as six feet of snow. Buying expensive winter feed, and getting it to the cattle in a blizzard, wasn't Arnie's idea of a good time. So they kept the herd small during the winter and bought yearlings in the spring to fatten them up.

He rode his ATV, keeping the cattle to be sold off separated from the rest of the herd. Daniel sat astride April, his favorite quarter horse, a sorrel mare with a blond mane. They'd isolated about twenty head, enough for a truckload to be sent to Bozeman.

"Okay," Daniel shouted from the far side of the smaller herd. "Let's move 'em into the pen."

While Daniel kept the herd leader heading in the right direction, Arnie cruised behind the group, the sound of the ATV making the cattle nervous enough that they kept moving. He gestured for Sheila to go after a cow that was trying to wander back to the bigger herd.

Leaping from the ATV, Sheila raced after the recalcitrant animal. She barked and nipped at the cow's hind legs until she reversed course back to where she belonged.

Maybe that was what Ellie was doing to Arnie—dogging his heels until he did exactly what she wanted.

But what did she want?

She'd run out on him eight years ago, abandoning him. Making him feel even more the cripple he'd become. Unworthy of her love.

He frowned. Could he really have told her to go away? Why couldn't he remember? Had he been that much of a fool?

Sheila's assignment accomplished, she jumped back into the ATV and sat up alertly, waiting for her next task.

"Good girl!" Arnie ruffled her fur and patted her rump.

The cattle funneled their way into the pen and milled around while Daniel closed the gate behind them.

He settled on his horse, lightly holding the reins in one hand, and tipped his Stetson to the back of his head. Despite the cool air, his denim jacket hung open. "I'll call the trucking company for a pickup in the morning."

"I hope we get a decent price for them," Arnie said.

"Yeah, me, too. The grass was pretty good this year. They put on some good weight. Luckily, we didn't lose a single head to wolves or mountain lions."

"Which doesn't mean we won't next year."

For a moment, both men admired the cattle they'd raised at the cost of considerable hard work, gallons of sweat and no small amount of the Lord's help.

The blue sky overhead, the sun turning the grass-covered hillsides golden, made for a perfect autumn day to celebrate their accomplishments.

"Tell me something, bro." Thoughtfully, Arnie stroked his dog. "Be straight with me. Do you think a woman would ever want to marry me?"

Hooking his leg over the pommel, Daniel turned in the saddle to look at Arnie. His interested expression lasered in on him, and Arnie hated himself for having brought up the subject.

"Forget about it." Arnie put his hand on the gear to shift the ATV into Reverse, to get out of there. "It was just an idle thought. Didn't mean a thing."

"Now, wait a minute. You can't drop a bomb like that and not tell me what's going on. Give, bro."

"There's no bomb. Nothing's going on. I'm sorry I said anything." He backed in a circle, then headed for home, aiming to get back to work on the wallboard job. Of all the dumb things to say, he'd picked a winner. He should've kept his mouth shut.

Daniel galloped up beside him and shouted over the noise of the ATV. "If you're thinking about Ellie, I'd say marrying her would be the best thing that ever happened to you."

Fear, like a summer twister tearing up the landscape, churned in Arnie's gut. The wind in his face made his eyes water and parched his throat.

He had to wonder, would he be the *worst* thing that ever happened to *her*?

So awful that she would leave him again?

Arnie didn't think he could handle that. It wasn't a risk he wanted to take.

He was better off just as he was. Living on the ranch. Soon in his own house. Alone. With no one around to break his heart again.

Sunday morning, despite her good sense and an hour's worth of lecturing herself about the error of futile thinking, Ellie looked forward to church and to seeing Arnie.

She'd also stopped by to see Pastor Redmond on Saturday to ask him to announce that Ability Counts needed community support for their expansion. She hoped he'd say something from the pulpit. She had flyers with her with information about Vanna's plans.

Choosing to wear a layered look for church, she

picked out a lime-green blouse and a knit vest to wear with her smoke-gray skirt. A couple of strokes with her hairbrush, a little lip gloss, and she was ready to go.

After she dropped Torie off in the child-care room, she walked around to the front entrance and found Daniel standing at the door, greeting parishioners as they arrived. Wearing a Western-cut shirt with a bolo tie, he looked very much the gentleman cowboy out on the town. What changes he'd made in his life in the past eight years!

"Hey, Ellie." He handed her a program. "How's it going?"

"Fine. Working hard to stir up community support for expanding Ability Counts."

"Yeah, Mindy said you came by the shop the other day with flyers." He glanced around, and when nobody was close by, he leaned toward Ellie. "Say, are you and Arnie…" His voice dropped below the sound of a breeze slipping through pine trees. "I mean, are you two seeing each other?"

Her cheeks burned with the heat of a thousand-watt lightbulb. She brought the church program to her lips, trying to cover the blazing evidence of her reaction. Evidence that she wished what he had asked was true.

"No!" Her denial was more of a burst of sound than a word. "Not at all. We're both helping Ability Counts, that's all." She shoved one of her flyers toward him.

"Oh." His lips formed a small circle, and his dark brows, so much like his brother's, lowered in what looked like disappointment. "I just wondered…"

She tried to force a smile, but it felt like her cheeks were carved of wood and would crack if she stretched her lips any farther. "See you later."

Her face still radiating heat, she fled into the church. Her mother was there, somewhere, saving her a seat, but Ellie couldn't seem to focus.

What had made Daniel think she was "seeing" Arnie? As in dating? Not a chance.

Scanning the pews, Ellie kept her eye out for her mother. She edged down the aisle and suddenly stumbled into Arnie in his wheelchair, parked at the end of a pew.

"Oh, sorry." Off balance, she grabbed the back of his chair to right herself.

"Easy does it. I'm out of practice having women fall for me." She saw a flash of something in his eyes. Anger that she'd stumbled over him? Or embarrassment that he and his wheelchair were often invisible to others, a frequent problem for those who were wheelchair bound? What a burden that had to be for a man like Arnie.

"Yes, well…" She stepped back. She'd looked forward to seeing Arnie, but not this way. Not by making a fool of herself or a spectacle. Or by hurting him. "Sorry. I wasn't paying attention. I was looking for Mother."

"Three rows down." He lifted his chin in that direction.

"Thanks."

The organist segued from a prelude to the opening hymn. Pastor Redmond walked out onto the stage, and the congregation rose.

Embarrassed by her awkward stumble, Ellie gave Arnie a finger wave and hurried to join her mother, who scooted over to make room for her on the aisle. Barbara held open the hymnal for Ellie to join in singing "Hail, Happy Morning."

The lively song settled Ellie's capricious emotions.

By the time the music ended, she felt able to concentrate on the worship service and ignore the niggling awareness of Arnie only three pews behind her.

The pastor stepped up to the pulpit. "Welcome to you all on this happy Sabbath morning. Before I bore you with my sermon…" He got a chuckle from the congregation with that comment. "I have some announcements.

"First, let me remind you about our annual autumn picnic at Riverside Park. The date and time are in your program. Mrs. Green, our lovely women's group president, is organizing a potluck, and the men's group will be arranging games for all ages. We're all hoping for a good turnout and a day of fun and Christian fellowship. We'll caravan from church, so, ladies, don't wear all your finery that morning."

That got another chuckle from the congregation.

Ellie remembered the church's family picnics, staid affairs compared to the afternoons and evenings she'd spent at River Park during her adolescent years. But Torie would enjoy the picnic and the games the children played, and her mother liked visiting with her friends from church.

Next, the pastor told them about Ability Counts and the expansion they were hoping to achieve. His final announcement was about the Paralympics marathon in Bozeman and Arnie's participation.

Under her breath, Barbara said, "I suppose you intend to be there."

Ellie stiffened. "You're welcome to come with me. I thought I'd take Torie, too. She's grown quite fond of Arnie."

Barbara wrinkled her nose.

If only her mother could see Arnie as he truly was,

strong and caring, a man who was defined by much more than his paraplegia, perhaps that would change her attitude. But Barbara clung to seeing Arnie as she had seen her late brother, through a distorted lens that showed only the pain and dependency of disability.

With a sad feeling of defeat, Ellie realized there was nothing she could do to change her mother's opinion. It was a wall Barbara had constructed years ago, one that had withstood the test of time and remained impregnable to any argument or logic.

Chapter Ten

"Based on the phone calls I've received this week, I'd say more than a hundred letters supporting our expansion have been sent to the city council." Although Vanna had dark circles of fatigue under her eyes, and there were piles of unfinished paperwork on her desk, she looked more than pleased with their campaign.

"Let's hope the council members listen to their constituents." Ellie had been busy all week and was glad Friday had finally arrived. In addition to her regular teaching assignment and being a parent as well as a daughter, she had attended a meeting of the local women's club to ask for their support. Vanna had been out making contacts, as well.

"Oh, I think we'll do fine," Vanna said.

"We may not get Robbins's vote. I think I really made him angry."

Vanna chuckled. "He'll come around when he sees how the other council members are voting."

From a pewter sky outside Vanna's office, rain dripped from the eaves, making pinging noises when the drops landed on a trash can. Very little light worked its way in through the window. The weather report had called for heavy rain in the nearby mountains, which were tinder-dry after a long summer.

"When will the item be on the agenda?" Ellie asked.

"We'll take another week to build support. I'll ask Mayor Knudsen to put us on the agenda a week from Tuesday." Rubbing her hand along her jaw, she said, "I assume you're going to Bozeman tomorrow to cheer for Arnie."

"Oh, yes. Torie and I will be there." No matter what Arnie said, Ellie had no intention of missing the race, rain or shine. He might become upset seeing her there, but it was one of the few ways she could show how much she cared, how much she'd changed.

"Arnie and the Paralympics have been a great help to us. Once we get the approval to expand, I think they'll play a critical role in developing ongoing funding for us."

That was Ellie's hope, too. But now she had to get to her class. Rain meant no Friday horseback riding for the children, and they'd be restless. She'd have to work at keeping them busy and active. A few rounds of London Bridge and Duck, Duck, Goose would help them use some of their pent-up energy.

By the following morning the storm had passed through the area, leaving only a few trailing clouds and air as crystal clear as a finely cut diamond. Overnight, the temperature had dropped into the low forties.

Both Ellie and Torie were bundled up in warm jackets. Holding her daughter's hand, Ellie worked their way through the milling crowd in the high school stadium to be near the starting line. Excitement and anticipation had Ellie craning her neck to get a glimpse of Arnie. She so wanted him to do well in the race.

"Can you see Arnie?" Torie kept bouncing up on her tiptoes to get a better view.

"Not yet." There were dozens of men and a few women in sleek racing wheelchairs jockeying for position on the tartan running track, each of them with a number bib pinned to their back. "I wish I knew what number he was wearing."

"There's Sheila!" Torie pointed to the far side of the track, where Daniel had the golden retriever mix on a leash. That had to mean Arnie was nearby.

Ellie scanned the racers close to Daniel.

"There he is." Her excitement rising, she squatted down next to Torie and pointed. "He's right up front, wearing a bright red track shirt and blue shorts. His cap is red, too. Do you see him?"

It took Torie just a moment to spot him. "Arnie! Arnie!" She waved her arm and jumped up and down. "We came to see you race."

He turned his head slowly. When he pinpointed Torie, a smile of recognition softened his angular features, and he waved.

"He sees me, Mommy. He sees me. Can I go talk to him?"

"No, honey. We don't want to distract him. He needs to concentrate on the race." What Ellie really wanted to do was race across the track to give Arnie a good-luck kiss. The thought of getting a negative reception, should she actually do that, kept the impulse in check.

Torie's slender shoulders sagged. "I could help him concentrate."

Ellie hooked her arm around her daughter's shoulders. "Not this time. After the race is over, you'll have a chance to talk to him."

"Is he going to win?"

Arnie turned to say something to Daniel. Ellie noted his racer's number was 314.

"I don't know," she said to Torie. "He's going to do his best, though. You can be sure of that." Although not as reckless as his brother, Arnie had always had fire in his belly when it came to competition. He'd been a star high school football player and had set some Potter Creek track records. Long before Ellie knew him. Before his accident.

The accident that had demolished much of what Arnie's self-image had been. Yet he was still a competitor. Even from a distance, she saw his grim determination. His intense concentration. His will to win.

He'd put that same resolve into restoring the ranch to a productive enterprise. Being in a wheelchair hadn't deterred him. So why couldn't she convince him being wheelchair bound didn't make her think less of him?

A race official raised his starting pistol. "Ready, set—"

Ellie jumped at the sound of the gun. Her heart slammed against her rib cage, and she drew a quick breath.

The racers sped forward at an amazing pace, maneuvering for position, their arms pumping hard. The onlookers cheered.

"I can't see, Mommy. I can't see."

Ellie hefted her daughter in her arms. She focused on Arnie's red cap and shirt as he kept his position at the front of the pack. Two other racers were neck and neck with him going down the track to the first turn, Arnie on the outside, trying to pass them.

That was a mistake, she thought. He should be on the inside of the turn, with the shorter distance to travel.

Unlike a speed ice-skating track or one used for race cars, a running track wasn't banked. The inside racer reached the turn going too fast. His chair tipped precariously. He was forced to slow.

On the outside, Arnie zipped by his two rivals and sped on alone.

"Go, Arnie! Go!" Ellie screamed.

Torie covered her ears. "That's too loud, Mommy."

Laughing, Ellie lowered her daughter to the ground as the racers peeled away from the track, out an open gate and onto the street to follow the twenty-six-mile course.

"When will Arnie come back, Mommy?"

She glanced toward Daniel across the way. "I don't really know. It's a long race. Probably more than an hour."

Many of the racers were young, in their early twenties. Most of them were probably accident victims or soldiers injured in the line of duty. All of them had had to rebuild their lives under the most difficult of circumstances.

I should have been there for Arnie, she thought. Dealing with such a devastating change in his life must have been terrible for him. If only he'd asked her to stay…

Ellie and Torie moved with the crowd to watch the racers pass on the nearby street. They found a spot to stand on the sidewalk among the fans, mostly friends and family members of the racers.

The ripple of applause and cheers started somewhere

to Ellie's right. Like a fast-approaching train, the noise grew closer until she could see those in the lead.

Arnie wasn't among them.

She craned her neck until she spotted him in fifth place and still in contact with the leaders, who were traveling a good thirty miles per hour.

"Come on, Arnie! You can do it." She pointed for Torie. "There he is."

"He's not winning," Torie complained.

"Don't you worry, young lady," a woman next to them said. "He's saving his strength by drafting behind the racer in front of him. He'll catch up at the end. That's my boy right behind him."

Although Ellie didn't think winning was the most important thing about any race, she couldn't help hoping Arnie would come in first at the finish line.

The wheelchair racers had barely passed when the crowd surged back into the stadium to watch the runners make their start. Ellie looked on in amazement as men and women with prosthetic legs, some even using crutches, accepted the challenge of running 26.2 miles.

She doubted she could finish a 10K race with two good legs, much less a marathon.

After the runners left the stadium, the time seemed to drag. Ellie checked her watch. The crowd collected on the infield grass near the finish line the racers would cross after returning to the stadium and circling the quarter-mile track.

She pictured Arnie. The muscles in his arms flexing with each pull of the wheels, his shoulders as broad and strong as those of a wrestler. His expression intent as he focused every ounce of his energy on the race.

Finally, a collective gasp rose from the onlookers

as the first two racers rolled onto the track, followed closely by a third.

Her heart slammed to a stop when she recognized Arnie's red cap in third place.

Without giving it any thought, Ellie raced across the grass, angling toward Arnie and the lead racers. Right behind her, Torie yelled, "Wait, Mommy!"

Ellie grabbed her child's hand and kept on running. "Come on, Arnie! You can do it! It's not far now. Keep going. Faster, Arnie!" Ellie's screams, rasping up her throat, strained her vocal cords, but she didn't stop.

Arnie closed the distance on the other two racers. Sweat ran down his face and soaked the back of his red shirt. With every turn of the wheels, he seemed to find a little more strength, apply a bit more power.

Torie added her shouts of encouragement as Arnie pulled to the outside lane to pass the competition.

The racer on the inside was having trouble holding his lane again. A rear wheel wobbled off the tartan track, banged against the low curb, costing him precious time.

Arnie took advantage of the error. He pressed into second place. Determination was written in the grimace of his mouth, the corded muscles of his neck and the way he leaned forward to get as much leverage as possible.

When they reached the straightaway, Arnie was only inches behind the leader. The crowd began to roar.

Touching the cross around her neck, Ellie closed her eyes only long enough to send up a quick prayer. When she opened them again, the two men were dead even and about to cross the finish line. Both men were working so hard, it was impossible to imagine them having an extra ounce of strength left.

A huge cheer went up from the onlookers.

"Who won, Mommy?"

"I don't know, honey. I can't see." Wheelchair racers continued to whiz by. The first woman finished in the middle of a pack of male racers, receiving another loud cheer.

Picking Torie up, Ellie forced her way through the crowd, past the finish line, to the spot where the racers were recovering their breath. She had to find out who had won.

When she reached the recovery area, she saw Arnie. He was congratulating a muscular young man who was waving an American flag high in the air, a big grin on his face.

The air escaped Ellie's lungs in a sigh. Arnie had placed second. An incredibly good showing against a strong field of racers.

With dozens of people greeting the racers they had cheered for, Ellie walked across the track. She lowered Torie to the ground.

"You were wonderful." Her voice sounded like she had a frog in her throat.

His hair damp with perspiration, his smile a little crooked, he beckoned her closer. He took Ellie's hand, tugging her onto his lap. His big, work-roughened hands framed her face.

She gasped with surprise and pleasure, his thighs firmly beneath her.

"I tried to win for you. I heard you yelling. I didn't want to let you down. Disappoint you. I'm sorry."

"Nothing you ever did would disappoint me, Arnie."

Slowly, not sure what his reaction would be, she brought her lips to his. Warm and familiar, she remembered his kisses. Longed for them. For a moment, he didn't respond, and then he relaxed. He kissed her back. She wanted to weep with the simple pleasure of being in his arms again.

"Mommy, can I sit in Arnie's lap, too?"

Reluctantly, Ellie broke away from the kiss. His dark eyes were as heated as his kiss had been. As needy as her own desire.

An unspoken message passed between them, bringing the past and the present together. A clash of lost love and broken trust.

This had been their first kiss in eight years, but would it be their last?

"Mom-my! It's my turn."

With a troubled smile, Ellie eased off of his lap.

Arnie shifted his attention to Torie. "Come on, squirt. Come up here and give me a high five."

"I cheered for you, Arnie."

"I know you did, squirt. Sorry I didn't win for you."

"But you did win. Mommy says when you try your best, you'll always be a winner."

He shrugged and gave her a high five. "If you say so, kiddo."

Others began to gather around Arnie. People from Potter Creek—Vanna and Ivy from the diner, Daniel returning Sheila to his side and draping a jacket around Arnie's shoulders so he wouldn't cool off too fast. Pastor Redmond congratulated him on his second-place finish, as did several members of his congregation. Others gathered around him were his friends from Paralympics and who knew where else. He was a popular guy.

He greeted everyone with a handshake or a hug, and regret that he hadn't won first place.

But the kiss had been Ellie's alone.

Suddenly, heat warmed her cheeks. All these people, Arnie's friends, must have seen her kissing him. But no one commented, for which Ellie was ever so grateful. She should have restrained herself in such a public setting but was so glad she hadn't.

After the runners had finished their race, officials of the Bozeman Paralympics made the presentation of awards. Arnie received a large gold trophy, and the young man who had beaten him accepted a trophy that was at least two feet tall.

"Ladies and gentlemen," the official announced over the loudspeaker. "Even more important than this race is the fact that more than $20,000 has been pledged for the support of our organization. I'd like to recognize our top fund-raiser, who, all by himself, collected pledges of $3,253.10." The audience chuckled at the ten cents. "Let's give him a big hand, folks. Arnie O'Brien, our second-place finisher."

Pride filled Ellie's chest as the official draped a gold medal around Arnie's neck. Life was about a lot more than simply winning a race.

It was about caring and giving back. How could she not love a man like Arnie?

Chapter Eleven

The row of spruce trees bordering the highway back to the ranch leaned to the west, victims of the frequent winds that blew through the area, stunting their growth, twisting their limbs. Making them less than perfect.

It was just as well Daniel had decided to drive the van back to the ranch after the race. Arnie figured even with power steering, he wouldn't have been able to get out of the parking lot.

He could barely hold on to the trophy he'd won for second place, the figure of a wheelchair racer on the top.

His arms had as much strength left in them as a gym towel that had been dropped in the deep end of the pool. Exertion had drained his energy. He'd downed three bottles of water to rehydrate. During the race, he had expended every ounce of strength he had, yet he was still on an adrenaline high.

From Ellie's kiss.

"You ran quite a race, bro," Daniel said.

"I had a good coach. I should've done better." During the final quarter mile he'd heard Ellie's voice above all the other screaming fans. He'd wanted to slow down.

His energy depleted, he hadn't wanted to push any harder. Finishing in third place wouldn't be so bad, he had told his weary body.

But he couldn't do that. Not with Ellie's voice in his head, urging him to go faster, push harder. Win. Because of Ellie, he had come so close.

How had she known he had more left in him when he hadn't known it himself? When he'd been ready to quit trying.

An errant thought popped into his head. Had he given up on Ellie too soon? When he'd gotten out of rehab, why hadn't he gone after her?

The answer came to him like a sucker punch to his chin. *Because you were too afraid she'd say no.* Better to blame her than discover what he feared the most, that she couldn't love a cripple.

"That was quite a congratulatory kiss you got from Ellie," Daniel said. "Looked like you were both into it."

"Yeah. Felt like it, too," he admitted. He'd been hungry for that kiss since she'd come back to town. Yearning to feel the old fire ignite between them.

Yet it had been more than before. Better than before.

How could he not want to kiss her again?

He didn't dare. The kiss had changed nothing.

He was still too afraid to find out the truth. To test the limits of how she felt about him.

Unsettled by Arnie's kiss, Ellie drove home from Bozeman, barely hearing Torie chattering away in the back seat of her compact.

She parked by the back door of her mother's house. As usual, Torie blasted out of the car as though she was rocket-propelled.

Sitting for a moment behind the steering wheel, Ellie touched her fingertips to her lips. The feel of him, the press of his lips, still lingered there.

Dazed, she walked up the steps into the kitchen, where Torie was regaling her grandmother with the details of the race.

"…was losing. But Mommy kept yelling at him to go faster, and so did I. We ran and ran to keep up with him. Then he started rolling faster and faster, and he just about caught up with the other man!"

"Just about, huh? Goodness, that sounds like an exciting race," Grandma BarBar said.

"He got a great big, gigantic trophy that was bigger than me." Torie held her hand high above her head.

Chuckling, Ellie slipped off her jacket. "Maybe not quite that big."

"But it was really, really big," Torie insisted.

"Oh, yes. They don't come much bigger." Ellie helped her daughter take off her jacket.

"After Arnie finished the race, Mommy sat in his lap and kissed him for a long time."

Ellie winced. There were no secrets as far as a talkative four-year-old was concerned.

Her mother shot her a stinging look.

"Then she had to give me a turn," Torie continued, "so I sat in his lap and gave him a high five."

Her jaw muscles taut, Barbara said, "I see."

Immediately jumping to defend Arnie, Ellie said, "You really should have seen him, Mother. Arnie is so incredibly strong and vigorous. Well, all the racers were, of course. But he was flying."

With a dismissive wave of her hand, Barbara stood.

"I'll fix us some nice hot soup and tuna sandwiches for lunch."

Torie wrinkled her nose. "I don't like tuna. Can I have peanut butter?"

"Remember, honey, at Grandma's house we eat what we're served. And after you eat your lunch, you and I are going to plan who to invite to your birthday party."

Her complaint deflected, Torie clapped her hands. "I'm going to be five years old."

"You certainly are." Barbara popped open a can of chicken noodle soup and poured it into a pan. "How did you get to be such a grown-up little girl?"

"'Cuz my mommy borned me."

And what a long way they'd come since then, Ellie thought. Her mother had come to Spokane to be with her when she gave birth. Barbara hadn't been happy about Ellie being an unwed mother, but she'd been as supportive as she knew how. She'd stayed a week to help Ellie recover; then she'd returned to the farm, leaving Ellie on her own. Trying to keep up with her classes that semester and care for a new baby hadn't been easy.

Overall, it had been worth every sleepless night and blurry-eyed morning.

Returning to her job as a waitress after six weeks had compounded her lack of sleep. Even so, she'd survived and baby Victoria Barbara James had thrived. At first a kind neighbor lady had taken care of Torie when Ellie was at work or school. Later, Ellie was able to use the child-care program available to faculty and students, sponsored by the university.

Barbara continued to be supportive and was more than loving with Torie when Ellie came home for brief visits.

But she had a blind spot when it came to Arnie.

A blind spot that hurt Ellie in a deeply visceral way.

After lunch, Ellie cleared the dishes and put them in the dishwasher, while her mother went off to take a nap.

Finding some notebook paper, Ellie sat down at the table again. "All right, Miss Birthday Girl. Who should we invite to your party?"

After some discussion, Torie agreed she should invite all the children in her class.

"And I want to invite Arnie, too," she announced.

Ellie's pencil froze above the lined paper. "Honey, he's a grown-up. I'm not sure he'd want to come to a party with so many kids."

"But he's my very, very best grown-up friend."

"Well, yes..." She mentally scrambled to come up with a reason not to invite Arnie, when in her heart she would love to have him here. Torie needed a man in her life as a role model. But would Arnie feel she was taking advantage of him, pressuring him to deepen their relationship? Assuming one kiss made theirs a relationship.

"You could ask him, Mommy." Her green eyes were round and big and pleading.

Rubbing her forehead, Ellie considered her options. "Tell you what, why don't we invite Arnie, Daniel and Mindy to the party? They've all been very nice to us, and that way there would be other grown-ups to talk to."

"Okay," she agreed brightly.

Together they planned a cowboy theme and the games the children would play. Grandma BarBar would be asked to make a chocolate cake and serve ice cream.

Hugging her daughter, Ellie thought of all the preparations she needed to make before next Saturday, and her stomach sank. She should have started planning a month ago.

* * *

With her computer-generated party invitations in hand, Ellie made sure to get to church early the next morning and drop off Torie in her Sunday school room. She'd either catch the O'Briens before church started or track them down after the service.

For once, her timing was perfect. Arnie's van was just pulling into the parking lot as she reached the front of the church. She waited for him on the sidewalk and watched as Mindy and Daniel exited the van, as well. Asking all three of them to the party made the invitation seem less pushy. Less personal.

And much easier for Arnie to decline.

"Hey, we've got our own personal greeter this morning." Tipping his hat back, Daniel strolled toward Ellie, and she remembered how she and Mindy used to call him Swagger.

"I'm here at Torie's behest to deliver some special invitations to all the O'Briens."

"Oh, oh." Arnie rolled up to her. "That sounds like trouble to me."

"Oh, hush, Arnie." Mindy whopped him lightly on the shoulder. "Torie's a sweet girl and you know it."

Ellie's gaze locked on Arnie's, his pupils as dark as charcoal. Her mouth dry, she couldn't look away. He was remembering their kiss, just as she was. Her stomach did a flip-flop, and her chest tightened.

"So what are we invited to?" Daniel asked.

The question snapped Ellie out of her reverie. "Torie's birthday party is next Saturday. She wanted you all to come, if you can." She handed them their invitations.

"Oh, how sweet." Mindy opened hers. "A cowboy theme. I remember my son's second birthday. I had broomstick horses for all the children. They galloped all over the house."

Ellie's heart squeezed tight in sympathy. She couldn't imagine the pain her friend must have suffered when she lost her son.

Daniel put a protective arm around his wife's shoulders. "Losing Jason is the reason we wanted to get started on our family as soon as possible."

"You'll notice my brother was glad to oblige," Arnie teased.

Daniel ignored him.

"I'd love to help you with the party," Mindy said, obviously not wanting to dwell on the loss of her child. "I could find some cute fabric and stitch up some bandannas for the children to wear around their necks."

"That would be perfect," Ellie said.

The sound of the organ prelude wafted out from the church.

"I'll give you a call," Mindy said. "We'll talk about how else I can help. And I'll ask Aunt Martha to watch the shop that afternoon."

"Thank you so much."

Taking Mindy's arm, Daniel headed toward the church entrance. Arnie started to follow them, but Ellie stopped him.

"Please don't feel you have to come to the party," she said. "It was Torie's idea to invite you. She says, and I quote, 'Arnie is my very, very best grown-up friend.'"

Cocking his head, he looked up at her. "You don't want me there?"

She flushed. "Of course I do. I can't think of anyone else I'd rather have come to the party. It's just that..." Her tongue suddenly as thick as a tree stump, she stumbled over her words. "After yesterday, I don't want you to feel you have any obligation to me. Or to Torie."

Slowly, his lips curved into a reluctant smile and crinkles appeared at the corners of his eyes. "No obligation. I get that."

The deep timbre of his voice vibrated in the air between them and resonated in her chest. More than anything, she wanted to kiss him again. Right there. In front of the church. She didn't care who saw them. But his tone didn't invite a repeat of yesterday's kiss.

"Tell Torie I'm happy to accept her invitation."

As he wheeled into church, Ellie wondered if Arnie had had birthday parties as a child. His mother had died when he and Daniel were quite young. His father had had a reputation as a drunk who got into fights, and had allowed the ranch to run down. If there had been parties for the boys, there hadn't been many.

Her heart ached for what Arnie must have missed as a child and what he had accomplished despite a father who likely neglected him or worse.

She wondered if he was aware of what he'd overcome. Or did he simply take life one day at a time?

Chapter Twelve

"Mommy, is it time to get up yet?"

Ellie peeked open one eye. Torie stood next to her bed in her princess pajamas. Outside it was still dark. The clock on her bed table read 5:32 a.m.

Groaning, Ellie pulled back the covers and patted the space beside her. "Not yet, honey. Climb in. Maybe we can get some more sleep."

"But I don't want to miss my birthday."

"You won't, I promise."

Torie got into bed, snuggling her warm little body next to Ellie. She pulled the blanket up over them, catching the fresh scent of baby shampoo on Torie's hair. She wondered how many years it would be before Torie no longer would want to climb into bed with her. She'd be too grown-up.

By six o'clock, Torie was squirming so much it seemed pointless to remain in bed, despite the fact that the party didn't start until one. The weatherman had predicted rain, late afternoon or evening. Ellie hoped it would hold off until after the party.

They both dressed in jeans and flannel shirts. Ellie

wore her old scuffed and worn cowboy boots; Torie a red cowboy hat Grandma BarBar had purchased at the party store.

Ellie had the tables covered and bales of hay arranged in the barn when Mindy arrived early to help with the setup. She had her blond hair pulled back into a ponytail. That would have made her look years younger except for her maternity top with a circular target on it, an arrow pointing directly at the bull's-eye, and the word *baby* written under it.

Torie came running out of the house to see what Mindy had brought.

"I found some cute fabric for the bandannas," Mindy announced, placing a cardboard box filled with red-checkered material with tiny horseshoes on the table.

Climbing up on the bench, Torie snatched a bandanna from the box. "Can I wear one now?"

With a silent eye roll, Ellie tied the bandanna in place.

Together, Ellie and Mindy strung crepe paper streamers around the unused horse stalls and set out paper plates and cups. They were contemplating how to tie a rope over a beam to raise and lower the piñata when Daniel and Arnie arrived. Both were dressed in new blue jeans and wearing their Stetsons.

"Ah, the cavalry has arrived," Mindy said with a smile.

When Daniel brushed a kiss to Mindy's cheek, Ellie felt a prick of envy. How lucky her friend was to have rediscovered love.

Arnie rolled into the barn right behind Daniel. "Sounds like we've got a couple of damsels in distress who need rescuing."

"My favorite thing to do." Daniel winked at his wife. "Assuming it's the right woman."

"It better not be any other woman," Mindy warned in a stern voice that contrasted to the hint of laughter in her blue eyes.

Torie came running out of the house, her red hat bouncing on her back from the cord around her neck. "You came to my birthday party!" She flew into Arnie's lap and kissed him on the cheek.

"Hey, squirt. That's some welcome you're giving this ol' cowboy. Happy birthday."

"You're not old, Arnie. You're just right."

Pressing her lips together, Ellie was tempted to agree with her daughter but thought Arnie might not appreciate her opinion in the matter.

"So what do you need?" Arnie asked Ellie, Torie now seated comfortably on his knee, as though she had always belonged there.

Ellie had been hugging the papier-mâché piñata, which was shaped like a horse. "We need a rope strung over a beam so we can hang this."

"No problem." He eyed the beam, which had to be ten feet high. "I'll hold the piñata. My little brother will climb up and risk his neck for the good of the cause."

With a start, Ellie wondered if she'd hurt Arnie, forcing him to silently acknowledge he wasn't able to climb at all. Did he focus on his disabilities, and not all the abilities he still could claim? She pulled her lip between her teeth and prayed that wasn't the case.

"I can climb up there, Mommy."

"Oh, no," Daniel said. He swept off his Stetson and bowed to Torie. "It is my duty as a cowboy to protect all females from possible harm."

The child folded her arms across her chest. "I'm not a female! I'm a little girl!"

Laughter broke the undertone of tension that was always present between Ellie and Arnie. When he gave Torie another affectionate hug, his eyes were on Ellie and his smile warmed her deep in her heart.

Everything was in order when the first children began arriving. Ellie greeted the children and their parents, meeting a few of their chauffeur fathers for the first time.

With a bit too much eagerness and not enough gratitude, Torie took the presents they brought and piled them on top of the table. Typical behavior for a five-year-old, Ellie assumed.

Her mother came out to the barn and organized Pin the Tail on the Donkey, while Mindy tied bandannas around the necks of arriving youngsters and supervised the children who wanted to decorate their pretend vests made out of brown paper sacks.

A scream raised the hair on Ellie's neck. She whirled, expecting to see an injured child.

Instead she saw Arnie and Carson racing their wheelchairs through the barn and out onto the asphalt driveway. The childish scream had been one of laughter as Arnie kept threatening to beat young Carson.

"I'm gonna get you, kid. Look out!"

"I'm faster than you."

"No, you're not." Intentionally staying behind the boy, Arnie gave Carson's chair an extra push. "Hey, no fair. Come back here."

Carson squealed, zipping farther into the lead.

Pulling to a stop, Arnie turned around, a big grin on

his face. He rolled back toward the barn, the picture of a mischievous, overgrown boy having fun at a party.

Laughing, Ellie thought that even if Arnie hadn't been given many birthday parties of his own, he certainly knew how to create fun for the children now. Eight years ago, she hadn't known or wondered how good he would be with kids. *Pretty spectacular*, she thought now. He would make a wonderful father—if he ever gave himself a chance.

"Arnie! Arnie!" Torie went running out to him. "Give me a ride, Arnie."

Seeking approval, he glanced toward Ellie, who shrugged. "Up to you."

"Okay, Miss Birthday Girl. I'll give everybody a ride. You first." He hefted Torie up into his lap and wheeled around. "Let's go get Carson."

Soon the children were lined up to take a turn in Arnie's wheelchair and he'd broken into a sweat from exertion. The kids were having so much fun, Ellie hated to stop them.

"They're loving it, aren't they?" Barbara commented, her tone mildly surprised.

"At the moment it's better than riding a horse, which the children adore."

Ellie waited until all the children had had a turn, then gathered them around while Torie opened her presents. Dutifully, Torie thanked whoever had given her a present but didn't linger long over any one gift. She was too anxious to open the next package.

Watching from a few feet away, Arnie downed a large glass of punch.

"I didn't mean for you to be the day's entertainment,

but thank you. You were a real hit with the children," Ellie told him.

He pulled a handkerchief from his pocket to wipe the sweat from his brow. His crooked smile made him look bemused. "If I'd trained with one of those kids in my lap, I might've won the marathon."

"There's always next year."

He groaned in mock agony. "Those kids will weigh ten pounds more by next year."

Laughter bubbled out of Ellie like fizzy water. Over the years, she'd forgotten what an understated sense of humor he had, often making her giggle like the teenager she'd been.

She wanted to go back to that time when they laughed together. When they'd been eager to spend time together simply because they liked each other. A lot, from Ellie's perspective.

But going back wasn't an option. Things had changed. So had their relationship. Could they possibly rebuild what they'd once had after so much time had passed? So many hurts had been inflicted.

After the presents were done, Barbara brought out the cake. Ellie snapped a picture when Torie, with a little help from her friends, blew out the five candles.

Thank You, Lord, for my beautiful daughter and the memories she will have of this day.

Barbara helped serve the cake and ice cream. Ellie poured the punch. Too excited to eat, most of the children didn't finish their cake.

After more games and the grand finale of breaking open the piñata, the children finally left.

Ellie sat down heavily on the picnic table bench. Her

mother had taken the remnants of the cake inside, and only the O'Briens remained in the barn.

"I can't tell you how grateful I am for all of your help," she said. "I could not have done this without you. I owe you big-time."

"I expect to see you at my little one's first birthday." Mindy patted the bull's-eye on her stomach.

"I'll be there, I promise."

Arnie spun his chair around. "I haven't had such a great workout since the marathon. Can we do this again next week?"

"No!" they all chorused, which was followed by laughter, hugs of gratitude and goodbyes.

After dinner and getting Torie to bed, Ellie sat in the living room with her mother. She picked up the sweater she was knitting for Torie. If she didn't get busy soon, the sweater wouldn't be finished before next summer.

The rain had held off until evening. Now there was a steady drumming on the roof. Windows rattled when the wind gusted, and a cold draft crept across the floor.

Ellie folded her legs under her.

When the program her mother had been watching on TV ended, Barbara muted the sound.

"I have to say, Arnie was very good with the children today." Her pensive tone caught Ellie's attention.

She looked up from her knitting. "He seemed to be having a good time."

"You know, I always did like him when you were dating him before you moved to Spokane. He was such a responsible young man."

"He still is."

"It's just that—"

"I know, Mother. I remember how painful it was for you to watch Uncle Bob being teased by other children and bullied. But that doesn't happen to Arnie. Everyone in town respects him. Even admires him." Tired of fighting her mother about Arnie, she drew in a shaky breath. "The children think he's wonderful." So did Ellie.

Despite the rain, after dinner Arnie put on a jacket and went out to his house to check what progress his friends had made while he was at Torie's birthday party.

He switched on the floodlight in the living room. Sheila gave herself a shake from nose to tail, spraying water on the unfinished subflooring. The rain beat against the plastic covering on the windows in a futile effort to slip inside the house.

Little Torie had done a great job of slipping under Arnie's skin. Her smile, her laugh, her quick intelligence had opened him up as nothing else had ever done.

Except her mother.

Ellie was doing a number on him, too. He'd thought he could keep being angry at her for walking out on him when he needed her. But every time he saw her, she managed to whittle another small piece of his fury away. The shield he'd hidden behind had become thinner and less substantial by the day.

What would happen if he lowered his defenses? Would everyone see how weak he was? Would Ellie realize what he'd been telling himself all these years was true—that he was only half a man?

He rolled down the hallway to the master bedroom. A room big enough for two. In his imagination he heard

Ellie's laughter, caught the scent of her citrus shampoo. Saw her smiling at him.

He scrubbed his hand over his face. It did nothing to erase the image he'd vividly conjured in his head.

"Come on, Sheila. Let's get back to the main house. Mooning over a woman and what could've been isn't going to get me anywhere."

Chapter Thirteen

Soon after Ellie had dismissed her preschool class to go home at noon on Monday, Jeffrey Robbins strolled into her classroom. Wearing an expensive leather jacket and slacks, he looked as out of place in a preschool classroom as a shady bill collector in church.

"So how were all your runny-nosed kids today?" He picked up a painting that had been left on the table to dry, the colors swirled together like a bright rainbow. "Not exactly a Rembrandt, is it?"

Instinctively, Ellie wanted to lash out in defense of her student. Instead she folded her arms across her chest and muted her response.

"I'm sorry," she said, lacing the words with false sympathy. "You must have said something that cruel because your mother burned all of your early paintings."

A quick frown lowered his brows as he struggled to find a suitable comeback. "Fortunately, I have other talents."

"I'm sure." She took the painting from him, returning it to the table where he'd found it. Robbins obviously had a far different attitude toward children than Arnie.

He would never have insulted a child's painting or expressed anything except praise. "Is there something you wanted other than a course in art appreciation?"

"Oh, yes, I definitely have something else in mind." He strolled around the room, touching books and toys, examining oversize construction blocks, sliding chairs under tables, marking the space as his own, giving Ellie a creepy feeling in the process.

Tapping her foot, Ellie waited. Although she wanted in the worst way to throw him out, Robbins was a member of the city council. No need to antagonize him more than she already had.

He stopped in the center of the reading circle. "I noticed Ability Counts's request for a building permit is on the city council agenda for tomorrow evening. I thought I'd give you one more chance to discuss the merits of the proposal over dinner this evening."

The man was more determined than she'd imagined. "I have other plans."

"With O'Brien?"

"That's no concern of yours. Now, if you'll excuse me." She looked pointedly toward the door.

Sliding his hands in his pockets, he rocked back on his heels. "Ms. James, I'm in a position to help you."

Said the spider to the fly.

"I appreciate your invitation, Mr. Robbins. While I must decline, I will look forward to seeing you at the council meeting."

His back straightened, and he removed his hands from his pockets, no longer making an effort to appear relaxed. "You're making a big mistake."

He marched past her and out the door.

The fine hairs on Ellie's nape quivered, as though

she were in an electric storm. Goose bumps sped down her spine.

What could he do? Vanna was sure she had enough council votes to have the permit approved. Robbins's negative vote wouldn't matter.

Unless he could convince three other council members to vote no.

Late Tuesday afternoon, while out checking the herd, Arnie got a call from his business associate on the Potter Creek City Council, Ted Rojas.

Slowing his ATV to a stop, Arnie flipped open his cell phone.

"Are you planning to come to the council meeting tonight?" Rojas asked.

"Yeah. Ability Counts's permit is on the agenda tonight, right?"

"Yes, which is why I thought you'd want to know about the email that's been circulating around town. Everybody in city hall and most of the town residents have gotten it."

A sense of alarm caused Arnie to straighten in his seat. "What email?"

"The one that suggests one or more teachers at Ability Counts do not have sufficiently high morals to work with young children and that Vanna should strictly enforce the morals clause in the teachers' contracts before she is allowed to expand the school."

Arnie's hand tightened around the phone. "Who sent it?"

"Councilman Robbins. The memo is long on innuendo and short on facts, but I've already gotten a couple of calls from concerned citizens."

"Send it to me, will you, Ted?" Since the ranch wasn't within the town boundaries, Arnie wasn't a registered voter for city issues and didn't get automatic notification of council agenda items.

"I'll forward it now. If you get a clue about what's going on, let me know."

"You got it." Having a pretty good idea why Robbins sent out the email, Arnie snapped the phone shut. A muscle pulsed in his jaw. He hit the accelerator so hard, he almost dumped Sheila off the back of the ATV.

"Hang on, Sheila. We've got a political mud-throwing contest on our hands." If he had his way, the only guy who would get dirty was Jeffrey Robbins.

Back at the house, Arnie headed directly for his computer. He booted it up and clicked on the email Ted had sent him.

It has been brought to our attention that one or more current teachers at Ability Counts Preschool may have violated the morals clause in the contract they are required to sign at the time they accept employment with the nonprofit organization.

While expansion of the school may or may not be approved, based on the city's land-use plan, we believe it is imperative that Ms. Vanna Coulter, president and CEO of the organization, strictly enforce the morals clause prior to any city council consideration of the request for expansion.

The letterhead on the email indicated it was from the office of Councilman Jeffrey Robbins.

Nearly snarling with fury, Arnie called Vanna and

found that she'd already gotten some irate phone calls herself.

"Ellie told me about his implied threat," Vanna said. "Even I didn't think he'd stoop this low."

"He's a snake and always has been. I can't figure out why the voters don't know that." Which didn't mean Ellie should have to sit through a council meeting and be dragged through the mud with him. "Maybe Ellie should skip the council meeting and let us handle it."

"I've already suggested that to her, but she'll have none of it. In fact, since Robbins didn't name names, all of my teachers are upset and in a fighting mood. They plan to stick together and face down Robbins."

Arnie wished them luck. But a guy like Robbins didn't give in easily, not with his ego. He'd have plenty of mud to sling at Ellie, and some of it was bound to stick, at least with some members of the community. Her reputation would be ruined. She might have to move away from Potter Creek, find a job somewhere else.

Please, God, don't let that happen.

Past Sins Revealed.

Her stomach churning with dread and her fingers trembling, Ellie pictured tomorrow's headline in the *Potter Creek Courier*.

She dressed in her most conservative navy-blue suit. She'd face her accusers. The whole town, if need be. But she wouldn't back down from Jeffrey Robbins.

And her actions could destroy any chance that Ability Counts could expand its program.

Torie hopped up to sit on Ellie's bed. She swung her legs back and forth, bumping against the mattress and springs. "Can I go to the city council with you?"

"No, honey. It's just a boring old meeting." Less boring than usual, from Ellie's perspective. "You wouldn't have any fun."

"Will Arnie be there?"

Standing in front of the full-length mirror in her bedroom, Ellie froze in place. The thought of Arnie hearing a recitation of the sins of her past propelled bile to her throat. She swallowed hard. How could Robbins have discovered details of her years in Spokane?

But Arnie already knew she'd had a child out of wedlock. What more could Robbins dig up—or make up—about her time in Spokane? Would Arnie believe lies about her?

"I don't know if Arnie will be there." She picked up her purse. "Tomorrow's a school day, sweetie. You be sure to be good for Grandma BarBar and go to bed when she tells you to."

When Ellie arrived at city hall, the parking lot was nearly full. She wondered if the crowd was there to support Ability Counts. Or drive an immoral woman from their midst?

Maybe some clever entrepreneur had developed a thriving business selling scarlet letters.

Once inside, Ellie saw the number of parents there to support Ability Counts, and the presence of her fellow teachers bolstered her spirits.

The knowing, sideways glances from others in the audience shook her resolve.

The seven members of the city council took their seats just as Arnie rolled down the aisle and parked his wheelchair next to Ellie.

He gave her hand a squeeze. "Don't worry. Jeff's a master at bluffing. He won't sway anyone."

Arnie's words and the warmth of his hand holding hers restored Ellie's optimism but did nothing to soothe the anxiety ripping holes in her stomach.

Mayor Knudsen, a brawny man who owned the lumberyard in town, called the meeting to order and made quick work of the routine matters on the agenda. Then he called for discussion about Ability Counts's request.

Robbins switched his microphone on and addressed the audience. "I'm sure we all support Miss Vanna's school and the services it provides, particularly for disabled children in the area. However, it is with regret that I feel it necessary to inform you that some questions about the moral character of her staff have been raised. I feel those concerns should be addressed before approving their expansion request."

The mayor interrupted. "Mr. Robbins, you'll need to be more specific. We can't act on vague accusations."

Ellie squeezed her eyes shut. *Please, God...*

"I have been reluctant to cause harm to anyone. However, if you insist..." He feigned regret with his brows lowered, his voice soft and apologetic.

Vanna leaned toward Ellie, whispering, "If you want me to withdraw our request, I will."

Her throat tight, Ellie shook her head.

"I have been informed that an individual in Miss Vanna's employ," Robbins began, "has an employment history that includes working for an unsavory establishment."

Ellie gasped and her head snapped up. "That was years ago. It was an upscale restaurant, not unsavory at all," she muttered only loud enough for those nearby to hear.

"At one point," Robbins said, "that business was

closed down due to a brawl resulting in several patrons being hospitalized."

"I wasn't even there that night," Ellie protested, her voice a hoarse whisper.

Robbins proceeded with a litany of her presumed immoral conduct, concluding, "Perhaps the most troubling evidence of this individual's inappropriate behavior is the fact that she consorted with a man of less than high moral standards and willingly admits she is an unwed mother."

A murmur of whispers spread around the council chambers like a prairie fire. Whether the audience agreed with Robbins or felt he had overstepped was impossible to tell.

Tears burning in her eyes, Ellie lowered her head. "I'll resign effective in the morning."

"You'll do no such thing," Vanna said. "You're not the only unwed mother in town."

"Don't do it," Arnie insisted. "There's no way Robbins can win this one."

Mayor Knudsen banged his gavel to silence the crowd. "Councilman Robbins has brought up some disturbing questions. However, his accusations do not *prove* actual misdeeds by the individual who he has yet to name."

The mayor looked to his fellow council members. "I believe we need to move slowly in this case. I'll entertain a motion to table the agenda item while further investigation is undertaken."

"Don't let him see you flinch," Arnie warned.

Her face as hot as if she were being burned at the stake, Ellie desperately tried to keep her chin up. When she'd read about the job opening at Ability Counts, she'd been so sure the Lord was leading her back home.

She touched the cross she wore. Would her credibility as a teacher now be totally destroyed in Potter Creek? And anywhere else she might go?

By the time the mayor adjourned the meeting, Arnie was steaming mad. He saw that Ellie's friends and fellow teachers were surrounding and supporting her. She'd be okay.

Arnie had something else he needed to do.

Spotting Amy Thurgood from the *Courier* across the room, he made his way through the departing crowd.

"Hey, Amy, I need a favor."

Her pencil stuck behind her ear, her glasses perched on top of her head, she smiled at Arnie. "Sure. What can I do for you?"

"Those accusations Robbins made tonight?"

"He was dropping a lot of bombshells there, if they're true."

"They're not," Arnie said. "Lies and distortions."

"How do you know that? He didn't name the individual involved."

"Ellie James."

The editor and sole reporter for the biweekly paper gaped at him. "You're kidding. She's a lovely young woman. I wouldn't think—"

"He asked her out, implying that if she agreed, he'd make sure the building permits would be approved. When she declined, he threatened her."

"Men! Some of them sure have their nerve." Amy plucked her notepad out of her shoulder bag and started to make notes. "Did you witness his threat?"

"No, but it's the truth." Flexing his hands, Arnie wished more than anything that he could personally make Robbins eat his words. Eight years ago, he would have gone after the sleazy character in a heartbeat. But no more. "He was talking about things that happened in Spokane while Ellie lived there and was going to college. I know you're a good enough investigative reporter to do a little fact-checking."

Her brows lifted. "I love it when a man tries to flatter me into doing something I want to do anyway."

He shook her hand. "Thanks, Amy. She deserves better than what Robbins is doing to her."

While Arnie couldn't protect Ellie's reputation with his fists, he figured—the good Lord willing—the power of the press could do the job just as well and not spill any blood.

Chapter Fourteen

"No, I will not accept your resignation." Vanna took the envelope Ellie had handed her, ripped it in half and dropped the pieces in the wastebasket beside her desk.

"After last night's council meeting, I've become a liability to the school," Ellie said reasonably, although the thought of leaving Ability Counts was breaking her heart. "If I'm no longer here, Robbins and the rest of the city council will have to—"

Vanna shook her head with such determination, her short gray hair quivered. "Jeffrey Robbins is all talk and no substance. By tabling our request, the mayor acted out of an abundance of caution. At next week's meeting everything will be sorted out. I promise."

Not as confident as her employer, Ellie started to object again. "But if the school loses the support of the community—"

"Here. This morning's *Courier*." She held up the Wednesday edition of the paper. "There's barely a mention of Robbins's wild-eyed accusations last night. See for yourself."

Taking the paper, Ellie skimmed the report of the city

council meeting. Only a brief mention of the school's building permit request being tabled appeared in the article. Nothing was said about the morals clause in the teachers' contracts.

Letting a sigh of relief escape, Ellie said, "If you're sure I'm not—"

"I'm absolutely positive." Vanna came around her desk and hugged Ellie. "You're a wonderful teacher. You take care of your students, and I'll take care of the politics for now."

As tall as Vanna was, and so slender she felt almost too bony, her hug and reassurance restored some measure of Ellie's confidence.

"If you change your mind about my resignation—"

"Hush. Go see to your children."

Ellie appreciated Vanna's loyalty and determination, but she wasn't entirely convinced it might not be better for her to resign and remove herself as a target of Robbins's ire.

Her spirits sank even deeper as she realized resigning would mean seeking another position. In all likelihood the new job wouldn't be in Potter Creek and would be a long way from Arnie. What chance would she have then to convince him of her feelings?

As the children began to arrive, one after another handed her a note from their mother or a small bouquet of chrysanthemums picked from their yard. In every case, the message supported Ellie and how much the children loved her. Obviously, the parents at the meeting had figured out Ellie had been the target of Robbins's attack.

Tears burned at the back of her eyes when Nancy,

walking with her awkward gait, arrived in the classroom and handed Ellie a huge zucchini.

"We didn't have any flowers and my mommy didn't have time to make zucchini bread for you, so she said I could bring this instead."

Ellie knelt to hug and thank the child. "Tell your mother I love zucchini bread. Maybe I'll make some tonight to share with the whole class."

Nancy beamed. "I like walnuts in mine."

"So do I."

In that moment, Ellie realized, beyond being near Arnie, just how much she wanted to stay at Ability Counts. This was where she could best use her God-given talents. Working with children who had a physical disability and hearts that beat with so much love, they could teach the world the meaning of the Golden Rule. Do unto others as you would have them do unto you.

"Mommy, Arnie's van is in our driveway."

Ellie jumped to her feet, nearly knocking over her half-finished cup of coffee on the kitchen table. Relishing a lazy Saturday morning, she'd slept late and dressed in her grubby jeans and an old pullover sweater that had seen much better days. She didn't have a smidgen of makeup on, either.

Torie made a dash for the front door.

"Wait, honey. Let me see what he wants." Frowning, Ellie wondered at his midmorning visit. Could he be bringing bad news? Even so, she felt a flutter of anticipation in her midsection.

By the time she reached the front porch, Torie had already snared Sheila's attention, the two of them playing chase around the small front yard.

Arnie parked his wheelchair at the bottom of the steps. He was dressed in jeans and a pullover sweater that didn't look any more stylish than Ellie's.

"Hi." Slightly breathless, Ellie hesitated. "I didn't expect to see you this morning. Do you want to come inside?" She gestured vaguely toward the front door.

His lips twisted into a wry smile. "Not unless you've got a ramp hidden away. Those steps are going to be tough for me to climb."

Her cheeks heated with embarrassment. "Not exactly handicapped accessible, is it?" She walked down the steps and sat down on a lower step so she'd be at eye level with Arnie. The day was cool, with a few high-level clouds floating overhead. Rain was predicted for the mountains later in the day. "What's up?"

"I brought you this morning's *Courier*. Thought you'd like to see what Amy dug up." He tapped his finger on an article on the front page of the paper, below the fold. The headline read: Councilman's Accusations Unfounded.

Curious, and not a little concerned, Ellie took the newspaper. She scanned the article.

Councilman Jeffrey Robbins insinuated a teacher at Ability Counts...multiple violations of morals clause...facts obtained from witnesses...no sug-gestion of impropriety...impeccable references... question the councilman's motives...council should immediately approve...

Ellie looked up from the paper. "How did Amy decide to check out Robbins's story?"

Arnie lifted a single shoulder in an I-don't-have-a-clue shrug.

She narrowed her gaze. "You talked to her, didn't you?"

"I might've mentioned something about slander and defamation of character. The reporting is all on Amy, though."

"Well, I sincerely thank you for whatever you did. She certainly did a great job." Leaning back, she rested her elbow on the step above her and smiled to herself. *Gotcha, Mr. Robbins.* "Now I'm extra glad I didn't agree to a date with Robbins."

"You were actually considering it?" Arnie asked, his voice rising. His expression darkened, and his brows lowered into a scowl.

As though her master had called her, Sheila came racing back to Arnie's side. Torie followed right behind the dog. She crumpled onto the ground beside Sheila, breathing hard from their game of chase.

"Not really, but I did start to wonder if it was worth it because it was the only way to get his vote. Potter Creek needs this school."

"Why didn't you trust me to take care of Robbins?" His grip on the armrests of his chair tightened.

"I had no idea you were going to get Amy to write an article to get me off the hook."

"You knew I didn't believe a word Robbins said. I wasn't going to let his insinuations stand if I could help it."

"Mommy, why are you and Arnie fighting?"

"We're not, honey," Ellie said. "We're having a little disagreement, is all."

"Then why are you shouting?" Torie asked.

"We're not." Arnie wheeled around and headed to his van.

"Wait, Arnie!" On her feet, Ellie hurried after him.

He activated the lift to lower it. "You can date any-one you want, Ellie. Like you said, it's no big deal."

"I don't have a date with anyone. I told Robbins no."

He rolled onto the lift and whipped around to glare at Ellie as Sheila hurried to join him. "I don't have any claim on you. Do whatever you want."

"But, Arnie—"

It was too late. He'd already wheeled inside and closed the door. Moments later the engine started. He backed the van and roared out the drive to the road, kicking up dust and pebbles.

Ellie's chin trembled. Tears she couldn't hold back crept down her cheeks. He didn't trust her. She'd bro-ken that trust eight years ago. Now he was breaking her heart.

Arnie made it back to the ranch in record time.

The knot in his throat was so big, he could barely swallow. His head pounded as though there was an army of carpenters inside. His chest ached.

Ellie could date any guy she wanted to.

So what's been keeping you from asking her out?

She wouldn't want to go out with me. She proved that when she bailed out of Potter Creek years ago.

She came back, didn't she?

She didn't come back for me. She came for the job.

Which happens to deal with handicapped children. What does that prove?

Maybe she's changed. Maybe loving someone who has a disability doesn't bother her anymore.

Shaking his head to dislodge the irritating voice that had invaded his thoughts, Arnie parked the van between two pickup trucks by his new house. The construction crew was installing windows today, anxious to get the place sealed up before winter storms arrived. The interior work could be done at a more leisurely pace.

Arnie hoped to be moved in by December, before Mindy's baby arrived. Not that he didn't like babies. He just wanted to give his brother and his wife some privacy. There would be plenty of time for him to play Uncle Arnie with the kid.

He rolled up the ramp into the house. Sheila's toenails tapped a rapid beat on the flooring right behind him.

"How's it going?" he asked Tim, who was installing the big picture window in its frame in the living room. Scott Derringer was helping from the outside.

Tim grunted. "If we don't drop this sucker, I'd say we're doing fine." He jammed a sliver of wood between the window and the frame to keep it straight.

Arnie glanced around, checking on the crew's progress. The kitchen windows were in place, and Daniel was installing insulation around the frames to keep out drafts. Arnie had installed wallboard as high as he could reach in all the rooms except the spare bedroom. He'd go work on that now.

Maybe pounding in a few nails would improve his mood.

By late afternoon, his buddies had packed up their tools, ready to head home.

Arnie followed them out. "Thanks, guys. Really appreciate your help."

They waved off his thanks as they piled into their pickups.

The last to leave, Tim slung his tool belt over his shoulder. "You going to the church picnic tomorrow?"

"Yeah, I guess." He'd forgotten about the annual picnic. There were lots of games for the kids, and the guys usually put together a game of flag football. Since he wasn't exactly mobile on a grass field, he was the designated quarterback. Occasionally overeager, the opposing players had managed to tackle him only a couple of times. No harm done.

"Great. I'll see you at church, then." Tim sauntered down to his truck, put his tools in the lockbox in the back and drove away.

Watching him leave, Arnie felt a sinking feeling. Chances were good Ellie would bring Torie to the picnic.

With a big crowd in attendance and decent luck, he'd be able to avoid her. He wouldn't have to apologize for being so stupid at the thought of her dating other men. He hoped.

Chapter Fifteen

Ellie drove her car out of the church parking lot to join the caravan of vehicles headed for Riverside Park and the church picnic. Although there were still rain clouds hovering above the mountain peaks of the Rockies to the west, overhead the sky was clear and the air crisp with a hint of Halloween on the way. A perfect day for hot chocolate and toasting marshmallows over an open fire.

With her mother sitting next to her, and Torie in the back seat, memories of the last time she'd visited Riverside Park swept over Ellie. She could almost feel the late-summer sun on her face, the icy-cold river water.

A half dozen couples were playing six-way keepaway with a Frisbee in a clearing near the river. The breeze, and the unpredictability of the flying saucer, resulted in more than one player having to chase the Frisbee into the water, which wasn't too deep that summer.

Arnie was the tallest among the boys and the best thrower. Regretfully, Ellie couldn't get the hang of the thing, which meant Arnie ended up in the creek. A lot. To the great rejoicing and raucous laughter of his buddies.

After his third dunking, they changed their position so she was throwing *away* from the water. But this time Arnie's effort went sailing over Ellie's head. His brother Daniel raced to intercept it.

"No!" she cried, stumbling backward to catch the Frisbee.

"Watch out!" Arnie shouted.

Daniel splashed into the water to snare the Frisbee. "You lose, bro!"

The slippery rocks and uneven footing made Ellie lose her balance. She fell backward. Gooseflesh shivered across her body as she slid under the surface. She swallowed a mouthful of water.

The next thing she knew, Arnie was pulling her up out of the freezing water, laughing at her. Her hair hung like a wet mop, dripping. He looked at her with such amazing love in his eyes that she shivered.

Lowering his head to hers, he soundly kissed her.

When he broke the kiss, he spoke in a voice rough with emotion. "We'll get 'em next time, Ellie. Nobody can beat us. We belong together."

We belong together. She still remembered his words. The joy she'd felt in her heart. The future she'd anticipated. She'd been so young, so sure nothing would change.

How could she have been so wrong?

Following the car in front of her, Ellie turned into the park entrance and drove over a bridge that spanned the river. The water looked higher than usual for this time of year, white waves splashing over the rocks lining the riverbed, carrying debris from upstream down toward the much larger Jefferson River.

"Is Arnie going to be at the picnic?" Torie asked from the back seat.

Ellie's heart squeezed an anxious beat, and she glanced in the rearview mirror at her daughter. "I don't know. I guess we'll see when we get there. I do know there will be lots of games for you to play and some of your friends from Sunday school will be there."

Dozens of cars and pickups were already parked at the group picnic area. The ladies who had organized the event had spread tablecloths on the sturdy picnic tables, and a handful of men were laying a fire in the stone ring. Nearby, children had claimed a turn on the swings and the merry-go-round.

Ellie pulled into a parking place. Her mother, who had been quiet the whole way, and Torie got out of the car.

"Can I go play on the swings?" Torie asked.

"Go ahead. But we'll be eating soon. Mom, you go on and help the ladies. I'll bring the ice chest."

Ellie opened her door just as Arnie's van drove into the handicapped slot next to her. She swallowed hard. She didn't want him to think she'd intentionally picked this spot next to the handicapped slot.

Within moments, the van door opened and the lift lowered Arnie and Sheila to the ground.

"So here we are," Arnie said, "visiting the scenes of our youth."

"We had lots of good times here."

His guarded perusal of her brought heat to her face again, and she knew he was remembering warm summer nights and the kisses they had shared. Kisses she had relished, memories she had left behind when she moved to Spokane.

"Why did you tell me to go away?" Her words were a whispered plea for understanding.

Wrinkles scored his forehead. "I don't remember telling you that."

"You did." The pain of rejection still had the power to bring her to her knees. "You told me two times to leave and not to bother to come back. The first time I figured you were still fuzzy from the meds. The second time…" She'd fled the room, crying. Nearly hysterical. The worst day of her life. How could he not remember when his words had been etched in her memory by the acid of betrayal?

He rubbed his forehead as though trying to recreate the moment. "I'm sorry, Ellie. I really don't remember. I was pretty much out of it for a long time. But I do recall thinking later on that you were smart to get on with your life without me."

In order to protect herself, to keep on going, she'd tried to believe that was true. She'd never been able to fully convince herself. Instead, she'd carried the guilt of leaving him for eight long years.

"I guess you still don't want me in your life," she said.

He wiped his hand across his face. "Nothing has changed, has it? I'm stuck in this chair for the rest of my life."

And Ellie was stuck loving him.

Turning away, she opened the back door of her car and pulled out the ice chest. "I need to get this over to the tables. We'll be eating soon." She walked quickly away so he wouldn't see the tears that burned in her eyes. Her love was pointless if he saw himself only as a man in a wheelchair who was unable to love her in return.

"Ellie!"

She turned at the sound of her name and found Mindy hurrying toward her, her advancing pregnancy giving her a distinctive waddle.

"Hey, Mindy. Looks like your pregnancy is progressing nicely," she said with a grin.

"Nicely, if you think looking like an elephant is in style this season."

Ellie laughed. "Your glow makes up for everything else. You look wonderful."

They visited for a few minutes, then Pastor Redmond called everyone together to say grace before they ate.

Too excited to eat, Torie managed only a few bites before she was off again to play with her friends.

Ellie lingered over her lunch, indulging in a magnificent five-layer chocolate cake for dessert. She'd worry about her diet tomorrow.

Most of the men had divided themselves into two teams to play football in an open, grassy area.

Squinting, Ellie gaped at the players. It couldn't be.

"Mindy, is that Arnie playing quarterback?" *In his wheelchair?* Was there anything that man *couldn't* do? How could he possibly think of himself as disabled?

"Sure is. Daniel says his brother is dead-on with his passes. His team wins every year. Of course, they have a rule that no one can rush the passer."

"I should think not." If they did, they'd probably squash Arnie and trample poor Sheila, who doggedly stayed near her master.

"Speaking of Arnie," Mindy said. "How's it going with the two of you?"

Ellie shook her head. "At the moment, it's not going anywhere and probably won't." To her dismay.

"I'm sorry to hear—"

A piercing scream penetrated the bucolic scene.

Everyone froze right where they were as if a snapshot had been taken. Only the breeze in the trees and the rushing water broke the silence.

Automatically, Ellie looked around to find Torie. A few minutes ago she'd been playing hide-and-seek with some of her friends. But now Ellie couldn't see her. An icy shiver of fear slid down her spine.

"Mom...my!"

The blood-chilling scream propelled Ellie to her feet. *Victoria!* Recognizing her child's cry, she raced toward the water.

Vaguely, she was aware of others running with her, but her entire focus was on reaching her child. Her baby girl. What had happened? Where was Torie? Why hadn't she kept better track of her daughter?

"Torie!" she shouted. "Where are you?"

Her heart pounding, she reached the edge of the creek, but Torie wasn't in sight. She looked up and down the fast-moving water, which seemed to be roiling even more violently than before.

"There!" someone shouted.

Her gaze shifted to follow the direction in which a woman was pointing. There she saw her daughter's dark red hair bobbing above the roiling water. *Please, Lord, help her...*

Suddenly there was scrambling downstream. Apparently while others had headed toward where Torie had fallen into the river, Arnie and some of the men had angled downstream to intercept her. In his wheelchair,

Arnie was perched on an outcropping of rock above the creek. He leaned forward. Waiting.

With his powerful arms, he launched himself forward into the creek only feet in front of a frantically crying, splashing Torie.

Ellie's heart stopped. No way could Arnie swim without the use of his legs. Not in this rapidly churning water. They'd both be killed. Drowned.

Breaking into a run, she dashed toward the spot where Arnie had entered the water. Brush whipped at her legs. Branches snatched at her face. She couldn't lose both of them. Not the two people on earth whom she loved more than life itself.

Yelling at his brother, Daniel leaped into the water, swimming after Arnie. Other men followed the path along the creek, ready to go in the water, as well.

Arnie's head appeared above the water. He spun around. Spotted Torie. With massive strokes of his arms, he swam after her. He bounced off a boulder. Just ahead of him, Torie became lodged momentarily between the rocks. Then the power of the rain-swollen river swept her downstream again.

Arnie didn't give up. He pursued Torie with the strength of an Olympic athlete.

Torie became lodged between other rocks. Ellie could see blood oozing from her daughter's forehead. She lay lax in the water, a rag doll, limbs akimbo, no longer fighting the pull of the stream.

Sheila, who'd been trailing along beside the creek, jumped in to aid her master just as Arnie reached Torie. He wrapped an arm around the child and held on to a rock to prevent them both from careening downstream, where a waterfall dropped into a steep canyon.

Daniel caught up with the pair, wrapping his arms around both of them.

Ellie prayed for their safety. All three of them.

Sheila paddled valiantly toward Arnie. The current swept the dog past her goal. She turned, fighting her way back against the force of the creek.

Slowly she inched toward Arnie, only to be driven back again by the powerful surge of water.

Covering her mouth with her hands to prevent a scream, Ellie held her breath.

Finally, Sheila reached an eddy near Arnie, the water smoother, and paddled closer to her master.

When the dog was within arm's reach, Arnie risked his hold on the rock and grabbed on to Sheila, looping his arm around her neck. Daniel latched onto Torie. Together they all swam for shore. Sheila's head dipped below the waves time and time again. Arnie's face contorted with pain. His black hair matted against his head. Daniel kept Torie above water as he stroked toward those waiting to help.

When they reached the shallows along the creek side, a half dozen men waded into the water to help Arnie. Daniel lifted Torie in his arms and staggered out of the creek. Her arms and legs limp, the child showed no sign of life.

All Ellie could do was drop to her knees beside her child as Daniel rolled Torie over and drove the water from Torie's lungs. Turning her onto her back, Daniel held the child's nose closed and began breathing into Torie's mouth.

Ellie prayed as she never had before.

Chapter Sixteen

Torie coughed up some water and moaned.

Ellie nearly collapsed in relief.

"There you go, sweetheart." Daniel rocked back on his heels and looked up at Ellie. The relief in his dark eyes reflected her own.

"Thank you," she whispered, kneeling beside her child and taking Torie's hand. She squeezed it gently. "You're okay, baby. You're okay now."

Torie coughed again but didn't open her eyes. The gash on her head created a river of blood that slid past her hairline. A purple bruise colored her cheek. Ellie couldn't tell if there were any bones broken.

Ellie's stomach nearly rebelled at the possibility.

"Wake up, sweetie. Mommy wants to see your eyes."

Ellie's mother squatted down beside her. "Is she all right?" Her whisper-thin voice trembled.

"I don't know," Ellie answered.

She dug in the pocket of her slacks for something to staunch the flow of blood. Daniel handed her a clean handkerchief. She pressed it to Torie's wound.

"I'm going to go check on Arnie," he said.

Keeping the pressure on Torie's wound, Ellie looked around for Arnie. He was still on the ground near the riverbank, several concerned-looking men hovering around him.

Her heart stilled and filled with so much love she thought it might burst. Without Arnie, she could have lost her child. He'd been the first to reach Torie. He'd saved her life, risking his own in the process, holding her out of the water until more help could arrive. *Please let him be all right, Lord.*

Apparently, someone had called 9-1-1. A yellow and white fire rescue truck roared into the picnic grounds, siren wailing. The truck pulled to a stop and the driver cut the siren, but the red lights continued to circle above the truck cab like the flashing eyes of a dragon. Ellie shivered.

The two paramedics separated, one running toward Arnie and the other to Torie.

A young man in a firefighter uniform knelt beside Torie and placed his stethoscope on her tiny chest. He listened for only a moment, then began gently examining the child, searching for injuries.

"What happened here, ma'am?"

"She fell in the water. That man on the ground over there saved her." Arnie O'Brien, her hero.

He glanced in Arnie's direction. "Good man."

"The best," she said with heartfelt emphasis.

"Mommy…"

Thank You, Lord! "I'm right here, sweetie. This nice man is going to make sure you're all right."

"Grandma BarBar's here, too, honey." Barbara's voice hitched. "You're going to be fine. Try not to move. Just let the nice man do his job."

The paramedic sat back on his haunches. "She's probably got a concussion. Some bruising and contusions, but no breaks that I can tell. I'm going to get a gurney and strap her down nice and tight just in case she's got back or neck problems. We'll take her to the hospital and let the docs take a look."

"May I ride with her?" Ellie asked, a plea in her voice.

"Sure. Glad to have you along." With a smile, he patted Torie's cheek. "You stay right here, princess. I'm coming right back, and I'm going to give you a ride in my chariot."

"Okay." She gave him a weak smile.

Ellie handed her mother the car keys. "Can you drive yourself home?"

"Nonsense. I'll meet you at the hospital."

A smile of gratitude lifted Ellie's lips. She didn't want to sit for hours in a hospital waiting room alone while doctors did who knew what to her daughter. Ellie needed her mother's steadying hand.

"Thanks, Mom." She hadn't seen her mother look so determined, so sure of herself in years. Because of her love for her grandchild, Barbara had risen to the occasion. Ellie would have to remember that and trust her mother had the strength to endure whatever came her way.

It took several minutes for the two paramedics to load both Arnie and Torie in their vehicle. One paramedic stayed in the back with his patients, and Ellie squeezed in between Torie and Arnie.

Daniel had to hold on to Sheila to prevent the wet, muddy dog from jumping up to be with Arnie.

"I'll see you at the hospital," Daniel said as the driver closed the door to the vehicle.

"How are you doing?" Ellie asked Arnie. His wet flannel shirt clung to his chest. The paramedic had covered him with a warm blanket, as he had Torie.

"I'm good. Couple of cracked ribs, maybe. I'll live."

She took his hand and squeezed his fingers. "I don't know how to thank you."

"Don't, Ellie." His expression unreadable, he looked away and removed his hand from hers. "Don't thank me."

"You saved my daughter's life." Her voice rose, challenging his statement. "You could've been killed yourself," she protested, stunned and hurt by his withdrawal.

His jaw muscle flexed. "If I had two good legs, she wouldn't have gotten so banged up."

The rescue vehicle lurched forward. Ellie held on to a safety railing.

"What are you talking about?" she asked. "You jumped in the river first. You were the first one to reach her."

"I couldn't let her drown." He turned back to her, his eyes bleak. "I didn't want you to lose her."

Ellie's heart expanded with love and admiration. The man didn't seem to realize that what he'd done was heroic. And he'd done it for her and her daughter.

Not caring that the paramedic was there, Ellie leaned forward and pressed a kiss to Arnie's lips, tasted the chilly water. It hurt that he didn't respond, but she was past the point of caring.

"Arnie O'Brien, you can't stop me from thanking you, and you can't stop me from loving you. That's just the way it is."

He scrolled his brows into a frown. "You stopped loving me a long time ago."

"No, I didn't stop loving you. I chickened out, I admit. I couldn't stay in Potter Creek after you told me to go away. I was young and foolish. I shouldn't have believed you. But I'm back now. And I'm here to stay."

Siren wailing, the truck bounced in a pothole, then rode up onto the highway.

Arnie grimaced. "Torie needs a man around who can climb trees with her, teach her to play soccer. A man with two good legs. You need a man who can love you in every way you have a right to be loved."

"And you can't love me at all." That wasn't a question, but a statement of fact. Ellie pressed her lips together.

He turned his face to the wall again. "I didn't say that."

His voice was so low, and the siren so loud, Ellie didn't think she'd heard him clearly. "What did you say?"

"Nothing. It doesn't matter."

Ellie thought it did matter. Wanting to drag the words out of him again, she fisted her hands.

"Mommy, I don't like this chariot." Blood had oozed through the gauze bandage the paramedic had wrapped around her forehead, turning it red.

Stroking Torie's head and brushing her damp hair away from her forehead, Ellie said, "It's okay, sweetie. It won't be a long ride." She glanced at the medic.

"Thirty minutes," he silently mouthed.

Ellie grimaced. Thirty minutes would seem like an eternity to Torie. In this sparsely populated part of Montana, hospitals were few and far between.

"Hey, squirt," Arnie said to Torie. "How're you doing?"

"My head hurts."

"Yeah, mine does, too. Next time we go swimming, let's pick a spot that doesn't have so many rocks."

"I don't want to go swimming anymore." Tears bloomed in Torie's eyes. Ellie wiped them away with a tissue.

"Okay. Where do you want to go?" Arnie asked.

"I want to go home!" Her tiny voice wobbled.

"How 'bout the zoo?" Arnie asked. "I really like to watch the monkeys climb around in their cage. What do you think? We could have a lot of fun at the zoo."

"I like giraffes."

"Terrific. We'll see the monkeys and the giraffes. What else?"

Ellie knew Arnie was trying to keep Torie's mind off her injuries and the swaying ride of the emergency vehicle. She blessed him for his thoughtfulness.

If only she hadn't been a coward about his injuries eight years ago, they'd be married by now. He'd be the father of her children.

But that would mean she wouldn't have had Torie. For that reason alone, she'd never want to erase the past. It was what it was.

She could only pray Arnie could find a way to trust her again, open his heart to her love and know that she would always be faithful to him.

At long last, the ambulance pulled up to the hospital emergency entrance. The back doors popped open.

"What have we got here, Walt?" a nurse in light blue scrubs asked.

"Female child with a possible concussion and adult

male with broken ribs," the medic replied. "Both patients are stable."

"Good enough. Let's get them out of there."

"Chariot ride is over, Torie." Squeezing her daughter's hand, Ellie eased out of the ambulance. She stood by while the medics retrieved the gurneys.

The nurse said, "Looks like your husband and daughter have had a busy afternoon."

"An unplanned dip in the river." Ellie didn't correct the nurse's assumption that Arnie was her husband. It took too much effort to deny what should have been and never would be.

Arnie didn't make eye contact as an orderly rolled him though the yawning doors to the emergency room.

Aching and heavyhearted, Ellie held Torie's hand as she was wheeled through the same doors.

Help me, Lord. Help me to let go if there's no hope.

"That was a pretty dumb thing you did, bro."

Arnie opened one eye to peer up at his brother from his hospital bed. Doctors had pinched, poked and jabbed him in the emergency room, x-rayed and wrapped his broken ribs. Finally they decided to keep him overnight for observation.

He hated hospitals. The smell of antiseptic. The rattle of food and laundry carts, the wheels squeaking and rumbling down the hallway, unseen. The bark of the loudspeaker paging a doctor—stat. Drafty hospital gowns.

It was the craziest stunt he'd ever pulled. What crazy impulse had made him, a paraplegic, think he could swim in a rain-swollen creek well enough to save himself, much less a helpless child?

"Everybody's calling you a hero."

"I was stupid." Just about as stupid as wanting to believe Ellie, wanting her to kiss him again, wanting to take her at her word that she'd never stopped loving him. Now that was *really* stupid.

He still wasn't the right man for Ellie. She and her daughter deserved so much more.

Daniel lowered the guardrail and sat on the edge of the bed. "I checked on Torie. The docs stitched her head up and sent her home. Ellie's supposed to keep her eye on her and wake her every couple of hours during the night."

"She's going to be okay, then?"

"The docs think so, or they wouldn't have sent her home."

Closing his eyes, Arnie said a prayer of thanksgiving. "What'd you do with Sheila?"

"Outside with Mindy. I've gotta get her to a vet for a checkup and a bath before the hospital will let her come up here with you. I put your chair here next to your bed if you need it."

"Thanks for taking care of everything."

"No problem." Daniel gripped his brother's hand in an arm wrestling hold, the way they had when they were kids, but he didn't take advantage of Arnie's weakened state. Not this time. "You get some rest. I'll come back in the morning to bail you out of this place."

"Come early. I don't want to stay here any longer than I have to."

After Daniel left, Arnie lay on his back, staring at the acoustical tile ceiling. If he had the energy, he could count the holes in each tile.

But what would be the point?

He was stuck here in the bed like a turtle rolled onto its back. Useless. Unable to escape. Any movement as painful as though somebody was stabbing him in the ribs with a sharp stick.

He curled his hands into fists.

It was just as well Ellie hadn't come upstairs to tell him she was taking Torie home. She didn't need to see him like this. Not again.

Not like he'd been when she'd left him eight years ago.

Ellie held herself together that evening until after dinner, when she put Torie to bed and was sure her child was sleeping peacefully. She continued to sit beside Torie, watching her breathe, the pink princess quilt gently rising and falling, and let the tears roll.

She'd been so scared!

Her lungs seized, and she reached for a tissue to blow her nose. What if Arnie hadn't been there? What if she'd lost Torie?

"Ellie." Standing in the doorway, her mother spoke softly. "Come on, dear. She'll be fine now. Come sit with me in the living room."

"I don't want to leave—"

Barbara held out her hand. "You don't want her to wake and see you crying."

Her mother was right, of course. But it was hard to leave Torie. To walk out of the room and not check her every breath. To not want to hold on to her all through the night.

Ellie stepped to the doorway. Her mother looped her arm around Ellie's waist, and they walked together down the hallway to the living room. Barbara sat down beside her on the couch.

"God was watching over us today." Barbara patted Ellie's hands, which had nearly shredded the tissue.

"God and Arnie," she said.

"Yes, and Arnie, too." She leaned back on the couch and sighed deeply. "I believe I seriously misjudged that young man. Years ago, when you were seeing him, I liked him well enough, but I was afraid for you. I wanted more than an early marriage followed by babies for you. I wanted you to have an education, something I never had a chance to get."

Ellie slid her mother a surprised look. She'd had no idea Barbara had even considered going to college. She'd never said a word. She'd seemed content being a potato farmer's wife.

"After Arnie's accident," Barbara said, "I knew if you stayed, you'd marry him and that would mean you'd never have the opportunities you deserved. So I encouraged you to leave. It nearly broke my heart. Your father's, too."

This was definitely news to Ellie. She'd believed the whole reason Barbara had insisted she move to Spokane was to prevent her from marrying a paraplegic and being tied down as her family had been with Uncle Bob.

"Then you came back home, and I was afraid you were going to take up with Arnie again."

"He doesn't want me, Mother."

"I'm not so sure of that." She brushed Ellie's hair back from her temple, much like Ellie had done with Torie's hair. "At Torie's birthday party, he was wonderful with the children. And I saw him looking at you. I know when a man is in love. I saw that same look in your father's eyes every day of our life together. With you and Arnie, it rather frightened me, I admit. I still didn't want you two to get together."

"Well, you're going to get your way. First, Arnie can't bring himself to trust me, because I left him before. And second, perhaps more important, I don't think he believes he's enough of a man for any woman."

"After what he did today?" Barbara snorted. "A man who has that much courage and gumption, who's that willing to risk his own life, is a man any woman would be happy to marry."

"I'm glad to hear you say that, Mother, but you don't have to convince me. It's what Arnie believes that's holding him back." There was nothing Ellie could do to change his mind.

Pensive, Barbara rubbed her fingertip over the slight cleft in her chin, a mannerism that spoke of deep thought. "Arnie has been quite active in church these past few years. The Lord has always been good about working through Pastor Redmond. Maybe you should ask him to talk to Arnie."

Ellie was more than willing to talk to the pastor about Arnie. She loved Arnie so much that she'd use the biggest megaphone she could find to get someone to wake him to what they were both missing. The love they had to share.

But would Arnie listen to the pastor?

Maybe she'd talk to him after the city council settled the Ability Counts issue...

Chapter Seventeen

Two days later, shortly after the city council meeting had been called to order, a cheer went up from the packed chamber. They'd won!

The city council had approved the building permit for Ability Counts.

As though lifted by the enthusiasm of the crowd, Ellie jumped to her feet. She embraced Vanna, her arms easily encompassing the slender woman.

"You did it!" Ellie said over the applause and cheers.

"We did it together. All of us." Her voice breathless, her eyes damp with tears, Vanna returned her embrace. Her emotions were so powerful, she trembled. Ellie recalled how pale and tired Vanna had seemed all day and then again when she arrived at the city council meeting. She'd been rubbing her left arm and jaw almost constantly. The stress of the past few weeks had obviously taken its toll, Ellie concluded.

Everyone who was involved with the school had turned out for the Tuesday night meeting. Everyone except Jeffrey Robbins, who had suddenly taken ill, according to the mayor.

Smiling a gotcha grin, and tickled way down to her toes, Ellie chided herself for not being concerned for Jeffrey's health. Whatever *illness* had kept him from the meeting, he'd brought on himself. And the Chronicle had put the facts in print.

Supporters gathered around Vanna, congratulating her, shaking her hand and giving her more hugs. Between hugs and good wishes, she rubbed her jaw and shifted her shoulders, as though trying to relax tense muscles. Understandable, given the situation and the weeks of preparation and planning for this night.

Ellie slipped past her, taking time to high-five her fellow teachers and thank some of her students' parents before she reached Arnie, who was sitting at the end of the aisle. She walked up beside him.

"I owe you another big thank-you." Ellie hadn't talked to him since the ride in the ambulance from the picnic and didn't know quite what to expect from him. Nor had she had a chance to speak to Pastor Redmond as yet. "If you hadn't sicced Amy at the *Courier* on Robbins, the outcome might've been different."

He shrugged, wincing a little, as though his ribs still bothered him. They probably would for another few weeks. "I figured I had to do something. The school means a lot to Vanna."

"To me, too."

"I know. It's the reason you came back to Potter Creek."

"True. But now there's another reason I'm glad I came back."

He gave her a sideways scowl. "Another reason?"

Was every man as dense as Arnie? She pressed in

on his personal space. "Maybe, after all this time, I'm hoping we might have another chance."

"You want a second chance? For us?"

"Does that seem so strange to you?" Her chest constricted with a mix of love and fear of loss. *Please God, let him see how much I love him.*

Straightening, she rested her hand on his shoulder, the breadth of his muscular upper body stretching his sweater, revealing his elemental strength beneath the fabric. She could feel his heat seeping through the cashmere to warm her palm. And her heart.

If anything, Arnie's expression was more confused than ever.

The mayor banged his gavel. "Ladies and gentlemen," he shouted over the crowd noise. "We have some more business to conduct. If those of you who aren't concerned with the next agenda item could step outside, we'd appreciate it."

Most of the crowd began to shuffle toward the exits. Ellie fell in step beside Arnie, her hand still on his shoulder as they moved slowly toward the rear of the chambers. Sheila walked beside him on the opposite side.

Outside, in a patio lined by willow trees starting to shed their golden leaves, the throng of Ability Counts supporters continued to chat among themselves, all smiles.

Daniel and Mindy, who'd been sitting in the back of the meeting room, made their way to Arnie and Ellie.

"Hey, you two." Daniel aimed a knowing look at Ellie and her hand resting on Arnie's shoulder. "You two are looking pretty proud of yourselves after your big win."

"You'd better believe it, bro."

With heat flooding her face, Ellie dropped her hand to her side. "Vanna's very pleased about getting the permit. It's been a long road for her. Now all she has to do is raise ten gazillion dollars to actually build the new classrooms."

"She's a master at fund-raising," Arnie commented.

"Better her than me," Ellie said. "I'm happy simply teaching my kids and watching them grow."

Tilting his head up, Arnie slanted her a look she couldn't read, somehow both serious and curious. "I'm guessing you're quite capable of doing anything you set your mind to, including fundraising."

She laughed off his comment. "I, for one, hope Ability Counts doesn't have to test your supposition."

"Oh, I don't know. You can be very persuasive."

Lifting her brows, Ellie wondered if Arnie meant that as a compliment. Or was he simply flattering her? Or maybe, she prayed, he'd finally gotten the message: she loved him.

From the middle of the crowd a man shouted, "We need a doctor over here."

"Somebody call nine-one-one!"

"I don't think she's breathing."

For an instant, no one moved. Then, in tandem, Daniel and Arnie shot toward the center of the patio, plowing their way through the immobile crowd.

Instinctively, Mindy placed her hand over her distended belly. "What do you think happened?"

Remembering the sight of Daniel hauling Torie out of the water, Ellie shivered. "Whatever it is, it doesn't sound good."

Whispered words sped through the onlookers like a dam had sprung a leak. The murmur spread, widening its wake, creating waves of gasps and soulful prayers, until the words reached Ellie's ears.

Vanna. Collapsed. Unconscious. Heart attack!

Dread thrummed in Ellie's chest. Tears stung her eyes. She covered her mouth to hold back a sob. Her fear was colored with desperation; her panic smothered in denial.

She'd just been talking with Vanna, applauding her success. She had sat beside her during the entire meeting. She'd been fine. Perhaps a little pale, her face had had a sheen of sweat, but Ellie had credited that to the importance of getting the permits. The strain Vanna had been under. And the excitement that followed.

She'd never considered Vanna might be ill.

As though drawn by the slender thread of hope, she eased her way through the crowd until she reached Arnie. He took her hand, squeezing her fingers as they watched Daniel press rhythmically on Vanna's chest.

The crowd remained silent, respectful, prayerful as Daniel counted, "One. Two. Three…"

"Where's the ambulance? The rescue squad?" Ellie whispered.

Arnie shook his head. "They'll be here soon." The concern in his voice matched her own.

The county fire department and police department served Potter Creek. The closest fire station was ten miles away. The response time was slower than the community would like, but a lack of funds…

Feeling helpless, heartsick and useless, she clung to Arnie's hand. *Vanna, her boss. Her mentor. Her friend.*

Minutes passed, until she finally heard the siren approaching. While she waited, she mentally reviewed the way Vanna had been acting. Had the frequent rubbing of her arm, and then her jaw, been a symptom of something more than simply stress? Had Vanna been on the verge of a heart attack for weeks? Or longer?

The crowd parted. Two paramedics dashed across the patio and knelt beside Vanna.

Ellie prayed they had arrived in time.

Two hours later, more than a dozen people waited in the hospital lobby outside the emergency room entrance. Some stood and paced. Others sat in uncomfortable plastic chairs, huddled with their friends, talking quietly among themselves. No one bothered with the array of magazines or hospital pamphlets available to while away their time. Their combined distress and concern for Vanna made even the air in the room feel heavy, as though an approaching storm threatened to overwhelm them.

Among those who had gathered for the vigil were Pastor Redmond, several of Ellie's fellow teachers, two sets of parents and a few of Vanna's friends who had known and loved her for years.

Mindy and Daniel had gone back to the ranch. Rather than drive herself to the hospital, after letting her mother know she'd be late, Ellie had ridden with Arnie, grateful to have his company and his calming strength.

Except her calm had worn off after the first hour of waiting.

"If the worst happens," she asked, "what will become of Ability Counts?"

"The school will go on as it has been. Vanna created a solid foundation for her dream. The school is more than a single person, which is what she wanted.

It's parents and teachers, supporters from all across the state, and the children themselves. In the worst case, the board would have to hire a new director, of course."

Ellie wondered how the board could possibly find anyone as devoted to the school's mission as Vanna was.

Instantly, she halted that thought. Vanna wasn't going to die. She'd be fine. People survived heart attacks every day. Vanna would be no exception. She might have to stay off work for a time, or perhaps work fewer hours. But with rest and rehabilitation, she'd recover. She had to!

The door to the ER swung open. Everyone turned as a woman in blue scrubs hurried out and turned down a hallway. She didn't spare so much as a glance toward those waiting in the lobby.

Unable to sit still any longer, Ellie popped to her feet. "What's taking them so long? Why doesn't someone come tell us what's going on?"

"Easy, El." Arnie snared her hand and rubbed his thumb over her knuckles. "They're doing everything they can for Vanna. We just have to wait it out."

"Wait. And pray."

"True." He glanced around. "There's a chapel down the hall. Let's go check it out."

"But if someone comes out—"

"They'll let us know." Giving her hand a tug, he wheeled around, heading for the chapel. Sheila fell into step right beside him.

Ellie had little choice but to follow.

Soft music, a string quartet, was piped into the dimly lit room. On a background of pastel green, murals of the Rockies, pine forests and prairies decorated the walls. A water feature at the front of the chapel showed a stream spilling out of the wall to cascade down a mountainside, splashing into a natural pool.

The serenity of the room, the peace and God's presence washed over Ellie as she sat down on a wooden pew. Her shoulders relaxed. Her worried frown eased. Breathing deeply, she caught the scent of pine in the air, heard the rushing water and felt the cool mountain breeze on her overheated cheeks.

Arnie was right. Prayer was the answer.

As though he'd read her mind, he took her hand and bowed his head. She leaned forward to the back of the next pew and rested her head on her hand.

"Dear Heavenly Father," Arnie began in a quiet yet deeply resonant baritone. "We are here to plead for Your help for our friend Vanna Coulter. We know she is Your devoted servant and that You have the power to see her through this crisis. We ask that You heal her and bring her back to us so that she can continue serving You and complete the work which has been her lifelong calling."

Tears crept down Ellie's cheeks as Arnie prayed, his voice steady, his words coming from the heart.

He finished the prayer with "Thy will be done. Amen."

"Amen," she echoed with a sob and turned to him, putting her head on his shoulder, her cheek caressed by his cashmere sweater. It was the most natural thing in the world to have his arms around her. He held her, patted her back and brushed tiny kisses to her hair and forehead, murmuring sweet words of comfort.

When she lifted her head, his shirt was soaked and there were tears in his eyes.

She looked up to find Pastor Redmond standing in

the chapel doorway. Lines of grief etched his face, making him look suddenly old and tired.

"She's with the Lord now." His solemn pronouncement rang hollow in the muted silence of the chapel. "She's sitting at His right hand, watching over us."

Sorrow clogged Ellie's chest until she could barely draw a breath.

"She would want us to continue her work," the pastor said. "The teachers and parents have asked that you come join them. They look up to you, Ellie, and need you."

Ellie swiped her eyes with the back of her hand. What could she possibly do to help them when her own grief was so fresh, so raw, weighing on her as though a mountain avalanche had buried her?

"Go, Ellie," Arnie said. "Be strong for them."

She studied him, the sorrow in his dark eyes as deep as her own. "I need you with me."

He responded with a solemn nod.

Arnie followed Ellie and the pastor back to the lobby, awed by the way she had set her own grief aside. Her back straight, her head held high, she approached her fellow teachers and Vanna's friends. To each she offered a hug and whispered words of encouragement.

"How will we tell the children?" Dawn asked, her voice unsteady, her eyes red-rimmed.

"We'll tell them the truth," Ellie answered. "The Lord called Vanna to His side. Her work here on earth is done. We'll all miss her. To honor her memory, we'll carry on with what she started. That's what she would want us to do."

"But how?" Marlene asked. "Vanna was the one with

the vision. She was at the center of Ability Counts. The core of it."

"She shared her vision. It's inside each of us." Ellie tapped her chest, over her heart, as she glanced around at the somber group. "That was Vanna's gift. Together we'll bring that vision to fruition."

The tightness of loss and grief in Arnie's chest eased, replaced with the hope and confidence Ellie imparted to the others. The fact that she was years younger than many of those she hugged and encouraged didn't matter. Somehow they sensed that she was a leader, someone to lean on.

She was not the same young woman who had deserted him so many years ago. The changes were more than skin-deep. With maturity she'd found her own core, her own strength.

Arnie wondered if he had lost more than he had imagined the day Ellie left town.

Chapter Eighteen

The week passed in a blur of grief and a battle to keep emotions in check.

For some, her pastor and her doctor, Vanna's death had not come as a surprise. She'd been born with an enlarged heart. She'd been aware, more than most, that her time on earth would be limited. She'd kept that a secret, a secret that had motivated her to strive as hard as she could to leave a legacy for those who would follow.

To her dismay, Ellie realized she should have recognized the signs of Vanna's impending heart attack—her sickly complexion, the way she rubbed at her jaw and massaged her left arm. If only she'd said something, perhaps Vanna would have avoided, or at least survived, her heart attack.

But Vanna must have known what was coming.

The morning after Vanna's funeral, Ellie was called in to the conference room to meet with the school's board of directors.

Ellie ran a quick comb through her hair, freshened her lip gloss and left her students in Dawn's care.

She shivered a little in the cool, crisp autumn air.

Below-freezing temperatures at night and a chill wind had stolen the last of the leaves from the poplar trees that provided a windbreak on the north side of the school property. The branches looked like skeletal hands praying for the quick return of spring.

Taking a steadying breath, she stepped into the main office building. She had no idea why the board wanted to see her and could only hope she wasn't about to be fired.

The board members sat around the same long table where she and the other teachers had met with Vanna so often. They had absorbed her dedication like blotters, had learned the lesson of commitment from her example and were better teachers because of her insights and what she taught.

Richard Connolly, the board president and manager of the local branch of Montana Ranchers and Merchants Bank, stood at the head of the table. He wore a Western-cut shirt with a bolo tie and Western-style dark slacks.

"Thank you for coming, Ms. James," he said. "I know this has been a difficult week for the entire staff, and we appreciate your time."

With a subdued smile, she returned his greeting. She was the most junior of the staff members. If they were going to let her go, she wondered where she'd be able to get another job, particularly at midterm. Would she have to drive all the way to Bozeman? A commute she wouldn't relish.

"I think you know most of the board members," Connolly said. "Arnie O'Brien, of course…"

She'd avoided looking at Arnie, afraid of what she might see in his eyes. But now when his gaze captured hers, she saw a twinkle she couldn't translate and a dazzling smile that set her heart beating double-time. What was he thinking? What did he know?

She'd lost track of Connolly's introductions. Fortunately, she knew Pastor Redmond and recognized most of the other board members, if not by name, by the fact that they had spoken for Ability Counts at both the school board and city council meetings.

Connolly concluded by asking her to sit in the vacant chair at the foot of the table, and she dragged her attention back to the meeting.

"As you may have surmised by now," he said, "Vanna was aware of her heart condition and what it meant for both her future and the future of Ability Counts."

Ellie wondered at Vanna's ability to live her life with the sword of mortality forever poised over her head. An amazing woman.

"In her inimitable fashion, Vanna provided a plan for her own succession and the future of the school," Connolly said. "The board has discussed and evaluated her plan and has agreed with her decision. On Vanna's behalf, we would like to offer you the position of executive director of Ability Counts Preschool and Day Care Center."

His words paralyzed her, and she gaped at the banker in stunned disbelief. Her face flushed, her palms turned sweaty and her ears began to ring. They weren't firing her? They wanted her to take over Vanna's position?

She shook her head. "That's..." Her voice broke. "That's impossible. I'm not qualified—"

"Apparently Vanna thought otherwise." He gave her a fatherly smile, as though she had been named the class valedictorian. "We've examined your record both here and in Spokane. While your experience is limited, we believe, as did Vanna, that you are the best person to carry out the vision of Ability Counts and lead us into the future."

Her mouth had become disengaged from her brain and remained open, but no words were forthcoming.

She cleared her throat. "There are so many things Vanna did for the school that I know nothing about. Fundraising. Architectural drawings. Supervising teachers."

"You're smart, Ellie," Arnie said, still grinning at her. "You'll learn."

"And we'll all be here to help you," the pastor promised.

"Naturally, we can understand if you'd like to take some time to consider our offer," Connolly said. "You have your family to think about and the commitment a position of this nature requires."

"Thank you. As you might guess, I'm beyond surprised." She glanced again at Arnie. Had he known this was coming? If so, he certainly hadn't given her a hint.

The board president walked to her end of the table.

"This is a copy of the contract we'd ask you to sign. You'll notice there would be a substantial increase in your salary and benefits. We're only sorry it can't be more. Nonprofit organizations, as I'm sure you know, operate on a limited budget."

Ellie did know the disadvantages of being a preschool teacher. As director she would have far more financial security, could perhaps have her own place and better insurance coverage for Torie. But she'd miss the day-to-day contact with the children.

She rubbed at her temple as if she could so easily bring order to her confused thoughts.

"Thank you all for this opportunity. I'll give you an answer as soon as I can. Next week at the latest."

Her head reeling, she stood, shook hands with Connolly and headed back to her classroom.

Was she capable of stepping into Vanna's more than capable shoes?

Equally important, was that what she wanted to do with her life?

Vanna had never married, had never had children. Her only family was a sister who lived in Florida. She'd been too ill to come to the funeral.

Ability Counts had been Vanna's family. Her whole life.

Was that what Ellie wanted? She simply didn't know. *Please, Lord, help me. Is this the path You want me to follow? Is this why I was called to return to Potter Creek?*

If she accepted the position, what impact would that have on her relationship with Arnie? Although their relationship already seemed to be at a dead end.

Then again, what had that grin of his meant in the board meeting? That he wanted her to take the job?

Grief was often a passing emotion with young children. That was the case Friday morning, when Ellie set off with her eager students to the O'Brien ranch for their weekly horseback riding class, the last one of the year.

"I bet Daniel will let me ride all by myself," Carson insisted. "He said I'm a real good rider."

"You certainly are," Ellie agreed, glancing into the rearview mirror. "We'll have to see if Daniel thinks you're ready to ride on your own."

"I am," Torie piped up. "I can steer Patches really good."

A tiny barb of panic zinged Ellie's heart. The idea of Torie riding off on her own gave her a good many second thoughts. She hadn't yet recovered from the terror of Torie falling in the river.

The van bumped over the cattle guard and rumbled up the drive toward the barn. Dawn, driving the second school van, followed.

As Ellie parked, she noticed the exterior of Arnie's new house appeared complete, the wood siding gleaming and the windows reflecting the long rays of sunshine.

She hoped Arnie was around this morning. She wanted to talk to him about the job offer and what she should do.

The children bolted out of the van before she could even turn off the engine.

Torie, spotting Arnie coming out of the barn with Sheila, raced toward him. Ellie, her heart soaring at the first sight of Arnie, trailed after her daughter at a more sedate pace.

"Hi, Arnie," Torie said.

"Hey, squirt." He poked a finger in her tummy, making the child giggle. "How're you doing?"

"I'm fine." Torie started to return the poke, but Arnie caught her finger.

"Easy, squirt. My ribs still hurt some."

"My mommy could kiss you and make it all better."

Arnie's rasp of husky laughter set Ellie's cheeks on fire and made her pray the earth would open up and swallow her. She really had to learn to control her reaction to the man. And control Torie's ad-lib comments.

"Maybe another time," Arnie said, winking at Ellie.

Fortunately, Daniel's appearance halted the conversation before Torie could demand more immediate or mortifying action on Ellie's part to reduce Arnie's pain.

The children, including Torie in her most insistent manner, clamored for Daniel's attention, pleading for the chance to ride alone without him or Marc leading the horse.

Without making a commitment one way or the other, Daniel headed for the barn. The children followed close behind, as though on a leash.

Ellie lingered with Arnie. "It seems like I'm always apologizing for my daughter's embarrassing remarks."

"She didn't embarrass me. I thought it was pretty cute."

He would! she thought, mentally rolling her eyes. She folded her arms across her chest, pulling her denim jacket tight. "At any rate, I did want to talk to you about the job offer. If you have time."

"Sure. I think it's a great offer. Wish there was more money on the table, but the board hopes continued fundraising will make that possible."

"I'm not too worried about the salary. It's certainly more than I'm making now. I'm just not sure if I'm right for the job or if I want to make that big a commitment."

He cocked his brow in surprise, took off his Stetson and finger combed his dark hair. "I thought you'd leap at the chance to take over Ability Counts."

"A part of me wants to." She glanced around, then strolled over to the pasture where Daniel's quarter horses grazed, and leaned back against the fence. "I have to think about what's best for Torie. I know Vanna had a lot of evening meetings she had to attend, and she traveled to Bozeman and Helena several times a year. If I took the job, I wouldn't be able to give Torie as much attention as I have been."

He rolled up beside her. "I hadn't thought about that."

"And there's my mother. I think she's coming out of the depression she's had since my dad died, but I hate to make her responsible for Torie all the time. She needs her own friends and activities. Plus, she is getting older."

"Isn't there anyone else you can rely on?"

Ellie gave the question some thought. If Torie had a loving father who was involved in her life, taking on a job like Vanna's might be easier. But that wasn't in the cards for Torie. Or Ellie.

She sighed. "Single mothers have to make a lot of hard decisions and juggle their lives around the needs of their children."

Growing pensive, idly Arnie petted Sheila and stared off into the distance, where two young colts were frolicking in the pasture.

"Guess I hadn't considered that," he said.

"But I have to." She turned to watch the colts with him, wishing she had someone special to rely on. Someone like Arnie.

Somewhere deep in her heart, she'd hoped having this conversation with Arnie would make him realize how much she needed him. How the three of them—she, Arnie and Torie—could be a family.

Tears burned in her eyes. Apparently he didn't believe her love was true enough, strong enough to be worthy of his. Nor, irrationally, despite all evidence to the contrary, did he believe he was good enough to love her?

Her fingers tightened on the top fence rail, splinters rough beneath her palms. She wished someone would knock some sense into the man.

Chapter Nineteen

"I don't think I can accept the job offer."

Pastor Redmond's brows inched upward. Ellie had made an appointment to see him Saturday afternoon in his office. Dressed in a maroon slipover sweater and chinos, he looked much younger than his fifty-some years.

"I'm both surprised and disappointed to hear that," he said. "Can you tell me why?"

"I'm concerned about the amount of time I'd have to be away from my daughter. Being the director is a huge commitment. I'm simply not sure this is the right time in my life to take on that big a job."

The pastor tented his fingers beneath his chin, his hazel eyes gazing at Ellie so intently, she felt a need to squirm in the face of his probing scrutiny.

When she arrived at his office, he'd led her to a grouping of comfortable chairs by the window. A leafless poplar tree stood outside on the lawn, the grass turning a golden brown with the arrival of near-freezing temperatures at night.

"When do you think you might be ready to move up into an administrative position?" he finally asked.

Ellie tucked a wayward strand of hair behind her ear. "I'm not sure. My daughter's only five. She won't be in school full-time for two more years. Even then, she'll need child care during after-school hours."

"You live with your mother, don't you?"

"Yes." The promotion would give Ellie a chance to get her own place and at the same time would remove the convenience of having her mother babysit Torie. Yet it wasn't right that she relied so heavily on her mother.

"Tell me…" Still studying her, he leaned back in his chair. "If child care wasn't an issue, would you want to accept the job?"

She chuckled. "In all honesty, the thought terrifies me, but yes, I'd take the job. To make Vanna's vision come to fruition would be an honor, if I could pull it off." She'd never dreamed she'd have that chance. She hadn't sought it. But now that the opportunity existed, she wanted to grab the golden ring.

But did she dare take that big a risk without knowing how it would affect her daughter?

"I can't tell you what your decision should be," the pastor said. "But let's take it to the Lord. The answers we seek are often with Him."

The pastor clasped both of her hands. Together they prayed for the Lord's guidance in the decision she had to make.

When the prayer was finished, Ellie stood. "Thank you for seeing me this afternoon, Reverend."

"Anytime, my dear." He walked her toward the door. "Tell me, how are you and Arnie getting along? I understand you two used to be close."

"Before his accident," she admitted. "I abandoned him when he needed me the most. Now he doesn't trust me, which I can understand. He also believes his injuries make him less of a man, which isn't at all true," she said with a vehemence born of frustration.

"Really? Arnie has always struck me as a strong individual. He's overcome so much."

"I agree, Pastor. He's the only one who thinks of himself as less than he was before the accident."

The pastor's hand rested on the doorknob to the outer office. He tipped his head to the side. "Forgive me for prying, but do you have feelings for Arnie?"

A rush of heat burned her cheeks, giving him the answer to his question. Her throat tight, she whispered, "I never stopped loving him, even though he'd told me to go, to leave him alone. I shouldn't have listened."

"He did?"

"In the hospital. He sounded like he meant it. It broke my heart. So I left and went to Spokane."

"I see." He opened the door for her. "Trust in the Lord, Ellie. He won't fail you."

She could only hope the pastor was right. So far no bolt of insight had struck her about taking—or rejecting—the job offer. She needed to give the board her answer soon.

Right at the moment, her answer would be no.

As for her and Arnie getting together? Even if the Lord and Pastor Redmond intervened, that appeared to be a hopeless cause.

To Arnie's surprise, Pastor Redmond invited himself to Sunday supper at the O'Brien ranch. He'd heard that Arnie had made up a batch of his award-winning chili, or so the reverend had said.

Arnie had the niggling feeling that the pastor had something else on his mind besides a bowl of chili. That feeling grew even stronger when he asked for a tour of Arnie's new house.

"This is terrific!" Pastor Redmond said, standing in the unfinished living room. "You've captured spectacular east and west views with the house placement."

Sheila sat on the floor next to Arnie, her head cocked as she listened alertly to the pastor talking.

"That was the idea. Tim Johnson helped me maximize the layout of the house and the views."

"He's a good man. Honest and hardworking." Hands in his pockets, Pastor Redmond strolled into the kitchen. The pinewood cabinets and granite counters had been installed. Tile floors were going in next week, along with the appliances. Arnie would move into the house before Christmas.

As planned, he'd be moving in alone.

"Did you want to talk to me about something?" Arnie asked, his curiosity getting the better of him.

Turning, the reverend leaned back against the counter. "Tell me what you think of Ellen James."

Arnie blinked and frowned. "I think she'll be a great executive director for Ability Counts. I sure voted for her."

"Yes, you did." Idly, he studied the empty spot where the stove would go. "How about personally? What do you think of her as a woman?"

That niggling feeling Arnie had had all afternoon turned into warning bells. "She's fine," he said with a sharp edge in his voice. "Why do you ask?"

"I was thinking…" The pastor wandered back into the living room. "This is a nice, big house. Three bedrooms, right?"

Arnie nodded.

"That's big enough so a family would be quite comfortable living here. But I don't remember hearing about you dating anyone lately."

Fingers flexing on the armrests of his chair, Arnie said, "Not that it's any of your business, but I'm not exactly an ideal candidate for a husband and father."

"Oh? Because you're paraplegic?"

"Obviously." He bit off the word with a staccato beat.

"That's odd. You're saying none of your paraplegic friends in the Paralympics organization are happily married?"

"Of course they are." They could do what they wanted, but Arnie wasn't going to tie down a woman who, sooner or later, would regret she'd agreed to marry him.

"But you're different. You don't think a woman could love you?" The words were said conversationally, but within them Arnie heard an accusation.

Arnie narrowed his gaze. "What's this all about? Have you been talking to Ellie?"

"We had a conversation," Pastor Redmond admitted. "Mostly about the job offer. She's not sure she'll accept the position."

Arnie hated to think she'd turn the offer down. She'd be good at the job. "You talked about me, too?"

"Some. She thinks you don't trust her."

"I trust her to do a good job as executive director."

"But you don't trust her enough to love her as much as she loves you."

Arnie's breath left his lungs in a whoosh. He wheeled his chair around so he was facing out the window, looking at the pasture with a handful of grazing cows. Not looking at Pastor Redmond.

"She left me once. She didn't stick around when I needed her. If the going got rough, she'd leave me again."

"Do you love her?"

Arnie froze. His jaw tightened. "It doesn't matter."

"Are you sure she left you? Is it possible you sent her away because you were afraid of what had happened to you? Afraid you couldn't handle being disabled?"

"No! She took off without even saying goodbye." *You told her to go. Remember? You were so scared she'd leave you that you beat her to it and told her to go away,* he thought.

How could he have forgotten what he'd done?

The meds. The pain. His head had been so muddled, he could barely remember his name.

The pastor came up behind the wheelchair and put his hands on Arnie's shoulders. "Sometimes the Lord works in strange ways we can't possibly understand. We just have to trust in the path God has given us to follow. That can mean trusting in a good woman's love. And trusting in yourself."

Arnie didn't respond. The weight of Pastor Redmond's words silenced him.

"I imagine you didn't know that Ellie had to go to the head of nursing to get permission to sit with you in the hospital," the pastor said. "The whole time you were in a coma, she barely went home long enough to take a shower and change clothes. That sounds a lot like love to me."

Pain, like a branding iron, burned into Arnie's conscience. "That was a long time ago. Water under the
bridge."

"Then, when you began to wake up," the pastor said,
ignoring Arnie's comment, "for all intents and pur-
poses, you told her to get lost."

Still standing behind Arnie, the pastor went silent,
as though he expected an answer. A defense of Arnie's
actions. A defense he didn't have.

Moments later, Arnie heard the pastor cross the floor
to the door and pause.

"Sometimes," Pastor Redmond said, "it takes more
courage to love, to take a leap of faith, than to deny
that love."

The door quietly closed behind the reverend.

For a long time, Arnie sat staring out the front window as the shadows grew longer. Nausea churned in his
stomach. His chest filled with a sea of tears he didn't
dare shed.

He'd never really blamed her for leaving. It was the
smart thing for her to do. But deep down he hadn't forgiven her, he realized. Had never forgiven her for *not*
staying, in spite of having every good reason to leave.
In spite of him telling her to go.

Sure, he'd gotten on with his life without her. He had
the ranch, his cattle, his own house and friends.

Sheila whined and looked up at him expectantly.

"Yeah, I've got you, too, Sheila."

He tried to remember the days right after Daniel had
driven them off the road, but the details were blurred.
He'd been on heavy pain meds. He vaguely recalled
waking up more than once, finding Ellie sitting next

to his bed, holding his hand. Talking to him. Then he'd drift off again.

How much time had passed? He had had no way to measure it then and sure couldn't remember now.

Then one day he woke up and she was gone.

He'd lost the one woman he had ever loved.

What a fool he'd been!

Ellie still hadn't told the board her decision, and it was already the middle of the week. The only other time she'd been so unsure of herself was when she left Arnie and went to Spokane.

She'd prayed about the job offer. She'd pleaded for the Lord's guidance.

Silence was the only answer He'd given her.

Working in Vanna's office after the morning pre-school session, Ellie sorted through the mail. There were letters of condolence that needed a response, invoices for office supplies that needed to be paid and checks from parents for their children's monthly fees that had to be deposited. Someone had to take care of the routine matters until the decision about a new director was made.

The board was waiting on *her* decision.

"Hey, anybody here?"

Ellie's heart leaped in her chest at the sound of Arnie's voice, and she was unable to tame her sense of joy.

"In here." She pushed aside the paperwork and stood.

Arnie rolled to the office door. His smile and the teasing glint in his eyes nearly undid her.

"There's somebody I want you to meet." He waved in a well-dressed woman in her forties who wore a conservative wool suit and practical heels.

Sheila remained at Arnie's side.

"This is Margaret Metcaf," Arnie said. "She's from the headquarters of the Children's Society in Chicago. She's been in Bozeman this past week, and I asked her to visit Ability Counts." He turned to Ellie. "Ellen James, one of our teachers and likely our next executive director."

Not wanting to correct Arnie's assumption in front of a stranger, Ellie extended her hand. "It's nice to meet you, Ms. Metcaf."

"Please call me Margaret. And I'm delighted to make your acquaintance. For the past two days, Arnie has been talking about nothing but Ability Counts and you. I wouldn't be surprised if your ears had been burning."

Ellie forced a smile. If her ears hadn't been burning before, they certainly were now.

"Margaret does a lot of the society's fundraising, particularly for expansion programs. She's working on developing a network of child development centers across the country."

"I see." Although Ellie wasn't quite sure how that related to Ability Counts.

"Arnie has described Ability Counts and your expansion plans in some detail. I'm quite taken with the model you've developed."

"I'm afraid the credit goes to our founder, Vanna Coulter, who recently passed away." Ellie stepped over to a nearby bookcase, selecting several brochures and the backup material about the school's services. "I can give you some of the materials we've used to describe our plans."

"Thank you. Although I haven't much time—I have

to catch a plane back to Chicago in a few hours—I'd like a tour of your facility. If you don't mind."

"It would be my pleasure." She started for the door.

"You see, Arnie has done such a good sales job, I'm thinking our society may want to approach your board with the idea of Ability Counts joining our network of child development centers."

Ellie halted midstride. "Joining?"

"Yes, a shared arrangement under the Children's Society umbrella organization. The local board would still make many of the operational decisions, and we would provide substantial funding to supplement what you raise in your own community."

A wave of dizziness washed over Ellie, and she reached out to steady herself.

Arnie caught her hand. "Now you know why I wanted you to meet Margaret." If possible, the gleam in his eyes had grown even brighter.

"That s-sounds…" Ellie stammered and swallowed hard. "Very interesting."

"Lead on." With a nod, Margaret gestured for Ellie to exit the office first.

In a daze, Ellie showed Margaret the classrooms and discussed the school's educational philosophy. The woman dutifully examined the children's paintings and commented on the layout of the classrooms. She smiled at the day-care students playing outdoors, a mix of disabled children and their able-bodied friends. All laughing. All sharing. Among them there were no differences that mattered.

Some left their playmates to visit with Sheila, who willingly endured their youthful attention.

During the entire tour, Ellie felt Arnie's unceasing

attention on her. It was warm and proprietary, as though his hand were resting on the small of her back, directing her. Encouraging her.

Margaret glanced at her watch. "This has been delightful, but if I'm going to catch my plane, I must be going."

"Of course," Ellie said. "Do plan to visit again whenever you're in the area."

"I'm quite sure I'll have that chance, my dear." Margaret bid them goodbye and hurried to her rental car, which she'd parked next to Arnie's van.

Arnie didn't speak until Margaret drove away.

He wheeled his chair around to face Ellie, his expression sober. "So, what do you think?"

"I think it would be amazing if they decide to underwrite Ability Counts." Ellie's fears about her lack of experience at fundraising and leading Ability Counts into the future would be eased. She could handle the teaching and coordinating functions of the director; with luck, over time she'd grow into the rest of the job.

"Ellie, I want you to take the job the board offered you. You're the best person they could hire."

His words and his support warmed her from the inside out. "I still haven't decided." But she was much closer to saying yes.

He glanced around the play yard. "Let's go back inside, where we won't be interrupted. I have something else I want to talk to you about."

Pulling her lip between her teeth, she nodded. Her lungs locked the breath inside her chest; her ears started ringing. Jake had told her they needed to talk and then he'd said goodbye. *No way am I interested in being a father.* He left her on her own to have and raise Torie.

Now she knew… She knew what Arnie was going to say. There was no chance they'd ever be together. He'd taken care of her future. She'd have a decent job. Money enough to raise Torie. Now he wanted to be done with her. Forever.

Her knees trembled with every step she took toward the office. Her shoulders rigid, she walked like a robot. Robots didn't need air. Didn't need love. They simply existed in an emotionless state day after day.

Arnie maneuvered behind her. Urged her to sit in one of the chairs in front of Vanna's desk. She sank onto the leather seat just before her legs gave out entirely.

He took her hands in his. Strong hands callused by the miles, the years, he had had to travel in his wheelchair.

"I owe you a huge apology, Ellie. If I could get down on my knees to apologize, I would. But I can't do that. I'll never be able to do that."

Her throat tightened. "It doesn't matter." *Nothing matters if you don't love me.*

"I hope you'll always be able to say that." His thumbs stroked lightly across her knuckles. "I've been all wrong about us. I wanted to blame you for leaving me and ignore the fact that I thought that was the right thing for you to do. For your sake. But you came back. And you've been trying to get it through my thick head that you love me."

Unable to hold his gaze, she closed her eyes. "Yes," she whispered. If only he'd believe her. If only her love was enough.

"I've finally realized that's all that matters. I can't figure out why you love me. I've been a fool."

A surge of all-but-forgotten hope straightened her spine, and her eyes sprang wide open.

"What I do know is that I love you," he said. "That's what I've been a fool about, denying even to myself that I love you and always have. Always will."

"Oh, Arnie…" Relief ran so deep, it drove the breath from her lungs. Tears blurred her vision.

"If you'll have me—even though I'm not the best candidate for husband of the year—"

"But you are," she protested. "You're a kind, good man. You're brave and honest. You love children and they love you. You're gentle yet strong." She lowered her voice. "Any woman would love you." But none more than Ellie did.

"I want to marry you and love you and take care of you as best I can for the rest of our lives."

"Oh, Arnie…" she repeated. "I love you so much. More than I'll ever be able to tell you."

She leaned forward and he met her halfway. Their lips touched tentatively at first, then with all the emotion that had been bottled up inside for more than eight long years. His were the lips that she had cherished and longed for. His sweet taste fed the yearning she had tried so hard to repress. His special masculine scent filled her with a joy that made her heart sing.

When they broke the kiss, they were both breathing hard, his pupils so black almost no color showed in his eyes.

"There is one other thing I need to do before we make this public," he said.

Immediately, she was wary. "What's that?"

He grinned, a lopsided smile that tugged at her heart all over again.

"I have to ask Torie if she'd be okay with me being her daddy."

Ellie tossed her head back and laughed out loud. He'd said he loved her, which she believed with all her heart. But his thoughtfulness of Torie, of taking her wishes into consideration, underscored his love as nothing else could. "I'd say that is a sure thing. She already knows she has you wrapped around her little finger."

"Just like her mother does," he said and kissed her again.

"Should I be asking Sheila if it's all right for me to marry you?" she asked when he finished kissing her.

"I've already had a discussion with her. She said if you turned me down, I'd have to pick up my own dirty socks that I leave on the floor."

Gazing into each other's eyes, they laughed together, the sound of their two voices in perfect harmony with the blessings they had received from the Lord.

Epilogue

Two weeks before Christmas

Ellie and Torie arrived at the hospital labor room a little after 3:00 a.m. They'd almost arrived too late to witness the big moment.

The doctor was already sitting on her stool up between Mindy's legs.

Clothed in a paper gown, Ellie took her place opposite Daniel. She squeezed Mindy's hand.

"You're doing a great job, Mindy," the doctor said. "Let's give her a push now. Make it a good one."

Ellie strained and puffed along with Mindy. Feeling her agony. Knowing her joy. With her free hand, she drew Torie closer to her.

"Here we go," the doctor announced. "Let's take a look…"

Mindy lifted her head.

"Congratulations, Mr. and Mrs. O'Brien. You have a handsome baby boy."

On cue, the baby let out a squall worthy of a cowboy rounding up a herd of beef cattle.

Everyone laughed, and Daniel did the honors of cutting the cord. Then the doctor laid the baby on Mindy's stomach.

"Oh, he's beautiful," she said, tears in her eyes.

Torie tugged on Ellie's paper gown. "Mommy, he's all red and yucky," she whispered.

"You were, too, honey. And I thought you were the most beautiful thing I'd ever seen in the whole world."

"What are we supposed to call him?" she asked.

Ellie looked to Mindy and Daniel for the answer.

"He'll be Robert Daniel O'Brien, named for his grandfather and his daddy," Mindy said. "We'll call him Robbie for short."

Her nose wrinkled, Torie studied the infant until a nurse swaddled him and took him away. She looked up at Ellie.

"I guess Robbie will be okay for a cousin," she said. "But maybe Arnie can help you make a prettier one that's not so squishy and red."

Ellie nearly swallowed her tongue to avoid laughing, but that didn't stop the others. She met Arnie's gaze across the delivery table. His eyes and his teasing smile held the promise of love and laughter that would bind their family together forever. *Thank You, Lord.*

* * * * *

Dear Reader,

I enjoyed returning to Potter Creek and renewing my acquaintance with the local residents. I hope you did, too.

In real life, returning to a community where you once lived may be an eye-opening experience. I remember several years ago I drove by the first elementary school I attended. How did it get so small? I had the feeling someone had slipped the school into an incredible shrinking machine.

Life is filled with changes, some good, some not so much.

I cherish the women I've kept in touch with who were my friends in high school and those I met in my working career. Although we all have acquired more wrinkles, and many of them have experienced heartache, inside they are still the loving, intelligent women I have always admired.

I hope you are blessed with friends like that. Keep them close, for they are the ones who know you best.

Happy reading…

Charlotte Carter

QUESTIONS FOR DISCUSSION

1. Do you think Ellie was right to leave Potter Creek after Arnie was injured?

2. Do you think Arnie shared some of the blame for Ellie leaving town?

3. Arnie and his brother, Daniel, are very close now, although they have very different personalities. Are you close to your siblings? What similar traits do you share? What traits don't you share?

4. What might Ellie have missed being raised as an only child? What might she have gained?

5. Are physically handicapped children mainstreamed in your school district? Do you think that's a good idea?

6. What problems and adjustments might a couple face if one of them is paraplegic?

7. Do you read a local paper? What articles interest you?

8. What are the advantages—and disadvantages—of living in a small town like Potter Creek versus a larger city? Which do you prefer?

9. Do you remember attending church picnics as a child? What games did you play?

10. Do you know a single mother? What difficulties and obstacles is she forced to overcome? Are there ways you can help?

11. Women's symptoms of a heart attack are different from those of a man. Ellie witnessed some of Vanna's symptoms of heart disease: apparent pain in her jaw and left arm, paleness and fatigue, sweating. What other warning symptoms might a woman experience?

12. If you were Ellie, how would you have handled Jeffrey Robbins's invitation to dinner?

13. Does anyone you know have a service dog like Sheila? What services does the dog provide?

14. Do you think children as young as Torie should attend the birth of a baby? Why or why not?